Appreciation for Scot C

"Savage and LOL funny, *Doublejack* is a picaresque page-turner with spark. This story's heroine is the baddest, most hilariously honest of survival-bent bad girls. Her ever-growing collection of scofflaws—from the rich and powerful to the desperate and hunky—will give you a cross-country run for your money. If Mark Twain and Cormac McCarthy got together to write a Western bodice-ripper, this is most likely how they'd go at it."

- Lynn Phillips (www.lynn-phillips.com); staff writer, *Mary Hartman, Mary Hartman*; author, *Self-Loathing for Beginners* (www.SL4B.com); columnist, "Dream On" at www.PsychologyToday.com

"Scot Crawford's *Doublejack* takes Ilya, a woman in flight from 1880s upper-class bourgeois New York, to the wilds of Montana. With more plot twists than a mountain trail, this violent, absorbing novel is the antithesis of the clichéd Western. The wily Ilya cannot be compared to any frontier woman, either fictional or historic, because she has more guts than anyone has ever before imagined a woman of that era could have. Crawford, a truly masterful writer, has created a page-turner which will have readers enthralled and excited."

- Zena Beth McGlashan, author of *Buried in Butte*

"I thoroughly enjoyed this book. I loved the characters and the situations, and Crawford's writing style is colorful and effortless. I was always eager to get back into the story, and I can see why people have said it would make a great film. I also can't help seeing a connection between Bridger and Huck Finn. If Huck had stayed with his Pap all those years, instead of getting away while he was young, he probably would have turned into a man just like Bridger."

- Jonah Lisa Dyer, screenwriter of *Hysteria*

"*Doublejack* is an anti-Western of rare humor and incendiary violence, the literary love-child of Robert Altman and Cormac McCarthy. In the beautiful and unyielding Ilya, Crawford has invented a woman bound for Tarantino's lens — a smart, caustic, larger-than-life stunner on a quest for freedom in the plundered West of Gilded Age America. Riding along with her as she leaves New York City and plunges into her new world is beautiful, and hilariously terrifying."

- David Newsom, series producer, "Shark Wranglers" at History (TV channel) and Co-EP at Undertow Films.

Doublejack

Ilya, Book One

SCOT CRAWFORD

ISBN-13: 978-0615878102 (The Ilya Series)
ISBN-10: 0615878105

Cover Design by Scot Crawford

Cover photo by Marlene Wusinish @ Vwphotography

Cover Graphics by Kathy McMillan

The cover model is Mandi Wilkinson

Her makeup is by Nicole Ratajczak

facebook.com/DoublejackIlya

ACKNOWLEDGEMENTS

I want to thank the following people:

Ginny Newsom, for her unfailing patience and tolerance.

David Newsom, ditto.

My mother, for her stubborn love for me.

My father, for making sure I seldom thought too highly of myself.

My family.

Jim Raglione, for demonstrating what being a fine artist and resolute friend looks like.

Mandi Wilkinson, my cover model, who managed to look like a mean, angry, beautiful woman, though she isn't any of those things, except the beautiful part.

Marlene Wusinich, who took a darn fine photo.

Nicole Ratajczak, my makeup artist, who made Mandi look right.

Kathy McMillan, who did the cover in a quick and easy way.

Lee Whitney, Administrative Assistant at the Butte Archives, whose ability to be helpful but amusingly cutting and self-deprecating made research a world of adventure.

Ellen Crain, the Director of the Butte Archives, and the entire staff, for doing a job well worth doing.

Zena Beth McGlashan, for personifying the kind of understated support that tends to work best for me.

Jo Antonioli at *Books & Books* in Butte, for running a small bookstore.

To Butte, Montana itself, and all the people there striving to preserve it against people who for some reason don't want to.

My friends in Driggs, Idaho, for populating that burg so I don't return to a ghost town.

To Lynn Phillips

I

1

Good evening, Herbert, Ilya said, as he entered the parlor. Byron growled.

Herbert flinched and stared at her standing by the fire, her face lit by the flames on one side, dark on the other. Good evening, May, he said, and frowned. He'd come in for a nightcap, and was dismayed to find her awake. He smirked, shook his head, took off his black overcoat and bowler, threw them on a chair, and squared his shoulders. Walking to the sideboard with an uneven pace he was trying to make dignified, he picked up a tumbler and filled it with whiskey, spilling some. Ilya watched the amber fluid splash onto the mahogany, and watched Herbert ignore it.

Ilya put Byron down on the divan. The sharp-bodied, little black dog yipped in disgust. She took a sip of whiskey, following it with a pull on her cigarette, blowing the smoke out through her nose in tusks. The gilt hands of the mahogany mantle clock she liked to wind pointed at five after three. It was the middle of the night, she hadn't been able to sleep, hadn't wanted to, and had come down for a drink.

She poked the fire and tossed in a length of sweet-smelling cherry with the hand holding her cigarette, watching Herbert peripherally. She thought to remind him that they had once agreed that he would call her by her given name when concealing her Jewishness wasn't necessary, but elected not to, because it made no difference anymore.

What remaining compassion she'd had for Herbert began to wane after his mother had died. He responded as if it had been Ilya who'd killed her, which, given his mother's dislike for Ilya, and fury at their marriage, may have been somewhat true. Compassion was not among Ilya's most prominent virtues, but she overcame her distaste for his mother, went to him, put her hands on his shoulders, looked him in the eyes, and managed to say, I'm sorry, dear. I am. Instead of accepting her paltry largesse, his face snarled, his eyes went stony and evasive, he shrugged her off, and left the house. He continued to behave as if she could not possibly know how he felt, as if her clumsy attempts at kindness were invasive, designed to hurt him, a suspicion which, she admitted, may not have been far off. His attitude reminded her of the way people managed to find Jews responsible for every misfortune, and that bias mingled rather uncomfortably with her suspicion that the bigots were right about Jewish omnipotence, and her hope that they were. Herbert's rejection of her efforts after Lillian's death was the culmination of his becoming increasingly loathsome toward her during their year of marriage. His behavior made her hate and doubt herself, her judgment, for marrying him, which in turn added another layer of hatred for him, until now there was a wheel of guilty derision toward him always turning the mill of her self-disgust. Now, after two months of stalking each other around the house in almost total silence, the death was behind them far enough for her to let any remaining sensitivity toward him wither. Though, part of her acknowledged that letting sensitivity wither was likely a poor strategy.

Herbert opened the humidor beside the array of decanters, plucked out a cigar, cut the end, and lit it from the top of the lamp globe. The wispy, black smoke from the kerosene mixed with the gray smoke of his cigar. His receding blond-red hair glowed in the yellow light. His high forehead gleamed. He'd shaven the soft skin of his pudgy face, leaving slim eyebrows, and a thin tuft of preciously-groomed beard that grew from the very end of his chin. The beard was a new addition, and Ilya thought, correctly, that he'd grown it in part to annoy her.

Crossing to the divan, he sat. Ilya smelled debauch on him — a mixture of alcohol, smoke, and sweaty body, partially masked by cologne a little too sweet for a male. He'd been out with Jackson again. She held her cigarette close to her face to mask the odor, and backed away a step. Herbert realized the way he was sitting made him look small. He dragged himself up straight, and yanked his black suit coat taut. Byron sat on the other side of the divan, staring at him.

Ladies don't smoke, Herbert said.

It's early in our social evolution. And you've remarked about this before.

Yet you don't listen.

I listened. And I heard you. I can do both. Perhaps I'm just not a lady.

You are not. You're a Jew.

Ilya made a short hiss, and narrowed her eyes. People got to 'Jew' so much faster than she got to 'bigoted ass.' But this was a new tactic, coming from Herbert. It had never been clear if he had been concealing his anti-Semitism, or just didn't feel it, but whichever it was she had liked him for it. Her cigarette began to burn her fingers and she threw it into the fire. Then she realized that doing so made it look like she was obeying him. She lit another.

True, she said, I am a Jew. Though, being too ladylike turned out to be something of a poor strategy for us Jews. Jesus was killed because he'd of rather hung drapes than people. And after a year of listening to the fatuous nattering of your Anglo-Saxon ladies, it's a relief not to be one of them. 'Fatuous nattering' is redundant, Ilya thought.

Well, he said. You do excel at smoking.

Thank you. One must find their passions in life.

If only you were adept at other things besides smoking. And drinking too much. I wonder, has it occurred to you yet that you might actually *do* something with your days?

No. It occurs to you, that seems enough.

My mother worked for my father. She refined him. He protected her from the filth of the outside world, and...and made money, and in return she cared for the house, she managed their lives, she educated me...she was a woman...a true lady. She completed him.

Ilya watched him as he said this. He wasn't looking at her, which, combined with the sickening tripe she felt this notion of women completing men to be, a notion Herbert had once himself disdained, irritated her further.

Yes, I know she did, she said. Or you think she did. She pulled herself up straighter, pulled her long, thick, black hair tight against the back of her neck, and retied the ribbon. Her high, angular cheekbones went starker beneath her sheer, pale skin, both bequeathed by her mother who'd died birthing her. Her dark brown eyes went darker, and the permanent crease between her eyebrows deepened. She placed her glass on the mantle, folded her arms under her breasts, and pushed her palms into her sides through her black, silk nightdress.

Of course, she said, completing two such disappointing men may have been what killed her, and pneumonia just an excuse. But you see, I married you so I would not have to do anything. Did I fail to mention that? Pardon me, it seemed obvious. And have you forgotten that at one time you didn't want me to be a lady as you've now decided to define one? Have you forgotten that in fact, you wanted me because I wasn't your mother? Because I refused to be beneath you? Because I was smart, and could speak, and did? That you wanted to pilfer those qualities from me for yourself — you do realize I knew you were doing that, don't you? You wanted me because I didn't want to complete you, as if that is something I would do with my time. You can hardly blame me for not being what you have suddenly decided you want after the fact.

Ilya felt the warmth of her power mix with the guilt of hurting him, felt the certainty that this is what she was meant to do in life — be a verbal archer. It was the few job openings for that talent which made her days so empty and long. She told herself she should soften, but to do so would make her angrier, which would in turn make her sharper. She took her glass from the mantle, drank it empty, went to the sideboard and poured, glancing at the puddle of whiskey he'd left for another to clean up.

I did not know you would turn out to be lazy and useless once you were rich, Herbert said, and drained his glass. Ilya turned, came to him, and refilled it.

Well, she said, looking down at him, I didn't despise you in the beginning, that wearies a person. And you may not have been looking at me closely enough, because you were drunk most of the time, speaking of excelling in that area.

Thank you, Herbert said, meaning his refill, cursed himself for his reflexive politeness, and drank. As Ilya replaced the decanter, he stood and moved in front of the fire.

Now that I see who you are, he said, I don't believe I want you completing me, it's true. I had a home before you arrived. Now I have a hole to descend into.

Now you're beginning to see my purpose. I am a holemaker, not a homemaker. We're starting to get along again. Seeing that he had taken her position, she crossed the room and sat in the chair by the door.

No. We are not getting along.

You've become so serious. You used to be fun, if not...challenging. Isn't it tiresome for you, to be both drunk and grim? People try to separate the two.

Age imparts seriousness.

Jesus Christ. You used to at the very least try not to be shopworn.

Don't put my God's name in your mouth.

Ah. Gone with God all the way now, have you? Well. I suppose that's natural, given your mother's...grinding piety. You're picking up her mantle of foolish, blind faith, I suppose, now that you've fallen over it and skinned your poor knees.

Ilya sighed, drank, and said to the air, Twenty years since *Origin of Species* and we still quibble. Incredible. To Herbert she said, The old you would have at least read Darwin and allowed yourself a doubt. Maybe even a thought.

I have no time for academic fads, for reading! Herbert said to the fire. When people have done with their foolishness with apes, God will still be there. I am a businessman. I do the work that brings you this house, this liquor, these cigarettes, your servants, your books, all of it.

My, the change in you is staggering to me. But it shouldn't be, I suppose. That's more words than you normally use in a month — you've clearly been working on yourself. It's not an about-face, it's more a...blundering retreat. Well, thank you for all the wonderful things you've given me, if I forgot to say so before. Though really, I should be thanking your father. You seem to take me for such a fool...it's surprising, and entertaining, since you married me for my mind. Or was it my beauty, and you just pretended to like my mind, because it made you seem superior to other men? You're not a businessman, you've just been putting on business clothes, and standing behind your father while he does the business. What do you do at the office, fill inkwells? Light people's cigars? You should have stayed with acting, actors get to be stupid. Your father came to the end of his patience with you, so you decided to become him before he started cutting you out for good. I'm not criticizing you — it's the best choice for a man of your limitations. The suggestion that it's you doing the work however, it's laughable.

Herbert glowered. The intimidation and envy he felt when with her burned him. In the beginning, those feelings, and the qualities in her which caused them, had been exciting, and novel, and drew him to her. Now he felt only resentment and shame. He groped around in his head, felt the way words fled his thoughts as if his thoughts were bullies. She always did this, took advantage, the way his father did, beat him down, because they could talk, and made everything he did manage to say seem stupid, and worse, he suspected that was because what he said was stupid. He cursed that he was not drunk enough for his tongue to come untethered, or that he had overshot the right degree of drunkenness, so that he would at least be unaware of what he was saying, or just not care how he sounded. How did she do it, be here, as if someone had told her when he was coming home, and she was ambushing him? Was she? This conversation was supposed to happen tomorrow, he wasn't prepared. He took a drink, longed for Jackson's strength and verbal dexterity, puffed his cigar, and kept his gaze on the flames. Her stark beauty made speech more difficult.

He struggled out, My father is grooming me for taking over the company from him. He is...letting me observe, and learn the way business is done. You are the fool who believes rebellion should go on forever. My father recognizes that rebellion is a...a...useful phase that ends. And you, my dear...you...are approaching your limitations right now with your mouth. This is *my* house!

So it is, Ilya said. She'd left her cigarettes on the mantle, so she crossed the room, lit one, replaced the case, and faced him. The fire glowed and crackled at their feet. He squared himself to her, and they stared at each other for a moment. He was her height, something she liked, because few men were. Her height was one of the things for which she was grateful to her father. But Herbert was heavier than she, paunchier. Herbert's indeterminately-colored, slightly watery eyes were dull and aggressive. His skull was tipped slightly forward, his shoulders up, cigar in his mouth. Ilya's heart quailed a little at his bracing her, and she clenched her jaw.

I've decided that I don't want to know my limitations, Ilya said. I can't recommend that approach for you, however. Your limitations are too evident to be ignored. There is no mystery.

You think glibness and sarcasm are courage. Discovering where the precipice is will be... harsher than you think.

Precisely the idea. It would be just like you to become somewhat thoughtful and attentive at this point. And verbal. I've taught you well.

What 'point?' Where is your infamous bluntness?

Oh, you want that now? No more 'ladylike?' Alright. I'm leaving.

You are leaving of your own accord? Hah! I don't believe you. You've grown too attached to being a layabout. You putter around thinking of insulting things to say instead of helping with...something!

But, thinking of insulting things to say is a grueling and depleting career, if one does it well.

You believe you're exceptional, and can put all this down. Herbert gestured at the room and Ilya followed his hand. But, he said, no one puts this down once they have it. However, it does sometimes happen that what is given is taken back. You are not leaving, you are being dismissed.

You want it to be your idea then? Alright. I suppose you should have at least one to start you off on your business career. Have you talked to your father? Is banishing me one of the terms for his not banishing you?

He has nothing to do with this. Herbert's eyes kept trying to skip away from hers, and his effort to hold them steady was obvious.

No? Your father saturates everything in our lives. He weakens you.

I am not the tedious sort who is weakened because their forebear is strong. On the contrary, he strengthens me. This is what you don't comprehend, with your insipid beliefs in self-creation. He is me, I am him, we are one thing...we...we build this country.

Ilya realized now that most of what he was saying had been rehearsed. He'd probably gone over it many times with Jackson, as he had with scripts when he was pretending to be an actor. Perhaps he'd even written it down. He was pitching his voice lower than normal, though the monotony of his diction remained the same. Each of them felt the urge to break this confrontation, but neither would, Herbert because he refused to let himself show frailty after working so hard to gain this moment of toughness, Ilya because she would not let herself lose.

Such melodrama, she said. See, acting was the way for you to go, the words are supplied. So then, what are the terms of my dismissal?

You go, he said. Tonight. Go live with your French whore, I don't care...

Jacques is American, Ilya snapped. Her husband is French. A whore, well, yes, perhaps...

I don't care. I was going to give you some time to make arrangements, but I've changed my mind. I am finished with you, and your mouth. You take nothing but your clothes and that damnable dog. He removed a paper from the inside pocket of his suit coat and placed it on the mantle. You sign this, he said, which is dated before the wedding, and which says you have no claim on anything belonging to our family. I have prepared an annulment to be filed later, stating that you wouldn't consummate, and left of your own accord with no warning. People will be given to think you ran off with a drunken actor, like a Jew would.

Oh, you don't understand Jews if you think that is their typical behavior. A Jew would make the actor famous and take a usurious commission. And have you forgotten that I'm not supposed to be Jewish? You'd best omit that when you tell your lie. So I've run off with the actor you once wanted to be? I ran off with the old you? And no consummation? Ilya gave a short, high-pitched squeal of laughter, the one that came from her when hysteria caused by travesty hit her. Her normal, seldom-used laugh was a low 'ha-ha-ha.'

She said, If only you thought of this to be interesting deliberately! But you haven't the imagination, and couldn't think of anything else. And I'm a woman of no means dear, I don't have to sign something to be entitled to nothing, it happens by itself.

I am very aware that you have no claim to anything. You will sign anyway. And people will think I made an understandable mistake out of youthfulness, which is the truth. And they will be nothing but relieved to have you gone from their society. By the first of the coming year, I am what I was made and born to be, and you are dead for us.

Oh, I can be dead for you now. Though, Christmas does sound like a good time for it, since I die then every year anyway. So. Nothing eh, you've decided? Not even a few shekels so I can buy back my father's dress shop and sew until my fingers are claws? Pick up my father's old moonlighting business, and tell fortunes until some drunk kills me for telling him I see death in his future — follow his footsteps to the grave? My Herbert, that's very chilly and ungrateful. What was it exactly I did to you?

That's of no moment. What is of moment is that you do not set terms, I do. You leave. Tonight.

He broke their standoff, took out his wallet, emptied it of bills, walked to the divan, and dropped the bills there without counting them. Ilya looked at the fire, rallying.

Purchase whatever future you would like, he said. Whatever it is it won't cost more than that, because without us, May, it will be short.

My name is *Ilya*, you'll recall. Did you know it means 'dirge?' There is much in a name.

I know. Herbert means 'illustrious warrior.'

Well, sometimes parents jest. She sighed. And it seemed so perfect, she said, 'Ilya smart, Herbert stupid, Herbert rich, Ilya poor.' What could go wrong?

Go to hell, Herbert muttered.

I'll need cab fare.

Herbert moved to the sideboard to refill his glass, and she roamed the perimeter of the room, running her finger over the chair rails, and the shelves with the show books on them, which she had broken protocol and read, intimidating Herbert further. She looked at the joinery of the woodwork, which was so tight as to astonish. She adored the workmanship, and stayed slightly amazed that the outcome of it was so morbid, that what had once been waving trees was this beautiful dead-room. In a way, excepting for the beauty and craftsmanship, the room reminded her of the food this family ate. The deathly stillness of a plank of meat lying next to a pile of vegetables boiled as if hated, a hard biscuit to further savage the tongue. Their investment in domination had no better example than their food.

She pulled aside the drapes and leaned toward her reflection in the night-black glass until her two faces met, and she could see out onto Washington Square. The twisting limbs of the elms waved in the steady, low wind, dropping their dead leaves and casting shadows in the pallid pools of gaslight. The Park was calm except for the air of malignity it had at night — the sense that things weren't going well for someone out there in the dark.

Lovely night for an annulment, she said.

Yes. I've given you good traveling weather.

'Given?' Hm. You are feeling powerful. Ilya turned and looked at Herbert, who stood by the sideboard staring at a portrait of his family — his father, mother, and himself, no Ilya. The way he was standing made her think of early in their relationship, when they had liked to get drunk and look at art together and mock it, when he'd been fun. She became angrier that he'd stopped being that man altogether, with her.

Well, she said, Henry promised me five hundred dollars if I signed an annulment and left. It is not only you and I that are aware that things have come to an intolerable impasse. I said I would have an answer today. Truly, you have much to learn from your father. He's a tyrant, but he doesn't bully without trying to deal for what he wants first. Perhaps he was the one to whom I was better suited, because I would be less superior to him than I am to you. Hm, I hadn't thought of that until just now. I wonder, now that your mother is out of the way...

Ilya watched him. He didn't respond at all, and she gave him credit for holding on to himself.

Your deals with him are not my affair, he said.

Oh? I thought you two were one thing, making the world...

Go.

Ilya stilled herself and softened her tone. Herbert, she said. Be...I don't know what...practical, perhaps? You are behaving as if you were deprived of something by me, as if I promised you something and didn't give it to you, so now you are allowed to punish me. That's not what happened. I am as surprised as anyone that you took your fit of rebellion so far as to marry me — I thought you would just diddle me and go. But you wanted to spit in your parents' soup — a fate too good for their soup by the way — and you wanted conquest over me. I accepted all that. Do you think I didn't notice that your rebellion fell short of allowing me to be Jewish? Not that I wanted to be, but it's an interesting point of information nonetheless. But I enjoyed it all really, because I was getting something in return — you were getting me up from the bottom. I mean, you didn't love me, that's fine, I didn't love you either, not really, but we both believed we did for while, we had...something. And now it's over, and that's alright. It was touching that you read Walden and wanted to be an actor, but I never thought it would last, and didn't care. But this punishment, it's unfair. I can leave with no ill-will that isn't naturally occurring in me, but this...dismissal?! You can afford to help me more than this. You have the option to not have me as an enemy, and you're not taking it? Why not? Who do you take yourself for? Do you think I'm supposed to simper and accept my banishment with insipid grace? Weep? Why? I have broken no deal. Be...honest!

Herbert felt a softening in him, and had the feeling that she was right, that this move was not a good one, or a fair one, but stifled all of it. He pulled gently at his beard, looking at her without expression. Ilya looked at the beard and rolled her eyes. The beard, coupled with the shame she felt for having just inadvertently asked him for money, drained the reason she'd summoned out of her.

Really, Herbert, she said. Please. He continued to just look at her, more safely from across the room, then moved to the hearth, and poked at the fire for no reason. The withdrawal and inarticulateness which everyone had been forced to speak of as virtues because of his stature, were back in play. She started to quake with rage, because his silence was an effective tactic, and she felt impotent.

My God, Herbert, that beard alone is enough reason to leave you. I was wishing to make it an honorable parting for both of us, but I see that's out of the question. Fine. I will leave now, if you need so badly to demonstrate your power. Give me a few moments to gather some things.

Certainly. Remember that everything is mine, however.

Ilya crossed to the hearth and picked up her cigarette case. His posture, standing there with poker in one hand and the other in his trouser pocket, looking into the fire, was affecting, domestic, and she had a fleeting memory of when she had believed he in fact did love her, when she'd believed his reticence covered tormented depth of an interesting kind. An anxious impulse to evoke that time to him, to try to salvage the situation, to try again, rose in her. But his speech had been given, and he would, as usual, leave resolution to her. Herbert stood, hands clenched, body rigid, jaw tight. She hesitated, almost squashed the impulse rising in her, then said,

Do give my regards to Jackson, won't you? I always liked him. Or should I say, to Jackson's asshole, to which you are far more attached?

The poker left a trail of red sparks in an arc through the dimness as Herbert whirled and swung it. Ilya jerked back, and felt the heat of it wash over her face as it passed. Surprise stifled the shriek that leaped into her throat. Herbert growled and stumbled over the raised lip of the hearth. He chopped at her when he recovered, but she had thrown herself away from him, stumbling and going to her knees. Byron went insane.

Ilya came to her feet. Herbert, silent, turned and came toward her with the poker over his head, clasped in his right hand, left pointing in front of him. At that moment, the thought that she should have perhaps not stressed her superiority so much flashed through her mind. She almost ran.

Fucker, she said, spit coming from her mouth. Herbert chopped at her again, and she lunged toward him, head lowered. His forearm hit her in the skull and knocked her to her knees. Herbert grunted as the poker flew from his hand to the floor behind her, and the bones of his arm rang. She grabbed the back of his thighs, drove her head into his crotch, and threw him down. He landed on his tailbone and the back of his head rapped against the floor. He groaned and cursed, rolled to his side, hands at his crotch. Ilya dug her fingers into his skull and banged it against the floor. He threw his weight against her, rolled her, and pinned her shoulders down. Terrified breathing was all they gave out, and each had the fleeting thought that this resembled their first sex, but was more impassioned. They saw into one another's eyes for a moment, in release, exaltation, and hate, and Ilya felt a crash of cold heat, and terror, and transport. Herbert let go of her shoulders and locked his fingers around her throat. Fucking bitch, he gritted out, saliva running. She grabbed him by the genitals and twisted with one hand, the other tearing at his fingers around her neck. He stood it for a time, trying to push himself back out of her grip without releasing his own. He couldn't bear it, let go with one hand, and hacked at her arm. She twisted her body hard, pushed him off her, and stood. He rolled onto his belly. Ilya snatched the poker, and when he turned toward her, getting his knees under him, she swung it at his skull like it was an ax to a standing tree, heard the leaden smack, felt the tremor run up the metal into her arms, and watched his eyes register surprise. He slumped to the floor.

No! Ilya said, panting, staring at him, and dropped the poker. She went to her knees, grabbed Herbert's skull. Blood smeared her hand. His eyes went to nothing, staring at hers, and his lips moved with his last lack of words. That image settled into her mind for good.

Fuck! Oh, *fuck!* Oh stop it, Byron! Stop it! She turned and grabbed the bouncing, yapping dog, and clenched his muzzle shut. His ears went down with his tail, he stared at her in alarm, and she shrieked a laugh at his expression. Once she started laughing she couldn't stop, and didn't want to, so she kept going, bent over Herbert, Byron clutched to her. Tears ran that she couldn't stop and didn't want to, and she knelt there, crashing out sobs, and unbelieving laughter.

When she was drained and stupefied, she stood, dropped to the divan, looked at her husband, and said, There, Herbert. I stopped thinking, and did something.

She sat for a few moments, breath easing, staring and trying to control her panic, then remembered trying to do so unassisted was foolish, and went up to her room. Her bottle of Mariani was full, and reassuring. She returned to the parlor, took a glass, filled it, smiled at the ecstatic woman dancing on the label — a woman who was becoming her steadfast friend — sat down away from the body, drank the wine down, and waited. Byron hopped onto her lap, and tipped himself over to a laying down position. It was her favorite move of his. She loved his total confidence that she loved him without relent and always wanted his company, neither of which were true. He felt warm and soft against her breasts. She kissed the top of his head, and he licked her face. In her arms, he was beautiful and calm. Out of them, an asshole who barked at everything.

The buzzing energy and feeling of insane well-being from the alcohol and cocaine in the Mariani came into her skull, her shock and nausea and panic fading. Her face tingled and grew warm and numb, strength filled her body, and she smiled in self-approbation for having discovered the stuff, then frowned in self-opprobrium for having taken so long to do it. She poured another glass and drank it down. The clock chopped at time.

Alright. Alright, little man, she whispered into Byron's neck, walking the room with him in her arms. What do I do? What do you do when a man uses you to commit suicide?

She put Byron down and looked at him for a moment, noting with some wonder, and envy, his total lack of concern for what had happened. He began to lick himself, and she snorted a laugh, and thought he had a certain wisdom. She lit a cigarette, trying to choke the fear in her chest with the smoke.

Goddamn you, she said to the corpse, and the fear became anger that this choice of what to do with herself, her life, which she'd welcomed before now, which had taken her so long to face, now had to be made under these circumstances, circumstances that made everything dangerous, and dire, that made her afraid, and she hated feeling afraid — it made her angry that for the first time in their relations this man had made her feel fear, that he had gone to these lengths to achieve it.

No, she said, and shook her head once, hard. I said, 'No limitations.'

She left the parlor and went up to her room. The house was achingly silent and still, and frightening, and she felt like a mad wraith. Snorting with impatience, she stripped her nightdress, put on her cotton chemise, went down the hall to Herbert's room, and got a pair of his coarse trousers that he pretended were for hunting to cast an image — the gentleman sportsman. But he never went hunting because he loathed physical discomfort and blood. The thick, tan belt she took from his hook smelled beautiful and new and she wound it around herself, but there was no hole for a waist as small as hers. She strapped on suspenders instead, and rolled up the trouser cuffs. In her room she put on stockings and ankle boots she wore for nasty weather. She went without a bodice, liking the sensuousness of her breasts free beneath the soft cloth of her chemise.

Byron ticking behind her, she went to the basement. The coal furnace breathed. It was new that year, and the subject of much familial pride. She'd not understood the pride, because the heat that came from the registers in the floors was weak, invisible, dull — being separated from its source made it seem inconsequential. Herbert had stopped lighting fires in his enthusiasm for the new equipment, so the rooms were tepid, though, the whole room was that way, instead of the fireplace heat withering as it got further from the source. Ilya thought the furnace an improvement that made things worse, so she kept the parlor fire, and her bedroom fire, burning, because she liked the smell of woodsmoke, and the intensity of open flame, and having something to stare at.

No, the furnace door is too small for him, sweetheart, she said. Byron's tail whipped. There will be no butchering. And it would smell worse than their cooking.

Ilya lit the wall lamps. She paced around the basement frowning, looking for a place to hide the corpse, but this family's insane puritan neatness made that impossible. A wild impulse to bag the body and drop it in the river went through her, but that was absurd. She thought to run into the street screaming, pretending there had been an intruder, but then she would have to maintain a lie while they searched for a murderer who didn't exist. She thought to simply tell the truth, to stop what she was doing and play it straight, but thought the truth would be irrelevant for her. They would want to blame the Jew, and this time they might be be right.

She had little time. She was to meet Henry at six. The servant Gertrude was in the house stoking the furnace by seven, having shambled over from her quarters in the Mews. By eight, Herbert's absence from breakfast would be noted — when he slept late, Gertrude looked in on him. By nine, Jackson would have been awakened with no knowledge of Herbert's whereabouts, and he would reveal that last seen, Herbert had been on his way home from less than three blocks away at three in the morning.

She swung open the wooden gate to the coal bin, grabbed the shovel, and went after the pile beneath the sidewalk. After a couple shovels, she stopped. Too much mess. She ran to the kitchen and took a paring knife downstairs, grabbed the large canvas sheet intended for the outings they no longer went on, made a cut in the hem, and tore the sheet in half. She spread half of it on the concrete floor, also new that year, and began to shovel coal onto it. After fifteen minutes she stopped, grabbed the other half of the sheet and a length of rope, and went upstairs to Herbert.

Ilya moved the divan out of the way and spread the canvas beside his body. Panting, she poured Mariani over her remorse and stared down at him. She grabbed his feet and yanked at the corpse until his head was toward the fire, his feet toward the door. On her knees beside him, she worked her arms beneath the body, and rolled it onto the canvas face down. Byron yipped and licked at her face.

Yes, little man, it's very exciting, I know...who would have thought death could be so thrilling? We must do it again someday.

She trussed the body, grabbed the canvas at his feet, and pulled him toward the stairs across the polished, red oak floor. At the head of the stairs she stopped and looked down.

Oh, this is going to be macabre...

Herbert's head banged on the treads as Ilya went backwards down them, pulling at the feet end. She kept up her momentum, continued across the floor into the coal bin, and kept on until her back was against the granite block wall beneath the sidewalk. She came around to the head end and got to her knees, pushing at the bundle and grunting, forcing the body back against the wall. A sob grabbed her throat. Oh Herbert, she said, I didn't want this, you fool!

She started shoveling coal onto him.

When she got most of the coal off the canvas, she gathered up the corners, worked the rest of it to the middle, picked it up, and dumped it over the top of the pile, then crouched, leaning against the gate jamb.

The furnace. If she left it, Gertrude would come down to stoke it, and she might uncover the body. If she put coal into it so it needed none, Gertrude would be suspicious. Being suspicious of Ilya was part of Gertrude's duties, in Gertrude's estimation at least, and Ilya often suspected that she had been explicitly told to watch her, probably by Lillian.

She opened the door to the furnace and put in two shovel's worth, splitting the difference.

She closed the gate to the bin, replaced the shovel on its hooks, grabbed up the corn broom, swept the errant coal dust under the gate, and stopped, leaning against the rough-sawn oak post that supported the stair header, standing in the lamp light, and the flickering of the furnace. Her hair was all over, she was coated in black dust, and sweat had soaked her chemise, the cloth clinging to her skin. The canvas. She rolled it loosely and jammed it into the furnace. The clothes. She stripped them off save for her shoes and stockings, and pushed them in, frowning. The fire wasn't burning hard. She added coal and waited for the fire to flare but it just laid there, the cloth smoldering, smoke coming into the room. Panic ran through her and she almost bolted. This was stupid, the Mariani was making her stupid. The damper! She turned the flue damper wide open, left the door ajar, and waited, standing nude before the furnace, smoke around her. A draft formed, the flames picked up, the smoke stopped gushing. She closed the door and opened the gate damper. The fire burned hard.

At last, not being a lady pays dividends, she said. One learns useful things talking to workmen.

She went back upstairs. It was half past four. She took off her shoes, put the parlor back together, cleaning up from her feet with a wet rag from the kitchen, scrubbing hard at the blood, replacing the poker. The knife. She threw the rag down at the top of the stairs and retrieved the knife from the basement, wiped her feet on the rag coming back up, and put the knife back. The rag. Gertrude would see it in the garbage.

Damnit. I see now why most people don't do this sort of thing. Being exceptional comes at such cost. She stood there. What day was it? Saturday. She went to the chest that held table linens and tucked the rag beneath Wednesday.

Her pace flagging, she put Herbert's coat and hat in his bedroom closet, and returned to her room, Byron with her.

Now darling, I'm unsure of the etiquette in this situation. Is it good form to break an appointment with the father of the man you've just killed? If I don't, what do I wear?

2

Fuck, Bridger said, looking at the downed section of barbed wire and posts. He and his father had done this stretch after the old man had started to come unhinged. The posts were too short, too thin, too far apart. Because of this, Bridger knew he would spend more time working on this stretch than any other on the shithole of a place the ranch had become for him. He hated it so much now the feeling went backward, and the place he had once loved now had always been a shithole, and the love he had felt was morning mist burned off. In better days, he might have gone ahead and gotten the wagon and more tools and replaced the posts with good ones, got earnest about doing good work, but he wasn't going to do that now. His father hadn't told him to come out here and work, Bridger had just muttered 'fix fence,' looked at the old man's eyes, which now looked like they'd been dug from the skull of someone dead, and gotten out. He'd thrown a small roll of rusted wire on Judy, mounted, and rode off.

He turned Judy to follow the fence down the incline. She was swaybacked, slow, and his big feeling about her was embarrassment, but that was loaded with pity and love. If trouble showed up, she couldn't do any more than be something to hide behind and cry, but trouble never had, making him feel dumber than his own horse for expecting it, and feel that trouble wouldn't even bother with him.

He sat and watched September clouds begin to pile up behind the Big Hole Range. The sun he was sitting in now would be chased off soon, replaced by what looked to be a hard, steady rain, maybe with snow in it down here, and lots of snow up high. The wind came up, carrying damp chill, and the beautiful smell of the approaching autumn death to which the land would soon surrender. Bridger loved the smell at this time of year, the sweet rottenness and cold clarity, the piss-yellow aspens and blood-red hawthorns. But, he hated that soon not having decent clothes would be even more of an embarrassment, and he would be cold. And the prospect of being trapped with the old man in the ranch house for months at a time was an unbearable thought, one that he couldn't face straight on.

The burning in his crotch rose again, who knew what from — downed fences, the smell of death, rain, could be anything — and he stood in the stirrups and quickly relieved himself of that grim chore with a cold hand and warm spit, rubbing the resulting goop into his gloves. When he sat again, the other feeling he'd come to expect and despise surged through his chest and into his skull with its usual abruptness, as it'd begun to do more and more often, and he lowered his face into his collar and wept below his hat brim for a short while, then rubbed that wet into his gloves.

Leakin' like a fuckin' cloud all th' time, he muttered, and swung to the ground. It was a new problem, this abrupt crying, and his concern that it would manifest around others had made him even more reclusive, like he'd become one of the squeakers that lived in the stone ledges — the little ground hogs that stood and chirped and dove into the earth when he got close.

Judy nosed for something green in the matted brown grass, snorted, and raised her head to stare, reins trailing. Bridger never had to picket her — she'd given up any idea of freedom. He liked to think that she wasn't sour about that, that it wasn't a sacrifice on her part, more just a realization that she wouldn't like to be free, not really. Then he would remind himself that she was a horse, that he was too old to fantasize about the inner lives of animals, and he didn't know what she was thinking, if she was at all.

He pulled the canvas sack that had once held coins from his saddle bags, and dug out a handful of the grain he'd scraped from the livery floor, feeding it to her in two cupped hands.

Yeah, he murmured. Don' fret. We ain't gonna git wet. The rain was an hour off, maybe an hour and a half, and it may not bend his way. He figured he could get some of this fence back up before getting to camp.

He sighed, surveyed the work, fished out his twist, and gnawed off a chunk. He went to the last upright post before the downed section lying on the ground, and pushed against it, seeing if it was good enough to be left alone. It wasn't, but he wasn't going to try and fix it, it couldn't be. The pliers and hammer clacked together when he slung the tool belt around his waist — he'd fashioned it from a gun belt he'd taken off a grave cross. The townsfolk in charge of morals hung the gun belts of men who were shot dead on them as a warning, illustrating what had killed the occupant of that hole, but they stopped when the belts went missing and showed up on other men.

Bridger cut the two strands of wire a foot to the bad side of the post and let that section sag the rest of the way to the ground. He wrapped the stub of the upper strand around his gloved hand, braced his foot against the post, and leaned back into the wire, trying to pull it taut. He got a couple of inches out of it — made it look a little better than soggy bunting. The post split when he started the 'U' nail, and he had to start three, grab the strand again, pull it tight, and pound all three nails home, leaving a shredded mess. The lower strand was now drooping.

Fuck. I fuckin' hate this shit. He grabbed the lower strand and pulled on it like the other, but it only tightened the section between this post and the next, where it was seized up on a barb. Beyond that, the lower strand still drooped, the upper too, but less so. The whole section just looked bad, like it couldn't keep the most lifeless cow in or out, like the members of the herd they no longer had would just nudge each other and snicker when they saw it. He went to the next post, dropped to his knees beside it, banged the pry bar into the wood, and worked the 'U' nail out away from the wire to free it. He went back to the first post, laid a hold of the strand, and pulled on it again. Still shitty, but a little better. He started some nails, pulled as taut as he could, bashed them home, turned the strand loose, walked up to the next post, and bashed in some new nails, splitting the post, because it was just too small to be a fence post, so he just kept bashing at it until his arm was tired, and the post near sheared in two.

Bridger pulled off his glove and sucked on the thumb he'd gashed open, and considered the sky, tears boiling his eyes. The wind was getting high and testy, throwing gusts like punches, and swirls that started warm and went icy. The weather was coming down the flanks of the mountains toward him, and the leading edge of cloud had passed over the sun. The temperature dropped hard. He almost just upped onto Judy and rode away from this, but imagined his father's disapproval, and felt that hot wall in him that he couldn't ever scale — the barrier made of fear and mortared with love — and turned back to the downed fence. He'd get the thing tethered back upright, and come back and finish it tomorrow. He was trained to work, no matter the futility of it, and he couldn't make the fact that they had no stock to lose relevant.

There were three posts in succession slumped over. The center one had snapped off at grade, the other two following it down like loyal friends. Bad job they'd done or no, the whole thing still looked strange being down so much — it looked like the wire had been cut — until Bridger figured out that this was a spot where they'd put splices, and they'd separated. He now regretted cutting the wire he just had in his pissed-off impulsiveness — it didn't make any sense at all now that he thought on it — because now he had four splices to do, and there might not be enough slack to do them. He looked at the two ends of the wires where the splice had been. This wasn't his work, it was his father's. He'd been doing work exactly how he'd shown Bridger to never do it. He'd only done a couple twists on the wire for the splice, and Bridger could tell that the twists had been too loose to hold for long. He had done a bullshit job knowing it was Bridger who would do the fixing. For a long while during his father's determined strut and stumble downhill, Bridger had had empathy for the man, in the form of confused, reflexive respect, and waning love. But, it had not ended or improved, the crash, it just kept going on and on, down and down, and Bridger couldn't feel much more than revulsion and anger now, and the tangle of fear and love that had always been there, that couldn't be untangled.

Fucking asshole, he said, inwardly shouting down the sense of betrayal thinking of his father that way brought up. He bent and looked at the bottom of the sheared-off post. The knot had shrunk and popped out, leaving a bit of wood the size of three fingers to hold the post up, which had then splintered apart, leaving a long dagger of wood pointing at the sky. The splices had come loose, and the snow had then piled over the three posts, and pushed them down.

Bridger remembered this post. He and his father had worked for three days straight trying to get this section done. His father didn't say much during those days, except to lay into Bridger for doing exactly as he himself was doing, which was twisting Bridger's mind because he'd been trained to do it right by the man now getting pissed at him for it. His father's face was set in a permanent stony rage, eyes bloody and bovine. Pissed and scared, Bridger had dropped the sack of nails on the ground, spilling them, and his father had turned and said, Do it right! and jabbed Bridger in the face with his fist. Striking him was not something his father did often, but when he did, it came from nowhere, and seemed to have no just cause — like he would have punched Jesus himself if he'd happened to be the one standing there. Bridger had stared at him, wholly surprised, then bit down on the rush of tears, and turned away, turned in a way that now seemed permanent.

This happened after Bridger had pointed out that this very post he was standing over had this knot in it, that the post shouldn't be used, and his father had said, Fuckit, used it anyway, then mangled the splices as Bridger watched him, holding the wire taut for him.

Bridger spat, checked the sky, grabbed the ends of the bad splice, and did two quick turns — the same job that had failed — did the same on the other strand, and walked back up to where he'd cut them. He grabbed one of the stubs coming out of the first post he'd dealt with, and the trailing end, and tried to pull them together enough to get a twist on them. Fuck, he said. The two ends overlapped by a couple of inches but it took all his strength to get them to do that and he'd never be able to twist them together without a third hand or a tail to work the pliers — he couldn't get enough overlap to grab both ends with one hand. And the weight of the broken posts was bearing down on the wire, pulling it through the leather gloves he'd fixed so many times they were more patch and thong than original leather, and were too big in any case so he had no real dexterity, and the wind was now filled with dead material blowing off the sage, and it was going into his eyes and mouth, Judy just standing there in a way that seemed knowing and insolent, and just...

Fuck. Fuck fuck fuck fuck fuck fuck FUCK FUCK FUCK *FUCK!!*

He went into a whirling, stamping, shouting fury. Posts crackled and went down under his boots. Wire tore his skin through his rotting jeans and long underwear, spittle flying from his face. Judy watched, shifted her ass away from him so he stayed in her vision as he laid waste to a hundred-foot section of the fence, ripping it into a mangled trail of twisted wire and splintered pine, hat gone, tangled, filthy hair looking like his skull had shattered and it had shot out. When he stumbled, went to the ground, and gashed his cheek open on a barb, he laid there, panting and sobbing.

The grass crackled under his ass as he sat up and stared at the storm coming on, his face snarled up, wiping off blood and looking at it. Easing down, he looked at the fence he'd fixed properly, smirked, said, Fuckit. His face relaxed, and he thought that he had, not nothing, but little to fear from what his father had become, but that inflated the fear instead of calming it, which he didn't understand, and he hated himself for feeling it. This section of fence was much too far away from his father's chair and jug for Bridger to worry about being punished, so he did. And his father had added a new twist to the business of cattle ranching and sold every animal they had, so they had none to rebuild a herd with. He then omitted the step of using the money to buy new stock, and drank what seemed like an impossible amount daily, and had Bridger carry on with the work as though there was a herd of ghost cows out there.

A vole skittered out from one of its tunnels of dirt that wound around the ground's surface, and winked out of sight beneath a sage bush. Bridger glanced up for a hawk, to see how daring the vole was being. Nothing up there. He imagined the filthy darkness the vole lived in, the long, twisting tunnels and shafts intersecting with one another, the feeling of having a threat always at one's back, the sense that there was no choice made in living like that, it just was that way. It seemed awful, but also, compared to his on-top-of-the-ground, free-wheeling human life here with this fence, desirable. Like being down in that tunnel would be warm and comforting, being hidden and having no one know quite where you were though they circled above and around. And not being rained on. Speaking of which...

Ahhh, damnit, Bridger moaned with a kind of relieved happiness, savored the release and exhaustion from raging, felt in the tool belt for the pliers, but it was just an empty scrap of leather tied to him now. The pliers were on the ground a couple feet away. He rolled over to them, picked them up, cut himself free from the wire wrapped around his legs, and stood up.

Shit, Jesus, he said, probing at the gashes in his legs through the cloth. The sting felt good so he pushed harder. He didn't feel rivers of blood rolling down, just trickles. Taking off the tool belt, he roamed around to find the hammer and pry bar, jammed them into it, started to pick up the nails scattered about, gave that up, went over to Judy, and slung the belt over the pommel.

He grabbed her behind the ears, pulled her head into his chest, rested his cheek on the knob at the top of her skull, and breathed her smell in. She snorted softly and pushed against him a little. Two fat drops splatted on his hat brim.

Let's go, he said. Fuck this. Sorry I waited too long. He grabbed up the reins and swung into the saddle. He wanted to run her, run her hard for the mile dash to the camp, but her running days were gone, and she acted like she felt she'd earned the right to pick her own pace. She cantered, knowing where they were headed, and as anxious to get there as he. Bridger felt good, even and resolved, not angry at Judy for being old, not embarrassed that she was his horse, grateful that at this moment she was the smarter of the two of them, that she couldn't lose her temper. He felt free, except for this broken fence, which he felt he was dragging behind him.

The rain intensified a little, then a lot. He fished the scrap of canvas with the hole cut through it that functioned as his slicker from his saddle-bags, and draped it over him and over Judy as much as possible. Through the lines of gray water he saw the stand of golden aspens where the camp was, and as they neared it, the rain came down in a loud, hissing, frightening rush, big saucers of snow in it. He swung down as he reached his wickiup, stepped beneath it, and pulled Judy under. He laughed a little, and stood looking out over her back at the deluge, soaking in the excitement and anger of the weather — the potential in it to lose all control.

Being here lifted his spirits more. Right now was the best he'd felt in he couldn't remember when. Freed from the grave of the cabin with his father and his mother's ghost, and her corpse itself beneath a pathetic cross of two sticks his father had made, made so that it looked like the short end was in the dirt, like he was mad at her, and had driven a stake through her. The careless cross made Bridger angry and uneasy, but also made him feel empty, because she'd passed when he was too young to form any but the most vague and instinctive attachment, composed largely of fantasy. Most of his feeling for her was annoyance that she couldn't get between him and his father, who seemed to only resent her for leaving him.

Years earlier, he'd dragged lodgepoles down from higher elevations to this slice of the piedmont next to the drainage that had water no matter how dry the year, and leaned them up onto a pole threaded through the aspen branches. The open end faced out over the valley floor, the closed end backed into the foot of a rise. Kept back from the edge of the trees, it was hard to see when the leaves were down, and impossible when they were up. Over time, he'd kept throwing on spruce boughs, dead aspen branches, leaves, a section of canvas, until now it was close to weather-tight. He'd weaved branches up through the aspens so three sides were closed, and with Judy standing in the open end, the wind was mostly baffled.

The first two years, it was almost entirely demolished by the winters, but he'd gotten better at getting it to hang together, taking green aspen branches and weaving them, tying them with strands of hide, learning to create stages of windbreak so when the gusts hit the primary shelter they were splintered and irresolute. He'd kept shifting the open side of it around, trying to figure out where the wind tended to push the snow so it wouldn't drift full. That wasn't happening — the wind wasn't predictable enough. So he'd laid boughs down as a carpet over the floor of the shelter, kept the butt ends of them sticking out and let the snow drift over top of them, so he could drag them out with the snow on them, unless the snow year was wet, and the floor became caked with ice. The weather tore at the shelter like vandals, but it had never come down once he'd gotten it figured out.

Night was coming down through the rain, it was cold, he and Judy were shivering. Bridger hurried, alarm grabbing him, and yanked the ammo box out from under the pile of branches and sod, threw it open. Everything was dry, and he pulled out the beginnings of a fire already laid, put it in the fire hole, pulled the leather bag of matches and flint and steel out of his shirt, took a match, and lit the nest. It flamed up, and Bridger fed kindling into it out of the box until it was crackling madly, made a pyre of dead pine over the writhing orange, and built it up until it would roar. He set larger pieces of wood beside the flames to heat up and dry.

Judy snorted and stamped when he stripped the saddle, blanket and bedroll off her, because the cold then got right to her, and her skin twitched like he wished his could. He threw the roll open on the ground, rubbed her down with the wet saddle blanket, and draped a dry one over her. On a flat stone he'd brought here from a cliff face up the draw because the stones down this way were all egg-shaped ankle busters, he poured out the last of the grain, fished the wizened carrots from Mary's root cellar out of his saddlebags, and put them down. He took the slicker and draped it over Judy to the ground on the outside, pinned and tied it in place, and stood a moment seeing if the wind was going to push the smoke from the fire back into the shelter — some, but survivable. It just stirred it, mostly.

The wind howling as though the world was pained mixed with the fire crackling as though things were looking up, and the last of the day's light drowned.

I'm hungry.

3

Good morning, May, Henry said.

Good morning, Henry, Ilya said.

Henry had gotten up when she rang him from Broadway, looked at his watch — 6:10 a.m. — pushed the door release, crossed to his bookshelf, taken down a random book, and was posing there with it when she entered his second floor office.

Please sit.

Thank you. She noted his pose. It reminded her that he had vulnerabilities, that she suspected he was an uncomfortable man, beneath thick skin. The book he'd chosen was Bleak House. Not his best effort, Ilya thought. If he'd chosen Guide to Gouging the Poor for the Contemporary Robber Baron, perhaps this posing would have been plausible. Though, she also thought Dickens was apt given his social position, believing the book had to do with rich and poor divisions. But she was only supposing, because she hadn't read it. And it was true that Henry did like Dickens, it just wasn't believable that he was standing in his office reading him right now.

Henry replaced the book, grimaced a little when he saw which it was, not having read it himself, and supposing the content was as Ilya imagined. He turned and stood looking out the enormous window at the changing of the guard from night to day on the street soaking in the dawn light. His suit was a straight, simple cut, pressed, the same dark gray as his hair, which was cut short and followed his small, well-shaped skull. He was thin and tall, slightly taller than Ilya. She thought he looked like a very well-made riding crop.

Henry watched a young man wearing a suit twisted like a rope around him vomit into the street, one arm around a streetlamp, and remembered the one and only time he had done that, let himself go to that point, remembered how much he hated the loss of control, and imagined how empty this chap's pockets now were, and how his tongue must feel to him. He watched another young man in a suit walk by, glance at the man vomiting, smirk, shake his head, and walk on, chin up and out, hat cocked, whiskers impeccable. Henry remembered looking and feeling like that man, too. He took satisfaction in the thought that more than likely this man around the lamp post would be run down and devoured by this city. It was a common outcome, and the city, the whole country really, quite brilliantly had many convinced the reverse was true. It was that eyes-wide-open, shit-eating grinning, back-slapping mendacity that was the huffing engine room of the country. No matter. They were astoundingly cooperative, people, so willing to feed themselves, their families, into the furnace. Henry had noticed that tendency early on in life, saw it in himself, but squashed the instinct. He adored the founding fathers for concocting this place where people would sit with their life, liberty, and pursuit of happiness like they were bath toys to enjoy in his cauldron. So perfect, this place.

The newsie took his place on the corner outside and barked out, Sun!...Sun, here!...Sun...Republicans destroy America in time for elections...a new Representative on the Ballot and he's a Nigger...

Henry smiled. He loved to listen to the newsie editorialize. This was the hour Henry normally went out for his papers, because he beat the newsies to work, something on which he prided himself. He began work so early because he liked to, because he liked the world best at that hour, and he liked to schedule meetings very early, believing it gave him an advantage over less driven people. When Lillian had passed, he'd moved into the upper floors of this building, and so far, he liked being a widower, and only having to walk downstairs to be at work.

Have you made up your mind? he said, when he felt he'd made her wait long enough.

I have.

He nodded once, returned to his desk and sat, the chair giving one squeak that ended fast. He took a thin cigar from its place sitting on his clean desk top in front of him, and lit it with a desk lighter shaped like a mining hammer — a new acquisition to accompany his new ventures. The smoke smelled excellent. Ilya took her cigarette case from her bag, removed one, and put it between her lips, looking at his eyes. They were colored like the basement floor she had just swept. His face was clean-shaven and lean, cheekbones strong, skin not heavily-seamed though that was beginning, and he was handsome and competent-looking in a way his pudgy son may have achieved, but it was unlikely. Herbert just hadn't had this man's sensuous power.

She stood up from the chair that was designed to make people wish they were somewhere else, smoothed her skirt with her hand, moved to the desk, bent over it with her cleaved bosom loud, took up the lighter and lit her cigarette, the flame spouting from the striking face of the hammer. Starting back toward the chair, she changed her mind, and roamed the room, wanting to be a moving target. The austerity of the room was such that it was as if the place had been built by a Shaker carpenter who had become offended by the baroque extravagance of the Shaker style, and rebelled. The floor was maple, every board the same 10-inch width, rubbed to a glossy yellow finish. It looked like tanned hide. The trim and doors were quarter-sawn white oak, and all the pieces with any knots or checks or areas of blight had been weeded out, creating a perfection that felt artificial. The furniture was either maple or oak, no flamboyant rosewood, which was currently fashionable. No inlays, no curly brass pulls. All of it was made with a symmetry and precision which was admirable but terrifying, as if each piece had something vicious trapped within it. It was a wail of a room, like the sound Bartleby would have made if he hadn't known it to be futile.

Well? Henry said.

I want more.

Mmm.

I know you didn't expect me not to make a counter offer.

No. No. I expected it. Even though you have no standing to make one.

Not legally. Not socially. Not culturally. But, I can make being you...unrewarding.

That's highly overstated, but I respect your hubris. You could never be more than pesky for me, but I am willing to pay to avoid even that. And, I respect the power of your French friend, though, not her. Henry noted to himself that this last was a lie. He respected Jacques, and somewhere, niggling down deep, there was fear of her.

He said, How much more?

Three hundred.

Ah. Eight hundred altogether. I see you've dressed for travel. Are you going abroad and want no one to mistake you for anything but an American?

Ilya's outfit was a lean dress of dull blue linen, a big, white cap with red trim into which her hair was tucked, red leather gloves to her elbows. She was a flag off to conquer. They loved their country, this family, and she had had the thought that the flag colors would give her a better bargaining position. It was also the only dress in her wardrobe with a neckline so low it made one think of crotch. Her choice now seemed silly to her — that to this man, the dress made her look weaker.

When one is so close to being a foreigner as I, she said, one must take compensatory steps, don't you think? For you, this is not an issue, since one can still smell the reek of Mayflower around you.

Well. I think I speak for all true natives when I say thank you for your patriotism. Have you removed yourself from my son's house? My house?

Yes. It's just a matter of picking up my bag and my dog.

'Bag?' One bag?

Yes. My father and I made dresses, which means I have few of my own. 'It is not the shoemaker who has good shoes.' You'll recall I did not come with much.

True. You did not come from much, either, so you're hardly to be blamed for that. In fact, I believe you're doing quite well for yourself, given your constraints. You've shown good business instincts.

True.

And so, I can trust that I needn't check on our silver as you depart?

You can trust me, I believe you already know that. I am difficult, yes, I've heard, but not deceptive. I considered scraping the gilt paint from the woodwork and taking it, but thought that might be perceived as too Jewish.

Good thinking. Never your intelligence that was at issue.

On the contrary.

Ah. You think I am threatened by your intelligence?

From inside your castle? Not at all.

Correct. That is in fact the point, or one of the points, of striving to build one. Though, I wouldn't feel threatened either way. Do you have the papers?

Yes.

And you have made your peace with Herbert? He has been informed? Not terribly distraught over the way things have played out?

He's accepted it with deathly calm. I almost think he wanted it himself.

Very good. It was a touching romance, and death comes to all romances, in one form or another.

Yes. If only we'd had your wisdom and seen that at the beginning.

No, no, that would not have been good...or possible, at all. There are few things as destructive as romance found and lost when you're old. This way, he is young, and he'll be over it quickly, and the stronger for it.

I daresay he is over it. I've never seen him with such quiet, strong resolve. It is as if he matured before my eyes.

Really?

I think he may have found someone who is better...suited...as it were.

So? Who?

Oh, I don't know. I never heard a name. I'm hardly the one he would tell. Better I don't speculate. I feel quite sure that whoever it is will be a better fit for your family than I. There will be a brilliant...symmetry, I feel sure of it.

Henry stared at her for a moment, twisting the cigar in his lips, exhaling through his nose, and felt the maddening pull toward her he was weary of smothering. He lifted his eyes and stared over her head, smiling.

I should have bedded you. It would have been unprofessional, however. And I would never have married you as he did, no matter my youth. He misunderstood the place of women, and the purpose of marriage. Something I never did.

He misunderstood many things, which was, of course, much of the attraction, since it made him manipulable. Well. I don't blame you for restraining yourself, and not seducing me. I prey on the inexperienced, of course. One predator doesn't attack another unless it's necessary. And I'm appreciative of your restraint, as soap and water only remove so much.

Henry smiled. Ilya took the paper from her bag, unfolded it, and placed it beside the others on the plain, blonde sweep of his desk. He glanced at the signature.

You're cooperating in a way that is unlike you.

Yes. And it's causing me not a little discomfort to do so.

I'm certain of it.

Would you care to hear the reason?

Trembling.

I would like the money in cash. Now. I have a train to catch.

The room went still. She stood across from him, leaning against the bookcase, looking at his slate eyes with her chocolate brown ones. The rising clatter and chaos of Broadway omnibuses went loud.

I see, Henry said. Sudden.

Yes.

A train bound for where, that you can't cash a check from me?

Oh, my train is for Boston. I will live with my relations there for a while. The cash is so that I can pay certain people here to whom I owe money. People that are not very...flexible, about the form their payments come in. Or when they come in.

Henry smiled in a genuine way.

You owe money to shylocks? Hah! I will give you another hundred just for amusing me.

They aren't called shylocks, Henry. This isn't a Shakespeare play, and they don't have horns. They are salary lenders. Ilya enjoyed the thought of Jacques, from whom she had gotten the money, as a shylock.

Indeed. Thank you for updating my lexicon. No matter. Just the irony that you are a Jew who managed to marry into a wealthy family, and you've managed to entangle yourself with...what do you call them? 'Salary lenders?' And have you recently obtained employment, that you have a salary to borrow against? What do you do?

Oh, I needn't show employment. My body and my address were enough.

Did you use my name in one of those places on Second Avenue?

I did not. I respect your need for privacy.

If I find out otherwise, and gossip about your...deed, and your connection to me comes out, I will punish you.

They are not terribly curious people, and I used my father's name, which they recognize. They weren't very demanding. And I can be very persuasive. They are becoming more so now. Demanding, I mean.

What did you buy with the money? We've given you everything. I have.

No. For instance, you did not give me cash.

Give cash to a Jewess?

In any event, it's probably better you don't know the particulars. It was a medical service. A woman's issue, in both senses of the word. It's why I didn't ask you or your son for the money. It would disgust a man your refinement.

Henry stared at her. His face went hard. She stared back at him, her body tense, waiting, measuring, regretting the risk she was taking but wanting to hurt this man more, now that she was committed to it.

I'm to understand that you...tampered, with my line?

Tampered is a lovely word for it. I did more than tamper. I ended it. Ilya realized she'd just indirectly admitted to killing Herbert. She said, I ended the line coming from me, at any rate. My replacement is of course free to amend that. You see, Henry, I was in a position where no choice could be a good one. If I had continued with it, I would have died, spiritually if in no other way. And that only to serve your son, you, and your family, which already has so much, you see. It was either I give you something, or I take something away from you, and given our relations, I thought to take from you was the best course. And consider, sir, the vile and dangerous concoction that the mixture of yours and my blood in one being would have been. That creature would have shamed Satan himself, don't you think?

Henry rose and walked back to the window, stood looking out, hands in pockets. Ilya watched him.

Your insolence, he said. I confess, I admire it, disgusting though it is in your sex. Your blood has saved you, as you know. If you were an Anglo, if your blood wouldn't have sullied mine, I would have seen to the punishment myself. Punishment that would have drawn the approbation of Satan.

Hm. And I thought you would double the money for my doing you this favor. You seem ungrateful, to me. I have set your son free, I have kept your line pure — at great personal risk, a risk you can know nothing about, being male. I have kept my mouth shut, and I have kept your house clean and in good repair, despite your son's protestations to the contrary. Why, just this morning I swept your basement. Yet, you speak as though not punishing me is an act of charity on your part. Your sense of entitlement is very evolved.

My sense of entitlement has been earned. And you will get the five hundred from me, but no more, and that is more than you deserve, you who connives for what they get. Though, you connive well, I acknowledge. And recall, please, that though your choice was the right one, it was not yours to make. My blood is mine the way this desk, this city, this country, is mine. I decide.

I knew what you would want, and thought it best not to trouble you with trifles. I also was smart enough to see this parting day coming, and thought simplicity would be paramount. Imagine the complexity if a child were involved. I apologize for my lack of judgment in the matter.

Accepted, with cynicism.

A wise codicil.

What's the interest on your loan?

Fifty percent. It doubles if I miss the due date, which is today.

Mmm. A line of business I should get into perhaps, with that rate of return.

Oh. Too literal for you, I think. No challenge.

True. Having others dig up oil for me has an attractive subtlety. I'm tired of this. Of you. Henry noted this lie to himself. I have work to do. I don't have five hundred dollars sitting in my office.

He returned to his desk, studied the paper she had laid there for a moment, slid another toward her.

Sign this. You now have absolutely no legal way to come for any more of my money. Your ties to my family are severed. I assume that meets with your approval?

It can't be overstated. She leaned over and signed.

That mouth. If a word of this appears in any newspaper, anywhere in the country, or the world for that matter, your life will take a turn darker than even you would enjoy. A remark overheard in a saloon brings my retribution. You are not, nor were you ever, a Jew who married into my family.

Put your mind at ease, if that's possible for you. It is not difficult for me to not be Jewish. That was much the point of the whole exercise, after all. Though it was difficult for me to be Anglo, impossible really, about which I'm disappointed in myself. It turns out that I am a poor actress. And no one finds this drama more dreary than I. I only want to be free of it.

He reached into his breast pocket, removed his billfold, took out all the cash, counted some out on the corner of the desk.

That's one hundred dollars. He wrote a check and handed it to her. That's four hundred. It will be redeemable on Monday morning, 9 a.m., at any bank in the city. Or in Boston, makes no difference. I assume one hundred dollars in cash is enough to keep your brethren from dismembering you until Monday?

Oh yes, plenty, thank you. They won't burn your house down either, if I request that they don't. Would you like me to?

Oh. Young lady. You must know that any mark of any kind on what is mine brings vengeance beyond your imagining. My reputation, my property, my family. Anything.

My imagination is quite vivid, but I'll accept the assertion.

I've had enough of you. You were an amusing bauble in my house for a while, but now you're an unbearable annoyance. Go wherever people like you go. He grappled with the mendacity of the stance toward her he was taking.

Thank you for your graciousness, Henry. I always believed Herbert got his gentlemanly qualities from you. He will go far in life with such equipment. He will be the fuel that drives the country.

Go.

Good day, Henry. As she turned, Henry watched her, watched her body, and began to miss her. When the door had shut, he said, If only she wasn't a Jew, and began the work of expunging her from his mind.

4

Mary sat on a high stool at a plank workbench in her workshop, staring east at the morning sunlight coming over the mountains, a bright penumbra of yellow-white light surrounding the highest peak. Her husband had located their house and store here partly because in early fall the sun came up in this spot, and it made for a very religious-looking morning. He had been religious in a way she was not, but he was kind, and had a sense of humor about it, wasn't oppressive, didn't proselytize. Good quality and beauty were the angels of his true religion. Good quality had to be supplied personally since people brought little here with them, and created even less, though they might someday do better. But beauty there was much of, a tiresome amount she often thought — the stark mountains that were somehow astonishing and ravishing no matter when you looked at them, the weather that was always severe, always overdoing it, always trying too hard, like she was living in the mind of a young artist with no control and no sense of balance, someone who didn't value anything other than 'more.' And always this beauty had an aloof, deadly quality to her, powerful and indifferent, like a massive, unwieldy, and vicious monarchy in which men had made a play democracy. But it was lovely to look at, from indoors.

She watched Bridger come out of the cottonwoods and walk quickly toward her back door, passing the cabin she and Gerald had lived in while they built this house. She smiled a little at his furtive, fearful haste, the awkward position of his body, the comically mangled clothing, the way he tried to hide himself behind just a wish for invisibility. The bleeding insecurity and sense of inadequacy which stoked his potential for rage made her grateful she'd never had a child, and also grateful this one had come along with strangely perfect timing — he seemed to have come slinking out of the storm of Gerald's passing. It was the sort of event that also made her think it was at least possible that a big someone with brains and a decent if conflicted heart was making a few helpful decisions here and there.

The wooden latch Bridger had made stuck when he tried to slide it back. Damn, he muttered, shame pulling down on him. He pulled on the handle and leaned against the door, working the two around until the wood gave and slapped back out of the mortise he'd chiseled into the jamb. He looked around behind him before going inside.

Good morning, Bridger, she said, and drank coffee from the white porcelain cup that was more a bowl. The coffee was rich, black, and sweet. She bought enough for herself, and sold the people of this town the dirt they seemed to enjoy for reasons she would never understand, and no longer cared to know. She and Gerald had spent some time trying to sell them good things instead of bad, but they were very attached to their horrible food and drink, and held most all else in contempt, with what she had come to think of as their peasant arrogance that swapped good with bad.

Mornin', ma'am. I c'n fix that latch fer y'...it swoled cuzza th' rain las' night.

It's fine. You did a nice job. It takes time, for the wood to become accustomed to its role. Better that you made a tight fit that will improve, rather than a loose one that will get worse. It will swell and shrink and wear against itself. Next year it will work smoothly. Gerald would have approved. And it was smart of you, or us, to put that roof over the door. Without the sun and rain beating on the latch, it shouldn't split too badly for a while.

Reckon so.

Mary rose, left the workshop, went to the black kitchen stove, took up the pot, poured another cup of coffee, dosed it with milk and sugar, and brought it to Bridger.

Thanks, ma'am.

Oh. Don't call me ma'am, anymore. I don't like it.

Yes, m...

She smiled. Sit down, she said. Today is a good day, I've decided. It seems that's something you just have to decide is true. It doesn't come on its own. Do you see it that way?

He shrugged. Never thought 'bout it.

Hm. You might start.

Bridger took his hat and coat off and sat on the stool beside her. They both looked through the glass at the onset of the day — the strange, malevolent creeping of light across the dying grass and pale, green sage sending up its fingers of brown fall seed, the aspens by the dry creek quaking in the low breeze as though shedding the night chill, making their low rattling Mary and Bridger couldn't hear but could supply for themselves.

How is your father?

Same, I reckon. Ain't seen 'im in a couple days.

Mary smiled faintly at the boy's disgusting English. She hated Bridger's father with a special ruthlessness, partially because it was he that got the boy speaking this way, or let him. She tried sometimes to correct Bridger with some success, but mostly put her energy into trying to coax him into not being the cramped-hearted asshole his father was, however he spoke. Bridger didn't take correction well. He seemed to feel it as harsh criticism. She had decided that it was best to just try to gradually get him to not pull away from her influence, rather than to exert literal influence. But now she instinctively felt she was out of time for delicacy.

You have to get away from him. You're old enough. Well. Not old enough really, but it will have to do. You're good enough, strong enough, you can learn the rest of life from here without him, and begin to unlearn him. Having so much of him in you, it's unlikely to go well. But, one never knows. Flowers grow in manure. I'm not calling you a flower, by saying that.

Reckon so. He jes gits crazier and meaner. Nothin' makes no sense. I'm out fixin' fence, an' we got no cows an' no money. He's down t' chewin' on bones. I brung 'im food from what y' give me, but he don' cook 'r nuthin'.

And he drinks heavily, of course?

Yep.

Well, whiskey makes everything better for him. Or, he believes that. It's medicine. He's sick. His brain is broken, like that latch there, but it won't fix itself being used, though I don't believe thinking was something your father ever did much of in any case. That latch is the more complicated mechanism. Some of it isn't his fault, I suppose. But, he can't be fixed. I'm not just making this up to influence you. The doctor has spoken to me. Your father won't see him, but the doctor guesses that your father is syphilitic, judging by the growths beginning on his face. He could live a long time, but he'll only get crazier and more unpredictable, and most likely, he'll eventually hurt you, or kill you. Or someone else. He hasn't the residual character to restrict the violence to himself. If this were the East, they'd put him in quarantine with others like him and let him gradually expire. But this is the wide and wonderful West. Here, they'll just let him go wild until it's too much, then kill him. Or take him out away from everything and leave him to die. I'm sorry. It's horrible. But that's your situation. And you're the only one who can make the decision about what to do with yourself. You need to have all the information there is before you do. I am probably the only one that will tell you the truth, but if you don't believe me, you can ask Will. He's not a man with a lot of initiative, but he's to the point, and honest, if not articulate or sensitive.

I b'lieve y'.

Thank you.

I know it, too...reckon I don' know it either, at th' same time...thinkin' he'll git better.

I understand. It's time to just know it, and proceed from there. It will hurt forever, it will hurt in ways you won't be able to feel, strange as that sounds, but not as much later. If you were much younger, I would take you in. I thought perhaps we could clean out the cabin and you could stay in it, like a renter, and work here. Your father would come after you though, wouldn't he?

Bridger nodded.

And in this town, filled with these...imbeciles and their vengeful hearts and bestial rules...they might react in some infantile way. Think things that aren't true because they want them to be. Working for me is one thing, living with me...it would inflame their ingrown imaginations unbearably. Will wouldn't agree with them but he couldn't stop them from doing whatever it is they would do. If I were the man and you the woman, it would be different.

How come y' don' go? If y' hate 'em so?

Oh. I don't know. I don't want to leave Gerald. And I don't feel well enough, really. I'm weak. I don't want any more of life. Not the kind where one struggles and moves around and hopes. I turned forty years old today. Few women live to be very old, and those that do are often awful. I only ever knew one truly old woman personally — a decent woman, who became a dried out, bitter wretch. She spat on people, and sat in her own offal. I suppose there must be those who don't go that way, who stay good and gracious, but I don't see myself as one of them. Certainly, I wouldn't like to gamble.

Y' might be one of 'em. If anybody would. Happy birthday.

Thank you, Bridger. We'll see what happens. I have this house, and Gerald built it, he's in it, and now it has you in it as well, and that comforts me. It's tight, and warm in the winter and cool in the summer. He located it so it's sheltered from the wind — he didn't just cut the trees down to build and heat with and then have no protection, like those fools down the street. The trees shade it in summer, but you see, in the winter, when the sun is low in the south, the sun hits the house directly. If I were younger, I would leave because the house hurts me and I would want more living, and change, but I'm old, so I want to be warm, and familiar. I can't have him, but I can have his workmanship, which is a lot, as it turns out, in this life, which is something one doesn't see when one is young and famished. Look at the carpentry in any other building in this town. Laughable. I was in the restaurant the other day, if you can call it that, and a nail just fell on me without provocation. The structure has moved around and dried up, and the nail just worked itself out and fell. The wood is twisting and shrinking and the building is essentially tearing itself down, as if the trees it's made of are rebelling against what was done with them. Gerald would have such sport mocking them to me. Those buildings will be gone in a decade, but Jesus will stay in this one when he returns for the Apocalypse, and needs lodging. You'll go, so I can't have you, but I can have your latches, and doors, and steps. This is not a very good town, but I don't think any are out here. It's not a boom town because the grass is good and there's a lot of water, so the ranchers will stay, and the town will last. And I can survive easily on what I sell, and what I've saved. My supply routes are in place, my suppliers all know me. The men here have all given up pursuing me, except the new ones who show up, and they don't last long, now that I've mastered the correct demeanor to discourage them quickly. Quite simple, really. Stare at them insolently, and never smile. That's good for you to know. If a woman is doing that to you, don't go towards her, or she'll despise you more. The men hate me, but that comforts me more than the reverse would. Except for Will. No. I'll stay. I'll just watch.

Aright.

Mary smiled and turned to look at him. He was sitting very upright beside her on the stool, elbows on the bench before him, hands cupped around the coffee cup, face serious, staring out the window. He was filthy — his ears clogged, eye sockets blackened, stubble filled with dust, a red-black gash across his cheek. One thing to thank his father for, he had a lot of hair as that man did, like he could survive the winter without clothes.

You're dirty.

He looked crestfallen. Yep. Well's dry. Creeks 'r cold as shit.

You should just come here to bathe. You don't have to wait so long between visits, you know.

I don' like t' burden y'...

I see. I think it's more because you don't want to bathe, and you know I want you to. I think you always want to see me because I'm the best thing in your life right now, but you always hold back because it feels wrong, because I'm not your mother. It's fine. Gerald didn't like to wash either. He always felt like he wasn't getting enough done, and wanted to get back to work. A beautiful man in a big rush, but not entirely bright, and too absorbed in accomplishment to enjoy the time he had.

He wadn't smart? With them books y' got?

Reading doesn't make you smart, it makes you someone who reads. Oh, he wasn't stupid, but intelligence wasn't his best quality. It was that he was good. Big-hearted, so that his brain seemed smaller. A big person. Most men are small. Most women too I suppose, but I don't know, and I don't care anymore. I like talking to you...you're not nailed shut yet. And you listen — extremely rare in anyone. I assume that's what you do as you sit there staring.

Bridger groped visibly.

Just say thank you.

Thank y'.

Perhaps an 'I like to talk to you, also,' would be appropriate. If it's true.

I like talkin' t' y'.

That's called being gracious. A simple reply, gratitude and recognition, and not trying to be too much. It's a good quality to cultivate.

I like talkin' t' y'.

She laughed, surprised.

That's funny. Did you know that would be funny before you said it? You didn't, did you? Don't lie, not to me, not over this. Lie when it's a good thing to do. To strangers.

I dint know.

No shame in that. Inadvertent humor is a very good kind. It doesn't mean you aren't responsible for it.

Ma'am? Sorry, I...

'Inadvertent.' Not on purpose. And don't call me 'ma'am.' She reached out and stroked the back of his head once. He flinched away a little. She grimaced, and wiped her hand on her skirt. I have an idea, she said.

Bridger looked at her.

This is Sunday and it's my birthday, so I get what I want, alright?

I dint bring y' nuthin'...I dint know it wuz yer birthday.

That's because I didn't tell you. Now you are the only one who knows. Will would try too hard to please me. And you're about to give me presents, so you needn't feel guilty. Starting with a bath, because you reek, sir. A real bath, which I'm certain you've never had. I'm going to show you how to take one. Don't worry, I won't watch. But you will be clean perhaps for the first time in your life.

I don'...I wuz gonna finish them shelves...I'll git dirty anyways...

Poor logic. It's alright for you to get dirty over and over but not clean over and over. If you do both, you'll have balance. You'll have dignity. The dignity may be misplaced, however, I've seen that happen more times than I like to remember. Don't worry. Don't resist. Ease yourself and trust me. It's my birthday. It will hurt your heart, but it will be for your own good. Has anyone ever used that absurd saying on you?

Nope.

Of course not. Who would? Come...

The building was long and wide, the store in the front on the street, the living area in the center, and the workshop to the back. It was designed that way so only two sides of the living space were exposed to the outside, to hold heat. A row of square-milled fir posts marched down the center of the structure, and reached up to the peak to carry a ridge beam, and allow for the building to be wide and spacious. It created the sense of a huge volume of space overhead, the sense of being in a coarse cathedral. Mary adored the knowledge that her home was larger and grander than the church, adored the crimped jealousy she felt creeping out of church people when she saw them.

She pointed into the bathroom with the tub but no window, and small stove that burned low all year except July and August, when it was the coolest room in the house. The floor was red brick, laid in a herring-bone pattern, grouted with concrete, sloped to drain water out the same hole through which the tub did, that into a ditch which took the water away from the house and into the hawthorns which hid the house from the town.

Fill the tub halfway out of the pump, and I'll get your hot water. Bridger looked panicked — a clown feigning the expression. His stoicism sometimes wasn't up to the task of concealment, or was itself the more revealing. She laughed, a rarity for her, and she enjoyed the rich, thudding baritone in her chest. She felt an easing in her, a sense of enjoyment, a kind of rediscovery of a brand of pleasure gone missing, lonesomeness retreating.

Please don't worry. Be at ease, if you can. It's Sunday. The store is closed. No one will come here. They're either drunk, recovering from being drunk, or in church, all very similar activities. We're alone. People need days like this in their lives or they become...like your father. Or like Mr. Anderson. Being strong is just a burden if you are also bitter and live in isolation. You see? It will be fine, and if it isn't, what of it?

She watched him try to rearrange his expression into one more benign.

That's a good start. You're very lucky I'm in your life. Please don't turn into a miserable shit that thinks he did it all himself, if you do anything impressive with your life. You are at high risk of that because of your upbringing. Or lack of upbringing. I'm doing a lot of preaching today, so I need your patience.

Thank you. He remembered to pronounce the 'you.'

You're funny. And so quick on the uptake. Tub.

He went to the pump in the kitchen and began filling the bucket. The indoor pump still shocked him some, giving him a feeling that he didn't deserve it, a sense of awe, and the sense that Mary was cheating, that life was supposed to be harsh, that acquiring the smallest necessity was supposed to be a grinding battle. They were silent for a time, as he filled the tub.

Give me that one, she said, took the bucket from his hands, and poured it into the cauldron simmering on the stove. Their two figures reflected in blurry marriage on the copper sheet Bridger had mounted to the wall behind the stove to protect the wood from the heat.

Gerald was a big man, Mary said, giving the bucket back to Bridger. He pumped. Big in stature, I mean. He loathed the tininess of the rooms in the West. He understood that they kept them small so they were easier to heat, but he said if all it was going to be was more work to feel like a man rather than a rat in a hole, he'd do it. He said it was as if as the sky got higher and the land got emptier, the people got smaller and more frightened, and built structures smaller and darker, like they were becoming burrowing animals, which seemed to be true in the mining towns, where they would spend their days rooting around in the ground, then come outside and go into another dark hole of a cabin or lean to or what have you. It was surprising they weren't blind, they were so often in the dark. Literally, I mean...

Like voles.

What?

Voles 'r blind.

Oh, yes. Those little mice that make those tunnels everywhere.

Yep.

How do you know they're blind?

Pap said they was.

Hm. I wonder where he got his information. He doesn't strike me as a...scientist.

'Fore he got bent, he wuz good with animals. Horses mostly, but...he knew some shit. He had t' figger everythin' out fer hisself...no one taught 'im nothin'. His pap wadn't but a storekeeper.

Like me?

No, well...

Don't worry. And you? Are you good with animals?

Got some skills, I reckon.

You do, I've seen you, and you're kinder than I imagine he was. Is. So you can surpass him in that regard. I'm sorry, I should be less harsh toward your father. I didn't know him much before he went mad. He was a good sort then, mostly?

Wadn't always like this...Ma went, an' that wuz bad, but, I don' 'member her much. But, we wuz like pards fer a while...an' th' ranch, it wuz hard, but we wuz aright. He'd go...I dunno...one day, he'd be aright...never smiled much...kinda...always looked like he was gonna git mad soon...but sometimes he wouln't...an'...he'd show y' shit...how t' do shit...and...y' c'd tell he was tryin' real hard t' do shit right, but he wuz learnin' all th' time...he never aready knew how t' do somethin' 'fore he tried t', so shit wouln't go good. Then, it'd be like he climbed from one side of a fence t' th' other, and he'd be kickin' and yellin' and throwin' shit...an' if y' was close enough t' 'im then, y'd git hit with somethin'...best jes git as far as y' could from 'im...wait a while.

Ah. And he would feel badly about it later? That's sometimes the way of it. Bridger took the bucket to the tub, dumped it, and returned. Another bucket will do it, Mary said.

Aright, he said, and resumed pumping. I dunno. He never said nothin' 'bout it after, but he wouln't be so mad. Y' jes had t' look and see who y' wuz gonna git, and ack whatever seemed right fer it. Now, he's jes all th' time on th' one side a th' fence. An' now 'is face is gittin' all puffed out an' shit. It's fuckin'...shitty...

I'm sorry. It's an awful thing to have to behold. But not your last.

Bridger shrugged, and lifted the bucket of water from under the spout. He carried the water into the bathroom and poured it into the tub. Mary loved that sound, and smiled.

Help me with this pot. Here. She handed him two potholders, nodded at one handle, and took the other.

Ready? He nodded.

They carried the water to the tub and dumped it in, a gout of steam rushing into the air and curling against the low, plaster ceiling. Mary took a long, wooden paddle and stirred the water gently.

Isn't that sound lovely?

Yep...like a crick eddy.

Lovely thought. She ran her hand through the water. Try that.

Bridger ran his hand through.

Will you die in there?

No.

Do you want it hotter? Whatever you want, it's your bath. It gets cold quickly, so hotter is better.

I b'lieve this's good.

Alright. Help me refill this so I can heat more. They stood together at the pump while Bridger worked it.

It took Gerald a month to dig this well. Sixty feet straight down, hit water at thirty in the dead of summer, but said he would die before his well went dry, which he turned out to be right about. He was prescient, in that case. What do you think 'prescient' means, after what I just said?

After a moment, Bridger said, He knowed what wuz gonna happen.

Yes. Watching him scramble up and down that shaft, pumping out the water, filling the bucket with this merciless dirt and stone, working the windlass...he seemed insane...

Pap on'y went twenny 'til he hit water...s'pose that's why it's dry now...

Yes, it is. Being thorough is a kind of genius. Few have it. Does it bother you that I talk about Gerald to you? I can stop if it does.

No. I don' think so. I ain't...sure...

Alright. If you become sure, say something. It's just...I don't want you to believe that men only come in one variety. There are two.

I think I knowed that.

That was a joke. There are a few varieties of men. Not many themes, but a few variations.

Oh...I...

Your water's getting cold. Get in the tub. You can leave the door open. I won't look in, but, I have to be sure you are thorough. Everything you need is in there. You only have to do this once with me, and for the rest of your life, you'll be good at it. It's important. Do you trust me?

He nodded.

Smile. It's not serious, just important.

Aright, he said, but didn't smile.

Begin.

She made herself another cup of coffee, tore off a chunk of bread from yesterday's loaf, buttered it, and crossed to the window in the living room, looking out at the street and chewing, listening to the rustle of Bridger. Her place stood apart from the rest of the town. Gerald had staked out enough property to keep them at a remove, to maintain privacy, to preserve his sense of proper distance from others.

The town was dead still, cool and dry. The sun had yet to stir up the inevitable wind, and its annoying friend, the dust. She hoped today the wind would stay down. When it decided to blow, and just did it all day, and turned the world into a gritty, beige hell, she hated life, all of it. Early, when novel, it had been frightening and exhilarating. Now, she closed the store, pulled the drapes, lit every lamp she had, and the fireplace, and read in as much light as she could make.

She looked at the men laying in front of Dooley's, the leavings from Saturday night. Three today, one with feet on the stoop, lying back on the boardwalk, hat upside down behind his head. Another curled up against the wall beneath the window. The third was the most amusing — belly down in the street as if he'd thought he was diving into water.

The clock on her mantel pointed at eight. Will would be along in a few minutes and scoop the men up, as he did the worst of the animal shit that accumulated on the street. She loved Will for that. He wasn't a terribly busy man, so he had plenty of time for it, but it wasn't part of his job to pick up shit, and he did it anyway. No one else bothered at all. He said he did it because when the drunks fell in it, it ended up in his jail, which was also his office, and his home, so he had to sit there smelling it. The combination of rancid cowboy, stale whiskey, and horseshit could make a man start thinking life wasn't anything but a shit river, he claimed, and he couldn't afford to have that low an estimation of life in his position. It had been Will also who finally insisted that the cattlemen not push their animals through the street when they arrived in town, but pen them a half-mile to the north, so the mostly southerly winds would keep their stench away much of the time. It was a common sense move that took a surprising amount of effort on his part to bring about, and that effort further lowered people in his estimation.

She sat and watched the street, waiting for what little would happen to happen. She lit a cigarette — smoking was by far the best thing about Gerald being dead, and she doubting there was a heaven for him to watch from. Even if there was, and he could see her, she had confidence in her ability to talk him out of his disapproval. She exhaled and felt the soft, whining buzz fill her skull and loosen her face.

How are you? she said, lifting her chin and talking loud.

Aright.

Do you see that glass jar with the blue and white powder?

Yep.

Wet your hair thoroughly, and use that to soap it, then rinse it out thoroughly.

I done used it on m' body aready.

Mary laughed. That's alright. My fault, I should have told you. I got distracted. The yellow cake there is for your body. The idea is to be patient and do the whole job, like you would do if you were building something for me, which you are in a way. Don't stop until you're finished, even though you want to. Do you understand?

Yes'm...yes.

And try to enjoy yourself. It feels good. Sometimes feeling good isn't immediately obvious. Have you had that happen?

I dunno.

Think about it. Is the water hot enough?

Yep.

Mrs. Havish came by, so punctual and purposeful it felt like her purpose was to ruin life for everyone else. Mary smirked at her. She so personified the word 'bustle.' Everything she did was done at this constant grinding pace, where even when standing dead still she seemed to be roiling about — a fussbudget trapped in a hairball. Mary felt she must grind her teeth as she slept, and that one could hook her up to some sort of mill and end up with a pile of corn meal in the morning. Mrs. Havish was on her way to open the church, and prepare for Father Michael to arrive, a man whose impeccable cleanliness made Mary question her decision to scour Bridger. People who were too religious disturbed her, but it wasn't bigotry on her part, she just doubted their intelligence and honesty and strength and character and understanding of existence. It wasn't personal. But these two people, this priest and his sycophantic amanuensis who Mary suspected showed up at the church so early for less than entirely devout reasons – a reason to like them more, really – disgusted her. She generally didn't bother with outright, pure hatred of others, but in this case she allowed herself the luxury. And, interestingly to her – and she was grateful to them because they interested her and so little else in this town did – they had actually never done anything to her. They were just so persistently and unfailingly who they were that she felt an urgent sense that they must be stopped, just, she didn't know from doing what, unless it was breeding, but they'd already done that, just not with one another, as far as she knew. But one thing, the woman could churn beautiful butter because of that incessant, mindless, sanctimonious energy, and Mary valued her for that, since it was a chore she loathed.

Ma'am?

Mary. It's Mary, now. We're making a man out of you in one day, you see. Men who are forever 'ma'aming' me make me think they're trying to apologize for placing themselves above me instead of just not doing that. What's wrong?

I'm freezin'.

Oh. I told you that would happen, but you didn't listen. She sighed. Hardly anyone does, she muttered. Even you. She looked at the clock. Well, you've only been in there fifteen minutes and you've been filthy for sixteen years, so I'm guessing there's more grime on you. Is the tub water still a liquid, or is it more like mud?

Kinda dirty...

I was joking. You're making me feel that I'm not amusing. It's ungentlemanly of you.

Sorry...

I was joking. If you run your finger across your skin, does it leave a trail?

No.

Is there soap in your hair?

No.

Mary stubbed out her cigarette in the tin plate she reserved for the purpose. Alright. I suppose that's enough torture. You're not going to confess, she added to herself. Amusement is wasted on you. Pull the plug and let the water out. Dry yourself off and hang that blanket around yourself, but don't put your clothes back on, whatever you do. I would have to paddle you if you did that. Just stand there. Don't stand right on the bricks, they're cold, stand on the rug I put there, you see?

Aright.

Mary pumped another bucket of water, and set it down inside the doorway of the bathroom. Done?

Yep.

Take this water and slosh the filth out of the tub. I don't want to see it. I'll consider myself fortunate if I don't have to throw the tub away.

She went back to the stove, tested the water, took a breath, heaved the pot off, staggered across the room, and set it down inside the doorway. Stopper the tub, pour this in there, get back in, take that big sponge there, and rinse off with just the water, no soap. When you stood up, you took a film of dirt with you, see it on the towel?

Yep.

So, you see how that somewhat defeats the purpose of the whole endeavor, yes?

Yep.

Good. So rinse off, dry off with a new towel, and...so on. At some point you may begin to use your instincts in the matter. They should be telling you something by now. Don't tell me what it is, please.

Aright.

She crossed to the stove and took a smaller pot from the rack overhead — a device the design of which she and Gerald had quarreled over before she had asked, Who does the cooking? and got him to follow her direction. She filled it, put it on the stove, poked in lengths of pine, opened the damper all the way, and listened to the growing wind inside, and the manic crackle.

She crossed the Douglas fir floor, aged and tung-oiled until it looked like flesh, to her bedroom, and took Gerald's toiletry bag from the shelf inside his closet. He deplored drawers, chests of them, of any kind. The house was filled with doors that opened onto shelves. He insisted it was better this way, because you could look at everything at once, and quickly find what you needed, without rummaging through things. He also believed building a door required far more skill than a drawer, because a door had no perpendicular elements to hold it flat. The carpenter had to understand wood and what it would do to keep the door from warping into a leaf. A drawer, pah, join it together, done, simple, he'd said.

Ready? she said.

I reckon.

I'm coming in. Mary laughed a little when she saw him standing there wrapped in the feminine blanket, hair wet and rampant, with stubble more befitting a thirty-year-old man, and a look of confused sternness in his eyes.

She pointed at the shelf across the room at counter height. Those are your new clothes. Put on everything from the waist down. She crossed to the pile of his old clothes on the floor. Is there anything in here you want? It's all going to burn.

C'n I go through it later?

Good thinking. She kicked the pile toward the door.

Bridger crossed to the pile of clothes, smelled their unfamiliar newness. He reasoned out what the underwear was, never having seen ones that weren't long. He shook out the black trousers, which were very soft, and put them on in a hurry. Mary came back into the room.

I could have just told those clothes to walk out on their own. Do they fit?

Yep.

How do they feel?

Dint know drawers c'd be soft like these.

It comes from having them be clean, and washed. Some more women's lore for you. It would serve you well to know some of what we know. She looked at him critically. Ever shave?

No.

Well, it's something of a relief that all that hair is a lifetime's worth. Anything less and you might resemble apes too much. People might lynch you for proving Darwin correct, or capture and dissect you, dear Bridger. She dumped hot water into the white porcelain bowl, and laid out the brushes, razor, strop. Come, stand here, face the mirror. Bridger complied. They looked at one another in the glass.

Some men like to shave, then bathe, Mary said. Some men like to bathe, then shave. Some men like to do both at once. That seems foolish to me, but do what you want, I just didn't want to be near you when you were so filthy, so I'm doing it after.

Bridger stood in front of the mirror, his shoulders up, back stiff. Mary stood beside him, a little away, nearly equal in height. Bridger, honey, she said, if you get any more rigid I'll be able to chop wood with you. Please, be easy. He looked unhappy, tried to will himself into softness. I'm not angry at you, she said. I'm not going to hurt you. Or, excuse me, I might, but it will be the kind of hurt that one is well compensated for. He looked at her in the glass, was still for a moment, nodded. Alright? she said. He nodded again.

Take that brush there, see? Put it through your hair, front to back, same as you normally do with your hand. Tilt it more, you're not plowing a field...yes...just keep doing it...do you want short or long hair? This is your head, you can have what you want...unless what you want is too awful, then I will be forced to intervene.

Long.

Alright. I suspected as much. A bad choice in my opinion, but your hair is good enough to allow that. But you must keep it reasonably clean, or you'll look...bad. At least rinse it out often, please? I don't want to waste my time. That's fine. You have a nicely-shaped skull actually. Your mother must have been something for you to turn out as well as you have. Sad that you never knew her as an adult...or, whatever this is you are. Do you want hair on your face? Keep in mind, whatever you keep you'll have to tend or you'll look bad...quite right away, too, the way your hair grows. Let's just take it all off right now, shall we, see how you look? The current fashion for extravagant facial hair is...idiotic. If you want a mustache, you can grow one before you leave today. He nodded. She shook her head. Sometimes people laugh out of politeness, something to remember in case you ever have to deal with actual living people in your life other than me. Take that brush there, get it wet, rub it around in this soap here...right...harder...alright, put it on your face thick...rub it in...not your eyes and nose...down to your collar bone...to here...alright...that's enough. I'm going to do this part for you, otherwise you'll cut yourself to ribbons, but you must pay attention, because I won't do it another time, alright?

Aright.

She took the razor and moved behind him. Hm, wait a moment, she said. She left the room, got a low stool from the kitchen, placed it behind him, stood on it so she could reach. Stay still. For obvious reasons.

It was quiet except for the sound of the blade against his face. Sounds a bit like sanding wood, doesn't it? She smiled into the mirror at him, he nodded. Don't nod your head like that again. He could feel her breasts through the cloth of her damp dress against his bare shoulder blades, could smell her, and the sweet, unfamiliar odors of the soap mingling with the steam in the air and the hot water. She could feel the intense stiffness of his body through her nipples, and his slight trembling, and felt a sudden, strong pull toward him.

The tautness of the skin of his face as it emerged made her feel sad and old, and tears welled up, a rush of forlorn longing for Gerald soaking her. She wrestled with the memory of the Sundays they had had together, trying to relish the memory but hold it away far enough to survive it, the day with this peculiar, unique flavor the other days lacked, this quality that removed whatever pile of irritation and sick-of-each-other had accumulated, if only for that one day. It didn't work every time, but enough to form an indelible fondness. It had been her church day.

She finished and stepped off the stool. Wipe the rest of the soap off your face with this, she said, handing him a small towel she had dipped in the water. He did. Now, look at me. Bridger watched her face, noticed the change in her expression from staunch attentiveness to aching sadness, saw the wet in her eyes, said nothing. She looked at him, turning his face back and forth by the chin, avoiding his eyes, reaching up with the blade and scraping off patches of missed hair. She dipped her finger in the soap, and slathered beneath his nostrils with a quick wipe. Hold still. She grabbed the tip of his nose, pulled it up, reached in and cleaned that bit off, put the blade down.

This is going to hurt, she said, reached, and grabbed the hairs trailing from a nostril and yanked them out. He flinched. One more, she said, and did the other nostril.

You're done. Or, that's all I'm going to do, in any event. Clean everything in here and put it back the way it was. This shaving gear is for you, it goes in that bag. You can figure out how to strop a razor yourself, same principle as a chisel, different movement. Then get dressed the rest of the way. I'll make breakfast. Are you alright?

Are you?

She looked surprised, noted that he'd enunciated, and her face softened, her breath caught. I am, yes. Thank you for inquiring.

Thank you.

You will be a problem when you realize you are good-looking and not a bastard. I'm sorry that won't be today. Maybe not even while I'm alive. Much too much to ask from this life. Finish up, and come out. She laid her palm on his cheek for a moment, and left the room.

Astounding, Mary said, looking at him from the stove, bacon cheering behind her. It's a very shopworn phrase, but you do look like a new man.

I feel purty diff'rent.

I'm sure you do. Do you feel bad?

No.

Do you feel better?

Funny.

Awkward, I imagine.

Yep.

That's good. Whenever you do something you haven't done before, you feel awkward. That's why I don't want to do such things anymore. Though, in your case, even when you do something you've done many times, I'll bet you feel awkward...no?

I reckon. Not all th' time.

What do you do that you feel comfortable at?

Shoot.

Ah, yes. That shot you made on the deer off my stoop was remarkable. Lovely to see it just go right to the ground. Though, having shooting be the only thing that makes you comfortable doesn't bode well. Sit down. Boots fit?

Yep. Little tight. I don' feel like I got all this clothes an' shit comin' t' me.

Well, you do. Trust me, not to have to see you going around like something being dragged behind a horse is payment enough. And you've done a lot of work here, and it's been good, except for that first set of steps, and that one door, but you didn't know what you were doing then. Anyway, accepting kindness is also a skill you should have. Everything in life is not an exchange, though in this country there are few who recognize that. Here.

She set a heavy, white ceramic plate in front of him with eggs, bacon, and potatoes arranged neatly on it, a cup of coffee above it on a cloth place mat – an article he'd never seen. He set upon the meal, and the small enjoyment she got from watching people eat her food was dashed as he carried on as if he were trying to devour something still alive. She got angry and opened her mouth, shut it, smiled a little. I'm too tired, she thought.

She sat across from him and ate, looking at the paper. He slowed his eating after a while and calmed, straightened his posture, noticed the way she worked through her food gracefully.

It isn't trying to get away, you'll notice, she remarked, nodding at his plate. The Comstock is playing out. They're not getting half of what they were out of it. And it seems they're discovering that cutting down every single tree for miles around to have a mine wasn't a very good strategy. Mudslides washed half their houses away, again. The trees won't grow back because the soil is now in their houses, or downriver somewhere. Good for the soil, I say. Can you imagine the idiocy? Wouldn't they just pause a moment and say, Well, let's not cut down every single tree? After they did that very thing in the East and have had problems? And Europe? Now, men stand around with axes trying to get a tree to hurry up and grow so they can lop it down. Hurrying a tree. Incredible, don't you think?

Reckon it's hard for 'em t' think they ain't 'nough trees when they look out there at all of 'em.

True, that happens, I'm sure. But, perhaps it's really that they don't think at all. The frightening part is not that they don't know what's going to happen, it's that they do. And, of course, that even as they cut down the trees where they will grow, the government is telling people to plant them where they won't. They don't appear to be very contemplative, these men, but perhaps they are and hide it because it makes them feel effeminate. Like women, that means.

C'd be.

It's entertaining, however, and I'm privileged to be able to watch them from here and mock them. Gerald was very smart to stay away from mining. He hated the rapacity. He rode the mountains around here for weeks with a mining engineer to make sure there wasn't anything in this ground worth having.

How'd he die? Ain't never said.

That is the central irony of my life, Bridger. My husband died of consumption, which is a lung problem, which are problems miners often have, though consumption and mining are apparently not connected, not necessarily. He suffocated and coughed himself to death, essentially.

Sorry.

Thank you. Nice of you to have concern of any kind.

Wish I'd known 'im.

Really? Why?

Seems like he wuz a...damn good man...

He was. Does it make you uncomfortable to be here, in his home, with his wife, doing his chores?

They gotta git done.

There was a long pause.

You needn't belabor the subject. I mean, does it feel...wrong...to you, to be here?

No more'n anywhere's else...'cept out where they ain't nobody.

You really enjoy it, being entirely alone, outdoors? Or is it more that you just don't want to be around your father?

Guess now they's th' same thing.

Hm. No. But, very tangled up with one another, certainly. I mean, generally people prefer to be around others. I am alone, but I wouldn't want it that the town wasn't right out there, regardless if I have any important society with the people. Would you rather be alone right now, than here with me, talking?

I dunno.

You have a profound romantic streak, my young friend. Girls will quite swoon at your charms. Well, here's what I would tell you if I were in the business of giving advice instead of selling handy things, but it is Sunday and I am your preacher today. Think about perhaps learning to be around people a little. Maybe you naturally just don't like people, that's fine. I can well understand disliking people, I do myself, but you don't seem to know any besides me, and that makes your stance perhaps a little premature. Maybe your father spoiled you for all people, that happens. Maybe you just need practice. But, you don't know right now, so try to consort some. The people in this town are almost like human beings, you could start with them. It's probably perfect that they aren't terribly...ah, refined, shall we say — you won't feel so inferior. Say, 'Hello, how are you,' on occasion. Or, 'Hot today, isn't it?' Or, 'What a lovely swarm of locusts.' It doesn't matter. It just shows people that you probably aren't planning to kill them right then, which, as it happens, concerns people quite a lot.

Yer sayin' I shouln't set a long ways off and shoot at 'em as a 'howdy.'

Why yes, precisely. That was sarcasm. Very good. You see, I could tell by how quickly you learned to use Gerald's tools that you were a bright one.

It ain't that I got somethin' 'gainst folks...I jes never see none. None ever come by, anyways...

Well. Why would they? Between you and your father it would be like going to hell just to be neighborly. Most people's sense of self-preservation stays them. Surely, you can see that?

Yep. Jes...whadya do 'bout it?

I just told you. Go to Dooley's and just talk to someone for a while, you're old enough for that. Dooley is a good man, and can read, and has had a thought or two in his day. And remember, I just made you look less dangerous, that will help. Though there will be the initial shock to get over for them, when they see you. But don't ever describe this day to anyone. Carry on like this is something you figured out on your own.

Thanks fer all this shit, by the way...

You're quite welcome. And it's not shit. School's out, my dear.

Aright.

The Comstock drying up means many more miners will be roaming through here looking for somewhere else to defile. Pitiful sight, really, all those poor men with no holes to dig. I'll have to increase my stock. I dislike it that I'm culpable in this madness. It makes your way of living make some kind of deranged sense. And it makes my cleaning you up perhaps the worst thing I've ever done to a person. Now you will have to engage.

What else y' done that's bad? Guess y'd have t' compare.

That's an excellent question. And impertinent, also.

Yep.

Coffee?

Yep...please...Mary. She looked at him over the pot and the steam as she filled his cup.

Oh, she said, I had some fun hurting people when I was younger. It made me feel powerful, and I suppose within that context, I was. I wasn't very beautiful then, but all the other girls in my town were homely...it made me shine...so I got to manipulate men, or boys really. They would come...I would act accepting, then when they were most excited and optimistic, I would reject them. It was fun for a time. But human mating rituals are quite disgusting and abject in general, though there are those who make it look very fetching. I stopped when I met Gerald. Those boys were roughly your age. I was fortunate in that I didn't do it to one who was...unstable.

'Zat what yer doin' now, with me?

Why, Bridger. Scrape the dirt off you and you become positively grown-up. And not a little brash. You know, I honestly hadn't thought of that until just now as you said it. I'm a little ashamed, me, with all this time to think, missing something so obvious. There are similarities, certainly, I suppose. But this isn't a deliberate effort to pull you towards me then hurt you, though, true enough, it wasn't then, either, at first, it just became so after I realized I had the power. Anyway, you're not a suitor. You're my surrogate child.

Ain't any kinda child.

I don't mean child in that sense, in an insulting way, in being young, I mean in the sense of being my...adopted child, in a sense. Are you offended?

Guess not.

Disappointed, in some way? Is there something more you want?

No.

Alright. Well, I have more for you, anyway. This is my birthday, and your Christmas. She lit a cigarette and stared at him. He rose and went to the pile of his clothes by the door to the workshop, fished out his twist, and returned to the table. He raised it toward his mouth.

What are you doing?

Chewin'...

I know what you're doing. No. No, you're not. May I see that? He held out the twist, she took it, looked at it, sniffed it, and pitched it out the open window over the stove. He watched her and turned red, which she could now see without the hair.

School's back in. I've been watching you chew that disgusting stuff long enough. It's in your teeth. Speaking of which, I should teach you to brush them. I just scraped tobacco off your face, you're not putting more on it. And you're not spitting at my table. What were you going to do, spit on my plate?

I ain't thought that far ahead...

Here. She put her cigarettes in front of him, and moved the tin plate to the center of the table. This is less barbaric.

He lit one.

Don't pull it all into your chest at once. He did, and started coughing.

It seems I spoke too soon when I said you listened. It's alright. It's something people don't do naturally, they have to work at it. Smoking as well, for that matter.

Hell, that's...fuck...

Language. If you hit yourself with a hammer, fine, swear. At the table, no, not mine. You'll grow accustomed to the smoke if you are less impetuous about it. She clapped her hands. Now! The rest of your gifts. Isn't this fun.

She rose from the table, and went into her bedroom. She sat on the edge of her bed, put her face in her hands and wept for a moment, then stood at her window looking out, drying her face. The saddle bags were supple and heavy, well-designed and made. She took them from the peg, smelled them deeply, returned to the kitchen, looked at Bridger sitting, holding his cigarette like it was explosive. He puffed it with more caution.

Happy birthday to me, she said, and put the bags before him. Happy Christmas to you.

I ain't thinkin' a travelin'.

I know. But I think that will change.

Howdya know?

I don't. But one should always be ready for the worst to happen.

Me leavin'd be th' worst t' happen?

For me? Under the current circumstances? It very well might be, but I probably shouldn't tell you that. You are one of two friends I have in this town, not to frighten you away. But it would be a good thing for you, to go. You're too much person for here, which isn't as great a compliment as it sounds like. Open them.

Bridger moved his dishes aside, and reached out for the bags.

Clear the dishes from the table. He stared at her a moment, then stood and moved his dishes to the sideboard.

And mine. He did it.

Thank you.

Welcome.

He sat and pulled the bags across the table to himself, opened up one of them, and pulled out a pistol. He held it and stared at it.

That's been fired twice. Once when he bought it to test it, once to scare a bear away from our tent when we first arrived here. That's why it looks so new. That, and that I take care of it. Do you know how to use one?

Shot Pap's. Better with a rifle. Never had no pistol.

Well. Pistols seem to be popular. There's no holster, he never had one. He didn't like to carry it around. He said two legs were enough.

I got one t' home.

Good.

Don' seem right, takin' his gun. Whyn't y' jes sell me one? I'll work fer it.

Because I don't sell guns, as you would know if you paid attention, just ammunition. It's bad enough I sell picks and shovels. Though, now that I think about it, since I prefer the land to the people on it, present company excluded of course, it would be more consistent if I sold them guns to kill themselves with rather than shovels to dig with. Thank you Bridger, you've made me reconsider a long-held hypocrisy. In any event, as far as I'm concerned, you have worked for it. I don't want it, I have my own. And I feel in a good enough position to say that he would have liked you well enough for you to have it.

Obliged.

Think nothing of it. Excuse me. Think something of it. I didn't mean to prevent you from experiencing gratitude. You could use practice there, as well. There are cartridges in there.

Bridger fished in the bag, brought out a box of cartridges, and set them down. He ran the functions on the gun, felt its weight, looked critically at the wood-to-metal fitting, pointed it out the window.

Good gun.

Yes. He liked good tools, as you know.

Ain't gonna load it in here.

Very polite. Thank you.

Bridger took four books out of the other bag. One was Webster's Speller. Another was McGuffey's Reader. One was The Black Princess. The last was Tristram Shandy.

I can't read.

Yet. You have a few words. You can write a little. Your father should have left you in school long enough to at least finish that. You'll probably never learn, I know that, but I thought if you had these always around they might provoke you into it. Make you curious. I'll help you if you're around to help. Either way is fine. I can't claim being able to read has led to happiness or contentment for me, but it is a good way to pass otherwise worthless time. They are bookends as well as books. That one, that's a speller. Start there. See how much you remember. That one is a reader. Everyone in it is a great writer everyone is supposed to know about, though I often wonder if that's true. If you work with those, knowing what you know, you might be able to learn to read passably well. That Princess book there is a piece of unutterable tripe, but it's easy to read, and it's popular, so it will give you a good idea of the poor taste of the vast majority of people. The other is an impossibly chaotic and rather ridiculous book of pure genius you will hate and not understand, so don't try. If you get to where you can read Tristram Shandy and follow it, you've graduated. If you can enjoy it, you've died.

This's more'n anybody ever give me in m' whole life.

Right. It's a good day for us both. Giving is good, often. It's not over. One more thing.

She rose and went to the workshop, returned, laid a large, black leather roll on the table, tied with a thick thong.

This isn't his, he just wanted one. I ordered it from New York, he died, it came. It's never been used.

Bridger loosed the thong and unrolled the black leather. In it was a line of five wood chisels 1/4" to 1 1/4" wide, a small shaping plane and a larger smoothing plane, each with a spare blade, a small-headed wooden mallet, four shaping knives with different shaped blades, a thin-bladed saw with fine teeth to cut curves, a fat-bladed saw with big teeth for straight cuts. There was a large whetstone fitted into a pocket, and two sharpening files, one for each saw. There were two rasps, fine and coarse. A shamrock in a circle with the words, 'William Marples and Sons,' was embossed in gold on the leather.

Travels well, Mary said. And here are these. She put a stack of six silver dollars on the table. They're more fun than paper. I won't worry about you spending it all too fast, since you would have no idea what to buy. That's the end of the gifts for today. Now you can clean yourself, build yourself, educate yourself, inebriate yourself, and shoot yourself.

Bridger touched the coins. He removed each tool and looked closely at it, touched edges gently.

Gerald said that new tools should be sharpened before you use them. Then, you should never let them get dull, but always keep sharpening them, whether they need it or not. It's something of a metaphor, ah...a lesson...for life, don't you think?

Don' git dull?

She smiled at him. Yep.

5

Ilya stamped up Broadway, chin up, teeth clamped, fuming, feeling Henry had bested her, hating herself for having accepted his dismissal. Scrofulous men gazed at her chest, not bothering to look up at her eyes to assess possibilities. One well-dressed man looked at her chest, then up at her eyes, tipped his hat.

You couldn't afford them, Ilya snapped.

His face went dead and angry and surprised, and he started to reach out to accost her as she passed. She jerked away from him, pulled her cloak up to her neck, covering herself.

I swear to you sir, any further movement toward me and your future will be brief. She stared down into his eyes. He stared back for a moment.

Hussy, he said.

Oh, yes. That is why you are not good enough for me. He flushed and began to raise his hand.

You overreach!

You have no say, sir. Good day. She walked away from him past the Old London Street Market, which had apparently been put up to make everyone glad they hadn't lived in Old London. It was her favorite neighborhood place to buy gruel and lumps of coal, and to watch mock lynchings in front of the Old Bailey she wished were real.

She went into Fleishmann's, stamping past the pines beside the flagstone walkway. They were just open, and filled with the hot smell of baking. The tang of yeast eased her somewhat, as she walked to the counter.

Your usual, Madame?

Yes, please, Hartmut. He nodded at her with his big, bald, bland head, reached into the pile of crosshatched loaves behind him, selected one after rejecting two, and bagged it for her.

Coffee today? he said.

She shook her head hard, expression taut.

You are alright, Madame? he said.

His words hit her, and she realized she was fuming visibly, as a lady shouldn't.

Yes, yes, I'm fine, thank you, Hartmut. No, no coffee, I am in a rush.

Very good, he said, slid the brown bag across the white marble counter, and took her money.

Be well, Hartmut, I will be away for some time, she said.

You are on holiday?

Something like that.

Very good. Please be well, yourself.

Thank you, Hartmut.

As she walked in front of Grace Church, wishing to raze it and the upper-class Episcopalians it supported to the ground, she passed an unconscious man with no legs sitting on a plank with wheels, wearing a purposely spliced soldier's tunic that was gray on one side and blue on the other. He wore a mashed kepi over a mangled face growing filthy hair, and was leaning against the wrought iron fence. A hand-lettered sign in his lap said, 'I lost.' Ilya took a dollar and pushed it into the palm curled upward in what remained of his lap.

Here. Drink yourself to death, she said. Just being alive is supporting the bastards.

She boiled past Union Square and down Fifteenth Street, raging at the growing crowds that seemed to only become worse year to year. At this time of day, on a Saturday, in this neighborhood, there had been a quiet and pastoral air to the city, but now to her it was as if some pustule had broken and flooded her streets with rabble of every stripe, as if the corners of the globe had been swept by a celestial maid into her parlor. The human variety that had at one time made her feel vibrant and titillated now ground at her, having to hack through this human brush not worth the effort to get to the presence of culture, since the presence of all of these grasping and oblivious fools made a trip to the theater redundant, and whatever production false.

She went right on Fifth Avenue and straight into the street, halting to let a landau clop past, the driver staring down at her with what might have been curiosity and chivalry, but in her current state was unbearable insolence.

She went up the white marble steps of Jacqueline's, past the two lions, one on top of each newel post, the one lying down and staring, the other sitting and roaring. My two testes, Jacques called them.

Fifth Avenue was less crowded than Broadway, and Ilya felt calmer. She stood there a moment, willing her breath to come down. The bell made a three-tone chime, the last note sad.

Good morning, Ilya! The small woman in the somewhat disheveled maid's uniform smiled warmly, and looked surprised.

Good morning, Zoe.

Come in, please.

Ilya passed through the enormous black door, the feeling of having come to a place of safety warming her.

You did not send a note you were coming, no? Zoe said.

No. I know I'm surprising you, I'm sorry it's so early, but it's very urgent...could you tell Jacqueline I am here? I know she is sleeping but it's very important.

Oh yes, of course, always she wants to see you.

Thank you.

Ilya felt ease and relief go through her, coating the fury from the street as she stood in the entry hall. She always felt this ease here. If Herbert's Greek Revival house on the Park was the skeleton of a living body, this place was the flesh and blood and imagination. The ceilings were high and coffered and gilded, and from the massive crown molding downwards was a fall of damask exuberance and lust for existence and pleasure, like cum down the thighs of a woman of surpassing beauty, and like the man who had supplied the stuff had gone off to do whatever it is they do — an apt analogy, because Jacqueline's husband Adelard was in fact away, trying to bring his notion of civility to some people in Algeria who maybe hadn't wanted it very much, and perhaps took strong issue. He hadn't been heard from in an alarming amount of time.

In his absence, Jacqueline had done the interior over. She hung the heavy, ornate damask tapestries down the walls and out onto the floor and into door openings. Carpets were everywhere, overlapping one another as if they were spills of desire on the florid, marble floor which ran out from beneath the fabric, and which the staircase, twisting down like a comforting encircling arm, ended upon. Sharp edges and hard surfaces were softened, made to feel like they were the fur or skin or claws of a living animal. Jacques kept the house warm, at the temperature of something alive. The Japanese erotic screens that had become popular that year were everywhere, though Jacques rightfully claimed to be using them before everyone else caught on. They were placed with no purpose or reason, the naked figures on them surrounding Ilya like a chain of dancers rejoicing in something Ilya didn't have, a gorgeous mockery of the living by the unreal. The place was faintly dusty, and smelled of perfume, incense, and sweat, all of it in a flickering, yellow glow from gas sconces with the flame turned low.

Ilya pulled off her cap and cloak as sweat started to come out of her, the moisture feeling acidic with fear, like it would rot through her clothes. She sat on a small sofa, stuffed to the point of splitting its floral skin, and she felt the softness of the room surround her, the muffled quiet, the sense of being safe and inside someone. She clamped down on the surge of tears and remorse and terror that bloomed in her now, watered by the anxiety and intense focus of the last hours. The Mariani was wearing off. There was a dirty, jittery feeling scurrying through her.

Come, Ilya, Zoe said from the top of the stair, smiling, from Ilya's angle looking like she was part of the gigantic, silly, crystal chandelier. Zoe was thin and gamin beautiful, with straight, jet-black hair to her shoulders.

Ilya went up the stairs, running her palm over the handrail, the breadth of which was her entire hand, past the balusters shaped like male and female arms in succession with spread palms holding up the handrail — Jacque's design.

Thank you, she said, looking Zoe in the eye.

Of course. Zoe smiled at her, presented her face, and they kissed both cheeks. Zoe took the bag of bread from Ilya, and walked away. Ilya passed down the hall and into Jacqueline's bedroom.

You want me dead, that you come to me at this hour? Jacques said. She was leaning against her pillows beneath the arches of gauzy red fabric over her bed like lips, her gray-streaked red hair spread around her face. The windows were tall, with drapes that were heavy, Arabesque tapestries pulled almost closed so the room was dim. The air was wet and heavy, and smelled of linseed oil, turpentine, oil paint, tobacco, incense, and perfume mixed with coffee and sweat and must.

Oh, Jacques, Ilya said. She threw her cloak, hat, and bag on a divan beside the door, walked across the area rugs that overlaid one another in no deliberate way, and sat on the side of the bed close to her, her shoulders sagging.

Ilya, you look terribly serious, even for you, who works so hard at it. And why are you wearing that insipid flag uniform? It isn't the Fourth again already, is it? Have I slept that long?

I've killed Herbert.

Why? Tell me he did not get you pregnant again? Then I should kill him myself.

No. I didn't do it on purpose.

Shame. I was interested there for a moment. He is really dead? Not the usual 'I'm Herbert and I am dead' dead?

No, the literal kind. Ilya lit a cigarette. Jacques watched her hands shake, and saw the way the exhaled smoke came out of her in hitches. She took the case from her hand and lit one of her own. As she lit it, she looked into Ilya's eyes for a long moment.

Hmm. You're not joking. Difficult to tell with you, you get exercised so easily over trifles. Well, that's very...something...my, I don't know what, yet, it's so early. Well. Thank you for coming before I am truly awake. Later in the day and I might have had an exaggerated response. Though, an exaggerated response to the death of that...man...seems difficult to imagine. Unless it's a city-wide celebration. She smoked and stared up into the fabric of her bed for a short while, looking sleepy and contemplative. Then she slapped her thigh through the coverlet and sat up.

Once more. You killed him?

Yes.

Oh, *mon Dieu*. The slight, imperious smirk that was Jacques permanent expression went soft and serious. Why? Oh, never mind. Foolish question. We need coffee. We need food, and some Mariani. We must plan...something...I don't know what. This is crazy news. How do you feel?

Ilya leaned over and laid her head in Jacque's lap. I'm tired, she said.

Oh, my darling, I'm sorry, I'm acting as if I am the only one here. Killing someone, I don't know, I've never done it, but it must be very disturbing. Though, in this case...perhaps not. It will be alright, my love, I will see to it. You are safe here. For a moment.

Zoe entered the room with a tray of coffee and sliced bread with butter and jam, and put it down on a table beside the bed. She poured coffee for all of them.

Zoe, guess what Ilya has done.

Mmm...I am sure I do not know. She sipped coffee and sat on a low, padded table beside the bed. A vertical band of light came through the drapes and sliced the gloom as the sun cleared the buildings across the Avenue. Motes dangled in the light. Did you...have an affair?

No. Ilya started to smile and the crease between her eyes smoothed. Jacques laid her palm against Ilya's cheek.

Zoe always thinks it's an affair.

Because almost always, it is, Zoe said. Did you...buy something wonderful?

Oh, much bigger, darling, Jacques said.

Oh! Did you...Ah, your husband, you left him!

In a sense, Jacques said. She killed that rodent Herbert. Can you believe it?

Zoe's face resolved into seriousness as if struck old. She stared at Ilya. Ilya felt awful that she'd brought gravity into this place where they were so adept at making things seem good. She nodded, the sound of her ear against Jacques' quilt loud in her head.

Oh, my friend. That is serious.

Yes, Ilya said. Zoe put her hand on Ilya's knee.

Oh, you two, how do you know it is so serious? Jacques said. It should be a national holiday. Zoe, we don't even know the details yet.

Details, they do not matter. This will be serious, for her.

Ilya raised her head, cheeks wet, and kissed Jacque's chest between the fabric of her nightdress sloping down from her shoulders, turned her head and laid her cheek against her breasts. Jacques held Ilya's head in her arms, and put her cheek against the crown of her head, inhaling the smell of her hair. Hooves clopped outside making time with the rattle of iron wheels on cobbles.

Darling, I'm sorry, Jacques said, of course you must be tired. Here you've already murdered someone and come all the way here to implicate me, and I've not even gotten out of bed. I really must start getting up earlier. I had no idea so much happened so early. So, who knows about it? How did it happen? Did he say something to provoke you? That's always made me want to murder him, when he talks...it's a wonder he stayed alive so long, really, when one thinks about it...all those long, staring silences followed by drivel...though, he never talked for long, which was courteous for such a boor.

We know about it, Ilya said. That's all.

How long will that be true?

I don't know. He's in the coal bin.

In one piece?

Yes.

Sad.

Eventually Gertrude will find him there, when she feeds the furnace. I don't know. It's chilly out. But, they like it chilly inside, so...who knows? At first they will think he just got lost on Friday evening.

Well, darling. Certainly, when you decide to solve a problem, you look for finality.

He tried to kill me. I let him know I knew about he and Jackson, and he tried to kill me because of it. It was insane. I didn't care about it, it made him more interesting to me, but...maybe I knew it would be the thing that would break him. We had just agreed I would leave...I was almost free of him...and I said something...I couldn't resist...but he was being so stupid and cruel!

The irony, Jacques said. He was murdered because of his only redeeming quality.

It wasn't murder! It was suicide!

Yes, I'm sorry. 'Murder,' it's a nice word to say. I've never been able to say it and have it be personal. He's been trying to kill you for quite a while, in his annoying, indirect way. So, there was a fight, and you won?

Ilya nodded. A fire poker to his head.

A hot one? Zoe said.

Only warm.

Shame.

Excellent question, Zoe. Promoting you from maid was a wise move, though, it's getting rather filthy in here, even for me. We can't have no one who cleans. Bravo, love! Jacques said. He must have been very surprised to find he was dead. Or perhaps he did not notice. Jacques removed the pins from Ilya's hair and toyed with it, pulling it free and spreading it over her, feeling it against her skin.

So, there is no time to lose, then, Jacques said, for...oh...for what?

No. If it gets very cold tonight, they might use enough coal to expose his body.

Lay down a moment here, we'll think. One day to flee. Are you fleeing? I suppose you must be. Do you have money?

Not very much. One hundred and fifty dollars. I have a check for four hundred from Henry, but by the time I can cash it Monday, they will know what I have done, and will have wired the banks.

Ach, Jacques said. You must learn to stop being impetuous. If you had simply waited to kill him on Sunday, much trouble could have been avoided. Though, it's very exciting, your way of doing things. I'm much too staid and cautious. You make me feel boring.

Jacques pulled her own hair back and tied it, then pulled Ilya to lean back against the pillows beside her.

It's too bad this is so much more serious than it should be, when one considers what has actually been lost, Jacques said.

He wasn't entirely...awful...Ilya said.

No. No. There have been worse men, Jacques said. And he might have become something like a man, eventually. But, my, he certainly went bad very quickly. I don't understand it. He made being tormented look very dull...and mendacious.

They are made of falsity, Zoe said. It makes their hearts work.

I know, I know, darling, Jacques said. But, they aren't quite consciously willing themselves to lie. Adelard doesn't lie on purpose. That's the interesting part about them...one of the few...

Ilya is going to understand it, eventually, Zoe said. She is so intelligent.

They consciously know they're lying, Ilya said.

Yes, but the impetus to lie isn't conscious, Jacques said. It's not like choosing a hat.

Well, so what? Zoe said.

Well, it means it's evolutionary, Jacques said.

Of course. He lies about which tavern he went to, something that doesn't matter at all, because otherwise a ferocious animal, it will leap out and devour him...it is not sensible...

Zoe! You've become so impertinent. That could very well be the case, though it does sound facile. It's just, in the context of this world now it makes no sense...

Well, and why are they not required to make sense in this world, then? Zoe said.

'Required?' I'm sure I don't know. But they're tools, not people.

First he became awful and unlike his father, then decided to try to be awful just like his father, Ilya said. But, without revealing his sexuality.

He would have been dead shortly, anyway, then, Jacques said One cannot conceal that for long.

How did you find out about that? Zoe said. You did not say.

He and Jackson behaved like we do, when they thought they were unobserved.

They were intelligent and witty? No.

Ilya laughed. No, they were...too intimate with one another for there to be any other reason. And...I can understand a man disliking me, in fact I relish it, but I cannot believe a man who does not want to fuck me, unless he prefers males.

They are not very creative, mostly, men, in living, am I correct, Zoe?

Of course, she said.

Jacques lit a cigarette, moving the freestanding ashtray in the shape of a blooming flower closer to herself. Though, she said, neither are we, it's just that we don't start off so awful. Though, there is Mrs. Beedle next door...did I tell you she cut limbs off my plane tree because it shades her bedroom? Without telling me. Now, why would she do that, do you think? I don't understand Anglos at all.

She does not like it that we are happy here and do not need her or her kind, Zoe said. She will always try to make us unhappy because she is not happy. It is not complex. We are complex so we naturally think others are, also. Not so. She is just a stupid, small woman whose heart is hard.

I'm sure you're right, she's just a...shit. So, now, really! We don't have time to try to understand men and Mrs. Beedle right now...

Oh, I think we have understood them already, Zoe said, it is just that we are saddened there is not more to it.

I want to stay with the two of you, Ilya said. This is the only place I have ever loved to be.

I know, Jacques said. I want you to stay here, too, but, my dear, next time you must not kill wealthy people. They take it very badly. Me, I don't care so much. They will come and look for you here. I would like nothing better to have you under the comforters of my bed forever, but it's simply not practical. You must leave New York. Or surrender.

I will not surrender. I will not. They will be merciless. I will not go from Orchard Street, to Washington Square, to the gallows.

It was self-defense, Jacques said. I could pay a solicitor to defend you. There is no one to refute your story.

But, I am a Jew.

That's so. But we wouldn't get you a Jewish solicitor.

It wouldn't matter. All people only wait for a reason to punish us, if they wait at all.

Yes, true. I have been lucky not to have that problem. And you have already made yourself seem...guilty. Were you drinking Mariani at the time?

Not before. After.

I see. That explains much of your choices. Don't worry. We will think of something. Let's have some Mariani now, so we can think straight. And we must keep our spirits high, it's the only way. Zoe, please?

Zoe nodded, smiled, rose, crossed the room to a table littered with paper, charcoal, pencils, paintbrushes, lingerie, creams, took up a bottle of Mariani and three dirty glasses, returned, poured them full, and passed them around.

Jacques nodded, raised her glass, said, Herbert. Farewell, *merde*. Ilya and Zoe said, *Merde*, and drained their glasses. They sat and waited for the feeling to come, staring at nothing.

As the warmth came up through her, Jacques gave Ilya a soft kiss on the lips and looked into her eyes. It will be alright, she said. Or not!

She threw back the comforter and went to the window, pulled back the drapes, and the sun flooded in. She stood and looked out at the Avenue and smiled a little — it was her favorite time of day because of the raking autumn light, though she almost always slept through it, so that when she didn't it would affect her. She put down the empty glass and slipped her nightdress off, let it curl to the floor. Ilya watched her. Her body was strong and heavy, breasts big and loose, and the hair of her crotch was rich, thick, and curled from her navel down her thighs. She came to the side of the bed and pulled Ilya upright, and she and Zoe began to undress her.

Come, Jacques said. We must get you out of this ridiculous outfit. What possessed you to wear this?

It shows my breasts, and I know Henry has always wanted them. I thought it was worth a try.

Well, it seems to have worked. You murdered his son...excuse me, killed his son, and then went to him for money?

Yes.

I believe surrender is not going to work.

From a man who cherishes it, you got money, Zoe said. Bravo.

I don't think he cherishes the money, Ilya said. I don't think he even cherishes the power.

What, then?

I don't know.

He is not our concern right now, Jacques said. Let's cuddle for an hour, and drink, and think. Something will come to us.

6

Beer, Bridger said. Dooley looked at him for a moment, turned and took up a glass, went to the barrel and twisted the tap, which made a sharp squeak, and let the amber fluid flow. 'Butte City Brewery,' the barrel said. 'Buh-tea' City? Bridger thought.

New brand. Tell me what you think, Dooley said. Bridger thought to tell him that he'd never had beer before, but didn't. He took some into his mouth, the foam warm against his lips. The bitter warmth, and the strong smell of something dying, but not today, fumed through his nose.

Good, he said. Dooley waited. Bridger stood there.

Well, don't slather it on, Dooley said. Not bad for a territory brew. Half the coin I gotta pay getting it from 'Frisco. You're Bridger Wallace, aren't you?

Yep.

Clothes fooled me. Thought you were dead. I see your Pap, never see you.

I ain't dead.

You're sure?

Reckon so.

I'll take your word on it. How is your Pap? Haven't seen him in a week or more. He must be dry by now. Is he dead?

Wadn't a couple days back. My Ma's still th' on'y dead one.

God rest her.

Hope so. Bridger groped, stomach sour and tight. Seems like snow might hold off some this year, he forced out. Mary's clothes and pistol were not boosting his confidence as much as they had when it was just her in the room.

Well, now. Hard tellin' not knowin'.

That's so. Bridger took up the glass and poured the remaining beer over his racing heart. Dooley's eyebrows lifted, and his face changed from benign curiosity to bemused dread.

It's not my affair, son, and I'll sell booze to a man drowning in it if that's what he wants, but you might want to take a study on your old man there, and think about where drinking like that can bring you. Runs in the family, that kinda weakness.

I ain't him.

Wasn't what I said. In fact, that's the opposite of what I was trying to say.

Wouldn't be the first time you wadn't followed, Doolio, Knot said.

Which is no reflection on me.

Hello, youngster, Knot said, and looked at Bridger with red, dull eyes. Bridger nodded, fought for something to say.

I believe snow will fly hard next week, Dooley said, long as we're gonna talk about shit we got no control over. Way the flies are all moving inside, the warm is gone for sure.

Flies were everywhere in the place, bashing themselves against the glass, having forgotten they were just out there. Or it may have been regret at having come into the wracked mess that was Dooley's Saloon driving them.

Dooley took up the glass, made a motion to Bridger with it, who nodded, and turned back to the cask to fill it. No offense, Bridger, but under the circumstances, seeing some dough will ease my mind a little. I've been treating your Pap because I feel bad for him, and Doc's too big an asshole to help anybody poor, but I don't want my pity to turn into the only thing he leaves you in his will.

I getcha, Bridger said. He took one of Mary's silver dollars from his pocket and placed it beside the glass.

Silver, Dooley said. And some very uppity duds to boot. Boys, seems our Bridger has gone out in the woods and had him a Injun manhood ritual out there. What'd you see, son?

Looks like he seen a preacher, shot 'im, and took his clothes, Knot said.

That'd make his new name Shoots The Preacher, Dooley said. Catchy.

That'll man y' up, Dink said.

That's how I got mine, Smitty said. Ain't a bad way.

Shut up, Smitty, Knot said, y' lie when y' jes' stand there and breathe.

Fuck you two.

Dooley, we're dry.

That hasn't been true in twenty years. He went down the bar, took up a bottle, slid their three glasses together and poured them full in one motion, walked away with the bottle.

Damnit, why'nt you just leave the bottle? Knot threw his drink down like he'd been shot in the forehead.

Same reason as always, you fucking sot. I can't make money off you if you drink yourself to death in one sitting.

Aright, then. Jes' askin'. Gimme another.

In a minute. Let that one trickle down first. And stop throwing your head back like that, you'll lose it.

Fuck you, Dooley.

I'm saving myself. Obliged, though. Dooley came back down to Bridger, took up a shot glass, poured it full of whiskey, and dropped the glass into Bridger's beer. The mixture frothed up, and all of them watched it roil to the top of the glass, and let one delicate finger of foam slide to the bar top.

Dooley smiled at Bridger. Now, there's a man who knows his job, wouldn't you say?

Yep.

On the house, Bridger. Kind of a rite of passage around here. Throw that down and we'll go from there. It opens up possibilities in life.

Then it closes 'em, Dink said.

True, Dooley said, but that's going to happen anyway.

There's a scientist in the house.

More like a philosopher, I'm thinkin'.

Artist...he's an artist.

Roll those three up and you still don't have me, Dooley said. Go on, son, I've never steered you wrong, have I? Go slow and steady. Bridger took up the glass and poured the drink into him. The warm whiskey at the end slimed his throat and made him gag a little. He locked his neck and kept it down, his eyes watered, and he turned his face to the street.

We got us a natural, boys, Dooley said. Runs in the family, like I pointed out. Guess I don't have to worry about going out of business any time soon. We have a little contest going around here, Bridger, because, well, as you have probably noticed, things can be dull when all there is to talk to is these three. Whoever comes up with a name for that drink right there drinks free for a week. And calling it a 'Dooley' won't go.

Bridger coughed a little. How 'bout 'poison?'

Dooley laughed. Now why didn't we think of that, boys? 'Poison.'

Nah, Knot said. Can't jes call it what it is. No fun in that.

True. A fine effort though, Bridger, for right off the front of your mind.

There's Spunk, Knot said. They all turned to the door, which was opened against the wall and held there with a hank of rope over the knob. In the oblique, wan sunlight of the street, Spunk Pilgrim came by, his small, pale skull thrust forward on a thin neck, in a tunic fashioned from a feed sack to the point of having buttons made of shards of bone up the front like vertebra, and breeches gone all the way black with filth stuffed into high, leather cavalry boots that had nearly separated uppers from lowers. A long, black shadow came behind him.

There's a cheerful vision of a Sunday, Dooley said.

Beats learnin' 'bout hell from Father Michael, Dink said. Knot and Smitty raised their glasses and intoned, 'amen,' together. At this, Knot's fear of an empty glass spiked and he said, Can I git another, yet?

Dooley looked at the clock that hammered rather than ticked when it was this quiet. It's time, I suppose, he said, and refilled him.

Knot turned to Bridger with a confidential air. I named that boy Spunk, didja know that?

Here we go, Dooley sighed. He poured and drank a shot in one liquid motion, moved towards the front of the bar and sat on a stool, newspaper flat in front of him.

I dint know. How c'd I? Bridger said. He knew who the Pilgrims were, but how he got the name Spunk, no. He turned to Knot. He'd been staring at a beam over his head where it butted straight into a column with no mortise, no shoulder cut, and was thinking about Mary while looking at the towed nails pulling free. His head was whining hard, and he felt good, but sick. He'd tried whiskey, sneaking gulps from his father's jug, but the vileness of the stuff, mixed with the effect it had on his father, kept him from indulging.

Well, that's why I'm 'bout t' tell y'. Talkin' ain't really yer winnin' hand, is it?

I got other skills, Bridger said. The hard note in his voice made Dooley look at him for a moment.

He wadn't always called Spunk, y' see...Knot said.

'Magine a ma that'd do that? Name her boy Spunk? Smitty said.

Like t' meet her, Dink said.

C'd you two mebbe shut the fuck up, so's I c'n tell a man a damn story? Knot said.

Easy, gentleman, Dooley said. It's not yet even noon. You can't have a pointless shouting match until two. House rules.

'Man?' Bridger thought.

Anyways, time was, he was jes Bill, an'...

'Magine a ma that'd call a body jes' Bill? Not even William 'r nothin'...

Damnit...

Children...Dooley intoned.

That'd be a Pilgrim woman fer y', Dink said, don't do a damn thing all fuckin' day, but don't have time t' call out a full name but gotta shorten it t' jes' Bill. Women beat all...

Fuckit, I ain't even gonna tell this fuckin' story...

Oh, do please tell it, Dooley said, it's faded in my memory since yesterday.

No. No. Tryin' to edjicate a man about his own community, an' you dumbfucks can't letta artist work...s'alright...ignorance is a fine thing...

I wanna tell it this time, Dink said. You git t' tell it every time.

No, me, Smitty said.

Jesus fuck me, there's a damn reason I git t' tell it, cuz I'm *in* it...I made it...you boys don' know shit 'bout nothin'...

Don' see why y' gotta be such a kid 'bout it, Dink said. C'd let a pal have a go once.

Well, now, Dink, there's a rule in storytellin' says the audience gotta stay awake through it. People nod out on y' too quick.

Fuck you, Knot.

Dint mean t' make a stir, Bridger said to Dooley.

Dooley shook his head. This isn't new, he said. If you decide to go, take me with you. Tell the story, already, Knot! My blood's gone solid.

Well, now, folks don' wanna hear a master at his trade, that's jes fine...

Tell it or I'll cut you off.

At that, Knot turned right off to Bridger, who turned, put his elbow on the bar and faced him. It was last year, 'round...well, hell...musta been right 'round this time, cuz the boys was 'bout done bringing stock through, and the whole valley smelled like cowshit, and the flies was all in every damn orifice like now...an' I was workin' ever' day at the livery...

Yes, Dooley said, that one month of hard work a year that you take eleven to recover from.

Smitty made snoring noises.

Fuck you, Smitty. Anyways, Mack hires Spunk, Bill at the time, t' help us, cuz it's the busy season, fuckin' horses and cows ever'where...on top of it all, Bill don' know shit from cake 'bout how much folks get paid, so Mack gits him fer two bits a day, when he pays ever'body else six. An' Mack says to us, 'Boys, don' tell Bill nothin' 'bout whut yer gittin' paid an' I'll have 'im do all the muckin' an' shit'.' An' we don' mind nothin' 'bout that cuz ever'body hates the Pilgrims anyways...

You mean they're scared of them, Dooley said.

...reckon that's in there, too...

I ain't skeered of 'em, Smitty said.

That's because you're stupid, Dooley said.

Oh, yeah...

C'n I go on? You boys 'bout done stoppin' up my flow?

Oh, yes. Do go on.

You with me? Knot said to Bridger.

Yep. Ever'body hates th' Pilgrims, Bridger said.

My throat's gittin sore...Dooley looked at the clock, came down, restoked him. Wouldn't want to upset the artist.

Good man. Anyways, fuckin' Bill's spendin' ever' day scoopin' up the shit, an' he ain't got but that one suita clothes we jes seen, so he's lookin' awful gritty, like somethin' a cat'd choke up...

You need to think of a new simile, Dooley said. That one's tired.

Whut?

Dooley shook his head. Never mind.

Anyways, hell, ol' Bill, he works at it an' all, ain't a slacker 'r nuthin', he's jes' fuckin' crazier'n shit...an' I start noticin' that ever' day, 'bout the same time, I'm goin', 'Where the fuck is Bill?' cuz, he ain't nowhere to be found, then, all at once, there he is agin', shovellin' and whatnot. So I decide I'm gonna watch 'im an' see where he goes...an' I'm thinkin', 'he goes off t' take a shit, but the same time ever' day? Ain't nobody that regular...'

Brilliant diagnosis. If Doc dies, you can step right in, Dooley said. He got up, came down and refilled Bridger's beer glass, took the shot glass and poured it full, but didn't drop it in. You'll need it to get through this tale, he said.

...so, I seen 'im snakin' up the ladder through the hatch an' onto the roof, an' I'm thinkin'...

'Even a Pilgrim don' shit on the roof,' all of them chorused.

...'zactly...so I skinny up the ladder behind 'im after a couple minutes, an' there's ol' Bill, peekin' over the top a the wall, an' I go, 'Howdy, Bill.' An' he comes 'round right quick, and there's his fuckin' little pecker bleedin' white over his knuckles...

This is a tasteful, upper-class establishment, you'll notice, Dooley said to Bridger. We're considering bringing this show to the coasts.

Aright, Bridger said.

...an' I'm goin', 'Ah, fuck,' cuz 'bout the las' thing I wanna see is a Pilgrim's pecker...

Less well-known than The Pilgrim's Progress, Dooley said.

...an' ol' Bill there, he's lookin' awful pissy 'round 'bout now, reckon anybody would be, an' lucky fer me he wadn't armed, cuz I wadn't, an' that woulda been it fer me if he was...

Unfortunate for us, however.

...so, I jes' go, 'Well, pardone ay moi, Bill, I dint know it was invitation only,' an' he's jes starin' at me like a fuckin' snake, so I beats it on back down an' leave 'im to it. Turns out he was goin' up there cuz Beth 'cross the street gits up at that hour, an' she always comes out on the balcony an' drinks coffee in her shift, an' she's got them titties could suckle the town fer a month...can't fault the boy on his taste in whores, anyhow...

And Knot in his infinite wisdom then came down and told everyone, Dooley said, dubbed him 'Spunk,' and turned the boy into an object of ridicule even more than he had been. Now we all live in fear of the day when he finally turns cream to curdle and starts shooting. We've decided to sacrifice Knot here, if it comes to that. Hope that satisfies Spunk. Can't imagine it would.

Hell, ever'body needs a nickname, Knot grumbled, I got one. Who the hell wouldn't tell that story?

'Knot' ain't yer proper name? Bridger said.

Hell, no. Y' crazy? 'David.'

His father is Big Dan Anderson, you know him, of course? Dooley said.

Bridger nodded.

Well, he's a big, tough, son of a bitchin', sure-enough man, and this here is his son, 'Knot an Anderson.'

Fuckin' asshole, is what he is, Knot said.

That also, Dooley agreed. Singing rose in the air outside, flowing out of the church and down the street.

Guess we're safe now, Dooley said. God's satisfied.

Bridger had had to take a shit for much of the story, but hadn't wanted to interrupt. He took a guess there was an outhouse out the back and weaved towards the rear door, his skull feeling detached from his body and buzzing.

Care for another to replenish your strength when you get back? Dooley said.

Yep.

Bridger stumbled down the two steps into the dirt, walked toward the little building with the big stink, and yanked at the length of rope knotted through a hole bashed through the door for a handle.

Hey, dammit! yelled Spunk Pilgrim, who was squatted there with one hand tucked between his pale thighs. Git the fuck outta here!

Sorry! Bridger said, swung the door shut, and headed back towards the door of the saloon. Shit!

He half ran to the bar and said, What do I oweya?

Six bits seems fair, Dooley said, looking at him curiously. Something odd come out of you out there? Came fast if it did.

Shit t' do, Bridger said. Dooley made change and put it in Bridger's outstretched hand.

Well, thanks for coming in. Stop by any time. Hope we didn't scare you off with that story.

Nope. Real funny. Bridger hurried out onto the boardwalk, across it, down into the street to Judy. As he stepped off the last stair tread, Mary's pistol slipped through his waistband, slid down his leg, and lodged in his boot.

Hey chickenshit, Spunk said. He was standing four body lengths away down the street at the mouth of the alley that ran beside the saloon.

Bridger turned from Judy. He'd had one foot in the stirrup. Hey, Spunk, he said. His voice was tremulous, and his head was swimming, and he turned to face the boy, trying to will himself into stone.

Whadja call me? Facing him, Bridger could see that Spunk had a pistol tied by a ring on its butt to a thong that looped around his neck and dug into the skin in what looked like a painful way, but which Spunk didn't seem to mind. The gun dangled beside his curled right hand. Bridger could see that it was rusty and battered, and looked like it was possible that it wouldn't shoot. He felt a fleeting impulse to offer to fix it up. From close up, Spunk's pants were a crazy network of patches that came from fabrics of every kind, the most disconcerting of which, a large, elaborate, and precisely-rendered rose which had once been among many hanging over a window, was over his privates.

Like bustin' in on folks doin' their bizness, do ya? Spunk said. His voice was ominous and malignant because it was flat and monotonous. He seemed distracted, like he had his mind on things other than this conversation, because he never looked directly at anyone, but off to one side. It was a quality that had contributed a lot to the unease he caused in people — his face would be pointed right at someone, but the eyes would be gazing over the shoulder, and he seldom blinked, and had never smiled that anyone had seen. Spunk relished this moment, because he hated Bridger — thought he was a pussy, and thought Bridger believed himself to be superior to him. From Spunk's perspective, Bridger was a wealthy heir waiting for his father's death before he could take over the ranch and loll in a luxury Spunk would never know, as the most he would ever come into was his father's shovel — he was the gravedigger, his livelihood and that of his family depended on the number of dead the town produced, a detail not lost on Spunk. Bridger would have been stunned to find out that Spunk thought of him as fortunate, that there were people to whom he was superior.

Bridger smiled with one corner of his mouth. Hell no, Spunk, he said. I dint know y' wuz in there. I dint mean nothin'.

I think y' seen me go in there and done come out t' set t' fussin' with me.

Hell no! I wuz jes gonna take a shit, Spunk.

M' name's Bill. Matter uh fack, it's William. Bridger thought to point out that he had heard otherwise, but didn't.

Sorry, Bi…uh, William...

Sorry ain't gonna git it done. Spunk's brain felt numb and hot and sure. He felt pointed at a destination for the first time. He wanted to shoot this rich pussy, but the rich pussy didn't have a gun on him. He looked at the rifle butt sticking out of the scabbard on Bridger's saddle. Spunk hadn't ever shot anyone but figured he was getting on in years now, and it was time to shoot himself a chickenshit fuck like Bridger. And Spunk had decided in a dim and fuzzy way, not unreasonably, that the only upward mobility possible in his life was to be a killer.

Spunk eased into what he felt was a confident, ominous slouch, his fingers touching the butt of the pistol. I'm gonna shoot off yer prick, first. If'n y' got one.

Hell, Spu...uh, William, it wadn't on purpose. I ain't got no quarrel with y'.

I'm thinkin' y' do.

Hell, why dint y' lock th' door?

Ain't no lock.

Howzat that my fault?

Howsit mine?

Dint say it was.

Ain't 'bout fault.

Whatsit 'bout?

You dyin'.

That ain't fair.

Ain't 'bout fair, neither.

Then I'm...stumped.

Yer 'bout t' git Spunked. Spunk almost smiled when this unexpectedly came out of his mouth. It was a good thing to say for future moments like this.

Hell, I don' even know y'.

I know you. You the fuckin' prick what's fuckin' the widder. She don' even let me in 'er store.

What?

Seen y' sneakin' 'round her.

Ain't no bizness a yours, an' it ain't true.

You ain't the one t' say what's my bizness.

Shit, what's this? Dooley said, seeing Bridger standing there talking to someone they couldn't see. They all turned and looked into the street, then walked to the door, and looked out.

Hell, looks like ol' Spunk's gonna shoot somebody, finally. An' it ain't me, Knot said.

People were trickling out of the church. Mrs. Havish watched the tableau for a moment, then strutted off to fetch Will, holding her skirts out of the dirt.

Desperation was mounting in Spunk. He knew that someone was sure to intervene if he didn't make a move. He felt he'd gone too far to back off, and he didn't want to back off anyhow. The wanting to kill Bridger was still hot. He also knew that if he allowed the situation to dissipate, he would be submitted to more mockery. He had the passing thought that a surname would be added to Spunk, he'd be called 'Spunk Yellow,' or some such.

Best not shoot 'im if he don' have a gun, there Spunk. You'll git hanged, Dink said.

Wouldn't that be a shindig, now? Smitty said. We'd be a real town. Be better 'n these damn picnics we's always havin' over some damn thing or another.

Ol' Knot there c'd play the harp.

Potluck'd be best, I'm thinkin'.

There y' go. G'head an' shoot 'im Spunk, we changed 'r minds.

Bridger's terror had subsided a little now that they had the town's attention. Spunk was standing there uncertainly now, indecision in his eyes.

Y' got you a rifle, Spunk said. Y'd best fetch it. I'll give y' time. A little time, leastways. Go on! he suddenly said viciously. Bridger started a little and stared into Spunk's off-shot eyes, which had evolved through blandness, to indecision, to sudden, feral surety.

Spunk, I don' wanna fight you, Bridger said. He was almost in tears from fear and from what this display of cowardice looked like. And how would he learn to consort as Mary had suggested, if he were either dead or branded a coward? He wished for her to arrive and cut Spunk down with a word. He looked about and saw Will tramping down the street, cursing. Will had gone on a grim, determined spree the previous evening, and had been sitting in his leather-covered swivel chair, feet on his desk, taking curative sips of whiskey with coffee, and staring at the sunlight wishing there was a way he could be dead for a day. When Mrs. Havish had burst into his office with the news of the fight, it had caused him to spill coffee down his front, and he'd almost cursed her to her face. She had stared at him a moment, then pointed out that he had work to do.

He plodded up to Bridger and Spunk and said, What in hell are you two doing? The sun was almost knocking him unconscious.

Bridger felt relief run down his body, but said nothing. Spunk also stayed silent but lapsed into a frigid rage that his moment was being taken from him, and just stood staring at Bridger.

Answer me now, Will said. The two stood there. Oh, for chrissake. He had an urge to step over and yank the gun away from Spunk and club the detestable little bastard to the ground with it. But Spunk was dangerous, and Will didn't want him to shoot Bridger, whom he liked and pitied, but wished would show a little damn spine once in a while. He empathized with Bridger however, recalling his own distaste for shooting people when he'd been young, a reluctance which had been approved of by the townsfolk and had helped to get him chosen 'the Man,' an outcome which he often regretted, and never more than now.

Look here, he sighed. Lemme explain the options. And I don't give a good goddamn what got you all snarled up like this. Spunk, if you shoot Bridger, I'm either gonna shoot you, or take that pistol and ram it right back up where it looks like it come from. Then I'm gonna hang your stupid ass from a tree, and the town's gonna thank me for it. Then I'll likely have to shoot your whole family just because I'm damn tired of lookin' at the whole sorry lot of 'em. Are you followin' me, son?

Spunk turned his face towards Will. His lip was curled a little, and his eyes had reverted to their previous blankness. He didn't look like he was contemplating the words. Will now noted with some consternation that Spunk looked like he'd finally busted off something important somewhere inside, which wasn't a large change from the norm, but was significant nevertheless.

Are you followin' me, son? Will said less aggressively. As repulsed as he was by Spunk, he didn't want to shoot a boy, though it was probably the best thing he could do for both the boy and the world.

Spunk stared toward Will for a few seconds.

I'm gonna shoot 'im, Spunk said. Then I'm gonna shoot you, too. The second statement was a vague afterthought. Will was shocked at the boy's hubris, or insanity. One thing about wearing the pistol around his neck like he did, it was easy to get to. Will had not freed the loop which held his pistol in its holster, not thinking that this would escalate. He also now thought that if Spunk had any brains he would shoot Will first, since Bridger wasn't armed. It wasn't intelligence that was at issue with that though, more experience and instinct.

Well now, son, Will said, holding his new fear cupped inside him. I might take some offense if you was to shoot me. If you don't kill me I'll surely kill you. And if you do kill me, I'll be waitin' for you on the other side, and I'm gonna be in a awful snit when you show up. And it won't take long, because they don't need me to hang you. On the other hand, if you give up the pistol, nothin' at all happens. What I'm tryin' to get you to see, son, is that whatever happens, if you don't turn the pistol over, you're gonna be dead today. I just wanna be sure you know that, before you make up your mind. Will tried to look into Spunk's eyes, feeling sweat trickle down his spine, and the dull throb of his headache.

Spunk was irritated at being called 'son.' The sense of being condescended to was tightening the knot of resentment he was, and the hatred of everyone in the town who had mocked and kicked him and looked down upon him was narrowing down to a pinpoint focus. The sheriff's point that he would die today one way or the other he didn't doubt at all, but he also didn't feel much concern about it. He felt a sense of eagerness and righteousness. He figured he was doing the right thing, and if the fight went on in hell, he'd take that on too. He felt that the last thing he could do was back out. It was too late, and he was glad of that. But he was uncertain as to how to proceed. One thing he didn't want to happen is Bridger to get away.

The townspeople had grown still and expectant. Knot and his boys held their glasses forgotten in their hands. They were surprised the episode had dragged on so long, expecting Will to diffuse the thing right off.

How do you want it, William? Will said. Your call. You know how I stand on it. He was gambling that being called 'William' would ease the boy.

Spunk grabbed the butt of his pistol and pointed it at the sheriff, who grunted, Whoa! and lunged away toward the ground, turning his body away, and grasping at his pistol. Bridger drew a sharp breath and turned to run, banging into Judy, who snorted and stomped as Bridger struggled to get around her. The gun report was sharp and flat, smoke flooding out of the barrel. The slug tore a deep trench through the meat on Will's hip. Will grunted and flopped into the street. Spunk turned, his face now twisted into mania and his eyes filled with a delighted malice that glittered through a sheen of water. He pointed the pistol where Bridger had just been standing and shot Judy, the slug plowing a shallow furrow through the hide of her belly. She screamed and jerked at the reins tied to the hitching rail, which came loose. Her shoulder rammed into Bridger and sent him staggering. Spunk kept firing, his next shot hitting nothing, the next one going through Bridger's neck as he tried to run, a hole bursting out the back in a little red shower of blood and muscle like a visible cry, and he screamed out as he went to the ground. The pistol had begun to come apart in Spunk's hand as he fired, the barrel disjointing from the cylinder armature, and as he pointed the gun at Bridger's writhing body and pulled the trigger, the last cartridge exploded in the gun. Shards of steel carried off two fingers and tore through his palm. The hammer blew back and crashed into Spunk's face, splintering off three of his teeth and driving them into the roof of his mouth, and hot metal slapped into the back of his throat and seared there. Blood gushed from his face, catching his cry and strangling it into a gurgle. Spunk stumbled back clutching his mangled hand to his mouth with his remaining one. Will had howled up out of the dirt, and now fired into Spunk, the shots booming thuds following hard on the splintering crack of Spunk's pistol shattering. Will spat curses as though they were the propellant for the lead hitting Spunk, who cried and gagged and fell back with each impact, and collapsed onto his back.

The descent of quiet after the shooting was broken by Bridger's wild sobbing, who clutched at his neck while blood flowed between his fingers. Will descended on Spunk and kicked the boy in the ribs, losing his balance from the blow, and staggered. He lifted his boot and drove the heel into the boys groin, and again into his neck and face, shouting and stomping Spunk's last breaths out of him. Will dropped to his knees beside the corpse and clutched at his torn side, lowering his head to rest it in the dirt.

For a few moments, the townspeople stood. The only sounds were Will's wheezing mixed with Bridger's low wails, and soft wind.

Who's the damn dumbass who fucked with a *Pilgrim!?* Will shouted into the ground.

7

I have to go, Ilya said.

Murder makes you impatient, Jacques said, holding Ilya's head against her neck and shoulder.

It wasn't murder.

If you flee, it is.

Yes. That's so. I left my baggage and Byron at the house. It's almost nine. It's almost certain that tomorrow at this time they will either have found him, or have decided that I am suspicious.

You are that, certainly. Jacques drank. It's lovely, the way it gives you energy and puts you at ease, she said, staring at the glass. I can't tell if it makes me paint better, or makes me believe I do.

Does it matter? Ilya said.

You are brilliant, Zoe said, staring at the ceiling of the bed.

Yes, it matters. No, it doesn't. Who cares?

You do.

True. Caring is so tedious, but it seems unavoidable. Quickly, let me show you my new paintings, then we will start moving!

Alright. A fine invention, it's true. Ilya looked at the glass with slurry eyes. I've heard the Pope drinks it. It must make him believe he's actually a god. A god invented by a man, sadly. But, now I don't want to leave. She had slipped over into a buzzing weariness.

Oh, but you do, Jacques said, it's just hard to feel here, inside this bed. It will be wonderful, it will be a great adventure for you! This is a good thing, I think. I haven't left this horrible, crawling city in much too long. Of course, being pursued for a murder makes things tense, but one must turn the bad to good. The tension will give us energy!

Ilya smiled. I love you.

Yes, I love you too. That will either protect us or kill us. Probably the latter, but so what, eh? I hate life! Every day, there it is, another day, as if we weren't paying attention and need to be reminded. Stupid, very stupid, this arrangement. I never saw why people thought so highly of a god they thought created this stupid thing...whatever it is.

Well, they are stupid, too, Ilya said. That has a shocking amount to do with it. Let's drink more. I need courage, I need energy.

Of course. You see darling, we have to treat this as if we are just going out to celebrate. Going down to the Points for a frolic like we used to, before they scrubbed it clean, remember?

Yes, I remember. Why do people insist on thinking that life will be better if they remove all the danger and dirt from it?

Because it is better, I think...it's just, still very disappointing. This, this is a great question...but not now. Come, look!

Jacques got off the bed and grabbed their hands and pulled them to the door of the studio and threw it open. She walked to the center of the room, twirled around and said, Observe! and giggled.

Zoe and Ilya went inside and looked about. There were two tall windows on the Avenue with light flooding through them. The other three walls had paintings up high in a row, paintings of landscape scenes and portraiture that were awful, unschooled attempts — childish trees, snowstorms that were just whiteouts, abysmally disproportionate buildings, dreary compositions.

Below them was a line of canvasses around the room that were of all different sizes and all solid, jet black.

I painted over my stupid paintings. It is a new series I call 'I don't paint very well because I couldn't go to University.' I was going to call them 'See you in hell, Marie Baskirtsheff,' but I don't want to seem angry. I will be in the next salon for certain, don't you think?

Of course, Zoe said. They are beautiful. Impressionism, bah. Boring.

Oh, I think it is like Impressionism, Ilya said, but you've made it just the one impression. You're a genius, Jacques.

I know. I fear I will never be appreciated in my time. So sad.

It is the best way, Zoe said. Recognition is a sign of mediocrity.

Isn't she a darling? Now, enough about me! She clapped her hands. To you dear, and your murder. What should you wear? Black?

Like one of your paintings.

Beautiful! And so metaphorical and true — you are my creation and I am not very good at creation. Otherwise you would not be in this predicament. Though, you thought of the metaphor, so I can't be all that bad, can I?

You're not bad. You're just out of place.

The best thing, I'm sure. How dreary, to belong. Black it is. What do you have, Zoe? I'm much too big and fat for her to wear anything of mine.

I have a lovely thing. Very strong, and not too restricting and clumsy, and too big for me. You may run in it if you must. I will get it.

We'll start there, then, Jacques said. Excellent. She began to pace the room naked. Now, this is a serious problem we have, much more serious than why people are so stupid, though we must not forget to consider that...not much risk of that, I suppose. Now, what should we do? We have to flee, but where?

Europe! Ilya said. I've never been there. Herbert never took me like he said he would.

You should have just gone without him so you could enjoy yourself. But you are young, you don't know how to just take what you want yet...a good start you've made, though. 'You won't take me Europe? Pah! A poker to the head!' You have ambition, that's good...though, it can be a killer...some caution is not a bad thing. No, no...Europe won't do...they've perfected that absurd cable now, they'll know you're coming in Europe before the boat has left New York. Why do they insist on making things so easy? I preferred it when you had to swim across the Atlantic to talk to someone on the other side.

Well, I've never been a fugitive before, but...

And are you loving it?

It's...I don't know yet...

Not boring?

No, not boring...but different than a spree that you take a cab away from when you're through.

True, true...a kind of depressing seriousness to this...too bad!

Oh yes, Ilya said, I know what I was about to say. If you're a fugitive, you should go where they don't expect you to go, I believe that is one of the first things they teach you.

Right. Exactly. And they will expect us to try to get on a ship, it's so obvious.

Or a train, Ilya said, and poured more Mariani for them.

We can't walk, Jacques said, though that might surprise them...searching all the ships and trains and carriages just to find us there ambling along the road, laughing.

Pleasantly surprise them, though.

This is quite difficult really. There are people everywhere, now! One always feels watched.

Where do two upper class women hide in this overflowing world? Should we pretend to be poor women?

Oh, no.

Oh, Jacques, Ilya sighed. The only quality of Jacques' that Ilya disliked was her contempt for poor people.

All the people were bothering me, Jacques said, but I never thought of it as quite as big a problem as it is until now.

I've heard of people hiding among the crowd.

Oh darling, I think we'll stick out...how many men drop dead behind you as you walk down a street?

All of them die a little, I hope.

Perhaps that's what makes them so...whatever they are...all those little deaths.

Well, West is all there is. They haven't filled it up yet.

So typical, though, 'Go West.' So boring. Is there nothing that sounds...original?

In a world this old and arthritic? I don't think so.

We'd be out of New York. I'm so tired of it here.

Ilya tried to pull back from the terrified hilarity she was in. She said, And...you know...I don't think I feel like a criminal. I'm just...irritable.

Yes. I understand. It's not as if you wanted a life of crime, since that's a contradiction in terms most of the time, though, it's probably true that few criminals wanted a life of crime.

Yes, probably so. No, I think what I want is to get away with this one crime...which isn't really a crime since he tried to kill me first...but not commit any more crimes. I mean, you know, I don't feel good about it, I don't feel that bad about it...but...I don't feel, 'oh, that was fun, I want to go kill someone else.' I don't want it to become a habit.

No. Though if that's the case, you shouldn't have left. You could have called it accidental, or self-defense, or a crime of passion, or something.

Putting your dead husband in the coal bin stinks of...deliberation...or fun...like the start of a habit.

I know. Perhaps I don't think well on my feet. I'm just a woman.

I know the problem.

I know you do.

We may be having it right now.

Maybe, maybe, but I also think we're making some excellent points, don't you?

Oh yes, yes, absolutely, but time is passing.

But not as much as we think...remember what our wine does to our perception of time...we think it's tomorrow but it's still only this morning.

Yes, I remember...but still...

Well, we should dress for travel anyway...I don't think staying is an option, do you? You're not going to turn yourself in?

I don't think I can. Not after taking money from Henry.

But you didn't kill him, did you?

No.

Now see, you're reformed already! If you were truly a dangerous person that must be stopped, you would have killed him as well. Certainly you don't need jail, or the law, or the government interfering in your affairs. This is America. 'Don't tread on me!'

No, jail won't do. Or a lynching. Anyway, remember that this is Henry. The law is whatever he says it is. He will not relent.

Well, there! Clarity at last. We run!

But you don't have to, Jacques. You should stay.

Oh, I know, but I don't want to. I want to be with you...I love your body...and you amuse me....I hate New York! It's getting too serious! But if I go, I would orphan my paintings...that's bad. And I'm old. That's bad as well. The West is for the young and durable.

I would hate to be without you. You make everything better. You know me...I get so...low...

I know, my love, I know...it's awful for you to have that blackness, that self-hate. It's your brand of stupidity to not be aware of how wonderful you are. Those paintings are portraits of you as well, you know that?

I thought of that.

Which is why you are so valuable, you would think of that. That bag of shit you killed and his father, they would never think that way. They are truly the black-souled, you are just miserable, they are very different things. There is the matter of Adelard, as well. He may reappear. This is an unusual length of time for him, but not an unusual occurrence. It's awkward, what should I do, leave a note? — 'Adelard, my darling, do forgive my absence as you've returned from being tortured and beaten by savages in darkest Africa for six months. Sincerely, Jacqueline.' It feels chilly, don't you think? Especially since my dearest is in fact a good man and pays for all this without thinking that I am indebted to him. He considers it an exchange.

You are extraordinarily lucky. If one leaves aside that your husband has disappeared and is probably dead.

Yes. Leaving me rather well-off. And it isn't just luck my dear, I can make his cum land on the windows across the Avenue, a thing he can get nowhere else. And it's great fun because I detest those people over there, and I like soiling their windows. It is curious though, that these men feel so insistent on meddling with Africans...are they so unhappy there?

I think they have things our men want. Rocks and trees and things.

Yes, but couldn't one just take them, or barter for them, and leave the people alone?

That I think they would find boring.

Perhaps.

Zoe came into the room. I have it, she said, and laid the dress out on the bed. This cloth, it is very strong. It is strong like denim, but not coarse, and it won't stain, it's so hard and black...it is nearly waterproof! It is perfect for an adventure.

Very good, Jacques said, the blood from her next victim will wash off easily.

Oh really, Ilya said, I can't take this Zoe, it's so beautiful. Oh, and look at the pistols!

You must take it. Yes, aren't those amusing? You have to look so close to see them embroidered in black like that. And look, there are pockets where you can carry real pistols...like these! Is it ok, Jacques? I thought what better purpose for them, than give them to Ilya. She held out two small, black revolvers with black walnut grips.

A beautiful thought darling, of course she should have them. Ilya, Adelard gave them to me thinking that I could protect myself while he was away. A dear thoughtful man, but quite insane if he doesn't know that I would simply seduce an intruder then emasculate him. Guns are much too loud and brutish. But you're going West, young man, you must have guns! And these are perfect, because as I understand it, they are smaller than normal guns men use, but quite potent nevertheless.

Ilya took the pistols, surprised at their weight. How do they work?

I'm sure I have no idea. But if men can understand them...

Let me show you, Zoe said, they are very fun, really.

You've shot my guns, Zoe?

Oh yes, I go up to Harlem to the woods there sometimes and shoot at trees. It is ok?

Yes of course, what a lovely secret to have. I suppose if I lose the house you could join one of those traveling wild west shows and shoot at playing cards. You could support us.

I would go to the very gutters with you, Jacques.

Ah, well. We should become highwaymen before that dear, now that I know you are deadly.

See Ilya, Zoe said, and took one pistol back. Like so. Push here, and you put the bullets in. They say to only put five bullets even though there are six holes, so in case you snag the hammer on your dress it will not shoot by accident. But, I suppose it depends on how many Herberts you are facing. Then, you pull back on the hammer like so, until it stops. Point it at something, pull the trigger, and pop! Very elegant, you think so? And simple. It is why men like them, it is easy to feel smart.

And less ungainly than carrying a poker everywhere I go.

So true. Though, you must stop somewhere and practice with bullets when you have a moment. They do change things, the bullets. They are very loud, and much smoke comes out and it stings your eyes, and the gun jumps in your hand like...like something has exploded inside it. I always dropped it at the beginning, but you will be ok. You have big, strong hands. Do not clench it with all your strength, just hold it very firm, and point it like it is your finger, and look at what you want to hit, not the gun, and soon, *voilà!* You are a dangerous outlaw, and they sing songs about you.

I read that the very difficult part is overcoming revulsion at killing something, not the act of shooting, Ilya said.

So see, Jacques said, you are almost there! You see already that killing things is natural and necessary, don't you?

But, I don't want to be a killer.

So you've said, and quite right. I'm only pointing out that should the need arise again, you will be in an excellent position. And darling, you are a very smart girl, the smartest I have known except for possibly Zoe. The two of you are so close together in intelligence it's as if you came from the same forebears. But you see Ilya, you can choose who to kill, correct? Don't worry.

Ilya wailed, How can I not worry! You won't come with me, I know you won't! I will be alone! I hate to be alone, you know that! I hate people except you two, I'll never have another friend! Especially in the fucking West! They don't even read out there! They eat...I don't know, shit *tartare!* They chew tobacco and spit. Who will I talk to? I don't care about Herbert, I care that I'll never have a decent meal again. And I'll miss you!

Oh darling, I know, Jacques said, but you must learn to change your outlook on things. It's a beginning, not an end. It's very cliché I know, but it's true. Even with Herbert alive, you wouldn't have been happy here, penniless, living off of me. Something was going to happen, maybe not the rudeness of this morning, but you're too much person for the life you were leading. This is a very *outré* approach you've taken to the problem of tedium. You should love yourself for your adventuresome spirit. Anyway, why don't you just go to San Francisco? That's almost like a true city now I've heard, even better than Brooklyn, though, so is a poker on the head.

The three of them started laughing.

But, what about my Mariani? What if I can't get any out there? Horrible food and no wine?!

Don't worry, Zoe said. The trains go everywhere. I will send some to you. And we will give you plenty today. For your travels. But, they must have some out there! It's so horrible and dry and windy, how else could all those people stand it?

Most of them are very poor, Jacques said, so I think they must be used to it, you know. I think of being poor as a kind of high.

I will be an orphan! Ilya wailed.

Ah! I have an idea, Jacques said. You can ride the orphan train! It's perfect! It's what you are, now! They will be looking on all the normal trains, and you can be on the orphan train. You can pose as one of the chaperones taking the little city Arabs to their wonderful new home in the country where they are worked to death. No one would ever think a woman like you would do something like that! You hate children.

Brilliant! Zoe said, smoking and smiling.

Ride a train with those...urchins? Ilya said.

My dear, I thought you liked poor people.

No, no, I don't like them, I grew up around them. I just don't blame them...it's not their fault.

Alright. I don't quite see what fault has to do with anything. But it's not important now. The point is they will never look for you there, they will look on the passenger trains, in the first class compartments, for you buying a ticket. Henry will believe that you are now spoiled by being rich and will never go back down in any way.

He is right in that regard, Zoe said. She was moving about the room collecting clothes for Jacques, stripping off her maid's uniform and putting on outdoor clothes. She clapped her hands. Ladies! We have much to do! Enough talk...

When does this train leave? Ilya said.

One pm from Grand Central.

It is all orphans, the train?

No, there are homesteaders and so on...people itching to shovel something of their own...

How do you know of this, Jacques? It's not like you, it's charity.

Oh, my somewhat friend Mrs. McCormick is very involved with helping children. I believe so she gets a better address in heaven. If they have a One Fifth Avenue mansion in heaven, she wants to be in it. She tells me about these trains ceaselessly, as though I'm an angel checking on her work and sending reports to God. We can take you to the station, we can tell Mrs. McCormick that you would like to help chaperone the little Arabs to their new homes, and *voila!* When you get to a station out there in the desert, simply get on another train, or horse, or camel, and there you are, a true fugitive.

I'm worried about you, Ilya said. What if Henry comes for you when I am gone? With Adelard not here? What if he hurts you? Come with me...both of you! We will be like a Dumas novel if he wasn't a man...the three of us...

Oh, Henry cannot hurt me, he is not the only one with power and information and money in this city. And he will think with certainty that you will be found...because you almost certainly will be, of course. The risk of hurting me outweighs the need for the information. He will ask me, I will lie, he will leave, and throw a net for you knowing I've lied. Then he will plot to hurt me in some other, less brutish way. He will never do it, of course. If my Adelard is truly dead, then I will be forced to join you wherever you are and all this is meaningless. Anyway, I will never leave this house except on my back...by that I mean dead.

My Byron, Ilya said. I cannot take him. 'Look for a woman with a small, black dog.' It's too easy.

I will love him like my own, and you will have him back when we are together again. The little bastard. You have such poor taste in men.

8

The following day, Henry handed Zoe his card, standing on Jacques' stoop. I would like to see Mrs. Reclus, please, he said.

Zoe looked at the card, and realization, resignation, and dread slid through her. She'd never met Henry, and didn't know him by sight. A late-afternoon September rain pelted Fifth Avenue. Henry stood there underneath his black umbrella, turned to the side, the cuffs of his gray trousers wet, his black boots shining with water. His landau stood at the curb, the driver curled underneath his umbrella, cape hanging. The horse stood in the downpour.

I prefer *'Madame'* Reclus, Zoe said. And you do not make prior arrangements.

Excuse me, *'Madame'* Reclus. I would appreciate it if she could see me. Something has come up. I apologize for the lack of warning. He looked at her, face stony, heart hot and cold and overlaid with relish for this new task, his tone betraying that he was not apologetic.

Zoe paused. She was wearing a glossy, green dress that came straight down to her ankles from a loose belt at her midriff, no hoop, no frame inside to inflate the skirt. Henry gazed at her green eyes.

She swung the door back and stood aside. Enter, she said.

Thank you. Henry retracted his umbrella, and stepped through the door into the foyer, dripping water.

Please, Zoe said, holding out her hand. Henry put his umbrella in it. She threw it in a corner. Stand there, please, she said. Zoe walked through the inner door — it was heavy, recessed-panel, clear-finished oak with no glass — and shut it. Henry listened to the lock snap. The floor was white marble with black veins. There was nothing to sit on, no hooks for coats, no table. There was a single, verdigrised copper sconce in the shape of an odd, pained cherub holding a tray of fire, which was the gas-fired flame. Henry pulled back the muslin curtains over the beveled-glass door panes and looked out at the rain, holding his hat.

Zoe walked into Jacque's bedroom, saw she wasn't there, and went into her studio. Jacques was standing in a tattered shift at a table in the center of the room, red hair splayed, angrily sloshing a brush in a can of turpentine. Black paint was spattered across her front, and a slash of it was across her cheek. A canvas stood on an easel beside the table. She was trying to do a landscape in black without painting over one she'd already done.

Zoe, I am no good, she said, voice low and gritty. She shoved the brush into the can, and swiped the can to the floor. Black liquid splattered over the layers of paint of all colors there. Even when I do not use color, I am no good. Fuck!

He is here, Zoe said.

Who is here?

Henry. Zoe held out the card. Jacques took it, looked at it, snorted, and threw it in the mess on the floor.

One does not simply appear at my house, Zoe, she said.

I know.

Then why did you not send him away?

You should see him.

Why?

Because he will then know you are not afraid.

I am not afraid.

I know.

Why do I care if he knows it?

Because of Ilya. We must protect her. There is no benefit to delay. We must know what he is planning.

Jacques sighed and rubbed her face, pushed her hair back, and looked at the window, which was draped, so looking was symbolic.

Where is Byron? Jacques said.

In my room.

Where is Henry?

In the foyer.

Just standing there?

What else?

I wish I could paint, Zoe.

Why?

'Why?'

Yes, why?

Because...I wouldn't feel useless...if I could.

Yes, you would.

Yes, you're right. But, still...

Jacques poured a glass of Mariani, lit a cigarette, and drank. She walked to the tall stool in the corner and sat on it, glass in one hand, cigarette smoking out of the other, shoulders sagging forward, hair over her face. Zoe waited.

I must? Jacques said.

No. You should.

How I hate that man. Put him in the front parlor where the painters aren't finished. Give him a drink. Bring him some of that *gruyere* we were going to throw out, he won't know the difference. Tell him I will be with him shortly. It is not wise to come and see me when I am failing, Zoe.

Exactly so, Zoe said. That is why this is a good time.

Will Byron stay quiet?

Yes. He is buried in my bed. He was walked in the garden. He wants nothing. Except Ilya. He is unhappy.

Do dogs get unhappy?

Of course.

Of course. What should I wear?

White.

Jacques looked up and smiled. The merino?

Yes. It is September. And cold. And raining. Like you, today.

Jacques stood and drained her glass, walked to her canvas, and looked at it. Perhaps it is not ruined, she said. Perhaps I can use color, still.

I do not think it is ruined. You must punish yourself to create. That is all. *C'est bon.*

Jacques came to Zoe and hugged her, kissed her lips. I will be down, she said. What should we tell him?

Nothing. We have not seen her. We know nothing. That is simplest.

He won't believe that.

So?

'So,' indeed.

Zoe left the room, went down the hallway, down the stairs, and to the foyer door. She waited a moment, listening, then threw the lock and jerked the door open. Henry flinched a little, then turned from the glass and looked at her.

She will see you, Zoe said, and held the door back.

Thank you, Henry said, and walked through the door into Jacques' entry hall. He looked around at the tapestries trailing down the walls and over the floor, the crazy array of rugs lapping over one another, the Japanese erotic screens. He looked at the balustrade, the male and female arms holding up the handrail. His face was a twist of contempt, repugnance, and envy.

I will take your coat, Zoe said. Henry looked at her. Her face was set and still, white, her eyes sea green and unwavering.

Thank you, Henry said, slid out of his black, dense wool coat and handed it to her. He held out his hat, an abbreviated top hat, in the other hand. She took them.

A drink? she said.

Brandy.

Certainly. Come this way. Zoe led him into the first room off the entry hall, a small parlor with windows facing onto Fifth Avenue. The walls were scraped and raw, the furniture had been collected in the center of the room and covered with canvas cloths.

I am sorry for our appearance, Zoe said. We are making changes. She dropped his coat over a canvas-covered chair, placed his hat over it, and yanked a cloth from over a divan. She threw the cloth in the corner, and shifted the divan out in front of a low table with the canvas still on it. Please, she said, and gestured. Madame will join you directly. I will get your drink.

Thank you, Henry said, and smiled at her provocations. Did they believe him to stand on this sort of ceremony, when they knew that he'd scrabbled his way to this level from near the bottom? That to him chairs were a kind of absurd luxury, ornamentation, that petroleum extraction was a brutal chore he had used to do himself? He swiped the canvas from the table, shifted the divan, and settled into it. He then rose, went to the windows, and pulled the canvas over them down so he could see the rain slash the glass. When he returned to the divan, he sat and slid a cigar from his inside coat pocket, looked around, and saw no ashtray. He went around the room stripping canvas and tossing it to the floor, until he uncovered a standing cast-iron ashtray in the shape of an upturned tulip petal. He moved it beside the divan, sat, lit his cigar, and looked at the rain.

Zoe returned with a tray, a decanter of brandy on it, with a plate of dry, flaking *gruyere*, and thin slices of day old bread. She looked at the canvasses on the floor, frowned, and placed the tray on the table in front of Henry.

You are comfortable? she said.

Perfectly, Henry said.

I will leave you.

Please do.

Henry sat smoking. He picked at the cheese, felt the bread, and left them.

Forty minutes later, Jacques came into the room. She had bathed, and was dressed in a floor-length, white merino wool dress with a deep neckline which clung to her torso until it reached her hips, then flared out moderately, and dropped straight down. She had black boots on that made her taller, and her hair was back in a loose chignon. She'd rouged her lips, powdered her face, and done her eyes with black in a way that made her look severe.

Madame Reclus, Henry said, standing. He braced himself against the violent pull toward her. She was devastating, and he hated her for it, hated himself for depriving himself of what she was.

Mr. Stewart, she said.

She shut the panel of the French door she'd come through, crossed the room to the tray, poured a glass of brandy for herself, and walked to the window. She lit a cigarette, stomach knotted.

Yes? she said.

There have been recent events concerning your friend May that have proven incommodious to me.

'Incommodious' to you. I see. It's unlike you to come here unannounced simply to cheer me up with your misfortunes.

That is something I should amend.

Not at all. I like it this way. Jacques crossed to the table, lopped off a piece of *gruyere*, put it on a piece of bread, and ate it. Brandy won't do for this, she said, and left the room. Henry sat back down. Jacques returned after a few minutes with a bottle of Bordeaux, three glasses, and Zoe. She set the bottle and glasses down on the table in front of Henry and said, Zoe, help me please. The two of them slid two chairs over to the other side of the table across from Henry. He made a move to help, but Jacques held up her hand to stop him. Jacques poured wine. Henry took his glass and sat back, looking at Jacques. Jacques and Zoe sat back in their chairs, glasses in hand. Rain crashed harder.

She is gone, Zoe said, after a couple moments had passed in silence. Jacques turned and stared at her. Zoe shrugged. I changed my mind, she said. This is less ridiculous, and we will reach our conclusion more quickly, and be rid of him.

Henry watched them, surprised at the parity of their positions, and that they weren't denying all. He nodded. I would think she would be gone, he said. I would like to know where. I would like to speak to her.

She mentioned France, didn't she, Zoe? She always wanted to go to France.

Yes. Also, Russia and Japan. She changes her mind so quickly. She is impetuous.

You think I want to hurt her, Henry said.

Of course, everyone does, Jacques said. If I could find her, I would tear her to bits myself for being so troublesome.

Hm, Henry said. He leaned forward and hacked off a lump of cheese, put it on bread, and ate it, struggling with the dryness.

Zoe, get the *époisses* you got today, and the fresh Fleischmann's. I can't eat this. Oh, and the olives. Is the hollandaise you made salvageable?

I think so.

Do bring it. And the cold asparagus. Men make me want to eat until I'm fat.

Zoe left the room.

I want to know where she is, Henry said. I won't hurt her.

You hurt her by breathing. I don't know where she is, and wouldn't tell you if I did.

She killed my son.

Your son was an imbecile who attacked her. Only an imbecile would try to dominate my Ilya. And he was a hypocritical puff.

I know. Those are not good reasons to kill him. She is stronger than he, and did not have to.

Jacques looked at him, surprised, but not betraying it.

It is a crime to protect a criminal, he said.

Jacques shrugged, sipped wine to buy a moment. He was not behaving with the cold brutishness she'd expected. She is not a criminal, she said, not by any sensible measure. And even if she were, mine is not much of a crime, and it can't be proven that I committed it. My solicitor would bury it without effort.

True.

Zoe came back into the room with the food and set it on the table.

Jacques dipped a piece of asparagus in the sauce, bit into it, wrinkled her nose, and put it back.

It's not in season, she said.

You knew that. I said, 'for soup.'

I forgot.

Jacques ate bread. No, Henry, she said. You cannot believe that I am this stupid. You are devious, but you are not complicated. I would tell you where she is if I knew, so she could kill you, too.

Henry smiled. No one will kill me. I believe that you may not know her exact whereabouts, but I don't believe you don't know anything. She may even be here. I will make a bargain with you. If you let me speak to her, I promise not to hurt her, and I promise not to make you a pauper. He leaned forward and sliced a piece of *époisses* from the hunk, put it on the new, fresh bread, and brought it to his face. He flinched a bit at the heavy odor but ate it, gorge rising, and gasping a little. He quickly poured wine behind it, and rinsed his mouth without letting it show he was doing so, much. Zoe cut a big piece of the *époisses* and ate it straight, rolling the goo around in her mouth, looking at him.

Then you consider me and Adelard imbeciles as well, that we would leave our fortunes vulnerable to your predations? Jacques said. What a lovely insult. The best I've received today. Perhaps you should come by more often, to amuse me.

No doubt, Henry said, you have protected yourselves. But Adelard has been absent for quite some time, and is likely no longer with us. And your reputation is hardly that of a woman with financial acuity.

I prefer that you refer to him as '*Monsieur* Reclus.' And he is with us. I have received word from him just this morning. Though, good as that news is, I do not need him to manage our financial life. My reputation is the result of small people with small minds and large mouths, and is meaningless.

Also, Zoe said, heart beating hard with rage she struggled to control, we have friends with acumen, and ruthlessness.

No, he said, you don't. Not among the people of this city who matter. Not like I do, anyway. He waved his hand to indicate the house in general. This, he said, the way you live, precludes having friends of the sort one needs for this kind of adventure. I, in contrast, have just precisely the right kind of friends.

Yes, Jacques said, pirates.

Mmm, no, Henry said, privateers. An important distinction.

A semantic one.

Not at all. A legal one. But I take your meaning. It's just not important.

Jacques leaned back in her chair, staring over Henry's head. So, she said, you have appeared at my house unannounced, and are threatening me. Zoe's face was hard.

Yes. But it is not something I am enjoying.

Yes it is, Zoe said.

Henry smiled at her. She killed my son, but I don't know the particulars. I would like to, so I can address the situation properly.

It is the word 'address' that is of concern, Jacques said.

Understandable, he said, and thought. I believe that you may misunderstand me. That your loathing for me is causing you to misjudge me. I am angry at May, it's true...

Her name is 'Ilya,' Zoe snapped.

Ah yes, true. I'd forgotten mine is of no use to her anymore. She has gotten the most out of using it, for which I give her due credit. That is something you do not seem to understand. I do not view her as my equal of course, she is not, but I have regard for her toughness, and willingness to do what is necessary to advance herself, because those are qualities of mine as well. And she is a woman, so has fewer avenues to go down. I believe she does not know about these attitudes of mine toward her, for which I partially blame myself. Killing my son, there must be retribution for that, I think you would agree, but it will not be as harsh as you are imagining.

And what is this retribution? Jacques said. Out of curiosity, of course.

I have not decided. That's the truth. I want to see her before I decide. I want the story from her. But it will not be the ultimate punishment. That is all I will say.

The two women watched him. His face was impassive. He didn't seem to be lying, and Jacques was surprised at his persuasiveness, and lack of visible anger. She was swayed toward him for a moment, as if she'd been walking a precipice over the edge of which she'd slipped and recovered. Zoe's visible contempt remained unchanged.

Jacques shook her head. No, she said. I would be an idiot to believe you. And I repeat, I do not know where she went. We deliberately remained in ignorance, predicting this eventuality. Knowing your savagery. Literal torture would prove futile, though your presence comes very close to being just that.

Henry looked genuinely saddened. Torture, he said. Hm. It pains me to be misunderstood.

Nonsense, Zoe said.

It is not, he said. But, no matter.

And your coming here, Jacques said, alone, to bargain like this. That is meaningful. No powerful friends with you? No law? You're infamous for your extreme desire for privacy. I think there is something you want to remain concealed, something Ilya knows.

He does not want it known that a Jew married into his family, Zoe said. That his son was a weakling, to be killed in a fight by a woman.

Perhaps, Jacques said, it is more than that. Perhaps something related to his way of doing business.

Henry smirked. You are imbeciles if you think that I need to resort to illegalities to get my way. I simply make the laws. With my friends.

He is lying, Zoe said.

No, Jacques said, that I can believe. His having friends, however, that part is dubious. It is how Adelard does it, though he retains a social consciousness.

A weakness that, Henry said. Society is an animal. It does not think, and it does what is necessary. Social consciousness is an illusion of the soft-hearted. Effective social consciousness, at any rate, that functions in the real world. As a fatuous belief, it is real enough. Henry lit a new cigar, and sat puffing as they watched him. He put his arm on the back of the divan, and crossed his ankle over his knee.

Well, I am disappointed, he said, though not surprised. I had thought to make this civilized.

As an animal would, Zoe said.

Precisely.

It is astounding that you have lost your son, and have no recognizable emotions about it, Jacques said.

Because he did not love him, Zoe said. This thought came into her mind and out her mouth unobstructed.

He blinked, his head went back a little, and he stared at her a moment. He said, I am not unfeeling. I am unsentimental. And it would be crass, and unseemly, to reveal my emotions to you.

And human, Zoe said.

He shrugged. As you like. This was merely a courtesy, not a necessity. I will find her. He paused for a moment, thinking, then shook his head. She is not here, he said.

How do you know?

Because I'm an animal, as you recall. I operate with instinct. I simply know things. And you will not believe this, but I also know her. And I know my son. Knew. I do not know the particulars of the killing, but her motivations...they're not simple. She is hungry, and staying and hiding...it would be foolish, and wouldn't serve that hunger.

She will devour you, if given the opportunity, Jacques said.

No. She couldn't. And I am not palatable. And she will not get an opportunity. He sighed. You do understand that your lack of cooperation will make the retribution harsher? For yourselves as well?

An idle threat, Jacques said. You do not have that kind of power.

Alright, he said, voice mild.

And I do not worry for Ilya. I worry for you when you find her. Which makes your threats against me more laughable. I hope you find her quickly.

Then help me.

No. I also don't want it to be too easy for you.

It will be, regardless.

Nonsense, Zoe said. Nothing about Ilya is easy.

That's so, Henry said. As it happens I agree with you, it won't be easy. I misspoke. But it is inevitable, and as you know, I don't give up.

You forget, Jacques said, that I have access to information, and power of my own, and can bring you precisely the sort of publicity you want to avoid.

I didn't forget. That is part of why I am here to bargain.

It is not bargaining. It is blackmailing.

He looked at Jacques, shrugged, and stood, thinking. The urge to bully was strong, but he waited long enough for his practiced chill to fill him.

This is how I predicted this would come out, he said. And I don't need you, it just would have been expeditious. And I have information now I didn't have before, so this has not been a waste. I will make you a new bargain. You are not so foolish as to believe my...threats...or offers...are idle. You know that, protected as you may be, and even with Adelard alive, which I believe is a lie, though well told, that I can do damage to you, if I choose. At any rate, I make a good enemy. And I acknowledge your power to effect me, though not in a way from which I could not easily recover. So if this...situation, remains our secret, I will let you alone. On my honor.

'Honor,' Zoe snorted.

He looked at Zoe, anger in his face for the first time. Yes. Honor, he said.

Jacques stood, went to the window and watched the rain.

I disapprove of gossip, she turned and said. Though as you know, a change in circumstance could change my mind.

Henry nodded. I believe you will find I am not who you think I am. He went to the chair and retrieved his coat and hat, put them on.

I will let myself out. Good evening.

They did not reply, and said nothing until they heard the front door close firmly but not loudly behind him.

Bastard, Zoe spat.

Yes, Jacques said. But, what kind?

It cannot be that he does not want to hurt her. It cannot.

No. It cannot. But, what else is there? I love you for telling him he did not love Herbert. That was inspired.

Yes. It came to me from somewhere. It is true, one could see. Even he could not conceal it.

Yes. That is interesting information.

Jacques sat on the divan, and they ate in silence for a time.

Alright, Jacques said. Our dear bitch Ilya is forcing me to be what I do not want to be. I will have to be the most beautiful robber baron in the world. Stupid Adelard. I do not believe he is coming back.

No, Zoe said.

But this worm Henry is correct. I don't know anything about money. I don't even know where mine comes from. I don't want to know. That is why I married a Frenchman with an inheritance, rather than an American like Henry, who is composed of only money. Because I wanted someone who would let me paint and leave me out of the rest.

I know money. I run a house, running a company, it is the same. I am good with figures. I will help. You must open Adelard's correspondence. You must talk to the banks, and the lawyers. You must assume control. It is not hard, it is only...disgusting.

Yes, yes. Jacques lit a cigarette and angrily shook out the match. We must find out more about Henry. His secretiveness, his reclusiveness, there must be a reason. He is a ghost. He never goes to balls, never to the theater, he is never in the papers. Ilya is not the reason for all that. No one with his money gets it cleanly.

No. They do not.

Is there anyone in society we have not alienated who can help us with this? I have no idea even how to undertake discovering the private business dealings of a man such as he.

Begin with the solicitor, they often lack scruples. And when you have money, many will pretend to like you and help you, and that is better than if they really do. And, it would seem to me, that Henry's name must appear as the head of some company, and that would not be secret. Their secrets only are secrets if there is something for them to hide behind. And we must stop reading only fashion and gossip and ridiculous politics in the papers. I will go, and find what there is about him, and his company, in the papers. No one so big can be invisible. But, he is not huge, not Rockefeller, as his kind...they cannot hide.

So much more than a maid, you are, Zoe.

Yes. That is why you love me.

So true. Jacques smiled, and stared at the ceiling. Well, I suppose this will be fun. We will be a part of Ilya's adventure. I was bored, anyway. Maybe I am a bad painter because painting is boring. I wonder where she is?

She will tell us, sometime.

9

It's Rex, I believe? Henry said, turning from the rain coming down outside his office window. He was musing over his meeting with Jacques and Zoe, earlier that day.

Aye, it is.

Please, sit down.

Thanks.

Henry sat behind his desk and observed the man across from him for a few moments, feeling dismal. The man was dressed in a garish green suit, blaring red cravat, and white bowler with a pale yellow, imitation feather in the band. His brown hair was combed straight down and plastered to his skull with a great deal of something sticky. He was clean-shaven, and pasty, and his eyes were pale blue.

Colonel Walker says you're proficient at what you do.

'E would know. A fly cove, that one.

Pardon me?

A smart man, he is.

Ah. Yes, he is.

Many a Johnny Reb heard the dismal ditty after I put me glims to him, working for the Colonel.

Ah-hah. I assume you wore different clothes while carrying out your assassinations and your spying?

Aye. I change me skin for the job. An artist I am, no rook.

Alright. Let me tell you what I need.

Do.

Henry slid a photograph of Ilya before Rex. I need to find this woman.

Why?

Henry hesitated, still unsure whether to let this man into his confidence, and remembered Colonel Walker's description of him as murderous but fiercely loyal, and someone who understood and liked his position in the food chain, so was not inclined to hurt his boss. And he had considered the second task he had for this man. She murdered my son, he said.

Did she?

Yes.

Rex picked up the photograph and frowned at it. A right nervy stunner, for hushin' a boy. Odd.

Yes. Evidently she is more dangerous than anyone quite grasped. She has the capacity to slip her moorings, clearly. I seldom underestimate people, but I did her.

Good she's pistol. Easy to mark.

I wouldn't count on that. If I understand your meaning. I wouldn't count on anything about this project being easy. She is smart. And now desperate. And evidently, deadly.

And you'll be wanting her in an earth bath then? Clean?

Henry paused to puzzle out what an 'earth bath' was, then said, Eventually, perhaps. But what I want right now is to find her. I don't want the police involved, nor the army, not that those bumblers would help much. I'm shy. I dislike publicity. And I don't want the Pinkertons in it, either.

Wise. Pack of ballocks they are. Go right to the barkers instead of their idea pots. Filthy buggers on top of it. Devious. No trust in them.

So I understand. Hence you, and your discretion.

Right. How'd she hush your kiddy?

Bashed in his head.

Mad was he?

I don't know. It's irrelevant.

When?

Two evenings ago we believe. There has been no sign of her since she was here yesterday morning.

She ogled you after she ended the kid? Nervy.

Yes. Under other circumstances I would hire her. But killing my son and then taking money from me...it's too much.

Bitter, that.

Yes.

Dreams on where she'd kite, 'ave ye?

No. She only has two friends that anyone knows of. Henry slid a piece of paper across the desk. This is their address. It's two women, living alone. She claimed to have family in Boston, but I don't believe that. She's a very prickly woman. Only so many would want her, and that wouldn't be for long.

Could be she'd ark it across the puddle. That's a safe play.

Look into it. If I were her, I'd expect me to put the whole world on watch for her. I have long reach if I choose to use it. I'd expect my picture to be everywhere. If she's on a ship she has limited choices. Few places to get lost on an ocean, and only a limited amount of places to dock. And a woman like her alone on a ship? Very unusual, and dangerous. For the men.

Aye.

What would you do, if you were her?

Rex stared out the window, smoking a cigar.

Wouldn't cross a gorger like yourself, for firsters. He thought some more. No notion, he finally said. Never fumbled for a doxie before.

You will be expanding your skills, then.

Well. Folks is folks. It won't be that fresh an employ. Her sacks are stuffed?

What?

She has money?

You should assume it. She took some from me, and her friends are wealthy.

Rex thought. I'll be after pullin' a brace of sharpers to help me. We'll twig the docks and Grand Central with the photo. Feel a breeze, maybe. I'll hover with the two fines, maybe there'll be a 'gram come in from our lady.

That would be a long time spent waiting outside their house trying to go unnoticed, then to intercept the telegram man at their doorstep every time, if I take your meaning.

Truth, that. A right knack for it, ye have. Rex thought, then smiled. I'll have a speak with the boy what brings them. Cop a squeal what stags the shakesters.

What?

Hire the telegram man. Not rich, them.

Oh. What if he tells his superiors? Some men are honest.

Rex smiled. Not when they get a 'gram from the Ruffian.

Who?

The devil.

And here I thought you were the ruffian.

As well.

Alright. But I don't want a lot of people involved in this. If you must hire people, don't tell them why you are after her. Don't tell them who I am. Only you, I'm trusting, and only because the Colonel said I could.

Aye. For the first bit I need help, only. I have to have lamps on the Fifth Avenue crib, if they go for a gather with our dearie, if she didn't fly the burg, and she's holed here. And best we know now if she took the go-away somewhere. Billet boy had to see her if she did. Once I have her string I can cut free my blokes, and chase her singular.

Do you always speak this way? Henry said. It would seem a liability.

Rex grinned, teeth yellow.

Why no indeed, my dear sir, he said. That would rather be a nuisance for a man in my line, wouldn't you agree? His accent was New York proper. Then he said, Ma, I got me a hole in m' stummick. Y' got some softkee an' at red-eye gravy y' done made yestiddy? His accent was southern.

Henry smiled. Are you an actor, as well?

Street theater.

I see. How much?

Five hundred will swing my pins for a wee stretch. Currency only, no vowels.

'Vowels?'

IOUs.

Ah.

We can respeak finance when I've got her in sees.

Done. Do this quickly, please. I don't want her to disappear. I would like this to be your sole project.

Coin's right, I'm yours. Hen got a moniker?

If she uses my name, which I doubt, she'd be May Stewart. If she uses her own, she'd be Ilya Kaempf. I doubt very much she'd use it.

Nay. Christ-killer tag. Too shiny.

And I trust that you understand that there will be hard times for you if you try to cross me.

The Colonel twigged me to you. Trust. And no troubles on this girl going spooky. She will leave scars. Rex looked sad. Glum I don't end her.

Yes, the Colonel apprised me of your relish for certain parts of your job. Henry slid a photo of Jackson across the desk. He frequents the

Blue Moon on Spring Street. A mysterious disappearance would be an apt outcome.

Rex picked up the photograph and smiled.

Aye aye, sir, he said. He touched the brim of his hat and left.

Henry sat at his desk, stomach tight that he'd made this last move, a first for him.

Damn you, Lillian, he said. Herbert was the best you could do, when you only gave me one?

II

1

Bridger came on their camp just before evening, as he was riding the fence but not fixing it, avoiding the ranch house, and town, and all people, even Mary, though he ached with missing her. He was riding the shame of Spunk, fixing that fence. He'd shot a whitetail, and was working his way through eating it, and smoking what would spoil before he could consume it, preparing to go he had no idea where. He was living in his wickiup, trying to teach himself to read.

They were in a copse at the bottom of the drainage east of his camp. He wouldn't have seen them if they hadn't been on the way he took to get home. That and the fire.

He kept himself concealed behind a rise, getting off Judy and looking down on them over the crown of the hill.

It was a woman and two men. The two men lounged on blankets and drank from a bottle, while the woman moved about, cooking and puttering. There was a rattletrap cart tilted far to one side, one of its side slats trailing over the wheel. Three horses were picketed. Bridger was about fifty yards away. An occasional snowflake drifted around in the eddies of wind, uncertain as he.

Bridger didn't know what to do, and his heart pounded. He was unbelieving that this was happening, wondered what collection of fools would willingly come onto his father's ranch. Didn't they know who he was?

It was almost dark. Bridger rubbed at the scars on his neck. It had become something he did to juice himself — the healing was at the point between there being no sensation and maddening itching. He thought about riding on to his camp and forgetting these people. On the other hand, Mary had said he should consort with others more, though his first foray into that hadn't gone well. And they were on his ranch. To say nothing, it would be cowardice. He thought of Will and the gentle, pitying disgust he'd shown for Bridger after the Spunk incident, and felt he had some redeeming to do. And in order to get where they were, they must have cut his fence, and that irritated him. He was possessive of his fence, and felt only he had the right to destroy it.

Judy snorted loudly. Bridger jerked his head around to glare at her and she stared back at him a moment before looking off across the land again. He had the feeling that Judy thought less of him since being shot on his account, and maybe she wanted retaliation. Though she was healing well, and was proving tough to kill.

He turned back to the fire and saw that the men were on their feet staring in his direction with pistols dangling from their hands, the woman standing still behind them. Their three horses were now looking at him. He stood and began to head toward the camp, glad that he didn't have to approach with piss and shit in his boots. Or a pistol — his ankle still hurt. As he walked, his new pistol felt unfamiliar on his hip, hanging in the tattered holster that he used to use as a tool belt, and of which he was ashamed. The leather looked ridiculous on his new clothes, and the gun flopped around in a way that made him feel stupid. He'd been practicing with the pistol, but wasn't good with it yet. He had few cartridges, and couldn't get used to the barrel being so short. He instinctively tried to shoot long-range with it, and was having a hard time remembering to go short-range first.

He wondered if he should stick the rifle back in the scabbard but figured they'd see him doing it and that would look worse than just walking up with it held in his hand, as if he were assuming they were no threat and they could take advantage of that. The rifle chamber was empty out of habit, and he thought to lever in a round, but didn't want to be seen doing that. He told himself that given the way his life was playing out, he should keep one in the chamber.

The two men stood still as he approached. Bridger raised the rifle and waved it, intending it to look like a salutation and a gesture of peace. They didn't return the wave. He stopped twenty feet from the fire.

The woman was beautiful, dark, and sinister. Bridger didn't take his eyes from her for a long moment, then he realized he was staring. Mary was the most beautiful woman he'd seen, but her age and weariness, and her manifest superiority to him, made the beauty distant, forbidding, a kind of rebuke. This woman was different. Young, and somehow sharp, and bright, but no less out of reach. The two men were nondescript, filthy, and expressionless.

Well? one of them said.

How... Bridger tried to reply, but his voice cracked. Howdy, he said.

Howdy, the man said. Bridger now noticed, like it had been a piece of information he could not at first take in, that the nondescript aspect of the two men was made perfect by their being identical twins. He'd never seen twins before, hadn't known they existed. Only, they wore different style hats, one flat-brimmed and flat-crowned which gave the man an evil aspect, the other a round-crowned type with a wide, curving brim.

Helpya? said the man with the flat-crowned hat.

Bridger cleared his throat. Well, uh... he said into his collar.

What's that? said the man immediately.

Uh, Bridger said again. The man looked at his brother, who continued staring at Bridger, which seemed to frustrate the flat-crowned man, like he expected his brother to look at him at the same time and share his amused wonder, but his brother had missed it. A flicker of disgust crossed the flat-crowned man's face as he turned back to Bridger.

Didja get yourself a new tongue t'day, and y'ain't used to it? There wasn't much insult in the tone.

Nah-hah, Bridger said, laughing and saying no at the same time. Uh, jes, thought I'd visit...seen the fire...

Nice a ya. Welcome to beans and coffee if yer hungry.

Nah. Much obliged an' all, I gotta...They waited for him to finish. Bridger had nothing to say much less do, and self-hate ran through him at his bumbling. He reminded himself that in the future, if he was going to always grope for things to say, he should prepare something.

The man smiled. He looked genuinely happy to be amused for a moment. Gotta what? he said. It's evenin'. Can't be all that much to do out there in the dark.

Bridger was eased a little at the man's geniality. No, well, I'm ridin' fence, but nah, no, I's jes...

Well, y' can't fix fence in the dark. I been a hand 'nuff to know that. 'Nuff to know it ain't no life for a man. Whyn't y' set?

Aright.

Sure. Trixie, get the boy a cup a coffee and a plate. We was gonna eat 'bout now. His talking to the woman brought Bridger's attention back to her, and that convinced him to stay, to look at her more. He left Judy saddled and hitched to a tree in the darkness, in case he needed something to hide behind as he fled.

The woman was crouched by the flames, wearing a black dress. She poked a flat wooden spoon into a brown mess of beans and gristly meat. Bridger noticed that she was overcooking whatever it was, and was cooking with the pot shoved into flames not coals, and that she kept burning her hand. He could hear the pot of coffee boiling hard and smell it burning. He stifled the impulse to give her some instruction, not that he excelled at cooking, but he knew enough not to do it this way.

He could see now that she was clean, and put together well, and contrasted to the men, that made her beam out as if her skin was lit. The man with the round hat had a big, ragged mustache, surrounded by stubble. The flat-crowned man had a smaller, neater mustache, but the same stubble.

The men sat by the flames staring into them and saying nothing. They drank from a whiskey bottle in turn, taking neither small nor large gulps, and wiping their mouths with their sleeves. Bridger squatted near them, feeling that to sit was too friendly, and tried to think of something to say. The flat-crowned man held the bottle cork in one hand and extended the bottle toward Bridger. Bridger drank, trying to look easy, and struggled to keep his face from betraying his nausea. He was becoming accustomed to the stuff, kept a bottle at his wickiup from which he drank while puzzling over the speller, but he still frequently vomited from it, and he was realizing that it stunted his ability to absorb what he was reading. He'd come to accept the sickness in return for the warm, buzzing fever that would come over him, that would mute his keening misery and loneliness. On occasion, the liquor would produce a brand-new feeling, something like hope and lightness would come over him, and he would feel less despair about the future he could never convince himself he had. Inchoate desire would take form, and fuzzy fantasies of a different life would come to his mind. The scraps of information he had acquired about the world would coalesce into a dreamscape of cleanliness, and women, and feeling good, and cities, and not being alone. He held the bottle out to the other brother.

The flat-crowned man lifted his forefinger from his knee a little and pointed it at his brother.

That's Bat, he said, without looking at Bridger. Bridger nodded slowly at Bat, who nodded at the fire.

I'm Rog, the man said. The 'g' was hard, so it sounded like 'bog,' rather than short for Roger. That's Trixie, there. The woman didn't look up at being introduced.

After a silence, Bridger said, I'm Bridger. No one replied to that. Trixie handed him a tin cup of burned coffee, which Bridger set hastily on the ground.

It's hot, she said without looking at him, and returned to her place. He stared at her, poising himself to look away when she looked up at him, if she did. Suddenly she did, and he was caught staring into dark brown eyes, one of which winked at him, her face expressionless. Cool sweat grew out of his skin and he twitched a little from the chill and stared into the fire. Bat poked a stick into the flames. Rog pulled his pistol from his belt and put it on the ground beside him. Bat did the same. Trixie kept on stirring the food, not seeming to care that it couldn't be more cooked.

Flurried thinking ran through Bridger's mind. He regretted coming here very much, the woman notwithstanding. What did the wink mean? Was she a prisoner and trying to tell him so? She didn't need his help, did she? Please not that. Was she flirting with him? Despite the surge of hope, Bridger dismissed this last thought as too absurd to be indulged. Should he wink back? What would he mean by it if he did? What the hell was going on here?

The whiskey bottle was being held out to him again, and he took it and drank. He forgot to drink only a little so he would remain alert, and took a healthy amount into his mouth. When the warmth flooded his stomach he got a powerful urge to get fully drunk, to become the angry, contentious but confident wretch his father became when drunk, which state Bridger both loathed and thought of as an indication of strength. But he remembered that he would puke and that would make him look bad.

Rog said, Ain't y' gonna ask us 'bout our names?

Bridger sat. It had only momentarily struck him that the names were a little odd. 'Bat' wasn't very odd. But 'Rog,' that was odd. But no stranger than 'Knot' and 'Dink.' The names of these two weren't that strange, when you thought about it. Though there was something strange about 'Rog,' something more than never having heard that name before. Bridger wondered if he'd broken some social rule by not asking, but he'd figured he'd of been breaking some rule to ask. He cleared his throat.

Where'dja git them names? he said.

Rog said, Well, Bat there got his on account he likes to sleep hangin' upside down durin' the day. Rog was looking steadily at Bridger, whose mind went dark at his statement. Bridger looked at Bat, who stared into the fire. Trixie stirred the beans.

Huh... Bridger said.

I'm named Rog on account of 'Rog-oo,' Rog said. Bridger was benumbed. What the fuck was 'Rog-oo?' He was scared to ask. He looked at Trixie entreatingly but she wasn't looking at him.

Know what that is? Rog continued.

Uh. No.

Y'ain't edjicated? This time there was mockery in his voice.

Not much.

Well. If you was edjicated you'd be awares of what Rog-oo means. There was now a definite note of scorn and self-satisfaction in Rog's voice. Bridger assumed that Rog would tell him what 'Rog-oo' was, but he didn't look like he was going to. Everyone just sat there. Bridger thought that probably he would offend Rog if he didn't ask him what 'Rog-oo' was, but wasn't positive. After a short, agonizing period he opened his mouth to ask.

It's a outlaw, Rog said, and Bridger closed his mouth. He had a stab of longing for Mary, wished there was someone around who was smart to help him. Trixie caught his eye, rolled her eyes, shook her head.

That's...mighty innerestin', Bridger said.

Ain't it? Rog took a drink of whiskey. His eyes, usually flat and benign, had taken on a wet, fervid sheen in which the yellow flames danced — they made him look like he was thinking. Bat began to cackle, sounding like a rasp on wood. Trixie scooped wet plops of beans onto tin plates and handed them around, serving herself last. Then she moved back from the fire a few steps and sat on the bole of a downed tree, plate in her lap. The men scooped food into their mouths with spoons. Bridger set his on the ground next to him to cool. It was still bubbling a little. They washed the beans down with swallows of coffee and whiskey. The whiskey was making Bridger feel unsteady, a little sick, but not bad, a kind of gleeful revulsion, but far from drunk-to-puking. Bat's and Rog's plates were clean in a minute. Bridger watched them with envious wonder that they could take the scalding material into their mouths without screaming. He also could smell the over-cooked gruel she'd made and wondered that they ate it at all. He thought of the smoked venison in his bags, wondered if he'd be breaking a social rule if he went and got it, if they'd let him leave the fire.

Bridger stole another look at the woman, determined not to be caught, but was. She winked again. Bridger blushed and took a drink of whiskey, glancing at Rog to see if he knew this winking was going on. Rog looked oblivious and idly took up his pistol. The chill wind soughed through the trees. Trixie took up a blanket and wrapped it around her.

Why'nt y' sing somethin', Trixie, Rog said. Too damn quiet. Rog had developed a small annoyed furrow between his eyes. After a short pause, Trixie began to hum a low, melodic tune, with no words. The sound was sweet and lulling.

Who y' ride for? Rog said. It was a moment before Bridger realized he was being addressed.

Uh, he said, my Pap...py . He stuttered over the word because it was seldom he had to say it aloud, like all words.

Y'r 'pap...py?' Rog now turned and looked straight at Bridger, but his eyes were in shadow.

Yep. This's his ranch. Bridger was trying to force himself to sound firm. Rog continued to stare at him.

Reckon that means we're yer guests.

Reckon so. He was looking at Rog's pistol held in his lap. He wondered if he was going to be shot with it. Why had he rode in here? Why couldn't he just be a lonely coward? What was so wrong with that? Mary would still like him, maybe.

Here's to th' host, Rog said, and drank from the bottle.

After a long, long pause, Bat cackled again. It was shriller this time, like a cricket. Trixie continued to croon, voice gliding from low to high register in no ordered fashion. Rog handed the bottle to Bridger. He began to raise it when it slipped from his fingers and clinked to the ground. He grabbed at it, just saving it from tipping over and rolling away. Liquor sloshed but none spilled. Trixie stopped singing, then resumed when the whiskey didn't spill. Rog looked at Bridger, who had broken out in a heavy sweat.

That'll put the fear a God in ya, Rog said.

Yah, Bridger said, and drank. There was no glee in his drunkenness now. For the first time, Bat was staring at Bridger. There was reproach in his look. He took the bottle from Bridger, and drank.

We ain't bank robbers, Bat said. Rog glared at him. No one moved. Bridger tried to think about the statement.

Me either, Bridger said. Trixie stopped singing at this, and there was a pause, then she started to make noise, which Bridger mistook for her singing for a moment before he realized she was laughing. Rog's face was moving like a body under a blanket, and it was becoming ruddy. He gave out a loud snorting gasp and took in a deep breath afterward. Then he shook his head hard, and said, Stop it, Trixie. She did, and resumed singing. Bridger had almost lost control of himself and begun laughing when Trixie did, but then sat still when she was shushed. Bat didn't move at all, and showed no expression. After a pause, when everyone had resumed their previous bearing, he cackled again.

That was funny, he said.

Wadn't 'at funny, Rog said. After the laughing, Bridger had almost felt the courage to ask them who they were, what they were doing here, to bring up the cut fence, not as a threat but to show he knew about it, but now he was afraid to. He felt sure they were bank robbers now. Or something like that. 'Rog-oos.' Regular folks didn't cut fence. Maybe he'd wait until they went to sleep then ride like hell to get Will. Anyway he was outnumbered, so doing nothing was justified. It didn't seem like these people were going to do anything to him. He wouldn't bring up the fence. But he didn't want to move at all, and wished he could go to sleep.

Well, Rog said. We give ya some work down that way apiece. He gestured with the bottle. Bridger didn't say anything.

We figgered we'd do some huntin' up here in these hills, but come to find there's a fence yonder. Can't get to the hills. Wadn't about to go back on account of a fence. I don't hold with fencin' off God's country. He'da put 'em there hisself if he wanted it all cut up.

Bridger wished the man would stop talking. He was exhausted from trying to gauge the meaning and the threat of all this. Every time he felt himself dozing off and looking sidelong at the woman with a sense of comfort, the man would say something and put him on edge. He didn't have anything to say to God's not being a fencing rancher.

Reckon so, he mumbled.

What's that?

Reckon God ain't a man that likes fences.

God ain't a man a-tall.

Reckon not. Bridger looked at Rog. Rog seemed to be becoming more and more agitated. He was sitting up like he was alert, but he was drunk and unsteady. He spun the cylinder on his pistol repeatedly. It was pointing directly at Bat, who seemed not to mind. Rog began to thumb the hammer back and release it, letting it down easy with his thumb. Bridger watched wide-eyed, sure the hammer would slip out of Rog's casual thumb and Bat would be shot. But Bat remained unconcerned, his eyes heavy-lidded, mouth slack. Trixie had ceased to sing, though she hadn't been told to stop, and Rog seemed not to notice. She sat still as though asleep, but Bridger couldn't tell if she was or not. The fire had gotten lower.

You reckon God ain't a man, Rog said, and snorted. Well, ain't that good a y'. Think God cares what you reckon and what you don't reckon? Rog pronounced the 'you' fully in this statement, maybe for emphasis.

Reckon not.

'Reckon not,' Rog mocked. He began to twirl the pistol in his fingers. The gun would swing around and hit his knuckles in a way that looked painful, but he ignored it. The hammer was back. Suddenly it dropped with a loud click onto an empty chamber. Bridger started. Bat heard the click and came out of his reverie, grabbing his pistol and pointing it in front of him, not intentionally at Rog, but just straight forward. Rog was pointing his pistol loosely at his brother.

Oh Bat, don't shoot me, Rog said.

Bat stared at him for a long moment, then he began to cackle. Rog's face writhed and his body shook with mirth. Trixie was statuesque and silent. Bridger had to piss, but was afraid to move. He began to feel convinced that he would die here tonight.

Bang, Rog said, making a play shooting movement.

Bang, bang, Bat said back, making the same movement and laughing. Bridger felt that he would go crazy with the fear and mirth mixed up in him. He also began to hate these men, and wished they would shoot each other for real. A searing impulse to pull his own pistol and shoot both of them right at this moment hit him, but he didn't. It seemed...wrong. Their food wasn't that bad. And he felt sure he would bungle it, and be shot himself.

Their mirth died away and they resumed staring at the fire. Rog tossed his pistol to the ground and walked a few paces away. They could hear his stream pattering on the ground.

You can just keep on pissin', son, Will called in an even and kind voice from twenty yards away. Rog came lunging back into the firelight, his trousers partially down. Bat came to his knees and raised his pistol at the dark in the direction of the voice. A bolt of cold terror and relief ran down Bridger's torso and into his legs, and he froze where he was, leaning on his elbow. Trixie curled up on the ground.

Leave it alone, son, Will said, as Rog groped for his pistol and at his crotch, his leaking penis poking out of his clothes. Leave both of 'em alone, he added.

Goddamn, Dink said weakly, and giggled. 'Leave 'em both alone...'

Knot, his own voice breaking, said, Damnit Dink, stop laughin'...

I might piss on myownself, said Smitty, voice high-pitched.

Gentlemen, please, Will said wearily. Rog and Bat were still poised and taut, guns pointed out.

Boys, you can shoot but you ain't gonna hit anything. You'll be cold and dead before you get off a second one. Will's voice was mild and reasonable. Rog's face was ruddy and angry and afraid. Bat looked disoriented and anxious. Rog was holding one hand over his crotch, trying to right his trousers.

Careful there, boy, it might go off and there goes yer hand, Knot said, and dissolved into giggles.

It'd be a Spunk gun, Dink said, and leaked squealing laughter.

Smitty tried to think of something to say, gave up, and just giggled.

Gentlemen, Jesus, Will said. It wasn't that damn funny. I gotta get to a bigger town. Knew you was too drunk to be a damn posse. If this wasn't a pack of dumbfucks, you'd be dead by now. He resumed his genial tone. Boys, what's it gonna be? Be sensible. You'll get shot to pieces and you won't even wing one of us. You're in the light, we're in the dark. Put 'em down. I'll buy you a drink myself when we get back to town if you make 'em into plowshares. I ain't a vengeful man. You just made a little mistake, no one's been hurt yet. Why don't you keep it that way?

Rog pointed his pistol at Bridger. I'll git one shot, Rog said, and it's goin' inta the kid.

There was silence outside the camp. Bridger looked at the gun muzzle pointing at his face, imagined the explosion when it went off, turned his face away.

Will said, What kid's that?

This one right here, Rog said. Bridger somethin'.

Ah, shit, Will muttered to himself. What the fuck is wrong with that boy all the sudden? he thought. He'd seen the shape of a man there by the fire, but thought him to be one of this crew. The woman, he didn't know what she was doing there, but her lying down out of the way was meaningful. He thought a moment, then said, Now, is that a good barter for yourselves? We're still gonna kill you.

Rog hesitated. Well...I'll kill the kid first, he said. Just as he finished the statement, Will started shooting, and gunfire erupted. Will put slugs into Rog and Bat in rapid succession until his rifle was empty. The others sent slugs into aimless flight, being surprised Will opened up. Rog's gun went off once, the bullet zipping by Bridger's head and digging a crater beside him. Rog and Bat dropped to the ground. Bat didn't fire at all. Rog was dead right off, Will's bullet having gone through his face. There was a pool of blood and brain beneath his head. Bat moaned for a couple moments, then died with a low, sad wheeze.

Bridger, Will said, you make it?

Y-yep.

Anybody else we gotta shoot?

No.

The men came into the firelight.

Trixie stood up brushing off her dress, and Knot, Dink, and Smitty stared at her, holding their guns vaguely toward her.

Will hunkered down next to Bridger, who remained curled on the ground.

Sorry 'bout that, son. I woulda made a different plan if I'd known it was you in here. I thought you was one of them. Y'aright?

Bridger tried to still his trembling.

No, he said.

Well, I don't suppose I'd be at my best right now either, was I you. You're having a rough few days. Will caught the smell coming from Bridger. He put his hand on his shoulder and said low, Hold on a minute, just stay down there.

He stood up and looked at Trixie. You ain't one of them?

No.

Hm. Can't say you look like you would be.

I have an explanation for this situation.

Do tell.

Yes.

Well, I ain't got time for it now. You strapped?

Pardon?

Are you armed?

I have two pistols in the cart. I have none on my person.

Will nodded. Boys, he said, roll these two up, put 'em in the cart, get ready to go back. Help her pack up all this gear, bring it all. Ain't worth shit, but I don't wanna leave garbage on the ground. We'll sort it in the morning. Leave this spot like they found it. Don't touch her, and don't shoot her, and don't drink any of that whiskey. Last damn time I make a posse outta you assholes.

You sure she ain't one of 'em, Will? Knot said.

Haven't I made that clear already? Hell, look at her. I don't know what she is, but she ain't one of them.

He grabbed Bridger's arm and helped him up. Come on, son, he said, and walked him out toward the creek. Clean yourself up. I won't say anything. I'll make like you got winged. You'll get yourself a nickname that's hard to shake if Knot gets a whiff of you.

Thanks, Will, Bridger said, feeling coated in shame the way his ass was in shit.

Sure. You wanna come into town with us? Mary'll put you up.

Wanna go home.

To your Pap? Funny pick.

Bridger thought to tell him of his place, didn't. It was his, alone. He said nothing.

Alright. Up to you. Don't worry about this-all too much. Your asshole'll start staying shut soon if you keep getting into jackpots this way.

2

Bridger dismounted, his ass chapped and freezing from the creek water, his hand and kerchief stinking of his shit. He ducked into his wickiup, heading for his bottle.

Hello, son, his father said.

The shriek stopped in Bridger's throat and he stood there. The old man took up a handful of pine needles and threw them into the embers, where they flared up and threw light. His face emerged out of the darkness, the skin overrun with balls of flesh seeming in a struggle to get away from the attack on his brain, his nose disappeared within what looked like a small skull emerging through his face. Black irises surrounded by blood shone. His battered hat sat strangely on his now misshapen skull. He was sitting on Bridger's bedroll, the reader beside him. He picked it up and held it. The roll of tools was open on the ground.

Hello, Pap, Bridger said.

Good t' see y' improvin' yerself, he said, waving the book, then throwing it aside. Y' c'd use it. Hell, son, dint know y' had such a nice place. How come y' never ask me t' supper?

Bridger was silent. The old man smiled, a cut through the papules.

Still can't find that tongue a yers, I see. Well, that's aright. I c'n do th' talkin' fer both of us, like I always done. Well, here I is, so whyn't we sit and have us a meal and a drink, an' we can catch up. Feel like we ain't had a chance t' talk much, what with you out mendin' fence all th' time. Always was a hard worker. Like all them words y' don' say come out as barbed wire.

Aright, Bridger said. He went out to Judy, pulled smoked venison from the saddlebag, and returned. His father was still sitting, this time with pistol out. When he saw Bridger with no gun in hand he smiled again, winced at the pain this caused him, and put the pistol beside him.

Bridger slid a bottle of whiskey out of its hiding place beneath a tangle of branches, leaned over, and placed it and the meat before his father. He sat. His father took a long drink and ripped a chunk off of the meat, chewing slowly, looking at the fire.

You part a that shootin'? his father said.

No...I...Bridger stopped.

Well?

Them...some folks...cut r fence, an' I...I come on 'em, an'...I was gonna...git 'em t'...

Git 'em t' what?

I dunno...dint wanna let 'em jes...git away with it...

His father snorted. Now, he said. You alive. Y' ain't gonna tell me y' done shot up them folks? That jes ain't like you. You the peaceable sort. Some say chickenshit, but I ain't mean.

No...I...they done robbed th' bank there...in town...an' I dint know nothin' 'bout that...an' I was jes' settin' with 'em...thinkin' t'...

T' what?

I...I guess I dunno what I wuz gonna do...

Now, that sounds like you.

An' Will, he come on us...an' he shot 'em up.

Kilt 'em all?

Yep. Bridger thought to mention Trixie, didn't.

Always liked Will. Gits it done. Not a man to underestimate. Folks underestimate me, y'ever notice that?

Reckon.

I always surprise folks, though. Not pleasantly of late, that's a fact.

Dunno.

Been admirin' yer work on my rounds t'day. His father's eyes were boring at him. Bridger couldn't hold them with his, and looked downward between his knees.

Seems y' got yer own way a doin' fence, now. Leavin' it on the ground so them cows trip over it. Easier, fer shit sure. Feelin' kinda stupid, never thinkin' of it m'self.

Pap, I...

You what?

I...

Y' thought I couln't see yer little mind in there, racin' 'round, plannin' how t' git away? Thought if y' don' talk, I won' know? There was a long silence. The old man coughed a laugh. Never c'd figger where you come from. Yer Ma, now, she wadn't a dribble mouth, but she could hold up her end of a conversation. I ain't no slouch m'self that way. But you, who done cut yer tongue out? Guess no point in askin' eh, no tongue and all?

Reckon not.

Well. I guess it ain't a bad way t' go. Sure as shit keeps th' rowels on th' other t' keep things innerestin'. 'Course, some folks c'd take it th' wrong way, an' think y' was bein' an uppity nigger. But not me, cuz I know you, an' I know y' jes can't help it. Or mebbe yer a fuckin' shit, jes fuckin' with folks, hard sayin'. Any thoughts?

No.

Aright. I love y' anyway. An' lovin' you ain't easy. He paused. Ain't y' gonna say it back? Impolite not to. I ain't nobody's notion of a perfect Pap, but I mentioned politeness a time or two, I recall.

Bridger coughed. I love y', sir...

Hell now, don' mean nothin' when y' gotta ask fer it. Yer gonna have t' give me somethin', so's I know y' mean it. How 'bout them clothes, an' that shiny pistol the widder give y'. An' them's some nice tools. Come in handy this winter. Seems like fair trade after me keepin' y' alive all these years. Wouldn't y' think?

Bridger's mind began to feel like his ass. He raised his eyes to his fathers'.

No, he said. I give y' 'nough. This shit's mine.

That so. Maybe y' don't talk cuz y' don' want folks findin' out yer a fuckin' chickenshit ingrate.

Maybe.

Hm. Sass, now. I guess I c'n unnerstan' this shit yer in. Feelin' like y' gotta be a man, but there ain't no man to y'. Feelin' like if y' open yer mouth folks'll find out yer jes a snot, so y' jes say nothin'. See, I ain't a monster. If y' give me a winder, I c'n see in.

Nothin' t' see.

Now see, that there is some kiddy shit talkin'. Might be what's in there ain't much, but ain't no nothin'.

I don' wanna be here no more.

Cotton'd to that. Little advice for y', boy. Next time y' wanna run away, do it sudden. You been gone inside fer a while. That wadn't hard t' see. The old man sighed and drank long.

Seems I raised a coward. Happens. Ain't gonna blame m'self. Thing is, it's kinda hurtful when yer blood turns on y'. I guess I c'n fergive folks not wantin' nothin' t' do with me, when I look like I crawled outta a swamp. But m'boy? Lightin' out jes when I'm gittin' on in years an' wantin' t' put m' feet up an' contemplate m' life an' times, good 'n bad, an' make an accountin', settle up? When I need a pal t' mop this fuckin' pus offa m' face, an' ease m' sufferin'? Yer makin' bein' fruitful an' multiplyin' a bad call. God there, he might be frownin' on you. 'Cept there ain't one. Who's gonna look after my estate if I let y' go? We ain't got deed yet, y' know. If y' leave, an' I die, y' can't come back to it. Anderson's jes gonna scoop it up, an' that fat Mormon fuck's gonna own the valley. Y' want them freaks walkin' r grass?

I don' care. I hate that place.

Y' hate it? Y' hate yer home? There was a pause, then the old man wept, staring straight out. Bridger stared at him. He had never seen him do that, and thought fleetingly that syphilis had an upside.

Y' are an ingrate fuck, the old man said. Mebbe that fuckin' whore of a Ma let herself git poked by a shitbird, an' now I got you. That'd be fair enough, I guess. Maybe that's how come I got these pus bags all over me now. Maybe that's whut I git fer tryin' t' do right. I git the damn fuck pox an' an ingrate son, all from a stranger an' a slut.

The old man took a drink, corked the bottle, tossed it at Bridger's feet. Bridger didn't move. The old man smirked.

Y'd haveta do more than drink behind me, boy, t' catch it. Y'd haveta fuck me to git started on lookin' like this. Y' don' wanna fuck me do y'?

Reckon not.

Y' ain't as stupid as that no talkin' makes y' seem. Yah, findin' a body wants t' fuck this ain't easy. Makes them churchly fucks seem right 'bout watchin' where y' stick yerself. Done any a that yerself, or are y' waitin' fer the right fuckin' chicken t' come peckin' along? It's shit sure ain't nothin' else gonna want coward prick like you got.

None a yer bizness.

All a you is my bizness. All a you! Y' don' seem t' be able t' grasp that. Lemme make it real clear. You is mine, 'less I decide I don' want yer sorry, useless, ingrate fuckin' ass. Y' got no *say,* boy!

The searing bubble in Bridger's chest burst, and he sobbed and shrieked, I ain't yers!

He lives. Aright, then. Y' ain't mine. Y' ain't yers, cuz y' can't handle yerself. Whose are y', then? The widder's?

Ain't nobody's.

Hmm. Sounds lonesome. Folks like that don' last long. They're wraiths.

Don' care.

Right now y' don'. Y' will, if y' live. Boy, lissen here, I c'n unnerstan' y' wantin' t' go. But I ain' gonna let y'. You is gonna stay, an' you is gonna take care a yer dear ol' Pap, jes like yer Ma woulda wanted. Yer gonna take care a that ranch so the fuckin' guverment don' take it back, an' it's gonna say 'Wallace' on it ferever. Spent years a my life scrapin' that place outta rock and scrub.

The old man leaned forward and tossed more wood onto the fire.

Bridger took up the bottle and drank, staring into the flames.

This 's how it's gonna play, the old man said. Yer gonna give me that pistol, an' we're gonna switch clothes cuz I ain't likin' lookin' all bunged up. My reputation's startin' t' suffer. An' we're gonna fire this hut, an' go on back home. Then, tomorra, when we're feelin' better, we're gonna jump in and start makin' that ranch there shipshape. Winter's comin' on, an' we got shit t' do. Y'll want it agin. I c'n see how y' don' want it now, I kinda let it slip some. I was otherwise engaged with dyin' a horrible death. But, I c'n muster up some doin' yet, an' you an' me c'n make it right. We done it before. We's a good pairin' when we put aside the mad. 'Member?

I give y' 'nough.

Damn boy, I'm tryin' to be reasonable here. There ain't no out for y'. When I'm dead, that's yer time. I ain't dead, I jes look like th' Reaper lately.

These'r my clothes.

Ain't nothin' a yers that ain't mine.

These are. Mary give 'em t' me. Dint say nothin' 'bout you. Nothin' good.

'Mary' is it, now? Ain't that fine. Best watch that bitch boy, she's a woman. Nuthin's free. He pushed his face into the firelight and pointed at it. Where y' think I got this mug? They carry disease. Anyways, y' think she wants a sprout like you when she dint want me? 'Fore I got this here gift, I mean?

Bridger went still.

Ah. She dint mention that, did she? They lie. All of 'em. Jes standin' there, they's lyin'.

Never lied t' me.

Howdya know?

Bridger was silent.

Can't know, can y'? I c'n know, cuz I'm old an' you ain't. Whatever they say, it's meant to keep y' from seein' what they mean. Git y' watchin' th' blade in one hand so y' miss th' gun in th' other. Mind me, now. I still got shit t' teach you.

She done nothin' t' you. She don' want no one but her husband, is all.

Yer gonna take th' word a that cunt over yer blood?

She ain't that.

Yer a hurtful little son of a bitch, I gotta say. Yer makin' it hard t' want y' 'round. That yer plan? Are y' a cunnin' mutt, makin' yerself disagreeable so's y' c'n run off an' be th' widder's boy she never had? That's th' kinda thing a man might take personal. Aright. Lemme make it more clear. I'll kill y'. I'll kill her too, long as I'm in that mood. See, this here pox, it hurts. It ain't jes I look a fright. It's like somebody's drillin' and blastin' in my bones all th' time. Soon 'nough, I won't be able t' walk, or move at all fer that matter. I needja boy. I needja t' man up. It's jes...fair.

Pap, I...

Now gimme that damn pistol, an' shuck them damn clothes. I'm done bein' nice.

The old man took up his pistol and held it loosely. This ain't a negotiation.

Aright, Bridger said, and stood.

Aright.

Bridger slid into the darkness.

The old man shouted Hey! and snapped a shot into the night. The slug zipped by Bridger's head and spanked off a boulder close in front of him, the stone and lead shrapnel tearing into his face, and he yelped.

His father cursed and growled and lurched into the darkness after Bridger. Bridger stopped, trying to silence his heaving breath. The old man went still, standing twenty feet away.

I'm gonna git y' boy, don't think I won't, he said after a few moments. His voice was slurred and splintering with rage and hate. An' when I do, I'm gonna beat y' near t' death, then I'm gonna let y' heal, then I'm gonna beat y' agin. Can't have y' dead. That there shot wadn't meant t' kill y'. Don' take it personal.

As he listened to his father speak, his face burning, hot blood streaking his skin, Bridger's fear was overtaken by hatred and rage and a burning excitement that numbed him, the numbness feeling like it was Mary holding him.

I ain't scared, he said.

His father turned and lurched through the dark towards Bridger's voice. Like hell you ain't, fuckin' little son of a bitch, he bit out. *C'mere*, damnit t' hell.

Bridger fled, scrambling through the trees, bashing into them and falling. His father came after him then stopped, because his own noise smothered the sound of Bridger's flight. He tracked Bridger again, and heaved off after him. Bridger stopped himself. He couldn't see anything but the weak glow of the fire a ways off. His father stopped when he realized Bridger had.

Y' ain't gonna make it, boy, the old man said.

Bridger pointed his pistol at the sound and said, I ain't scared, again, and felt a swelling, bestial comprehension of the point of faking courage, a quick understanding that he'd been foolish waiting not to feel scared. As his father's pursuit of his voice began again, Bridger fired at his sound. The muzzle flash blinded him. The report from the pistol was loud, the hard spank of the report put a ringing in his ears, and echoes called through the valley. The slug went by his father's torso, the hard whine of the bullet audible to him.

Surprise burst through the old man's rage, and he shouted, God*damnit!*

Bridger flashed on Spunk, and fired again. This slug tore through the old man's bicep and broke the bone. He screamed and went to his knees. Bridger took off through the dark. He could hear the strangled, sobbing shouts his father spewed behind him, as if they could pursue Bridger in his stead. The old man's rage devolved into malevolent determination. He lurched after Bridger, and fired twice at the sound of his son. Bridger shot twice at the muzzle flash. The first slug zipped by his father, the second punched into his abdomen, and the old man grunted hard and went to his knees. He shot wildly at where he took Bridger to be, missing by far. The old man hunched over his stomach gasping, trying to stay silent. Bridger stood still in the darkness, panting.

Fuckin'... fuckin' damn you...boy, the old man gritted, and he growled hard against the pain.

I'm right here, motherfucker, Bridger said. His father snapped a shot at the sound, and Bridger shot at the flash. His father's slug passed Bridger, Bridger's punched into the old man's chest and killed him.

3

What am I gonna do with you, now? Will said. He groaned as he sank into his chair, shifted to ease the pain in his side, and sat there a moment staring at the ceiling, coming down from the day and the ride in from the killing. He'd thought about the shooting as he rode in silence, adjusting himself to it, manipulating the guilt and distaste killing brought up in him, though, because of the war, it wasn't a new thing.

I don't know, Ilya said, standing in the middle of the dim, rough office, looking for photos of herself. There were none. But there were no photos of anyone, no wanted posters, nothing that looked official. Just wood floors, wood walls, a wood ceiling, a couple windows, a desk, a couple simple chairs, a small gun rack, the smell of gun oil and not entirely well-bathed man.

Will leaned forward and adjusted the wicks upward on the two lamps sitting on either side of his desk.

Start by sitting down, he said, waving his hand at the chair across from him.

Thank you, Ilya said, and sat.

This has been a lot of evening, Will said. Whole point of living in this flyspeck is not having to deal with robbers and killing and all.

Sorry to shatter your peace.

That's alright. Gets dull.

Ilya took the case from her dress pocket and lit a cigarette, then put the case on the desk. Will reached over and picked it up, examining it.

That's smart thinking, he said.

Thank you.

Your idea?

Yes. It used to hold rouge.

Hm. Never seen them rolled so perfect.

It's a machine. They have them in New York now.

I'll be. New York, you say? May I?

She nodded. Will lit one, inhaled deeply, coughed a little, and exhaled. Brings it right into you, doesn't it?

Ilya smiled. A little caution is wise in the beginning.

After that, you can just go wild?

That's up to you.

Obliged.

You're welcome.

Will leaned back in his chair and smoked, gazing at her. After a moment he said, I should thank you. I've never had a situation quite like this present itself in my years as what people think of as the law around here.

You don't think of yourself as the law?

Nah. More just the one whose ballsack shrivels up last when things happen. No offense.

Not at all.

Didn't peg you for the sort that gets the vapors easy.

What betrayed me?

Getting out of the shooting back there so smartly for starters, then being stone cold and helpful packing up with those brains all over the ground. Are you a nurse or some such? Most women would at least blink a few times.

No, I'm not a nurse. That's not my temperament. It simply didn't bother me that those two men received that treatment. It seemed apt for them. And inevitable.

Yes. Mostly is with their sort.

You've seen a lot of them?

Some. There's not as many as Eastern people think there are. Most of them think it's just going to be a hail of bullets, and the streets paved with dead men out here. Oh, and scalping. They love scalping.

Yes, I suspected as much. The lifeblood of New York is hyperbole. Without it, no one would countenance the place for a moment.

Wouldn't know.

Would you like to?

Nah. I hunger for some civility and some education now and again, but having too much of it all piled up in one place doesn't sound good.

It's often ugly, true, but...intense.

What were you doing with those two men? Probably should ask.

Are you going to charge me with something?

No. As far as I know there's no law against being in the company of thieves. Not that I would know. Like I say, I'm not the law.

I don't understand your situation. Are you the law, or not?

Will stared at her for a moment, weighing whether to talk to her as a person, to let her not be a stranger. She looked back steadily. He shrugged, to himself more than to her. She just didn't seem like someone low and stupid and untrustworthy. And she was so beautiful, it made him want to see her as a person, in case that would help him have her, though he recognized the stupidity of that feeling.

I don't understand it, either, he said. People here, they got a thing about government, about authority. They get real touchy about feeling like somebody's telling them what to do, laying on them and crushing them, messing with their freedom. It's why they come so far out to live. That's fine, but thing is, mostly they're a bunch of weakling children who can't deal with their own problems. So they come to me, but they don't give me tin to wear, so they don't feel confined by me having authority and power over them — so they don't feel smaller, but they still do, so there's not much sense to it, but there rarely is. I get this place to live. He waved his hand at a normal door with a lock hanging from it. There's my jail, not a bar in it. It's amusing, because sometimes they forget themselves and call me 'sheriff' instead of 'Will,' then they catch themselves, and look damn foolish, and very...young. I don't care. They pay me okay, I have things to do but not too many, and I don't have to wear a target on my chest. And it cuts both ways. They don't get to demand much in the way of personal behavior from me, and there's nobody to report to if they have a problem anyway. If something terribly big happens, I'll send for someone with law skills. Nothing ever does, though. Until this week. This week's been very exciting. No, I'm just curious. We don't get many of your kind through here.

'My kind?'

Women that have no rope tied to them, of any sort. I guess those two fools were a rope of a kind, but I guess we can call that one cut. Also, tall, pistol-hot women like yourself are exceeding rare. What's your name?

Ilya hesitated. Trixie, she said.

Will nodded, his face in a bemused twist. You look like a Trixie. He took a bottle of whiskey from his drawer, set two tumblers beside it, poured one half full, and gestured at her with the bottle.

Ilya nodded. I've been waiting.

Pardon my manners. Not a lot of call for them here.

All the more reason to use them.

Sensible. He poured the other glass and placed it before her.

You don't use shot glasses. I appreciate that.

Always seemed foolish to me. I always think I have an advantage over a man that would shoot himself in the head with a drink like they do.

Sounds plausible.

Are you going to tell me your story? Something entertaining would be nice. We don't get a lot of variety out here.

Certainly. I think I can amuse you for a while. She hesitated, buying herself a moment by drinking and smoking, deciding what to reveal, thinking to spin an entire fabrication, but the thought of concealing who she was, it was repugnant to her. The point of this adventure was to be who she was. And this man just didn't seem like a threat.

I left New York three weeks ago, she said. I was a chaperone on an orphan train.

Will frowned. I thought they were nuns and priests.

A popular misconception, born out of the excessive religiosity of most people, and the assumption that the only people who care about others are those who want to get into heaven for it. In fact, Mr. Brace — he's the compassionate man who is scouring the streets of New York of its human offal and sending it to the West...

Thanks.

...yes, you're welcome. He's a passionate Darwinist, so one wouldn't have to be a nun to chaperone the street rats.

A 'what'-ist?

Darwin. No?

Will shook his head.

Hm. I could try to explain it all, but it's very complicated, and I confess I don't understand it very well. He believes that humans come from apes, similar to the way an adult is an old child. Rather than humans being fashioned by a god. He cleverly called his book *Descent of Man*. It's an open question whether he was being ironic. The theory applies to every creature, but we seem to be the only ones who care enough to quarrel over it.

Huh. I remember hearing something about that now. Neither one seems very flattering.

I think the point is that we shouldn't want to be flattered. It causes us trouble.

Well, I don't want to be flattered but I get trouble anyhow. I can think of a few people who would take the ape news poorly.

Almost all of them I should think, which is much of the attraction of the theory for me.

Likely.

You're not upset by the news?

I was in the war. If you told me we were hatched by snakes, I'd see the hitch.

Well, taken far enough back, the theory says we were.

Clears things up.

Doesn't it? A wonder more people don't feel better about it.

I don't wonder that hard about people's foolishness, anymore. So, there you are, riding the train with a bunch of...'street rats' did you call them?

Yes.

Not so fond of the little ones, but there you are caring for them as they go on to a better life?

Do contradictions make you uncomfortable?

No. They make me curious, though.

To be truthful, children have never moved me very much. I was doing it more as an adventure, you see. I was bored, and the opportunity presented itself, and I thought that I might see something of the much vaunted and mythologized American West, and it allowed me to travel alone, but not quite. But when we reached Salt Lake, one of the little darlings pinched my reticule as I slept, and jumped off the train before it reached the station. I was nearly penniless.

This Darwin is looking smarter and smarter all the time.

Indeed.

And this event curdled you on kids, so now you call them street rats?

It's more that I call them that without guilt now.

Well, we're supposed to think that they can't help themselves.

It's likely that's so. Why that should matter to me is less clear.

Well, that's a sad story. Welcome to the West.

Thank you.

That doesn't tell me how you got here, and how you ended up with those two boys.

The door rattled open and Mrs. Havish bustled in. She looked at Will and Ilya, at the bottle, glasses and cigarettes, and her face puckered.

Will, the Dodson's have their stock on our grass again.

Come in, Will said.

Are you going to do something?

You're up late. Well. It's evening. And cows eat grass, ma'am. That's just the way they are.

It's our grass.

Will sighed, took up the bottle, poured a drink for himself and Ilya, motioned at Mrs. Havish with it. She frowned deeper.

I'll talk to Dodson tomorrow.

I think it's time you did more than talk.

Want me to kill him? I told you to build a fence.

Why should we have to build a fence to keep their stock off our grass?

Will shrugged. Because Darwin works in mysterious ways, I guess, he said, and motioned at Ilya with his glass. She smiled.

What?

Never mind. As I've told you before, cows are very important out here. Sometimes they outrank God and his church grass. Build a fence.

You're not going to do anything?

I did say I would talk to him.

But you know that won't accomplish anything. Please be competent.

Will looked sad. Tell you what I'll do. If you can raid God's pockets for some coin, I'll get a couple of the boys over at Dooley's to build you a fence. Maybe they'd be better at that than being a posse.

A drunkard's fence.

Those are the affordable kind. If you want a teetotaler's fence, God's going to have to miss a meal or two. Up to you.

I will speak to Father Michael.

Fine. You let me know.

Thank you, Will.

You're welcome, Mrs. Havish.

I like her, said Ilya, when the door had shut.

She's not so bad as she appears, but it's so close it's not worth contemplating. Beats all how folks can come out here where you don't need a boss looking over you, and avoid government, but bring God with them. You were saying? So far this is a decent story. Not overpowering, but better than scoopin' up poop.

You flatter me. Ilya smothered the urge to tell him of Herbert, to save her reputation.

I'm a charmer.

So then, there I am in Salt Lake City, with no money.

In hell, you're saying.

A terrible place. The Jews were at the very least direct and dramatic enough to call theirs the Dead Sea. 'Salt Lake.' Very dull.

Like the people who live there. I was hoping they settled there so they would have a big enough lake for us to drown them in.

I suppose it's good that there is a place for them.

That's the way I look at it. They spread though, is the trouble.

Ilya lit a new cigarette and drank. In any event, as I was enlisting the help of the local law enforcement to help me find my bag and my money, my train left.

The other chaperone wouldn't wait? Wouldn't do anything?

We did not get along. Anyway, it's not an orphan 'train,' it's more an orphan car. An entire train of those kids would be too much.

I didn't know that.

And the train doesn't wait for anything, they're very strict about that.

Still, that's a pretty serious disagreement with the other chaperone, for him to leave you stranded.

I made the mistake of mentioning my thoughts about Mr. Darwin. He took offense.

Thought they weren't religious folks.

This gentleman was. It turns out to be very difficult to find godless people who want to do good deeds. He also made advances toward me, and didn't respond well to being rebuffed.

Now that sounds almost like the truth.

I'm glad you think so.

Alright, so the shitty man strands you in Salt Lake to take revenge on you.

And Salt Lake is grave punishment.

The religious kind prefer that. Do go on.

Well, I ask you, what is a woman in that situation to do?

Wire home for money.

Panic grabbed Ilya. She hadn't predicted that answer, and it was the obvious one, so she hated herself.

Yes, my thought as well. However, I am an orphan myself. She congratulated herself for coming up with this, but got a bolt of fear because she didn't know where to go now.

Oh?

Yes. A wonderful parity, don't you think?

And that's why you were helping the children? You know their plight?

On the contrary, that's why I didn't want to help them, and only wanted an adventure. I know from experience what wretches children are when they aren't parented properly. Even when they are, frankly. Witness the rat who stole my baggage.

Ah-hah.

And as if this run of poor luck wasn't sufficient, my fiancée turned away from me. I wired to him, and he wired back only two words, 'engagement terminated.'

Cad.

Perfectly so.

You seem too smart to have chosen a person of such low character.

In what world do you live where poor women have choice in that way?

Point taken. But you don't seem like any poor woman I've ever seen.

I read. A lot. And dislike the coarse illiteracy poverty brings. I strive. And desperation can cloud a woman's judgment, leading me to choose a man of means when the opportunity arose. Ilya struggled to keep the tension out of her face.

A lot of things can cloud judgment. Greed. Lust. Stupidity.

I assure you, it was simply a confluence of misfortunes. My fiancée turned out to be intolerant of women's freedom. He expected me to stay at home and keep the furnace stoked. Must I supply every detail of my history? It would be a long night.

No, no. That would be entertaining, but I'm content watching you wind your way through this chapter. It's been a long day, I don't want you to get too tired. And this is far better than having crazy young men shoot me.

Your job sounds lovely. Poop, and shooting, and Mrs. Havish.

That about covers it, these days. And they're not all that different.

Perhaps being free is not all it is cracked up to be, and women are erring.

That is a fact. The being free part, anyhow. Can't speak to the women part. What happens next?

Well, you see, the next choice was to appeal to a church for their charity.

Of course. Mormons love to help infidels.

Well, I'm a Jew, so for them I'm not an infidel, I'm almost a god, except that I'm a woman.

Too bad. You could have commanded them all to go back to wherever they came from. Done us all a favor.

You seem to almost have antipathy toward the Mormons.

I don't like to hate much, but I make an exception for them. I came out here to get away from folks like that, and here they come slithering along behind me. Can't trust people that up and decide they're special.

My quarrel with the Jews.

They're a popular bunch in their own right.

Much beloved, it's true. So there I am, a female Jewish atheist in a Mormon city with no money at all. Of course, I feel terrified now, but also exhilarated, you know. Alone, left with only my wits to find a way through, in the wild West. I am in a dime novel. I only want for a male hero.

Well. You have a hell of a lot more than just wits.

True.

This is becoming the best story I've heard in a long while.

I would think it would be. So I am hungry, and alone, and attracting more attention than seems healthy. And I conclude that selling myself for a short time is the only way to acquire the funds I need to move on.

Really? This is more a biblical homily than a dime novel.

As you like.

You don't seem made for that sort of work. Not that I have anything against it. Comes in right handy.

Well, to continue to be perfectly honest, I have had experience with the job. Many female orphans do.

Ah. I had forgotten that you were an orphan.

Please try to follow along.

My apologies.

Accepted. For obvious reasons, I am able to find employ quickly.

Your wits?

Precisely.

And I begin to make money. However, problems quickly arise.

No.

Sadly the case. The man who ran the establishment...

What was it called? Just so it's less of a mouthful for you.

It was called 'The Establishment.'

On Commercial Street. Has that chandelier with all the crucifixes for lamps. The Momo's hated that place when they weren't going to it. I know it well. Fairly well.

Good. This man's character changed dramatically once I began to work, and he began to keep more of my earnings then we had agreed to. And he began to behave as if he had purchased me, which was the case with many of the other women. And he struck me.

A mistake that, I'll allow.

Very much so. Also, I had lost my taste for this kind of work, not that it was ever very strong. And being an orphan myself, and seeing the outcome of children born bastards on the train, and all through the streets of New York, I was, shall we say, reluctant to allow myself to be impregnated by the nauseous creatures that frequent those places, most of whom refuse to wear protection, and the owner backed them over us. He didn't like to pay for skins. He preferred to let the women become pregnant, then replace them, over discommoding his customers.

The Establishment gets mostly the uppity sort, as I recall.

They get all kinds. The uppity sort are the ones who won't wear protection. The lower ones, they are usually less objectionable because they are so frightened and grateful, and they'll do what is asked of them. With them it is simply a matter of breathing through my mouth. There are exceptions to that of course, and when they except themselves, they take it far. But as a rule, the upper ones are worse, because they feel entitled, and superior, and that quite ruins their superior manners. Makes their training something they like to ignore, to liberate themselves from. Being low is an adventure for them. You see?

I believe I do. That's something I had never considered.

Interesting, isn't it? I see myself as something of an anthropologist.

That a special kind of whore?

Exactly so. Of course, there are exceptions to the well-bred-sinking-low type, as well. Sometimes they are the gentlemen their clothes imply. In any event, I am in the habit of slipping out from beneath these sacks of excrement as soon as they've loosed their slime into me, and I wash myself out quickly with astringent, to dispatch their seed before it has a moment to gain a purchase. Sometimes I would jump up and down and beat my abdomen with a wooden paddle, but I admit that was only to enhance the drama. I *am* Jewish.

Will chuckled with amazement. He'd never heard a woman speak this bluntly who wasn't herself the low sort. Even Mary had more scruples.

I appreciate your candor, he said. Less so your attention to detail.

Pardon. I forgot about the strange squeamishness of men. What is a story without candor and detail, I ask you? Also, in pursuit of my anthropological studies of men, and aside from shaming them and making them pay with something more dear than money, I wanted to see how they would respond to my...scourge of their seed.

And?

The vast majority simply slunk away looking hurt. Some became furious, but did nothing. Some became furious and wanted to strike me, but there was an enormous man there to prevent that.

In the room?

Of course not. A shriek away. And it was made quite plain to the men that he was there before they were allowed to be alone with me. One man forgot about him, or was just beside himself with outrage at my treatment of him, and he struck me. The chucker-out pitched him off the balcony after savagely beating him. It was a scene I will treasure.

Enjoyed it, eh?

I'm not altogether certain what my response was. I was appalled certainly, because the poor fool hadn't a prayer, and was just coldly hammered to bits by this giant. He didn't break anything in the room, or even disturb a hair on his own head doing it. He simply held the naked man by the neck and pummeled his head, then picked him up, walked out onto the balcony, and pitched him into the street. I had to open the door for him, he wasn't quite strong enough to carry the man with one hand. I wasn't cheering, but it was fascinating, no question. But all of the men, with one exception, responded in a very negative way.

Odd.

Can you now see where my story is taking you?

I can't. I'm enjoying it very much, so that may be hiding the obvious.

Excellent. So, then Bat came to see me one day.

Who?

Oh, excuse me. The men you just killed were named Bat and Rog.

'Rog?'

Ilya rolled her eyes and shrugged. He was the one who was in *deshabille* when you came upon us.

In 'what?'

He was urinating.

Ah.

He was illiterate, and had apparently at some time heard the word 'rogue' mispronounced, and took the name for himself. He was the leader, though that word seems laughable used to describe him. Bat was his half-wit twin brother, though, if Rog was the full-wit, it would seem to make Bat more an eighth-wit compared with a normal person.

Will snickered. All that fits well with their methods as robbers.

Doesn't it? At any rate, I subjected Bat to the same treatment at the brothel, and he did not respond like the others.

Ohhh.

He laughed.

Being an eighth-wit.

Yes, but I hadn't grasped that at the time, and thought he was an interesting man, and I felt very refreshed that he laughed. And he restored a small amount of my regard for men. And then, when the owner accosted me, because I was gaining a reputation that was costing him money — men came in enthused by my beauty, but left very...ill at ease, and unlikely to revisit — Bat beat him senseless, and we fled.

Will laughed hard. Then he stood and stretched, took another of Ilya's cigarettes and lit it, fed wood into the stove, returned to his desk and sat.

So the three of you have been on a crime spree since then?

Well, I wasn't on a crime spree, but as it turns out, they were, which I didn't know, though I certainly should have intuited it. They didn't kill people, they were more just badgers, pilfering whatever they could. Sometimes they held people up for some dinner, when they likely would have just given it to us. It was somewhat sad, really.

And they just kicked it up some when they went for the bank here?

That was a first while I was with them, certainly. Ambition got a hold of them, it's true, and that goes very poorly for some. I assure you, it wasn't my affinity for them, or for their habits, that kept me with them. They were protection. Traveling alone as a woman is not advisable, even for me. One constantly has vultures circling.

We call them buzzards out here.

Thank you. It's so important to speak the language. Frankly, those two were easy for me to control, so it seemed a good fit, temporarily. All I cared about at the moment was getting out of Salt Lake. And having little to return to in New York...

Why come north, though?

Rog said he had friends up this way. He wanted to join up with them and I suppose become a proper gang. I didn't inquire very much.

I can believe the easy to control part. The way they robbed that bank, they may as well have shot themselves. Saved us all a lot of trouble.

It wasn't their intellect and sparkling *repartee* that attracted me. And they were curiously reluctant to force me to bed them.

Many men are. And dumb as they were, they probably figured it wouldn't go the way they wanted it to with you. Well, I think I believe over half your story, and that's a pretty good percentage.

That sounds about right.

What are your plans now?

I have none. The day's events call for making new plans.

True. Well, I'll tell you this much. It wouldn't trouble me at all if you stayed on here. You'd be an entertaining addition to this menagerie of mine, and Lord knows...or Darwin knows, we need some entertainment. But that woman-like creature Mrs. Havish and her mongrel priest aren't going to much care for you. In fact, there is probably nothing about you that wouldn't rub their fur the wrong way. And I say 'fur' with all possible meaning.

I appreciate that.

So if you want to stay, be my guest, and I'll do what I can to get between you and them, but they have a lot of power, being the king and queen of our morals, and this being such a little place. You might be an outcast. Why they think that's a hurtful thing, I'm not sure. There's a small bunch of folks who aren't so...stiff, but by small I mean maybe four, five people. I'm thinking we may not be enough to keep you...feeling alive.

Thank you, I'll proceed westward. Perhaps to the coast. I have the sense that I'm not well made for your wild, wild West.

Based on that story, you may be better made for it than you're allowing.

Perhaps.

Well. Stay the night, anyhow. You're poor again, I'm betting.

No. I have my earnings. It's a fair amount. Paper money is a wonderful invention, it was easy to conceal from my men.

Good. Well, I don't like trouble and we've been having too much of it lately, so please don't take it upon yourself to earn more money and exterminate cowboy seed in my town, if you don't mind. The boys around here wouldn't laugh.

Would you?

I doubt it. Be pretty hard to know what to do. Laughing sounds about right, but I doubt I'd think of it. Not at first, anyhow.

Precisely. I'll control myself, easily. I'd like just a bath and a bed and a meal. It's been a long time.

We have those. Go over to Molly's there and tell her I sent you and she'll give you a crib for a night without vermin, and get you some food. Mary's closed now, but her place is off down at the end there. In the morning you can buy some supplies for the road off of her. You and her are somewhat alike, come to think of it.

I appreciate your kindness. And your credulity.

Think nothing of it. I don't know what that last word was, but I'll take it on faith it's a good one.

In your case it is.

Alright. Best pack it in. I have to get those corpses where the dogs won't chew on them. We'll plant them tomorrow. Any parting words for your protectors?

It was a pleasure, gentlemen, and my thanks.

That'll do. Will opened the door and held it back for her, and Ilya passed through it onto the boardwalk. She stood there a moment breathing the sharp, woodsmoke air of the evening, listening to the clatter of Dooley's. She considered that Will had no notion of who she was, that New York had not followed, or preceded her. There not being a poster of her on his wall could be explained by his being not quite the law. But there had been no photograph, no newspaper article, nothing, in Salt Lake. It was interesting information, but she could not fathom what it meant. It was not possible that Herbert's death would be unavenged. She wondered what Henry would do, and it was chilling not to know. But it was also like Henry to keep himself shrouded from others.

She and Will stood side by side, looking at the paltry row of lights that was the main street at night.

Belle Manque ain't much of a town, I guess, he said. Compared to New York.

No. But, New York 'ain't' much of a town compared to...'Belle Manque,' you said?

I did. 'Ain't' sounds damn funny coming from your mouth. 'Trixie.'

I feel the same. 'Belle' so, 'Beautiful'...but beautiful what?

'Lack.' Boy first staked it out thought he was going to be rich off gold, and called it Belle Grande. Turns out he was too optimistic. One of the folks who stayed was a French Canadian, old boy, used to trap when there was money in it. He changed it when the first boy left.

Ilya laughed. That is perhaps the first time in the West where the name of a place wasn't ridiculous to me.

You're welcome. Come look in on me in the morning. We'll get you set up for travel someway.

Thank you, Will.

Thank you. I'm in arrears to you for that story, far as I'm concerned.

I agree. Good night.

Good night.

4

Oh, Bridger darling, what happened? Mary said, standing at her stove, startled, staring at his face. He had walked right into her kitchen, something he had never done before. It had been an unspoken agreement between them that he was allowed to just walk into the workshop, but not the living space.

Mary, I...He came toward her as though falling, and crumpled into her.

My baby...

Her face grew stony. She held him hard against her body and at first tried to still his convulsions, then just let him wrack himself against her.

You're safe here. It's alright.

When he ran dry, and pulled himself from her, blood from the wounds on his face streaked her cheek and neck, blotched her dress. She held his face in her hands and looked at him.

Bridger, what is happening with you? Her face took on an expression of soft bemusement. I've seen men have a difficult time with this part of their lives, but this is positively melodrama. Did that fuck do this to you?

Bridger shook his head and shrugged and turned from her, sagging onto a stool.

Come. Bring the stool. She led him to the bathroom, got hot water, carbolic, and cloth.

Jesus, she said, and winced as she dabbed at the grit and clotting blood from the gashes in his face, and picked at the shards of stone and lead with a needle. His eyelids flickered at the sting, but he stared through her, eye sockets dark, eyes both blank and pained, mouth in a hard, tight line cut through hollowed cheeks. She laughed a little at the haunted intensity of his look. At that his gaze fixed on her, and more hurt came into it.

Oh Bridger, you know I am not laughing because I enjoy your hurt. I like *schadenfreude,* but not at your expense, darling. *'Schad'*...never mind. She kept dabbing and picking at his face. These won't need suturing. They'll close up shortly. You'll have little scars, but you'll still be beautiful. She put her fingers gently on the puckered wound in his neck. How does this feel?

Gittin' there. Don' hurt no more.

Good. Well my dear, you certainly are coming to look like a dangerous man. The irony of that is something to be savored.

She took up a heavy, white cloth, poured carbolic into clean, steaming hot water, soaked the cloth in it, folded it, and put it over his face, pushing it hard.

Come in here and sit. Just keep your head back and keep the cloth on it. Be easy. If you can.

She poured whiskey, added warm water, took his hand from the arm of the chair and put the glass in it.

Drink it down. I'll be right back.

She went to the front of the store and looked out at the street for a moment, pulled the shade down and locked the door, and returned to her kitchen.

I'm going to bet you haven't eaten. She lit a cigarette and stoked the stove.

She said, Nursing you is becoming something of a career for me. I'm beginning to suspect that you leave here and deliberately get into a scrape just so you can come back and have me fuss over you again. It's very flattering, but you could simply come to see me.

I kilt Pap.

Mary drew in a sharp breath, and stared at the cloth on his face.

Oh, my. She pulled a chair back from the table, sat, and laid her arms across the white cloth, cigarette trailing smoke. She looked straight ahead, expression sad.

Oh, my baby, I said be thorough, not become a lunatic. Must you overdo everything? I said to simply leave him.

He took the cloth from his face and said, I *tried*, his voice shattered.

Shhh, shhh, alright, alright, it's alright. I know you didn't kill him on purpose. Depending on what one means by 'on purpose.' Tell me what happened.

Bridger gave out the story like a ragged fusillade.

That fucking shit, she said, when he finished.

Why dint y' tell me he come fer y'? his tone pathetic and aggrieved. Did he? Was he lyin'?

Mary was stunned. Bridger had left that part out when he had told the story. Why, I...oh. She took a breath and thought, and her face resolved into stern melancholy. Because, honey, he did more than come for me. He wasn't a suitor, he was a beast. How do you suggest I tell a boy that his father is a rapist? I wanted to protect you, and to pull you away from him, but not to utterly destroy your regard for him, because it would be an act of violence against you. I thought it was better for you to see him as ill, rather than evil. I still don't know which is true, probably both are, but Bridger, if I did it wrong, I am so sorry. I am so sorry.

He took y'?

No. He wanted to. He felt entitled to me, and could not accept that I disagreed with him. That's all I want to reveal. It doesn't matter now. It was a long time ago.

I wanna know.

But why?

I don' know.

Oh, God. Mary snatched up the bottle, poured, drank it down.

It must be so wretched to be male, she said. First an attempted rape, now an attempted mind-rape by the son. The torment that must lead to that. Alright. He just wasn't strong enough. That's all. We struggled, wrestled really, and I won, because he was weak, in every way. He slapped me to try and force me to submit, but I slapped him back. He did not know how to deal with powerful resistance. He might have won if he persisted long enough, but he hadn't the...sand, I guess you'd say, though that seems wrong. I almost told Will, and he would have dismembered the bastard with his hands. But I held back. Here is what I think, and you are of course free to ignore my opinion, as millions profitably do, but after this I do not want to talk about it again. Too much life has disappeared down that man's gullet. Your father may not have been strictly a piece of shit man, but he was certainly a very weak one, and a manipulator as they usually are, and his illness merely made what was bad about him all he was. It's not uncommon for strong men to sire weak ones, but it is quite uncommon for a weak man to sire a strong one. I suspect you are one of those, knowing that I am most likely wrong. I was trying, not well perhaps, but I was trying, to nurture the strong in you. If I had simply let loose on you altogether with my estimation of your father, you would have felt doomed by him, to being him. But you are not. I'm sorry if I did not handle it perfectly, but I am childless and quite new at the chore, and anyway, imagine your life if you had not had me. I will tolerate only a little remorse in myself, and a little opprobrium from you. After that you are on your own. Being strong and being hard are not the same, but this may be a moment when the latter should take precedence.

I ain't mad at y'. At you.

How very good of you.

Bridger sat forward, elbows on knees. She went to the window and stood there, staring out, one arm straight down in front of her with elbow into her hip, cigarette pinched between forefinger and thumb, lit end pointing into her cupped hand pouring smoke, other arm across her abdomen, hand over her forearm. He could see the wet on her face. He stood and went to her, put his arm around her waist, and laid his cheek against her shoulder. She stood stiffly a moment and then eased, raised her hand and put it on his head, pulling it into her.

I apologize, my baby, she said. I forgot you just slew your father. That can put a person out of sorts.

I never meant nothin' like I thought shit wuz yer fault, he said.

You and your eloquence. At the very least, now I can teach you to speak without it being so futile. She turned in his arm and they held one another.

Let me cook, she said, and pulled away from him. What do you want to do now?

Dunno.

'I don't know.'

I don't know.

You left him just laying there?

Yep.

Well. He's solved a world of problems by getting himself killed. Do you want to tell Will? He won't do anything to you. No one will. Between Spunk and your father, this town has had a much needed cleansing. And you had a lot to do with both of those, which is so strange I can't quite grasp it. They may make you mayor, should they ever decide they want one. On the other hand, they may decide you're a devil and pitchfork you out of town. They're resisting progress very hard, apparently believing the state of nature is preferable. Fools. You, on the other hand, seem not to be able to escape the state of nature. Do you want to fetch him and bury him?

Might put 'im next t' Ma on th' place.

Men simply can't stop punishing women. Alright. We'll eat, go get Will, and you two can go out and get him. The animals have probably already begun making a meal of the man. Soon the forests will be overrun with poxed beasts running amok.

They were silent for a while as she cooked. Bridger sat dabbing at his face, smoking and watching her, longing for her.

She put the skillet with ground venison and eggs and peppers mashed together on the table, jammed a big spoon into the mess, and clattered some plates and silverware beside it.

Eat. Not my best effort, but it will give you strength.

Bridger came to the table and sat, arms hanging between his knees, shoulders pulled forward, staring.

I think your big troubles are over for a while, she said, and came to him, and stroked his head. God, they better be. Ick. You need another bath.

They heard the front doorknob rattle, then sharp raps on the glass.

Some people have a hard time with rejection, Mary sighed. It might be Will, he comes around at this hour sometimes.

She went to the door, raised the shade, and saw Ilya standing there, Will beside her. She unlocked the door.

Good morning, Will, she said.

Mary. Like you to meet a new acquaintance of mine. This is Trixie, from New York, by way of those two thieves I dispatched yesterday.

Mary looked at her, then back to him. 'Trixie?' she said.

Will shrugged.

Alright. I'm Mary.

Pleased.

I as well.

Yes, Will, Mary said, I overheard something about the shooting this morning. It's been a very exciting time for you. You must be quite depleted with all the doing good, and being shot, and saving damsels, that's been demanded of you of late. I know it's not first nature for you to be heroic.

Damned straight it's not. Are you closed for an important reason? We weren't aiming to disturb you, the lady here needs to buy some things, and I was headed this way to see if you had your very special coffee only I deserve.

Well, as it happens I am involved, but I was about to come for you, anyway. It seems your trials are not yet completed, Hercules. Come in.

Ilya and Will stepped inside and paused there while Mary relocked the door and drew the shade. She gestured around the store and said, Please,

Miss, shop, I have to talk to Will. Come Will, let me show you something. They walked to the back and into the living quarters, where Will looked at Bridger.

What the fuck?! he said, when he saw the boy's face. Excuse me, Mary.

Don't be silly. Coffee?

Please. And a slug of that whiskey in it would be nice, also. I got a feeling I'm going to need it. Anytime Bridger shows up these days, blood and bullets start shooting out all over the place.

It's not bad news, really, Mary said. Will sat facing Bridger, watching him eat, and looking bemusedly at his face. Mary put a cup before him, and poured in a dollop of whiskey.

Thank you, Mary, he said. He took a long sip, swallowed, put the cup down, and looked at Bridger again. Mary sat at the table, poured herself a whiskey and coffee and lit a cigarette, blowing the smoke out hard.

Boy, you just look like shit, Will said, and laughed with a mixture of wonder and bitterness.

Thanks, Bridger said. Feel like I been rode hard and shot dead.

Do you want to tell him, or should I? Mary said. Bridger waved his hand at her and looked away.

Boy ain't stupid, anyway, Will said. Lay it on me, Mary. Be gentle.

You know that's not my way, Will. He shot his father. Killed him.

Will sat for a moment, took up his cup and drank, replaced it, took up one of Mary's cigarettes, lit it, and exhaled, looking at it. Why is it you women know about these new things before I ever do?

Because women are inherently progressive and like new things, Mary said.

I see you haven't been dealing with Mrs. Havish much.

You have me there. I take it back.

So, Bridger. I know your Pap wasn't much to look at, but was murdering him the best you could come up with? It's awful...biblical.

Oedipal, really, Mary said.

I'll take your word on it.

I dint murder 'im.

Alright. That's good. Tell me about it.

Well, he...Mary said.

Hush Mary, let the boy tell it. You aren't objective.

I beg your pardon...

Will reached out and patted her hand. I have to tell the people something. You know how they get about blaming somebody for shit. I need to be able to truthfully say I got the story from the boy, and I believed him. It was a human life, and they don't care all that much about whose it was, they just know somebody has to pay. You know that.

It wasn't a human life. But, you're right. Telling me to hush won't do, however.

Agreed. I forgot myself. I'm sorry.

Alright. Tell him, hon...Bridger.

Bridger told the story again, watching Mary wince at his language out of the corner of his eye and trying to mend it before it came out of his mouth. When he finished, Will sat there and thought.

Tried to take your clothes, huh?

Bridger nodded.

Boy was some cracked. Is that Oedipal too, Mary?

I could reread it and let you know if I missed that.

Do that.

It's hardly about the clothes, Will.

Thank you, Mary, I snagged on that myself. Well hell, son, that's a sad story. Second one in two days for me. You're getting the little end of the horn all the time. How are you taking it all, if you don't mind my asking? This sort of thing puts some people right down.

I couln't help it, Bridger said. I tried t' jes git away, but he kep' comin' at me. I dint wanna kill 'im.

Well, I'm skeptical there. Everyone else did. I kinda feel bad we couldn't do more to help you, but...the parents are the parents. As it turns out you didn't need help. Been nice if we could have taken your Pap and shackled him to the whole Pilgrim clan and put them on a ship of fools, but we don't have enough water out here for ships. 'Canoe of fools' doesn't have the right ring to it.

He wants to bury him next to his mother on their place, Mary said.

Alright, Will said. I guess that means at one time you all were pretty good together, Bridger?

The question drew tears into Bridger's eyes, and he nodded and looked away.

Just my luck to miss that part, Will said. Alright. At least I don't have to kill folks before I bury them this time. This makes you the owner of 160 acres of crappy ranch land, son. Ain't you lucky.

I don' wannit. If it wuz attached t' th' next chunks it'd be aright, but it ain't fer shit th' way it is.

True story. The dumbfuck government drew the lines like they was drunk at the time, and they probably were. Your father wasn't savvy enough to see that, and picked the worst parcel of the lot. Too far from the river so it's all rock, can't grow anything. Crick only runs a month a year. Grass is alright but the critters die of thirst. Anderson is the only one that can use it.

Then let's sell it to him, and give the money to Bridger.

That's sound. Anderson won't give much for it, tight as his Mormon asshole is, but he likes to get bigger if he can. Makes putting your Pap in that ground not very sensible, though. Up to you, boy.

They're in your head, Bridger, Mary said, I'm sorry to say. Their bodies don't mean anything. Food for the animals is as good an end as any. Your mother, though, that might be different.

I never knew 'er anyhow, not really. Let 'em rot, Bridger said. I jes want done with all this fuckin' shit. I don' wanna see him, I don' wanna see th' ranch, I don' wanna see nuthin'. I'm fuckin'...done. Fuck!

That's showing some spunk, Will said, then raised his hand. Easy now...that just got out before I knew what it was. It's not going to be so much rot as he's going to be devoured. Just want to make sure you understand that. A lot of folks, that's more than they can bear.

Bridger shrugged. I don' give a fuck.

Well, that makes my day easier. Do you have your Pap's horse and all? Do you want anything from the house, anything at all?

There ain't nothin' in that house I want. Everything I got, I got with me. Y' c'n burn it.

Well, no need to waste a standing structure. I might be able to squeeze a couple of dollars more out of Anderson if it's got a house on it. His hands can live in it if they need to. I'll write to have the right papers sent out here, it's still government land. I ain't got any idea how that goes, but I know if the government's involved it's gonna be fucked. And I'll talk to Anderson, get what I can for the place. In fact, he probably knows just how to do it, what with all the practice. Where are you going to be?

He can stay with me for now, Mary said. He can live in the cabin. It's very early to make decisions like these.

Folks'll want to see him mourning.

Ridiculous. He's been in mourning most of his life. It's time for living.

Just saying, that's how they like it.

They're idiots. The moment the shackles are removed from him, they want him to put them back on.

True. No need to go over all this now. And our Eastern lady is waiting on us, Mary. She probably wants to be on her way.

Oh, yes. I forgot.

Finding what you need? Mary said, as the three of them came into the store.

Yes, thank you, Ilya said. She was sitting on a chair by the window.

I apologize, Will said, didn't mean to leave you out here like that. We had some important business.

No trouble at all, Ilya said. Hello again, she added to Bridger. She frowned. That looks painful, she said, when she noticed the state of his face.

Ma'am, he said, and got very still. The shame of the night of the shooting rushed him, and the maddening attraction to her. He didn't stare at her this time.

You two know each other? Mary said.

They got acquainted at the party where I shot up those two thieves.

Ah. An auspicious way to meet. So very Western. Being from New York, that must have been a strange way for you to make a new acquaintance.

Not so far off from a cotillion, really. Out here they use real blood and bullets, is all. Mary glanced at Ilya and smiled. 'Trixie' at a cotillion? I see.

Ilya regretted not giving Will the name she used on the orphan train, Sarah, but she'd grown used to Trixie with Bat and Rog, and hated Sarah, because it made her sound weak and common, and was too Jewish. Trixie was at least absurd and amusing.

Would you like a cup of coffee, Trixie?

Yes, please.

Bridger would you mind? He nodded.

How do you like it? Mary said.

Milk and sugar if you have them.

Alright Bridger?

Yep.

We need to outfit her with enough gear and grub to get her down to the Terminus so she can get herself on a train to the coast, Mary, Will said. Probably a week's worth.

Why not take the coach? That's only two days.

I prefer to travel independently, Ilya said. I dislike being on the timetable of another. I'm in no rush. I'm a tourist, somewhat by accident.

Hell of a tourist, Will said.

Will, we've gotten old, Mary said. Imagine traveling through this region because it's fun. And alone. What about the natives?

Not much risk there, Will said. One might stagger out and die on you, but that's about the worst of it now. Down this way anyways. Up north I wouldn't advise it.

Still. Alone, Mary said. No offense, Trixie, I'm certain you can take care of yourself, but some things no one can defend themselves from. Highwaymen, beasts, common men who lack self-control...

I'm not for it, either, Will said, but she's seen her share of scruffy on her way out here, and I gather she come up through rough circumstances in New York. I told her she was welcome to stay, but this isn't her kind of place.

No offense, Ilya said.

Oh, of course not, Mary said. It surprises me that anyone stays here. I suppose it's because one is away from it all, whatever 'all' is, and the illusion of independence and freedom is much easier to maintain. One pays dearly for it, though.

Oh? Ilya said. In what currency?

Independence and freedom are deeply tedious. Nothing you do matters to anyone else, so doing something seems pointless.

A point not mentioned on the handbills in the East encouraging settlement.

They're cunning, aren't they? If one is stupid enough to believe them. No my dear, you have the right idea. Pass by and look, but don't stay.

Why don't you pass by?

I like it here. Well enough. It's ridiculous, and I like that.

Bridger came out and handed Ilya her coffee.

Thank you, Bridger.

Mary rummaged through the pile Ilya had gathered. This won't do. This is the wrong food and not enough of it, anyway. One blanket isn't enough...no cartridges...are you armed?

I have two pistols, but I'm out of ammunition.

First tell me what you already have, dear.

Figure she has nothing, Mary, except what she's wearing, and those two dinky pistols. Those two boys weren't much for traveling in style.

Will, this is impossible, what's the matter with you? We can't let a young woman fresh from New York go roaming through Montana Territory by herself. Come to your senses.

I agree with you, Mary, but it isn't my way to get in the way of someone wanting to do something. It's a free country.

It's a tedious country, as I believe I mentioned. Trixie, you aren't traveling alone because you absolutely must have it that way, you just have had poor luck finding companions, correct?

Yes, something like that. I have nothing against other people on principle. Sometimes.

Then Bridger should go with you to the Terminus, and then he can return. He looks more dangerous than he is, but that seems to be changing.

That would be fine with me, Ilya said. I'm not experienced with...wilderness.

Bridger?

Yep.

Alright, Mary said. This seems like it will work. What are you riding on? Or in?

She has a cart outside, Will said.

Mary went to the window and looked out at it. Insane, she said. Alright. Bridger, do what you can to fix that thing. Will, what are you doing right now?

Well, I was going to get drunk and piss the day away. I've been working too hard lately.

You've earned that. But, how about you get drunk and go get Arnold out of whatever ditch he's laying in so he can fix the rims on that cart, instead?

I can do that.

What about horses?

Judy ain't gonna make it, Bridger said, sad about it.

We're good on mounts, Will said. We got Bridger's Pap's horse. Got the two from them thieves, plus the one pulling the cart.

I don' wanna ride his horse, Bridger said. He treated it bad. Needs tendin'.

Alright, Will said. Let me go get Arnold, and I'll look at the flesh we got. If I have to cut you one out of my string, I will. I got a mustang geld that's steady and can go all day. Hasn't been named even. We'll work it out.

There is far too much to do for you to leave today. Trixie, may I suggest that you leave tomorrow? By the time we have you in order there will be little left of the day. We can eat together tonight and you can get up fresh. I haven't cooked for a party in a long time. I have two people I like under my roof, and one more I believe I could. That by itself is novel for me.

I recommend you take her up on it, Will said. You'll not have food like Mary's for a long spell.

Alright, thank you very much, Ilya said. I haven't had a good meal since New York, and I love to eat.

Coming West was an extraordinarily foolish choice then, Mary said.

Oh, I know.

Over the years I've figured out how to eat quite well here. I think I can accommodate a woman of taste, especially one named 'Trixie,' and I'd be happy to see one eat. That ass Molly can make a raw carrot seem overcooked.

I discovered that last night, Ilya said.

I've always been partial to her meat pie, Will said.

I haven't trained you yet is why, Mary said.

Well, I've been waiting for you to open your own restaurant, Mary. I don't know why you don't.

Watch these people root around in my food? I think not. Molly is perfect for them. Anyway, that is far too much work. Excellent, then. Bridger, does all of this sound alright? You've never been out of the valley. It will be good for you. Or not, given the way your luck is playing these days.

Never seen a person have a streak like he's having, Will said.

I don't know what luck is, Mary said, but it seems there is such a thing as a hard-luck person. She took Bridger's chin in her fingers and examined the cuts.

You'll be fine, she said. Try not to smile or laugh or grimace or blink, you'll heal faster.

Aright.

Humor, my darling Frankenstein, humor.

5

The morning sun raked the chill off the street and the frost began to sparkle and die. Ilya and Mary embraced.

That meal, Ilya said. Thank you. Elk ragout. It was indescribable.

Yes, Mary said. A triumph, even for me. I impressed myself greatly. Claret gives an entirely different savor to elk than it does to beef, far superior in my opinion. It seems to make beef too gamey and bad, and elk less gamey and good. And one learns that root vegetables are almost the only ones you'll get here, so one had best learn to use them well.

I thought johnnycake was something people ate to punish themselves for sin, but yours...

Well, Ilya — a much more suitable and beautiful name, by the way — if you come back I'll show you the trick. It has to do with butter, as most cooking does. But I can't give away my secrets when I hardly know you. Sad we devoured all of it, or you could take it with you. Thank you for giving me a reason to protect my reputation.

Pleased to do it.

I'm sure. Mary took Ilya's arm and turned her aside from Will and Bridger. She held Ilya's eyes. Remember, she said, I want him back. Not to be mine, to be his. He's not ready for you. Probably won't ever be.

Ilya felt a brief shock, then nodded. I have no designs.

That could easily change. The desire and adulation and lack of aggression coming out of him...the kind of aggression he feels righteous about at any rate...it could be like opium for you.

Ilya thought of Mariani. I see. You have my word.

No, I don't want it. You can't give your word about something like this. Promise me you will try. That you will be gentle, and smart.

I promise. I'm infamous for my gentleness and intelligence.

That is not terribly reassuring. Goodbye, dear. You are always welcome here. It's hell but it's home, as they say, too often I suppose. Mary turned to Bridger and tucked bills into the breast pocket of his coat. That's a hundred dollars.

That's a lot of money, Mary, Will said.

Shut up, Will, Mary said.

He flinched, opened his mouth, then closed it, realizing that this parting was hurting her more than he'd grasped.

She touched the gashes on Bridger's face with her fingertips. Bring me a present. Clean your face every day with the mixture I gave you. Alright?

Aright.

I'll see you in a couple of weeks. She went up the stairs and into her store. They heard the deadbolt smack. Bridger watched her, feeling desolate.

She's shut more than she's open these days, Will said.

Alright Bridger, Will went on, it's two days down, cross the Madison, and you'll hit a T. Go left, that'll be south. The Jeffersons will be on your right, the Gallatins on your left. Keep going, you'll hit 'Ginny City couple more days, maybe three, depends. Spur's still there even though the city's mostly Chinks picking tailings. There's probably one emigrant a week. The terrain's flat, the river's shallow. It's dead easy all the way down. And the leaves will be pretty as shit. You probably don't care about that but she might. Seems like a long time since she looked at something pretty from a position of being somewhat safe. You remember how them two thieves I shot looked, don't you?

Bridger nodded.

If you see men look like them, don't trust 'em. There's agents out there. Where you'll be, there won't be much cover, so you oughta see people coming a ways off. Don't trust anybody, but don't haul off and start shooting unless you have reason. If they're being too nice is a good time to look sharp. Might be best if you just kept your rifle in your hand, chambered up. Might scare off the wavery sort. Don't ever let anyone get real close to you, like I am now. Closer they are, the less time you have to react. He reached out and gave Bridger's new, black holster and cartridge belt a tug, and slapped a bit of leaf off his coat lapel. Least now you don't look like...your Pap.

He lowered his voice, nodded at Ilya, and said, All men would eat a mile of her shit to get to her asshole. They'd regret it right off when she noticed them back there, but they'd still do it. That's a serious problem for you, because they're gonna see you as something they gotta go through to get to her. She's also way smarter and way touchier than they're gonna have experience with. Stupid, ugly, tough, touchy sluts, yeah. Her, no. She's unlikely to finesse her way through for long if one of them starts up. Don't worry too much. She'll likely have them dead and buried before you realize there's a problem. Mind me?

Yessir.

No need for 'sirs.' Your Pap was the last fuck you oughtta have to 'sir,' and you punctuated that part of your life pretty smart.

Will stood and hesitated, looking at the mountains, thinking of what Mary had said to him in private earlier, gathering himself. He reached out and put his hand on Bridger's shoulder, looked hard into his eyes and said, One more thing. There is one hell of a big difference between cowardice and competence. You had you a problem with the first one, but that shit's on its way out, trust me, because I have been there. No one is steel right away, and most not ever. It's best you know what fear is. Though you overdid it a mite, but that's probably a good thing too, somehow, and overdoing things seems to be your way. It's experience, almost all of it, and you've got some now. Too much too quick, but it goes that way mostly. Competence, you have that, a lot of it. Sometimes having a crap Pap ends a man, sometimes it doesn't. It ended Spunk. But not you. I know it seems like you been shit on. Something to that. But hardly anything in the world wipes off easy as shit. You living out there all this time, making it mostly by yourself, no Ma, that thing you had for a Pap...you got real sand, it just doesn't feel that way to you, yet. But, it will.

Will paused, struggling. Bridger stood still, alarmed.

There's no shortage of things to be scared of, but you got nothing to be ashamed of. Stop doing it. I see you...you...looking for things in your head to say, but you're looking right by them. You can just say, son. I know you're thinking in there. You ain't dumb. And from what I hear, you're hell itself with that rifle — Mary told me about that pick you made on that whitetail off her stoop. I don't know you all that well, and I hope you don't take offense at me talking to you this way, but Mary does know you, and she says you're it, and that's good enough for me and it's more than enough for you. She reached out, grabbed you by the collar, and saved your ass, and you owe her your life. That means preserving your life so she ain't so alone. Just do what needs to be done, and you'll be alright. And if not, who gives a shit? He nodded at Ilya again. Keep in mind, she's smart and all, but she doesn't know shit about the mountains and you do. That makes you two even. Alright?

Bridger looked at the ground out in front of him a ways and nodded slowly. He looked up into Will's eyes and held them for a moment.

Aright, he said.

Alright.

Will stepped over and put his hand out to Ilya. You take care of yourself, Ilya, he said. Come on back when you got a new story. She took it.

I will, Will.

Funny.

They went west. The sun rose higher behind them and warmed their backs, and the melting frost wet the grass and covered the hard, red hawthorn leaves, making them look licked. Then the water disappeared and it was dry and faintly dusty, and the air smelled sweet, fetid, and delicious. They stripped out of their coats. The wheel span of the cart was shorter than the ruts, and Ilya worked it up and set one wheel between and one to the side. Bridger watched her handle the reins for a while and figured she was new to it but good enough to leave alone. He was afraid to talk to her, and rode beside the cart, twenty feet or so away, his rifle across his thigh and resting against the pommel. The road followed the creek, but up away from it on the hillside away from the thickets that lined its banks, and the road straightened the constant snaking of the water. The land was gentle, weaving rolls of dull green sage and tawny grass stretching away.

He missed Judy, missed the sense of reliability she gave him. Will's brown mustang was a good horse, though. Will had sat on him, pulled his pistol and shot a hole in a tree to prove his steadiness, and the horse stood still, ears twitching. Name him if you want, he had said. Judy'll be here. He also switched out the nag the cart came with for a young, black mare with experience pulling.

Ilya wondered at the distance Bridger kept from her at first, then pushed it from her mind and lapsed into a watchful reverie. The wagon's creaking and rocking, which she had once found maddening, now felt comforting and rhythmic, and the cart was fixed, so she didn't worry about being dumped on the ground. Bridger had fashioned a back for the plank seat of the cart, she could lean back into it and prop her boots on the foot board. After a few feet she fished a blanket out, folded it, and put it on the seat to sit on. The first of the days out of Salt Lake without Mariani, all of which she'd consumed on the train out from New York, she'd been gritty and ill, unable to sleep. Now there was none of the craving for it, and her body had settled into a sense of strength and health.

She took her hat off and shook out her hair. She was clean, her clothes were clean, the weather was clear and seemed ready to stay that way, she was well fed, and she was with a man, or boy, she didn't care which, who didn't want to talk and didn't want anything from her bad enough to pester her yet. That idiot Rog was forever pawing her, though in exchange for a few contemptuous handjobs and the vain hope she would stay with them, he'd shown her the basics of handling a horse and wagon, and riding, and she could handle her pistols now and liked them. The cart was filled with blankets and oilcloths, and Mary had filled a basket with potatoes, onions, garlic, and her last very sorry-looking tomatoes that still tasted good. There was Bridger's venison that Mary said came right back to flavor if boiled with salt, and small, angry-looking apples that were absurdly tart but good. She'd ground salt and pepper in a burr grinder and combined them in a tin with thyme, and put in a small pot and skillet.

You may not want to cook on the road, she'd said, because it's a difficult, painful skill to acquire, but it also tastes marvelous, campfire cooking. Just don't cook over flame, only coals. After that it's fairly simple.

Herbert's killing felt far away and inconsequential, and though she felt that she couldn't feel safe from Henry permanently she felt like she could feel safe right now, and felt that she had learned a little about savoring that chance since she'd fled. The West provided a place for that, the feeling of safe removal if one could stand the hell of getting to it. And she felt like a boss now, or if not a boss, without one for the first time. No one in her current world had more power than she did. Having to come to Montana Territory to feel that seemed absurd and made her angry, but she let the anger slide through her, let it become amusement, which faculty the West itself had provided, adding to the strangeness of all of this that her life had become.

Her hat was low-crowned and black. She'd cut the skirt of her black dress between her legs and sewed them into pantaloons out of which Spanish-heeled, black boots with vicious-looking rowels that she loved as ornaments and hated as tools protruded. The hat and boots were from Mary, used like new. Ilya had cut the sleeves of the dress back to above the elbow and hemmed them there because they were tattering at the wrists, and her forearms were growing muscled beneath her now-tanned skin. A gray, woolen vest kept her torso warm. She had a knee-length, charcoal-colored man's wool coat with a high collar, a black woolen scarf, and black woolen gloves that came to her elbows, also from Mary. She had one pistol in a black holster and cartridge belt, worn up against her belly cross-draw fashion, Mary had had cartridges. The other she left in the black leather valise she'd pinched from the owner of the Establishment with what little she had left of belongings — she was wearing what she owned. She and Mary had spent the previous day washing and tailoring Ilya's clothes, chatting, and arranging for what she needed, Mary constantly going into her kitchen to keep her meal rolling.

Bridger rode in a low thrumming panic, being over-watchful and feeling ridiculous. His face stung and crawled, healing. Every so often a mild pang of itching pain would shoot through the wound on his neck. He observed Ilya, noticed the softening of her expression, an extension of that from last night when he'd sat silently while they ate, and watched the other three talk and laugh. Ilya had told her story again, this time confessing that 'Ilya' was her real name, and the three of them laughed hard and loud, especially at Ilya's description of her prophylactic measures. Mary had wept with laughter at the wooden paddle, something Bridger had never seen her do, not even close, and he'd never provoked that sort of free mirth in her and that made him resentful. It hurt that he felt he had nothing to contribute, but what was he to say — 'Oh, y' think that's funny, I kilt my Pap today!'? But he was able after a while to lay back into his role and drink and try to absorb their way of being, and he mastered his technique of watching Ilya without being caught at it — holding his head pointing forward and slewing his eyes toward her so he could snap them away quickly. Ilya's beauty made Bridger feel glum and seedy and afraid when he was close to it, and that lent itself to his keeping away. In his red-rimmed imaginings of her he'd not had to face his own intimidation. Now, with her being real, inadequacy came upon him like the filth he'd been encased in before Mary scoured it off. Femaleness itself was enough to demoralize him, and having her be beautiful enhanced it. Her peaceful expression, broken by the slight, bitter smirk around her mouth, broke his heart. He longed to be already liked by her as he was by Mary, and was convinced that she could never care for him as Mary did.

There had been a low, scurrying feeling of betrayal that moved through him when he looked at Mary during the supper, but he couldn't face it and it couldn't survive the heat of his pull towards Ilya. And when he looked at Mary there was a warm sense of security and a powerful, angry, and defiant feeling of protectiveness and need, and a guilty sense of resentment at Will and his easy, dignified gentleness with her. All of it gave him a strong wish to be back in his wickiup with Judy, but he was glad he wasn't.

At midday they stopped and ate, chewing apples and venison, standing by the side of the road easing their asses. They'd seen no one.

Is it usual to have no one on the road at all? Ilya said.

Time a year. No one much come up t' r town anyhow from this direction. Come from th' east when they do.

Hm. Ilya stared around her at the terrain. This land was different than any she'd seen getting here, and that felt ridiculous somehow — mountains, rivers, plains, that's all there was in the West, what was compelling about this place? And she couldn't say what it was exactly that made it different, that made it feel superior to what she'd already seen. It had a quality of overwhelming and melodramatic beauty but so had most everything else she'd seen out here. Montana land had life in it, she guessed, in a way other places didn't, an intensity similar to New York's, but coming from beauty rather than being busy. She imagined that there were times of year when that wasn't true. She couldn't think of words to describe the feeling she now had adequately, and her mind resisted trying. She was tired but easy, and wanted to only be in this place with no effort, to be apart from the angry roll of her thoughts.

Shall we? she said.

Yep.

Bridger's reticence at first was a relief, then was alarming because it was so steady, then she became easy with it because, compared to Bat and Rog, he was beautiful to be with. She started to see why Mary valued him. He was distant but polite, and deferential, and seemed to be without any compelling need to dominate, or demonstrate his stature, or prove something to her. She'd been mildly concerned that he would start doing shooting tricks for her benefit, because his prowess with a rifle was a short topic of conversation the previous evening, when his reticence and distance had made the others pay attention to him. She didn't want him to haul off and blow away an eagle to seduce her, but he seemed to have no urge to do anything like that, so she stopped worrying.

They continued on through the afternoon, camped, and Ilya made a clumsy stew out of the basket. Mary had been right about trying to assemble any kind of decent meal outside, it was comically difficult. With

Bat and Rog her unhappiness, and their lack of discernment, had made her not even try. Ilya chided herself for doubting Mary, for believing that for someone such as herself these things that others found challenging would be easy. The result was undercooked and had dirt in it — a clumsy, watery soup that was sad and tepid. She doused it with enough of the spice mix to make it edible, and the flavor from the fire saved it some. Bridger tended the fire and the horses, cleaned the dishes and stowed them, checked the weather and decided it would remain clear, and they slept on either side of the fire in the cold, and bright starlight.

The weather the next day was the same. They stayed in an almost wordless state — only speaking for a practical purpose — for which each was grateful for a different reason. Bridger didn't want to feel more awkward, Ilya didn't want to expend any kind of effort beyond the bare minimum. She felt herself to be on holiday from speech. Bridger had initially been worried that Ilya would want to converse a lot because of her performance at the dinner. When he found that she didn't, that she didn't seem to want anything from him but his presence, that his presence was enough, he began to feel stronger, calmer. Will's words had gone into him deeply, and as he rode he thought about them, and was able, after reviewing his past, to believe them some. Having Will and Mary show such confidence in him, such regard and kindness, had made him angry at first. He suspected that they were playing him in some way, that they were setting him up to hurt him, though these weren't conscious thoughts, just feelings that were driving him inward. He was rejecting Will and Mary while he was needing them badly. Now he thought about what Will had said and came to believe that there was no maliciousness, or wanting to deceive, in him. As he rode through the second day his spirits rose. A new horse, good clothes, proper weapons, being severed so thoroughly from his father and that hateful ranch, a job to do, leaving the valley, the insistent autumn sun that didn't cook him, the sheer blue sky, and the rolling land that was both new and familiar, with Will's words about his competence, he felt good. Good in a way he never had before, good with strength in it, good with heart, as opposed to the fluttery and faint bits of short-lived happiness he'd felt before. And he came to be able to see Ilya not just as being superior and stronger, and astoundingly foreign, all of that strangely mixed with the need for him to protect her, but he came to see her as a source of strength. She helped him feel safe, and eased the loneliness he had come to feel was permanent. He still felt threatened and inadequate but was more easily able to conceal those feelings from himself and her, weakened as they were.

Midafternoon on the third day they stopped on a rise.

What do you think, Bridger? They were looking down at a collection of buildings tucked against a bluff where a small, brown river curled out and rolled off to join the Madison far out where their valley cut into a massive north-south directed plain, too wide to feel proper calling it a valley.

He shrugged, looked at the sky, nodded at the purple clouds curling over the Jeffersons. I c'd see that droppin' somethin' on us tonight. It's fall-in' up high fer sure. Might be an early dump. Wakin' up under a blanket a snow ain't fun.

Alright. We've done two nights on the ground. They might have some rooms there. A bed and a bath might be nice. If they have a store we could pick up a couple of things. It doesn't look like much, whatever it is.

I c'd use some range clothes. These ain't good fer out here, an' I don' like t' fuck 'em up. Shoulda got some from Mary, but...she give me a lot aready. My old ones is gone.

Ilya looked at him. She likes giving to you. No shame in accepting if you keep the sheets more or less balanced.

The air had taken on a bitter tinge and the sun was gone. She stood up in the cart, wrapped the black woolen scarf around her neck up high, shrugged into her coat, and pulled up the collar. She shoved her hair into her hat, sat, and said, Alright. Let's go in.

Ilya began to regret their decision as they approached. The buildings were low, dark, fungal growths that seemed to barely have escaped the ground before dying of discouragement. There was no street, just cabins scattered like dice over a trampled meadow, too far apart to be called a community. Beyond them, beside what had been a creek connecting with the small river, was a scape of small pyramids of gravel and dirt packed tightly throughout the bottom of the drainage. Uprooted trees and wild snarls of tangled brush surrounded the pyramids of gravel, and brambles grew out of the ravaged ground and pools of stagnant water trapped by the gouged earth. Fires burned and men slopped through the mess, dragging brush and piling it on the flames. Three steel chutes pointed into the sky like insanely long cannons, iron wheels with blades welded to them for traction beside them, and up the barrels of these machines a succession of cupped blades attached to a chain rattled, carrying a load of creek bed out of the sloshing water and dumping it in a constant feed into a sluicebox that shook hard, as if palsied. Steam engines worked, pounding their effluence into the air, and men moved in a constant stream wrestling cordwood in stages toward the fire-box. Trees that had once carpeted the slopes rising out of the narrow floor of the draw were strewn down the hillsides, and men dragging cable crawled through them, hitching on to butts and motioning, the cable going taut in time with the higher pitch of the engine, and the downed tree skidding out of the tangle and down the slope to splash into the water, to be set upon by other men with axes and saws. Great raw patches of exposed earth reared up out of the creek bed where sections of slope had been undermined and had slid down in a heap of root and rock and sloppy mud. Men scurried through the bed with picks and shovels clearing the mud and dirt, keeping the current of the creek moving enough to find its way through the mess.

What is this? Ilya said.

Dredge minin', I'm guessin', Bridger said. Never seen it but can't be much else with them machines goin' at it like that. Ain't hydraulic.

What metal are they after?

Gold, probly.

What are those pyramidal things?

I'm gonna guess that's how th' tailin's come out. They sure as fuck are tearin' th' piss outta th' crick.

Do they then drink that water?

Sure as fuck hope so. Serves 'em right t' get a bellyful a dirt fer their trouble. Bridger got a sharp pang of wanting Mary, wanting to see her hurt these people.

Perhaps we're better off camping again, Ilya said. This seems like we'd be lodging in a...factory.

Won't bother me none t' sleep on the ground, even with snow. C'n git a oilcloth goin'. This shit's...Bridger looked grim and melancholy and alarmed. He'd never seen mining in action, and couldn't find a word.

Pandemonium, Ilya said. Oh, it's unspeakable it's true, but I've had two days of the pastoral and idyllic. This is no adventure if there's no variety. Let's stay one night shall we? We'll be back to our wilderness paradise tomorrow. If they have a hotel or boardinghouse or something. If not we'll camp. It's going to be dark soon.

Bridger shrugged. Aright. Gold sure got power gittin' men t' do that shit all day. Couldn't pay me 'nough.

Try not to go about mentioning your position to people. Not that that's your habit. Oh and, not that consorting with these people is what I'm after, but if it comes up we're brother and sister. They may be less apt to trouble me that way. And we look convincingly alike.

As this unexpectedly came out of her mouth, Ilya looked at Bridger and realized it was true. Bridger glanced at her and realized it, too.

Aright, he said. Bridger wondered what it made the people here more apt to do to him, this lie.

They came down the incline through a field of stumps into the meadow. There was a bunch of cabins in a rough semicircle around the centerpiece building of the camp — a two-story, stick-framed, false-fronted structure with no porch or boardwalk. A plank was spiked to the clapboard beside the entry, the word 'tel' slathered on it with some black substance without a lot of longevity.

I'm going to assume that used to say 'hotel' in better days, if there ever were any, Ilya said. She laughed a little and stared around, apprehensive and amazed. The cluster of cabins was on a shelf above the dredge operation, below it was another meadow filled with filthy, mud-spattered white tents letting gray smoke into the air, beyond that the bellowing grind of enterprise.

I'll get us rooms if this fine establishment has vacancies, Ilya sighed. Can't imagine they have anything but. What should we do with the horses?

Bridger looked around and said, Ain't no livery here. An' I don' like 'em bein' far off. I'll picket 'em out backa here. I seen a little grass, an' there's some aspen leaves still hangin' back there got some green to 'em. Some willow bush. They'll eat. They got watered good 'nough comin' in, don' haveta drink this shit.

Alright. Ilya dropped to the dirt and sod roiled together by wheels and hooves, and walked up the two steps and through the plank door into a low, cold, dark room that reeked of something unfamiliar, and she briefly felt glad she didn't know what it was. The windows were small and filthy, and were the only light, except for a single tallow candle burning on a plank set across two barrels. There was a woman seated behind the plank. Ilya let her eyes adjust for a moment.

Hep y'? the woman said.

Ilya started to walk toward her and stumbled, almost went to her knees. The floor was very uneven.

Careful there, the woman said.

Thank you, Ilya said, and came up to the plank. The woman now standing behind it was a foot shorter than she and sapling skinny. Her skin was an angry red as though she were a welt in the air, and her black hair was cut close to her skull. Ilya could see there was something wrong with her eyes. One seemed frozen, looking to the side, the other seemed milky but at least responded and followed what was being looked at. Her dress was a black, heavy, sleeveless shift that came to her knees, and below that she wore heavy, black engineer's boots. Beside her was a low, barrel-shaped, cast-iron stove that flickered yellow light through draft apertures and cracks in the skin at the joints.

Is this an hotel? Ilya said.

'Pends on who y' ask.

Alright, Ilya said, irritation flashing through her. What if I ask you?

C'd call it that, if y' dint mind stretchin' fer what's true.

My brother and I would like a room for a night.

Which night?

This one.

One room fer two of y'? That ain't gonna work too good.

No. A room for each of us.

Ten dollar.

How much?

Ten dollar. Each.

This entire town isn't worth twenty dollars.

Dint ask for th' town. Anyhow the shit in that crick's worth a fuck of a lot more'n 'at.

Jesus. Is there a bath?

Out back. Man called it a bath once, I dint fight 'im on it. It's a dollar.

Is there a restaurant?

Nope. C'n buy a hunka buffler offa the hunters just come in, an' I'll let y' use my skillet and stove fer a dollar.

A brace house in Pandemonium, Ilya muttered. Excellent. And how much are you charging me for these answers?

Them's are free cuz so far they's easy. Y' start to push on me, I might have to take a fee.

These prices are very high.

See them clouds on yer way in? They make prices go up like a sucked pecker. At noon them rooms was a dollar.

Is there a store?

Riley's place got some gear, minin' stuff. Spendy though. He's a gougin' fuck, bein' alone in th' enterprise. I like t' be fair.

I'll give you twelve dollars for everything. If that doesn't suit you we'll move along.

That'll work.

You don't want to haggle over it?

W'd that change yer thinkin'?

No.

There y' go.

Ilya put the money before her. Do you have keys?

Ain't hardly got doors.

Which rooms are they?

Don't keer. Ain't nobody stayin' here. Clientele dried up, still ponderin' why.

Bridger picketed the horses under a single remaining frail cottonwood in a field of stumps, looking at the sky unhappily. It looked like someone had set a stone over the valley. He put an oilcloth over the top of the cart, decided to keep his saddle on, and draped the mustang and the black under an extra blanket and oilcloth. He kept their rig as together and hidden as possible. The sense of unfamiliar responsibility was making him more serious than he normally was.

Bridger headed toward the back of the hotel, looking at the building. The builder's ambition to have two stories was not matched by his abilities. The upper story was detaching from the lower because one corner of the structure had been perched on the edge of an embankment which had been undermined by the redirected stream, and the carpenters had not fully thought out the connection between upper and lower, and had decided that the sheathing which could have kept the structure from wracking was an unnecessary step. The clapboard had begun popping away from the studs under the strain, and the ends of boards waved in the air with a strange beckoning motion. Bridger could see through the siding to the cloth and newspaper they'd nailed on the inside to stop up the holes. He pushed through the buffalo skin hanging over the door opening — the door itself was leaning against the wall inside, because it no longer fit the opening what with the building slumping. They had adze-hewn logs flat on one side for floors, but they had twisted and rolled their curved undersides upwards — a mockery of a puncheon floor. In a detail he'd never seen before, at which he smirked in disbelief, they had used mud chinking to try to close the seams between the floor logs. The mud had broken free and was now scattered around the floor in hard, jagged chunks, and he could see through the floor to the ground beneath.

He stood there in the dimness, looking around.

There was what had been intended to be a bar on the other side of the room, but it was made of unmilled logs stacked on top of one another and spiked together, on top of which were three logs maybe left over from the floor laid side by side, with rounds of sapling laid laterally across the three and nailed to them to keep them together. The weight of this furniture was too much for the floor, so the whole rig was sagging through. The owners had taken to pouring whiskey glasses only half-full because of the radical slant of the bar top, and this had caused consternation among the patrons. At some point someone had wedged sticks beneath the forward edge of the bar to prevent it collapsing altogether.

Who's 'at? the stripling behind the plank said. With it so dim he hadn't known she was there.

Woman come in here? Bridger said.

Upstairs.

Bridger looked at the stair treads, shook his head. They were fat, short planks the ends of which had been hacked into the exposed studs, and the outside ends of which were held together by one long plank spiked to the endgrain, which was splitting. He went up them quickly and found Ilya sitting on her bed, staring at the wall with a look of stunned, angry disgust.

Make yourself comfortable, she said, and gestured to the room next to hers. And just wait for death.

Bridger walked to it and tried to pull the door back, but it was wedged against the floor in a way that was now permanent. He squeezed through the gap it left and looked around. A sawn log twelve inches in diameter and eighteen inches high with crispy bits of bark clinging to the pale, yellow bole, and a crooked branch sticking up from it as a back, was the chair. The bed was two feet wide, made of more branches, these tied together with knotted lengths of rope and untreated hide string. Dried and cracked hide straps formed the mattress springs beneath lumpy sacking and a torn piece of canvas left balled up in the middle — a pillow. Light came in from an opening chopped through the siding, and a scrap of canvas dangled beside it to keep out the rain or snow by hooking it over protruding nails. On the chair was a piece of jagged quartz with a candle stub melted over it. The flooring planks had shrunk and he could see down into the room below.

He could see Ilya through the gaps between the horizontal boards that formed the wall. She was sitting on the edge of her bed with her face cupped in her hands. Bridger thought that she was crying, and stood there, worried. If she started crying he might as well. She stood up and came around to his doorway.

I'm going to bathe. Then I'm going to the store and get us some supplies. I'll get you some clothes. We'll stay here tonight because there's no choice now, but unless it's a biblical blizzard tomorrow, we're leaving first thing. I've quite had enough of this part of our adventure already. It's a flogging. Go and get us some blankets out of our gear or we'll freeze. This is worse than being outside. Her face was seamed and rigid, the crease above her nose was deep, her eyes gone black. Her barely-controlled rage cowed Bridger a little, and he whipped up enough insolence to repel it.

Aright.

Ilya took her bath in a glaring fury that the sense of peace she'd been able to maintain for two days had been stripped. The tub enclosure was outside and barely as large as the tub itself, and the water came from a gouged-out ditch that trickled past. One filled the tub by dipping a bucket in this furrow, which they had troubled to dig out a little to create a small pool for this purpose. The tub was too small to sit down in, there was no warm water and she was not going to barter with the hag for some, and the sides of the sheet metal tub were encrusted with hair and rust and some sort of fungus she tried to keep away from. Every so often she would lift her leg to slog down some part of it and she would touch the sides, the feeling amphibious and filthy. She had a simple but adequate set of toiletries, but didn't use them because she would feel that she should throw them away after, along with her body. She settled for a quick swabbing with a cold, soapy rag.

Standing tiptoed on a scrap of cloth, she put on a clean shift and her black outfit and fled the tub shanty, releasing a pent-up breath as she did so. In her room she pinned up her hair, put on her hat, shrugged into her coat, strapped on her pistol, and felt better, felt armored. She found Bridger standing in his room shaking out a blanket.

Now you can bathe. If you don't want to bother I don't blame you, there is little point to it.

I'll bathe, Bridger said. He didn't want to, but Mary would want him to.

Your life. We'll figure out a meal after. One travesty at a time.

Ilya stamped across the big clearing, past the line of wagons heaped with hides toward the cabin that said 'store.' She saw a cluster of burned-out cabins that were close together, the inspiration for spreading their re-placements apart.

The air was now bitter and unruly, and snowflakes were floating about with strange gentleness, going in all directions. Night was poised.

The three jacked-up, gabbling buffalo hunters in the store went quiet when Ilya came through the open door. They and the storekeeper stared at her.

She stood there a moment, trying to see. Carcasses of flies covered all flat surfaces except the counter in front of the keeper, and live ones buzzed and bumped.

The three hunters sat on wooden crates, each holding a brown bottle of whiskey, and sprouting wild thickets of brown, matted hair underneath battered slouch hats. Their clothes were caked with dried blood.

Christ, Ilya blurted as she regarded them, not concealing her bitterness and revulsion at all because she was surprised by the reek, and the appalling look of these men, and her anger made what little inclination she may have had to do that evaporate. She raised her hand to her face against the stench and walked to the counter.

I need an outfit for a man. Very quickly if you don't mind. Pants, shirt, socks, gloves, underwear, she said. Medium is fine. No, she said, after recalling Bridger's shoulder width and the length of his legs. Large.

The storekeeper was a fastidious man. His shirt still resembled the white it had started as, and his black vest was sharply pulled over it. He was bald and had a gigantic mustache with ragged, errant hairs covering his mouth.

Whuttaya needem fer? he said. That there's a fine getup you got on as it is. Sir.

The hunters chuckled, and the storekeeper looked at them and laughed too happily at their approbation to be becoming for a man. Ilya watched contempt flash through the blood on the face of one of the hunters, and briefly marveled that he could have that faculty.

A hunter said, Ain't gonna git far 'thout barrel and balls out here, little squaw. Man clothes ain't gonna be 'nough, by themselves.

Ilya pulled bills from her pocket and said, How much? Please, my things, I'm in a hurry...

Well, we got us a sale goin' on. I reckon I can let y' have all 'at fer...mmm...fifty dollar. Coin only. Oh, an' four humps fer me an' my partners here. Good ones, not doggie. The storekeeper looked into Ilya's eyes. Her fury and disgust went icy, and quick regret slid through her. She looked back at him for a moment, then turned her head and looked at the window to think and to see if Bridger was maybe in sight, but the window was thin-scraped hide stretched over a hole, and was slightly translucent but opaque. Flies were pounding themselves into it. The light in the place came from the door she had left open, and a lamp before her on the counter. She felt her heart boom in her with the realization that she had done something very stupid, and she felt a flash of self-hate that she'd stomped past all the signs that this situation could be a possibility, and then she got angry at Bridger that he hadn't warned her. What was he for?

All she could see of the hunters was the pale of their faces above their beards, and the glitter of eyes.

I will give you ten dollars, Ilya said, voice less than firm. That's fair.

The storekeeper looked annoyed. Well now, as I recall, we's fresh outta all 'at shit. Guess them's r' gonna be charity humps. Girl, you took a wrong turn comin' here. We got two hundred miners an' six whores that'r now 'bout stretched to death. Ain't a pecker touched a pussywall in months 'round here. Not a lotta gentleman left in nobody. An' these boys here, they been out shootin' down bison, how long, Lemmy?

Month. None left in th' whole damn country neither, now that I'm done.

There. One month. Dead buffler pussy ain't much good, neither. Can't speak to the live kind. You c'd leave this place plumb wore out but with some sure 'nough specie if you was to cooperate. Other way, yer just fucked dead. Probly before the night's out, them minin' boys find out yer here, which ain't gonna be long cuz shift's 'bout over.

Ilya stared at his eyes, which were large and close to the sides of his skull. His face was jaundiced from the yellow light shining up on it. He held her gaze for a moment, then looked nervous and irritated and turned his face away. Lemmy had gotten to his feet and had stepped to the end of the counter. Ilya was enveloped in the smell. She tried to still her violent trembling.

Ilya looked at Lemmy. His face was fervid and malignant to a degree she'd never seen. She turned back to the storekeeper. Please get the things I requested, she said. Her voice shook beyond her controlling it.

Y' heard the terms.

Lemmy took another step forward, which put him an arm's length from her, and put his bottle on the counter, keeping his fingers wrapped around the neck. Another hunter shut the door and shadow rose.

Ilya's knees were vibrating enough to make her doubt they would hold her up. For the first time in her life her voice wouldn't work, and that frightened her badly. She took her pistol, jammed the muzzle through the storekeeper's front teeth, and shot out the back of his skull. The report was a muffled thud and black blood spattered behind him.

Jesus holy *fuck!* Lemmy said, and stepped back. The storekeeper dropped. Ilya turned her back to the counter, stepped away from Lemmy, and pointed her pistol at his face. The other two hunters went still, one still sitting, the other standing, both with their hands partially raised, bottles dangling. Ilya's breath came in sharp, ragged pants, and cold slime coated her skin. Her knees steadied, her voice came back, borne on a new pleasure.

You were thinking of fucking me whether I cared to or not, she said to Lemmy. She smiled at him, her eyes bright, her lips a straight slice.

What th' fuck I care what y' care t' do or not do? Lemmy said.

I appreciate your candor. Are you a patriot, Mister...?

I'm Mr. Man-gonna-fuck-you-apart-like-a-wishbone.

Ah, of the Fifth Avenue Wishbones? A fine family. But are you a *patriot,* sir?

I cum red, white and blue honey. An' all up in you in a minnit. You gonna be a goddamned flag.

True? I thought so. You seem like someone who's just come from the Tea Party. Well then, you must be aware that our dear founder Thomas Jefferson recommended castration for men who rape women. Who rape anything, as I remember.

Cunt.

Yes. One you'll not experience. Jesus, you should be hanged for the stench alone. She lowered her gun to his crotch. You can show me your prick if you like, so I won't miss and make a mess of it. Otherwise, I'm going to guess. Either way you are being castrated today, unless you and your...whatever these are...get the fuck out of my way. Ilya's trembling was still evident, and her chest heaved, but talking, the feeling of her brain working, the warm rush of hatred, being *right*, gave her a sense of giddy abandon, of lust for this time she was in, of the way it now felt like her words and her pistols were wed.

Lemmy lunged to the side and slapped at her gun. She shot him in the belly, wheeled, and shot the hunter who was still sitting through the face as he rose, trying to free his pistol from his belt. The third had his pistol out and partway up when she shot him in the chest. She turned and put her final slug through Lemmy's forehead as he got off one round from his position kneeling and clutching his abdomen. His bullet put a hole through her new coat but not her. The third hunter had life in him still, and was trying to rally. When her hammer fell on a spent cartridge, she holstered her pistol, crossed the room, snatched the rifle leaning against the wall, pulled back the big hammer and put a bullet through his head with his Sharps. The heavy recoil of the rifle was unexpected and pain shot through her right wrist as the gun flew from her hands, and the barrel clapped her in the forehead. She twisted away and held her head with her left hand, her right against her stomach. She stood there a moment heaving out ecstatic sobs, gasping in the flies and smoke, ears clanging, eyes burning.

Wiping the tears from her face, she wrenched the door open and looked out. There was no uproar, everyone was at the dredge. The gunshots inside the small, sod-roofed cabin filled with men and cured hides, blankets and other goods, at close range, hadn't traveled, not through the constant clatter of the machines. She made a mental note that a stupid man's skull muffled gun reports very well, and thought with a tinge of hysteria that she must tell Jacques and Zoe that she'd found a new use for them. A long whistle from the dredge operation blew, and honed the fear that was making her mind sharp, now that the dullness of indecision was taken care of.

Bridger started when Ilya jerked open the shanty door. He was standing naked, thinking that this was probably not the kind of bathing Mary would insist on.

Put these on, we're leaving. Fast, very, very fast, she said, and threw the bundle of clothes at him, which had the shopkeeper's blood and brains splattered on them.

What...?

Do it please, Bridger...quickly, quickly...now! I'll explain later!

He began pulling them on and Ilya went to her room, grabbed her bag, looked in Bridger's room, but he'd shaken out his blankets already — nothing to easily grab. She banged down the stairs and toward the back door.

Don' a bath jes change yer whole outlook on a day? the thin woman called.

Bridger was coming in as she was going out, pistol on and rifle in hand, suit rolled under his arm.

Come, she said, grabbing his arm and pulling him. We have to go. Right now.

What th' fuck?

I had to shoot some people. Come.

Shoot 'em? Why...

Trust me.

Shouts rose from the store, as off-shift miners came for food and whiskey.

There, that is for us. Are you coming with me?

Fuck shit, Bridger said, what th' fuckin' hell...and ran to the horses. His heart banged hard, and fear and panic ran into his throat. He started to hitch the black to the cart, hands shaking.

There's no time for that! Ilya said. We have to go! *Now!* She struggled onto the back of the black, clutching her valise. Bridger swung up onto the mustang, trying to keep a hold of his suit and rifle, and they pounded out from behind the building and up the hillside they'd earlier come down.

Miners shouted and fired on them without aiming. Ilya was leaning forward, her arms around the neck of the horse, fighting to stay mounted with no saddle. As they crested the slope, the blanket slid from beneath her and she flopped to the ground, slamming her banged-up arm and losing her valise.

She shrieked and curled up there, her hat off. Bridger swung his horse around and slid to the ground, dropping his suit, rifle in hand. He ran to Ilya to help her. She was trying to get to her knees, but her arm was useless as a prop, and she didn't want to turn loose of it with her other hand. There were men running up the hill shooting, and behind these, others standing beside their tents watching.

Bridger let go of Ilya as she got her knees under her. He hunched and looked at the men shooting, turned to flee the bullets that were now passing close enough to hear them, then froze, heart banging like the dredge.

Don't you fucking leave me, Ilya said. She shrieked a little as a slug kicked up dirt beside her.

Bridger straightened, mind burning, shouldered his rifle, and shot the closest man, who had stopped chasing them when he saw Ilya fall, and was standing still and firing his pistol with some care, having figured out that shooting and running did not mesh well. This man, when Bridger's slug hit him in the center of the chest, froze, then somehow toppled and fled at the same time. Bridger levered, the casing glittered in an arc over his shoulder, and he put his bead on a man standing like him, rifle raised pointing at him, and put a slug through his torso as that man's rifle fired and his bullet missed Bridger. The other men started to go to the ground and scramble for cover. Bridger shot another man fleeing in panic, then another who almost made it behind a stump, another who made it behind a stump too small to hide him, and with his last round he took a moment to aim with care, and shot a man running away from him who had just crested a hillock and was nearly out of sight. Bridger's bullet entered the back of his head and blew out his eye exiting, and he dropped to the ground.

Ilya had gotten to her feet clutching her wrist and seen Bridger's final shot, and looked at him. He turned, and came up to her. His face was a stew of panic, gritty exhilaration and bitten-down stoicism. His eyes were bright.

Let's git, he said.

The horses had stood placidly through it all and Bridger went to the mustang, sheathed his rifle, grabbed the reins, and was about to swing up when he saw Ilya struggling with the black.

Fuck, he said, pulled his pistol, and snapped shots down the hill as he wrenched his horse over to them, grabbed Ilya around the waist and shoved her into the saddle.

Go. I'll catch y'. She hunched over, reins in her right hand, wrist screaming, and clutched the pommel with her left, and the mustang began to run when Bridger slapped his ass. He got himself up on the black, grabbed a fistful of mane, and roweled her hard, hating himself for hurting her.

6

Night came down and Bridger led them into a copse before it became pitch black.

Jes' wait, he said. He kicked leaves aside beneath a tree, pulled tinder out of his saddlebags and struck a fire, hunching over and feeding it until it was strong.

Aren't they going to see that? Ilya said.

They ain't gonna go fuckin' 'round in th' dark. They'll wait 'til tomorra.

How do you know?

Cuz fuckin' 'round in the dark gits y' kilt out here. 'Less you kilt somebody they can't do without and they're all hot an' crazy, they ain't gonna come t'night. Not when they're knowin' we ain't easy t' kill. Git down, strip th' saddle, we need that blanket. On'y one we got.

My arm, she said, and slid down. He stared for a moment, nodded, went to the horse and stripped the saddle, got the blanket, and draped it around her.

Hell, we ain't got shit fer gear, now, he said. He went into the trees and began snapping dead wood off the boles of the cottonwoods, and kicking branches toward the fire, hurrying and piling the fire high. He kept at it until he had a mound of fuel, banging around in the dark.

Ilya stood wrapped in the blanket staring at the flames, cupping her arm, freezing from the inside out as exhilarating fear turned to depressing fear.

Bridger stopped and looked at her forehead. Good lump there. How bad's yer arm?

She held it out, turning it and looking at it. I don't think it's broken, she said.

Y'd know if it wuz broke. He stood and thumbed cartridges into his rifle, right at that moment realizing he had neither crapped himself nor started crying. Pride and terror swirled in him, formed itself into some version of grim, hopeless confidence, necessity and circumstance smothering panic. He pondered that he had simply reacted to what was happening to him and it hadn't gone badly, that fear needed thinking to flourish. The memory of that moment when he had almost fled ran through him, became one that would forever make him flinch. Ilya pulled her pistol, handed it to him, and he filled it, standing close to her and sliding cartridges from her belt.

Gonna tell me why y' shot people? Git bored?

You wouldn't understand, Ilya said, then regretted it, felt ungrateful and mean.

His face went black and grim. Who wuz they?

I believe they were buffalo hunters, judging by those hides.

Y' like buffler that much, d' y'?

No special affinity no, but I feel quite sure I would prefer the animal over the man hunting him, if those were any example.

They ain't hunters. Settin' on a hill and shootin' down couple hunderd head a day ain't huntin'. Bridger stamped his feet against the cold. Flakes that had wound their way through the tree lit on them and slowly disappeared.

Fuck, Bridger said. We's fucked evry which way, now.

Well, I could have let myself be raped by them and saved us some inconvenience, but I'm saving myself. I had no choice, Bridger.

C'dn't finesse it?

Ilya stared at him, then coughed a bitter laugh. If only you knew what that word sounded like coming from your mouth.

Bridger flushed.

I'm sorry. No, I couldn't finesse it. They would have left nothing of me, and if I hadn't acted first I wouldn't have had any chance at all. I killed four men Bridger, and got away with only a banged-up arm and a bump on the head. Aren't I a true western woman, now?

Yer gonna be a dead western woman when they catch us.

Then let's avoid that.

How'd y' git banged up anyhow, if they never got t' y'?

They made it clear they were going to rape me. I shot the storekeeper. I shot the hunters, but I was empty and one was still trying for me, so I took a rifle and shot him with it, but it was a cannon.

Sharps. Lemme see.

She held her arm out and he took it, gently turning her hand. She winced.

Jes wrenched it good. Be aright in a week. Lucky it dint break yer arm. Always wanted a Sharps.

Had I known I would have brought it for you. To thank you for shooting down those men so...efficiently. That seemed like very...proficient...killing.

Pretty easy when they jes come runnin' right atcha, not even troublin' to aim. Seems like somethin' a fuckin' miner would do. Can't be all that smart bein' willin' t' do that shit. Mebbe they'll reconsider cuttin' all th' damn trees down now they got nothin' t' hide behind when somebody shoots at 'em.

Maybe they thought that getting shot down was preferable to a lifetime of that work. Maybe it was suicide. That last one you shot wasn't coming at you. That was something different.

That there wuz a sweet pick. Never thought I'd git 'im.

But, why did you shoot him? He was not a threat any longer.

Bridger thought. I don' know. I like t' shoot I guess, an' they give me a target. An' mebbe I don' like these shitty fuckin' cocksuckers tearin' up my damn country like it's on'y theirs. Hadda 'nother gun I woulda kep' goin' an' kilt all of 'em. Fuckers. See what they done t' that crick? Anyhow, who gives a shit, now? They'll be careful tomorra when they come on us. Guess it'd be better fer us if they wadn't careful, though.

Speaking of tomorrow, what are we going to do?

Run like hell, I guess. Get up inta th' Jeffersons. They ain't too far off. Them boys ain't gonna wanna go up there. We stay on th' road they'll git us fer sure, us with jes these two horses and one saddle.

You don't want to try to do it the honest way? Tell the law? Say we had to do it?

Bridger thought. Ain't gonna be no law 'til Ginny. I'm thinkin' there ain't nobody t' say we wuz in th' right. An' I'm thinkin' there ain't nobody in that town gonna feel like bein' square with us, now. Mebbe we c'n tell r side when we git t' 'Ginny, but not right now.

And they will tear me apart, those men, if given a chance.

Yep. Bridger looked nervous, thought of his father, thought of Mary, thought of Will, felt all of them watching him.

I would like you to keep that more to the front of your mind. Alright? There is no man on earth that gives a woman being ravaged the importance it's due. Either it's something they would do themselves, or it's something they don't think is very important, or it's something they deplore until it comes time to punish someone for it. I'll die by my own hand before I'll let that happen to me. I can protect myself, but you're going to have to know that it's a very big problem. I want you to be prepared to shoot down any man that comes near me with that in mind if I can't do it first. Including yourself. Alright?

Bridger looked at her and nodded. Aright.

Will is going to like this story.

Bridger took stock of what they had left. He was in the clothes Ilya got him, which were stiff as hell, but his black suit was gone. He had his coat on. He had ammunition, an extra shirt, a half bottle of whiskey, and an oilcloth in his bags, but they had no food. There was one canteen, half full. One blanket. It was bad. Ilya had her outfit on but had lost her valise. He bit down on fear. It was harder to smother with nothing to do but stand there in it.

As soon as the first light leaked into the sky and showed him east so he knew west, Bridger headed them out at a canter he thought the horses could survive. By mid-morning they were climbing out of the valley, and by nightfall they had crested a ridge and were looking at the high peaks before them. Intermittent flurries persisted and the sky stayed slate.

It was surprising to Ilya how devoid of wildlife the West was. In New York, she had imagined that the land must teem with animals, that one couldn't go a step without kicking some bear or elk or something, that the plains would be covered with bison like the store had been with flies. Since they'd left Mary's she'd seen nothing but chattering birds, floating raptors, and squirrels.

Bridger stood on an outcrop and stared into the valley down their back trail.

Can't see nobody but that don' mean much. Squirrels rattled hard overhead, and pine cones plopped to the grass around them.

Cut south agin tomorra, stay up 'bout this high, kinda skid 'round. Ain't gittin' 'cross them 'thout a hell of a fuckin' trial, he said, nodding at the peaks.

How about eating?

Don' think 'bout it. If I see somethin', I'll shoot it, but ain't no guarantee up here. Couple days 'thout food ain't gonna kill y'. Eat a squirrel in a pinch, but might's well eat a boot 'thout a way t' bile it. Fuckin' bullet'd splatter it all t' hell anyways. Be pickin' squirrel meat outta trees.

Alright. My appetite seems to have waned for some reason, anyway.

Bridger assembled a small fire, and they crouched beside it as darkness fell. They didn't try to sleep. The flurries became a steady, dreadful, hissing fall of big flakes. The temperature dropped. There was no wind.

Hell, Bridger said. 'Fraid a this.

Jesus, Ilya said. She shivered hard and stretched her wet hands to the flame. Her gloves had gotten wet.

Bridger reached out and pushed her hands back. Not s' close, you'll git chilblains. Fuckin' hell they are. They ain't gonna track us now, anyhow. Come light, we'll drop back down outta here.

How are we going to see to travel in this?

Wanna sit here an' freeze? We'll see what th' snow does. Keeps comin' hard we stay here and keep warm. Lets up, we try t' git down.

Light brought seeing the snow drop like a curtain. They stood there with the horses being buried for a while before Bridger said, This ain't no fuckin' good. Gits too deep we ain't gonna be able t' move outta here at all. This don' feel like it's got stop t' it any time soon.

What do we do?

This ain't a situation where a body jes picks th' right thing cuz they done it so many times. You got a say innit. This shit could go another minnit, another hour, or not stop 'til it's over r heads. I'm thinkin' it ain't gonna stop soon. Don' feel like it, but no tellin'. We c'n stay an' figger we got horse t' eat, an' if we work at it we c'n probly keep this fire goin' awhile. But...I dunno. If it gits too deep an' stays, we might as well jes shoot ourselves cuz spring's th' next time we c'n move. Ain't likely t' jes keep on. Too early in th' year. I say we go. Can't see what direction, but anythin' downhill 'll have t' do now. Ain't goin' back an' walk right inta them fuckers.

Let's go. I don't want to just stand here and drown in snow.

Bridger cut a length from his coil and roped the horses together, took the reins and stomped off. He made a guess about direction but it was very much a guess.

They kept on all day, going the way the land offered passage, and the snow continued to descend. Pines emerged out of the white, their boughs holding tall heaps of snow. The light, puffing snow fluttered into any crevice in their clothing, filling their boots, working up their sleeves and down their necks, and it grew deeper at an astounding rate. They grew parched and filled their mouths with the stuff which was so dry Ilya was convinced that it was not made of water. Their inner layer of clothes became soaked with sweat and melted snow, and their stomachs gave sharp pangs.

We jes might not make this, Bridger said, as the next round of darkness descended. Can't make no fire. Dint hit a crick. We stop movin' we freeze t' death.

I suppose I could have let myself be raped, Ilya said through blue lips. I would have lived. I'm sorry. I didn't see this eventuality at the time.

Not havin' that, Bridger said. We ain't done yet. Jes...don' stop movin'. We got one more night in us. Keep movin', stay next t' th' horses, keep yer hands pushed on 'em. We'll eat one tomorra if we gotta. Hate t' put us afoot though...

Eat raw horse? Horse *tartare*? Ilya squealed a small giggle. I loathe adventure.

They kicked a circle into the snow and tamped it down, and kept themselves and horses within it. They paced around, pushing their hands against the horses, cramming them into their armpits.

Do this, Bridger said, and held up his hands and threw them down to the end of his arms. Don' blow on 'em. Ilya, with skepticism, did as told, and it helped more than she could believe, forcing the blood into her fingers.

He took the oilcloth and put it on the tamped down snow. Sit there, he said. We're gonna lose toes. She sat down and he wrenched her boots and socks off. Tuck 'em inta yer coat, don't let 'em git snow in 'em. He knelt before her, opened his shirt, and pushed her feet against his underwear, gasping a little as the cold and wet bled to his skin. He wrapped her feet in his clothes and stayed that way, hunched before her, wrapping the blanket over them both.

Can y' feel yer toes?

Yes.

Tell me when they feel warm, we gotta switch.

They hunched there listening to breathing horses and the steady exhale of snow.

Have you done this before? Ilya chattered.

Been fuckin' cold as shit an' stranded? Yep. Not this bad. But close. Bein' up here ain't smart.

We're done for, aren't we?

No way a knowin'. One thing I found out gittin' caught out in it is shit changes real fast. Don' go fuckin' crazy an' wait. Y' can be near dead at th' bottom of a cut with a busted leg an' live, or y' can die with yer hand on th' doorknob. Jes ain't no point t' decidin' th' end ahead a time.

Alright. They're warm. I suppose.

Aright. Stay on th' cloth.

Ilya tried to get his boots off but couldn't with her bad arm, and he slapped her hands away and strained at them until he got them off. She gasped as he pushed his feet against her belly. Her feet began to freeze again.

We gotta keep doin' this all night is all. One night. Long fuckin' night but we won't die. When we c'n see, we'll think it agin.

The snow stopped before dawn, and the ice blue air retreated before the sun rising over the Gallatins, lighting up the treetops, and creeping down toward them over the heaps of snow on the boughs. It was astoundingly beautiful, and the discouragement it caused was a blow.

Fuck, Bridger said.

What?

Mighta shoulda stayed where we was. Or gone back.

Why?

We wadn't lucky where we come down, he said, nodding east. There was a tangle of ridges and a bare, rocky skull sticking up out of the white and green, the sun just topping out over it all.

Fuckin' valley's gotta be on th' other side a all that. Fuck me. Might as well have fell inna well down here. I'm sorry, Ilya. I fucked it up. He stood staring at his boots in the snow. Shoulda gone back. Best chance a gittin' down. Probly c'dn't a found it, though. Might not a made no diffrence. Dunno. Fuck me.

You're saying that's it? We're going to just squat here and die?

No. I'm sayin' we got a hell of a chore gittin' outta this. An' a short day t' do it in.

Ilya looked up into the shocking azure sky. Well. It would be great sport to blame you and punish you, but I think it's better we move on. I'm cold...

C'mere, open yer coat. He opened his coat, slid his arms around her inside hers, and roughly rubbed her torso.

Do me dammit, I ain't an oven.

Sorry. She started to rough him.

Better? he said.

Astoundingly, yes.

Keep throwin' yer hands an' feet. Wanna eat a horse? We're gonna start gittin' weak.

I don't know. What do you think?

Ain't there yet. We git out an' got on'y one ride, that ain't good. Doublin' up...wears 'em right down. An' horses r spendy as fuck.

Then let's save them as a nice treat for later. We'll want a slab of raw horse meat after a long day of foundering.

Aright. Might be we can git inta a place where we can git a fire up. Couldn't burn kerosene in this shit down here. Gotta go slow a little so we don' git too soaked agin.

They pushed through the powder, sidehilling when they could, trying to stay in the sun. The gorge they were in snaked around, and Ilya got angry at the configuration of the land, angry that it didn't simply travel straight like a New York street, and thinking that the scorn she had had for the up-town grid, for the numbing monotony of it, might have been premature.

The gorge they were in became a *cul de sac.*

Fuckin' hell, Bridger shouted, then stood, mouth moving, staring down at his feet.

What now?

We gotta climb. It's gonna wear us out. We're gonna freeze up agin.

Well, which way?

There. That's lowest. Fuck me.

When the sun was at its zenith Bridger took them out on a ledge and kicked a spot clear.

We gotta dry everythin' now, while we got sun, he said.

They arranged the horses as a screen from the steady, low wind and stripped off their outer layers, standing on the cloth in bare feet, trying to dry their socks and boots.

This is deranged, Ilya said. Aren't we wasting time we don't have?

Mebbe. I jes know bein' wrapped in a sheet a ice ain't good. Bridger stood looking at the rocky skull thrust out of the cliff band before them, squinting hard against the snow glare.

Dry fer an hour here, we c'n git up against that knob there 'fore dark...might find a deadfall...might live...He trailed off. He was having a hard time keeping his thoughts following one another. Ilya stood there bak-ing and freezing, her head pounding from squinting against the glitter.

As you like, she said, feeling herself slipping toward a semi-con-sciousness that seemed comforting, an inability to care.

Ilya was struggling along, eyes almost shut, feeling her mind seize, when she flinched at a rifle shot in front of her. She opened her eyes, and over Bridger's shoulder she watched a cloud of snow tumble down a face of naked rock. Bridger turned and smiled at Ilya, which made him look frightening.

I hit it.

The snow?

Goat.

Oh. What does that mean?

Means...means if we git it we c'n eat it, an' not horse. We gotta hour 'fore dark. An' see...he pointed to the right. There was a talus slope at the top of which was a black hole punched into the cliff band, beside it an avalanche path, live and dead trees sticking up out of the fresh snow.

There was an avalanche already this year? Ilya said, looking at the swath of destruction and intuiting what it was.

Last year. Ever' year probly, but not this year yet. We got us a hotel better'n that last one right there, if we c'n git to it. Shelter, food, an' fuel, cuzza them deads in the slide path. An' there's standin' dead right there, if th' downed ones git buried. Y' see?

She looked at him, then nodded. She couldn't follow her thoughts, and for a moment didn't know what troubled her. She gazed off towards where the goat had fallen.

How. How do we get it? she said. Her voice sounded helpless, enraging her. She was so thirsty. He looked off toward where the animal had fallen.

I dunno. Wouldn' 'at be a hell of a thing? The goat was on the other side of an expanse of deep snow which lay in the lee of a clean-swept mound of gray stone. Bridger cupped his hands around his eyes, and could see now that the animal had dropped through a sharp-edged cornice of snow, the beginning of what would be a massive overhang later in the winter, the shaded underside of which was a deep, cold blue. The goat's fall had broken a chunk off, leaving sharp, fragile teeth sticking into the air. Swirling, fine clouds came from it as the wind sharpened the edges. Ilya felt a pang of remorse that the clean, beautiful sweep of pristine snow had been spoiled by the animal's fall. Bridger, as the significance of all this came on him, growled.

Ilya watched him for a moment. What's wrong with you?

That fuckin' snow's ready t' come down. He pointed at it. See? And that snow's gonna be deep as fuck t' git through where that damn goat fell. Wind jes drops it all right here.

Oh. But we have to get it. We'll starve. It's that or horse meat. I don't want to have to eat you. No offense.

Wouldn't like it neither. Tell y' what. I'll try an' sling it outta there, an' if it ain't gonna work, we eat horse.

It'll be dark soon, she said.

Good fer th' fuckin' dark. He took up his rope and set off through the snow toward the goat.

Wait, she said, and he stopped. Give me one end. He handed it to her.

The snow was to Bridger's chest in a few moments. He couldn't feel the ground beneath his boots, which were packed with snow. He flopped and swam through the powder. She came behind him, trying to keep her body from sinking. At the midway point to the outcropping, Bridger fell and disappeared altogether. All Ilya could see was the shifting snow over him. She tried to reach him, plunging her hands after him and grasping. He emerged out in front of her, a sea creature blowing spume.

Rocks. Here, he said. Ilya floundered forward, almost disappearing into the snow herself. Bridger grabbed her collar and pulled at her until she could get a purchase on the buried rock, and they scrabbled to the crest of the clean-swept knob of stone.

We should be tied together, she said.

Bridger shrugged, face pinched. Don' mean shit. He was looking down into the depression where they could see the scar the goat's body had made in the clean skin of snow.

Ilya looked up at the cornice, the wind tearing its edge away in clouds that blended with those floating across the field of darkening blue beyond.

You'll be killed under there.

Git kilt out here. He slid down the stone incline toward the animal. Don' let yerself freeze, he said.

Ilya beat at herself with her arms, kicking and throwing her limbs, snickering in a crazed way about the lack of dignity. Bridger fought through the snow.

Ilya pulled at the rope but could get no purchase on it, it was slick, and her fingers numb. Phlegm was frozen and caked in her nostrils, and her breath came out of her mouth in whimpers. She could feel the cold creeping through her limbs toward her heart. When Bridger reached the goat he was in deep, blue shadow, and she could barely see him. The wind gusted, throwing snow into her eyes. She looked at the cornice, wanting to fix it in place with her gaze.

She wanted to shout at him to flee, that this was stupid, that she didn't understand why they were doing it. Bridger had to flop forward into the snow to reach the animal. He groped, trying to orient himself to it, and managed to find a horn and pull on it, but he sank deeper. He fought, trying to find something beneath him to stand on. He got a loop around the neck.

He wanted to shout to Ilya to pull. He gestured at her, and he could see her leaning backwards, rope wrapped around her hands. She could not see him well enough to understand his motions, but was pulling out of fear of losing him. The goat wouldn't move. Bridger growled and slobbered, snow clogging his nose and mouth. He began to violently thrash around, beating back the drifts, trying to clear a path for the goat to slide upon. He sunk deeper down. He was chest deep, sweat pouring from him, icicles of phlegm and sweat dangling from his nose, when his boots struck something solid. He hunched and got his shoulder beneath the body and wrenched it up and out. The release of tension in the rope sent Ilya to her ass on the stone. She didn't feel it, just got to her feet and began pulling again. She was having no effect. The animal was too heavy. Bridger was off his footing, trying to move the body. He couldn't. He was crying and cursing, the tears freezing to his cheeks.

Bridger! Ilya whispered hoarsely. The wind whipped the words away. Bridger! she said louder. Finally she shouted, Bridger, Bridger, Bridger!! Her voice pounded against the face of stone and echoed away. Bridger heard her and stopped straining. They waited for the snow that didn't come down. He stared at her.

Just cut a piece off! she said, her voice a loud rasp.

Bridger considered the idea. It was a good one. He felt stupid for a moment, then wrenched the goat's mouth open, gouged out the tongue with his knife, and pushed it into his coat pocket. He sawed at the rear leg, the hide and hair resisting his blade, checking to see if he was using the sharp edge. He wrestled the animal to its back, raised his knife over his head, and plunged it into the stretch of skin between belly and thigh. Once he'd pierced the hide the knife made progress through the flesh. It took him some minutes to free the leg, hacking and wrenching at it, probing for the ball joint, finally seeing the ivory knob roll out of the meat, and jamming his knife into it and prying and ripping it apart. Ilya felt herself losing her resistance to freezing.

Bridger emerged out of the shadow, bashing back through the snow. He made it back to the stone, leaving a bloody trail.

Go, he spat, and waved his arm wildly at the talus slope. Take this. He pushed the leg into her arms, and went for the horses. Pain shot through her arm, and she shrieked a little and set off.

No! he shouted, and waved. There, that way, in th' trees. Next t' th' slide path, not in it... She went towards it, and saw what he meant — in the trees beside the path, the snow was less deep, the ground less treacherous.

Wood, Ilya said when they'd made it inside, and felt the deadening, still, cold of the air in the cave, worse than outside. Energy and desperate anger juiced her. Bridger scrambled out into the wind to a dead, snow-covered pine and fell upon it. When he had an armful of needles he went back to the cave and threw them on the floor. Ilya had put the horses before the opening to block the wind, was standing there, embracing one of them. He went to his knees shaking violently.

C'mere, c'mere, y' gotta do this.

She clamped her chattering teeth and knelt.

Oh, God, fuck...

These'll flare right up, but they'll be gone in a heartbeat...git th' snow off 'em, git it ready...He fished his fire bag out of his shirt and threw it down. Git some matches outta there.

He bashed out to the tree and came back with twigs.

Aright fire it, now, now...

She couldn't hold her hands steady, couldn't get the tip of the match to the striker. He knelt beside her and took the box and held it in both hands. She held the match in two hands and slashed at the box.

Oh, fuck, she said.

C'mon, c'mon...

The match caught, flared, and went out.

Take a bunch of 'em, he said, and dumped them in the dirt. She grabbed up three of them, clustered them, and slashed at the box until they burst and caught and held. The needles flared up and the pile burned.

Keep feedin' it, th' needles'll be done quick...

He forced himself back out into the snow and began making trips as fast as he could, wheezing and snorting through the twilight and the rising cold. He stood up on a branch and jumped up and down on it until it snapped off the bole, and he wrenched at it, pulling it free, a long tongue hanging.

Bridger dragged in the branch and stamped to the snapping fire, pushing his hands toward the flames. Ilya was huddled as close to the heat as she could get, weeping.

That ain't gonna work, Bridger said. Take everythin' off. Quick. They wrenched their soaking, frozen clothes off and crouched there naked on the oilcloth, shuddering beside one another, the blanket over them. The strange numbness was replaced by agony as blood pushed back into their limbs. It was an astounding, unspeakable amount of pain, as if their bones were being torn out through their flesh. It couldn't be borne sitting still, and they paced around the flames, growling and shaking their arms and sobbing.

The pain escalated, and Ilya was shattering, could feel her mind coming untethered, and Bridger could only just keep himself from screaming by giving out an incessant, grinding moan. They weren't able to tell themselves that there was an end to this, and they were consumed by this physical agony and mental anguish that felt like a pool they were submerged in, and the fire was just there to give them light by which to see their end.

The pain began to give in to a relentless burning which was less excruciating but more aggravating. The burning began to be tinged with maddening itching, until everything from the wrist and ankles out felt like it was trying to crawl away from their bodies.

In an hour they were sagged together beneath the blanket. The fire had a bed of coals which pushed out heat in a steady, warm breath beneath the yellow flames above them. The cave was small and shallow, and the ambient temperature had risen some. Their hands and feet had yellowed and gone waxy, and itched madly.

Bridger stood, slid his knife out of the sheath hanging from his belt on the floor, and snaked the goat's leg to him, getting back under the blanket. He got the tongue from his coat and threw it into the fire. He pulled on the hide of the leg and tried to cut it loose from the flesh, but his fingers couldn't grasp and the meat was slick.

Y' gotta pull th' skin, he said.

Ilya grabbed a flap of the hide and pulled on it with vicious hysteria.

Easy, jes...pull steady on it...so I c'n use both hands...yer gonna eat inna minnit...

Ilya inwardly screamed herself into calm and focused on pinching her fingers closed as hard as she could, and pulling the skin toward her. She felt ashamed of herself.

That's good...pull steady on it. In long, probing strokes, Bridger cut at the pale veil holding flesh to hide. When they had it back enough, Bridger hacked off chunks of the meat and tossed them into the coals. He fished the tongue out and gnawed a chunk off of it, and handed it to Ilya. She took it, bit into it, tore off a piece, and chewed, the hard springy meat bouncing her jaws apart, the taste buds coarse against her own. She swallowed, it almost came back up, and she shut her throat to keep it down. They finished the tongue and Bridger flicked the bits of leg out of the fire with his knife, and they crouched there, eating. Their bodies slowly stopped quavering.

You cook well, she said, when surviving seemed likely.

Thanks.

Needs salt.

I'll keep it in mind fer nex' time.

Please do. Perhaps we should open our own restaurant. Or our own cave. When we get out of this.

When they had eaten, Bridger stood. Git up a minnit, he said. Ilya stood up in the blanket, and Bridger took their damp coats and laid them on the cloth as close to the fire as possible. Freeze t' death layin' on rock. Lay there. Ilya laid down on her side facing the fire and Bridger laid against her back, and pulled the blanket over them.

I'm not sleepy, Ilya said. Tell me a story.

7

Ilya stood in the cave mouth, blanket around her, blinking hard, her hand over her eyes like a salute. The mouth pointed due south and the sun was directly before her. On the other side of a series of low peaks to her left she could see the Gallatins in the distance, and could see a small slice of the valley floor. Before her the range reared up beneath the sun, to her right, peaks rose high. Lodgepoles and firs carpeted everything, heaped with snow, with aspens running through the bottom of the drainage, now stripped of what leaves had remained, their branches carrying a delicate coating of snow which was beginning to drop off in the sun. The ground just outside the cave mouth was a sharp slope of jagged, snow-covered scree, with boulders and slabs of stone that had sheared off the cliff face behind her pushing up out of it.

Bridger sat on a slab of stone he'd kicked clean of snow, the sun melting what remained. The uppers of his long underwear were around his waist. He was baking his face and torso. His skin was the near the color of the snow, his forearms brown. Black hair sliced through it on his back. She'd fallen asleep close to dawn, Bridger never had. He'd stayed up, shifting their clothes to dry them, keeping the fire going, and the horses calm and dry as he could. It was late morning. The horses stood on a more or less level spot, looking miserable.

She got her shift and slipped into it, went back out with the blanket, scrambled up the side of the slab, and sat beside him. The heat was stultifying and beautiful and made her high. The glitter of the sunlight off the snow blinded her.

Hello, she said.

Hello. He didn't move his face from the heat.

Lovely day.

No complaints.

I'm thirsty.

He picked up his canteen from beside him and handed it to her. Ain't much. Fill it back up with snow an' put it in th' sun. Gotta keep doin' it. Horses need some.

She drained the tepid gulp of water, slid back down off the slab, and spent some minutes trying to push snow into the mouth of the canteen, which was comically difficult, and hurt her hands, and felt intensely futile.

She clambered back up and said, Move, and nudged him, showing him the blanket. He stood up and aside, she folded it long ways, laid it out on the stone, and they settled on it.

How can it be so hot? After yesterday?

Happens. Bridger lowered his face and opened one eye, nodded out towards the valley floor. Snow out there, wouldn't surprise me if it's gone tomorra. Git down a thousand feet, probly on'y a couple inches, none at all on south facin'. Sometimes it'll snow like it done and jes go straight on inta full winter, but ain't likely this time. Too early. Be second mud season a th' year down there I bet.

How irritating.

Yep. Lucky fer us though. We'll be able t' git down outta this in a couple days. It'll be deep at first, but we leave early, fight it out, we'll make it. I c'n fuckin' see now. If it don't snow agin, but I don' think it will. One thing though, we ain't gonna git many more a these bluebird days we got right now. It'll go gray and wet soon.

I don't understand why everyone out here isn't blind from the sun off the snow.

Cuz soon it's gonna be gray and wet mosta th' time.

You just said that didn't you?

Yep. Y' c'n do this too. Help some. He cupped both hands around his eyes as though holding binoculars. She mimicked him.

Amazing, she said. That works very well. Somewhat inconvenient not having your hands. What if there's a duel?

Guess it's a tossup 'tween th' blind guy with th' gun, and th' guy that c'n see but can't shoot.

I don't want to contemplate the metaphorical implications of that statement. I'm exhausted. Dying is tiring.

I ain't pushin' fer it. He stood up and ducked into the cave, came back out with the whiskey. She stared at him as he took a swallow.

Why didn't you bring that out when we were dying?

If I did, that's jes what we woulda done. Pap tol' me a story 'bout people gittin' snowbound, gittin' drunk, got stupid, an' died a mile from town. Fucks up yer blood too. Y' freeze faster but y' think yer warmer.

Doesn't seem fair.

Nope. Woulda brought it out if I thought we wuz done fer.

You believed we would be alright?

I b'lieved I dint know yet.

He held out the bottle to her, she took it and swallowed, felt the angry warmth flow into her and join with the heat soaking her skin. She felt liquid, about to flow out over the stone and into the valley. He slid the bottle out of her slack fingers before she dropped it, corked it, and sat down.

You were a hero, she said, face into the heat, eyes shut. I've never had a hero before, which is somewhat disappointing. I'm attractive enough and that's all heroes care about. Seems unjust. I would have died. And been glad to.

Sorry t' fuck y' up.

I forgive you. Please ask next time, however. Imagine how angry at you I'd be if I hadn't wanted to be saved.

Aright.

Thank you, Bridger. In earnest.

He took a moment to consider before speaking, so his pronunciation was proper, You're welcome.

Was I a lot of trouble?

Bridger's face crunched up and he got a bolt of panic that he'd gotten something wrong, that he had not said, or not not said, the right thing.

Hell...no, you wuz....fuckin'...real tough 'bout it all. Shit, I wuz jes lucky my bad calls dint get us kilt. Coulda, easy as not. I thought mebbe there'd be some goat on that face, cuz that's where they go in th' shit, but I wuz jes dreamin'. I wuz gonna pack it in when I saw we wuz up so high when I wuz tryin' t' git us down. Every damn down made us go up more. He jes moved at th' wrong time an' I seen 'im. Wadn't any skills to it. Jes found a goat 'thout any luck of his own.

Thank you for not being boastful about it. It would be insufferable. I'd have to kill you, now that I've become practiced at it.

Guess we's both jes some dangerous shit now.

Indeed.

Lemme see yer feet. She glanced at him, then raised one leg and put her foot into his cupped palms. He looked at it and rubbed it. Can y' feel all that?

Yes. It doesn't feel quite right, though.

Wouln't. I got frostbit once...my feet never felt quite good fer weeks after, but they did after some. We wuz lucky, got warm 'fore it got too bad. Gimme th' other. She swung her body and put her legs in his lap, and he cupped the other foot. Same?

Yes. What about yours?

They're aright. Seems like y' git nipped once, they're tougher next time.

Oh, good. Let's do this often then. Let's stay out here until we can never get cold again.

It's a plan. He stopped rubbing her feet and put his palms on the stone behind him. His shoulders were up beside his ears.

Keep rubbing them, she said. He stayed still for an instant, then sat back forward and went back to kneading her feet, staring out away from her, eyes slitted. She took up the whiskey and drank, gave it to him, he took the bottle, drank, put his hands back to her skin. She laid back, hands over her belly.

Fuck, Bridger said.

What's wrong?

You, too. He took up her left hand in his right, grasped the little finger in his thumb and forefinger and squeezed it. Can y' feel that?

No. Not...quite.

That ain't good. I got th' same thing. Diff'rent hand.

She sat up and looked at her blackened finger. He was holding his hand out, palm to her, wiggling the small finger. The tip was black fading to blue, to yellow at the second knuckle. Above that the skin was covered with fragile, translucent blisters.

They're dead, he said. He probed at the blisters and they gave out clear liquid.

Well, better them than us.

Hafta cut 'em off. Flesh rot c'd spread.

Gangrene, you mean.

Couln't thinka th' word.

Well, it's an unpleasant word. Well, my dear Bridger, my hero, you are having an uncharacteristically lucky day.

Howzat?

I think this what we have is dry gangrene. Wet gangrene is the one you need to amputate for. When you get shot, for instance.

Huh. Howdya know?

I'm rich and I'm from New York, and doctors are high society there. They like to talk about their work, and I like to listen to stories of men being insane to each other. The war made amputation a very popular topic, depending on your social set.

Yer hidin' th' rich part pretty good these days.

Well. Excuse me. I *was* rich.

Decided y'd rather come out to th' Rockies and git frostbit?

Precisely. An opportunity to get gangrene is not to be missed.

So we jes walk 'round with dead fingers?

I believe it means we have a choice. It means we don't have to take the rather cliché step of cutting each others' fingers off in a mountain cave to metaphorically imply an intimate psychological connection, you see, but with the touching contradiction of the removal of something being the creation of the bond. I don't want my adventure to become hackneyed.

She squinted up at him. He looked puzzled and embarrassed. She hated herself, her pretentiousness.

I suppose you didn't understand much of that.

Not much.

You're ashamed?

I guess.

Oh, she sighed. You're that kind. I was beginning to suspect. Do you see how ridiculous is it for you to feel ashamed of not knowing something you have no way of knowing? And after you just knew so much we're not dead? I don't feel ashamed — well, I do a little, I suppose — that I knew nothing about how to survive what we just went through. How could I? You see?

Aright.

A metaphor is just something that means something else. Cutting our fingers off would be a symbol that we had grown closer, in a story, you see?

Bridger stared at her, not with incomprehension, but with a look that made her feel metaphors were stupid things.

Now, she said, how can I explain 'hackneyed?' How can I explain anything, for that matter? Let me see. Have you ever heard the same story many times?

No.

She laughed to where she could not stop, and he smiled and his shoulders shook, but nothing came out. She laid there, one hand over her eyes, giggling. He sat with his arms draped over her thighs, and laughed in his chest, his face working.

Well, my occasionally very amusing hero, can you imagine how you would feel if you did hear the same story many times?

Bored.

Yes. That's what hackneyed means. A tired old story that makes you bored. I don't want my adventure to be hackneyed.

Aright. Me neither.

It's rather nice, I think. We get to choose whether to cut our fingers off or not.

Free country, I heard. He wiggled it around. Hurts, he said. An' don'.

Mine, too. Ilya laid staring out over the range, felt his prick against her thigh. She swung her legs off him, swung around, pulled him out of his underwear, and took him in her mouth. He gasped sharply and flinched, feeling like a man fumbling behind some drapes. She worked gently for a few seconds, and swallowed. She pushed his prick back into his drawers, swigged from the bottle and sloshed it around in her mouth, swallowed.

Cum and goat do not mix well, as it happens. Even for my sophisticated palate.

She handed him the bottle, looking into his face and smiling until he smiled in a small way.

She put her hand out and pressed it against his rigid, thudding chest.

Panicking is generally thought of as a poor response to fellatio, she said gently. Calm yourself. You'll get through this.

She watched him try to will himself into calm and smiled, and shook her head. You are a very tightly-wrapped hero, she said, and reached out with both hands and pushed down on his shoulders. Maybe they have to be, heroes. Down. Down boy.

He forced his shoulders down but wouldn't look at her. She laid her head in his lap, pulled his arm around her and held his hand against her breast.

I want you to know, she said, that I would fuck you. But I am not getting pregnant again. It happened once and I had it taken out of me. You can't understand, but for comparison, it would be like someone using blacksmith's tongs to reach up your asshole and pull out your heart. You see?

Not good, I'm gittin'.

No. So it's not personal, me not fucking you. I suspect a young man like you, your juice might impregnate me just from swallowing it. Anyway, based on your response just now, fucking me might kill you with anxiety, and I still need you. For the moment you should stick to horses, goats, and shooting things. We'll save the fucking for another time. It's far more complicated and difficult than killing, and far less satisfying most of the time. When we can get protection for me from your criminal seed perhaps we'll try it. I owe you.

You don' owe me nothin'.

That's good. There's a small chance it will be better if I don't feel obligated. Are you angry?

No.

You're either lying or a fine man. Though it could be that a fine man would lie right now. I don't want to know. I want to sleep for a while.

'Man?' Bridger thought.

G'head an' sleep, he said. We'll stay t'day. Eat th' rest a that goat. Rest up. Git down next mornin'. Them horses don' eat, they gonna bolt.

Alright.

8

Is this our life from now on, Bridger? Sitting outside of wretched communities, wondering if it's safe to go in?

I dunno. 'Pends on what we do now.

This is more adventure than I care for. What town is it?

Got me.

Well, let's rest a moment and think about it.

They dismounted and stood, torn apart and depleted and filthy and hungry.

Bridger had gotten them down on the southeast side of the Jeffersons, but they'd decided the train was a bad idea given that they'd become fugitives, as was the road. But Ilya still was set on San Francisco, so Bridger had taken them around the south side of the range and west, keeping close to the foothills. The snow down low did melt quickly, and the temperature stayed up, which produced mud for them to become splattered in. They'd been three days from the cave to here, and had seen no game to shoot.

We're a war photo, Ilya said, looking at them. She rubbed her face with both hands. I don't know what to do. This is...hard.

Bridger stood silent for a moment. His ass hurt from riding the black without a saddle.

Still c'd go t' th' law.

Then we would be prisoners. They would get to choose what becomes of us. You might be able to get through it. I'm a Jew, and a woman, and a

New Yorker. They'll burn me just for making them feel inferior. No, dammit, I didn't run from New York to the West just to...She stopped. Bridger watched her.

Bridger, she said, you've done your part. Far more really. You don't have to stay with me. It's probably better if we don't stay together.

Ain't nothin' t' go back to. He thought of Mary and hated saying those words, hated fearing that he'd disappointed her. He wanted to know what she thought of his actions, but was scared to know. Was this, now, what he was, her definition of strong?

Rather be out here in th' country...in America...anyhow, whatever happens, he said.

Ilya looked into his eyes. You know, if you are not with me you are not an object of suspicion. No one saw you there, correct? Not the hotel woman?

He looked back at her. Nope. Not clear. Not up close.

Then you should stay away from me. She saw me up close. Though it was dark and she was dumb, and her eyes were...off. That could help matters. Those miners weren't close enough to see either of us well.

He looked at the ground for a moment. S'posed t' protect y'. You.

You've done more than enough of that. And I don't need protection that badly, as I believe I've demonstrated quite amply. Save yourself.

Bridger stood there with a curious lack of sensation. He wanted to tell her that he'd rather be dead than apart from her, but couldn't. Whatta *you* want? he said.

She stood, feeling stretched to the point of breaking. Feeling like she didn't want to be having this conversation, and was tired beyond belief of what her life had become, the incessant tension and fear and hardship. She couldn't visualize the future, couldn't assess the risk she was taking accurately, couldn't tell if a description given by the batty hotel woman was something to worry about or not, if she had even given one. She thought of Mary and remorse slid through her, followed by defiance. What choice had she had? She tried to picture making it across the country from there without Bridger — being in a constant defensive state alone, fending off the strangers who wanted to hurt her, and the ones who didn't, the chivalric ones, who were in their way worse — and couldn't. She opened her mouth to tell him that she could go either way, it made no difference to her, but couldn't say that.

I want you to stay with me, she said.

Relief drained through him. Then I stay, he said.

It's foolish.

He shrugged. Don' care.

Alright. Is it exciting for you?

The corner of his mouth went up as he looked at her. Beats ridin' fence.

I should think being with me would top that, yes. She hesitated. I killed a man in New York. That's why I'm here. He was my husband. He tried to kill me. He failed. I can tell you everything in more detail another time, but there's that. Alright?

Bridger thought a moment then shrugged. Aright.

Well, I can see how after the massacre you must feel like much too much man for that little town you came from.

Somethin' like.

She looked around them and shivered. Fuck, she said. Her reek gagged her. Her clothes were filthy and mangled, her hair was a clotted mess, her skin felt like she was wearing that of a corpse, her finger ached maddeningly, and her feet seemed permanently half numb. The lump on her forehead had gone down but her arm still ached. They had finished the whiskey the first day and had had no tobacco.

The fucking West, she said, looking around. Whoopee.

Hell, I ain't never been a outlaw. I don' know. What d' y' think we should do?

I'm sure I don't know. I let my subscription to the Outlaw Review lapse with my Godey's Ladies Book. I have to say, being an outlaw is an incredible inconvenience.

Reckon that's what makes most folks take th' other road.

Mm. That and fear of punishment, and lack of rebelliousness and creativity.

Ilya fumed. She wanted a bath, a good meal, a soft bed, Jacques and Zoe, a bit of money, a few books around, decent whiskey, maybe see a show, not be a whore, have stupid men leave her alone, be better than everyone around her, and maybe some traveling where you don't freeze and starve to death, and you get to come back to where you started with some dignity. Just a normal life. Here she was, right outside of a town, and she can't go in because she'd be killed or jailed.

I wanna drink, Bridger said. Ilya glanced at him. He looked miserable and comically ragged, the dignity he'd acquired with Mary's clothes gone. She didn't want him to turn into a drunken sniper, reeling about the country picking people off just because he was good at it. She thought of his father.

If Bridger was going to turn into a version of him she was going to have to separate from him. She recalled him telling her the story of killing that man while they were in the cave, and the Spunk story, and reminded herself of how warped that would almost certainly make him. That eventually he would betray her, and probably not realize he was doing it, because to him all he had done is become interested in something, or someone, else. And now he would expect always to be betrayed, would feel himself to be cornered before he was. Trouble was, he didn't seem to be that way at all. He seemed steady, loyal, whatever frailty in him not the sort that made someone a shitty person.

Be careful with the drinking, please, she said. You don't want to get to the place where you need a drink to work up the courage to have a drink. Though I want a drink, also. I want a lot of things. I wonder if they have real cigarettes in there.

Might. Big town.

Alright, she sighed. We'll go in. There's no way to know where the next town is. We can't survive out here with what we have, your skills notwithstanding. Yes?

Bridger nodded. Ain't good we git seen t'gether.

True. We're going to have to have a talk about the way you talk. It would be a brilliant disguise for you to use English.

Mary been workin' on that. I'm tryin'. I fergit.

That's understandable. Speaking proper English while freezing to death probably doesn't seem important. It's time to get you to where you can speak it when you don't happen to be freezing to death, or shooting people. Although, the likelihood is you'll shortly be dead, so...why bother?

There oughta be schools.

Ilya turned to him, brow furrowed. There are...oh, she said. Then she snorted a short laugh.

That's funny, she said. I think you're in the school right now. You're being home schooled. Or cave schooled.

Dint git much a th' reg'lar kind.

That's too bad. Maybe. Who knows what they would have had you read out here? Probably Genesis over and over until you're a halfwit. But it's alright, you're learning to be a murderer, and it's an old, respected trade. Alright. We'll go in separately. But if I go in dressed like this they'll know me right away. I don't have a proper dress anymore. It's best I fool them by appearing to be a woman. And I don't want to have to shoot anyone. I want a nice, quiet time. I want some good food if they have any in there.

Bridger was glum. It was so complicated. He wanted to just say to hell with it and ride in and let the chips fall. This was too much thinking, and he got nostalgic for the easy purity of the moment of shooting, but then remembered the chaos and trouble that followed it. He shook his head.

You'll have to get me a dress, Ilya said.

Bridger frowned. Me?

Who else?

You. Yer dress.

They're looking for a woman in man's clothing. There's no disguising me, right now. I'm not going to sneak into this town inside a wooden horse. You're just a man like any other, and no one saw you at that camp. They're not going to notice you if you aren't with me. We'll tidy you up a little.

How'm I gonna look comin' in buyin' a dress fer a woman that ain't there?

You're a man, you can do anything you want. Tell them your sister's sick or something, it really makes no difference. Tell them nothing. She thought a moment, her mind fighting her over having to strategize. I suppose you're right. You walking into a modiste asking for a dress looking like that would be suspicious. Or just terrifying. Steal one.

Howzat less fucked up than buyin' one?

I don't know. I mean steal one without being noticed. I think walking up and shooting everyone in sight to get a dress will arouse suspicion, though I realize that's now your most comfortable approach. But it's time for you to acquire some subtlety.

Does subtlety go good with whiskey an' goat?

Oh, it's plumb tasty.

Shit. Where'm I gonna steal a dress?

You can shoot men in the back of the head as they run from you in terror, but you can't steal a dress?

Yep.

You're more complicated than you look. I understand there are some manhood matters at stake here for you, but you must be more rational. The whole advantage to starting a life of crime by murdering people is that all the other things just don't have the magnitude, you see? At this point we are allowed to lose our petty sanctimony and social fear. There are those who even may hold that the point of murder is to avoid those very annoying prejudices that plague humans normally. Do you understand?

Yeah, mostly. But I hafta skip over all th' words y' use t' do it. Ever jes say a thing? I ain't arguin', I jes don' know nothin' 'bout dresses.

When did you know something about murdering people, before or after you did it? You're not going to wear the dress, unless that's something you think you'd like, and we can talk about that if it's the case. That may be the way for you to go. Maybe that would just clear everything up inside you. But for right now, I just need you to go into town and find a dress, and get out of town without being caught. I don't care how you do it. And you know a lot about dresses. You know women wear them, and they make everything women have to do a lot harder than they need to be. And here's another piece of interesting lore for you — men invented dresses so women would be easier to catch and rape. You probably didn't know about that last thing but now you have something to ponder while you gun some more men down.

I thought a that a few times. Never seen why women wuz always wrapped up like they wuz one big, busted bone.

Then you are already superior to most men. I got to you in time. Or Mary did. You have a great future, if you don't mind that it's so short.

Ain't happy 'bout it, but...I wadn't happy before, anyways.

It is elusive. Don't steal me a sack. Look for something with a little lace.

Where d'ya think I should steal one from?

You'll think of something.

This town was the biggest Bridger had seen, which, though it intimidated him, was a good thing. It was a clattering, busy, noisy place sprawled out over the land. He saw with some wonder that they had secondary streets beginning to grow off the main thoroughfare. Someone with engineering ambitions was overseeing some crude drainage system and men were spreading coarse stone. There were continuous wooden sidewalks down each side. There was enough activity for Bridger to go unnoticed among it. He was tempted to ride back out to Ilya and tell her not to worry, they would be stones in a riverbed in this place. He chose not to. She would be angry at him, and she was shitty when she was angry.

All the dresses seemed to be dangling from clotheslines over the street from the second story, waving at him from balconies like whores.

The saloon was nearly empty and quiet. The Imperial, it was called. A couple cowhands stood at the bar staring. A woman was sitting looking out the window in a red dress with a low-cut and lacy bodice from which her breasts erupted in a way that looked unhealthy, looked attractive and compelling but taunting and repulsive. Bridger considered asking the woman if he could have her dress, or just shooting her and taking it.

He went to the long, polished bar. The refinement in this place made him nervous. It made Dooley's look like someone had taken a shit on the ground and started serving drinks out of it. There was a polished brass foot rail at the bar. There was a big, carved rail at the front for his elbows to settle into. It had a tight, fir floor, the wax on which squeaked under his boots and made him feel he would be punished for walking on it. There were two mirrors in ornate, gilded frames behind the bar, but he couldn't see himself where he decided to stand, and didn't want to. He felt intensely watched and didn't want to add himself to the crowd. The back bar was an ornate spread of carved oak, with grooved pilasters and a pediment filled with carved, naked gods who weren't fucking but didn't seem to be doing much else of consequence either, just hanging there in bas-relief. The bartender loafed down the bar to him from turning cards over. He looked at Bridger.

Bridger cleared his throat. Whiskey, he said.

The bartender said, What kind? Bridger hesitated.

You wanna go and ponder it some and come back? the bartender said. Maybe in a few years? One of the cowhands turned and looked down at them.

The urge to take his pistol and shoot the bartender through the face crashed through Bridger like a lout, followed by a bouncer of fear. I want the cheapest whiskey you got, he said.

That's easy, the bartender said, took a scratched bottle sitting behind him, pulled the cork, and poured into a shot glass. The glass was clear, unscratched.

Quarter.

Bridger put one of Mary's silver dollars on the bar. Obliged, he said.

My pleasure.

When the whiskey hit Bridger's empty stomach, his abdomen flared up hard, and the urge to puke came all the way to his teeth. He stared away from the others until his gorge retreated, and his stomach became a soft, burning soup. His anxiety fell through him and the skin around his eyes relaxed.

Yep, Bridger said, and pushed his glass towards the man. He noticed with sickly pleasure that his voice was now a manly croak. His eyes were bright and fixed on the bartender's. His face twitched.

The bartender's eyebrows lifted in mild surprise and he shrugged. Bridger threw the shot down and stood there feeling the burn. The cowboys watched. Bridger gripped the edge of the bar and stood with his brain reeling and his eyes swimming, keeping still. When he could he picked up his change, and nodded to the bartender.

Obliged, he rasped.

Don't be a stranger, the bartender said, still watching Bridger. Bridger walked a long parabola from the bar to the door and exited. He turned the corner of the saloon, plodded into the alley, and when he'd gone as far as he was able he vomited down the side of the building. When his stomach was purged it kept twisting. He curled up and laid in the shade, eyes closed, and waited.

He watched the motions of an indistinct, contorting object. He blinked, willing his eyes to clear. When he could see he realized he was looking at a red and white dress floating on a line with other clothes. It was flapping at him over a fence made of pointed vertical boards. He got up weaving, looked through the slats of the fence, noticed that whoever had built it had some skills. The builder had left gaps between the boards to allow some wind to pass through. But there was too much of everything in his vision, and he kept wanting to close his eyes. When he tried to look around him to see if he was observed he plunked down on his ass. He clambered to his feet and reached for the dress. The hem of it flicked at him out of reach. Terrified but sick, and predicting Ilya's anger if he came back with nothing, he flopped over the fence into the dirt yard and snatched the dress, vaulted back over, caught his foot, and crashed back into the alley. He balled up the dress, jammed it under his shirt, and made for his horse.

Gingham, Ilya said. You stole a gingham dress for me?

Hell, it's a damn dress...

She stood there, hands on hips, glaring at him. Her eyes narrowed.

You're drunk, she spat. She wanted to shoot him. Another bumbling, incompetent, drunken, stupid, heroic man getting in her way, imposing their idiotic visions of women on her, wanting to dress her up in frilly whorish garbage, or now this silly little peasant girl gingham dress, as if she should go gamboling about the fields with a straw in her mouth and flowers in her hair while some slobbering fool flopped along after her.

Bridger was weaving in the saddle from whatever he had drunk, from the sun beating on his skull and his tongue cracked and dry, from the shock of having angered Ilya after trying so hard not to, but he was becoming enraged himself, which further wracked his brain. All he'd wanted was a drink and they poison him. Never seen them before in his life and the first thing they're up to is kill him or shame him. Try to do a good thing for Ilya, be a proper partner, hold up his end of the bargain, and she blows up on account it's not the right kind of dress, as if he should know anything about dresses. He'd rode out here fairly proud that he'd gotten the thing and without getting caught or killed.

He snorted and threw the dress on the ground. Ilya looked at it. And now it's dirty, she said.

Bridger put his hand on his pistol butt. Go t' hell, he said.

She looked at him, thinking that conflicts were serious when everyone was armed. And she thought that not fucking him might make him more demented than he was already prone to be. Sucking a man off could create expectations.

She could see Bridger's chin and hand trembling, and the maddened look on his face. She waved her hands in front of her and shook her head at him.

Be calm, she said. If you shoot me it will be a very short time before you regret it, isn't that so?

Bridger relaxed in the saddle. He was relieved that he'd made a stand and hadn't been killed or shamed for it. He'd been afraid Ilya would take his guns away and spank him.

Well...I jes ain't feelin'...too good.

You don't look well. What happened to you?

He shrugged his shoulders and looked bewildered. Hell, I dunno. Just hadda couple drinks. Asked fer whiskey, but that shit, I dunno. They like t' poisoned me.

Oh, Ilya said, tanglefoot. It's turpentine and neutral alcohol and tobacco and other unmentionables. They give it to the people that are too broke, or too destroyed, or too young to know any better. They do it in New York as well, it's a more crass version of putting turnip juice in champagne to turn it pink so the codfish aristocracy feel good. Why it does that to them quite mystifies me.

I don' know what th' fuck y' jes said.

They deliberately poisoned you. It probably didn't help to have an empty stomach.

Hell, I dint know.

Happens to everyone once. If you can keep it to just that one time you win the game of life. She picked up the dress and shook it out. It's big enough. I can wear it while I buy a new one. And perhaps I'll look perfectly innocent in it, and no one will suspect me of being a ruthless killer. I suppose I'm to blame for coming to a place where people wear fashion a century old. Maybe this was a good choice you made. Most people are probably not expecting their outlaw to murder them wearing a little girl's frock. This is fine, you did fine. Go on back into town and get a room for yourself. A decent one. Do you still have Mary's money?

He nodded.

That's plenty. I'll be along later and find you. Sit out in front of where you check in so I can see you. I don't want to go to the same place. We'll stay one night to get cleaned up, pick up supplies tomorrow and leave. We'll meet on the other side of town. We can't be seen together. You get what we need for the trail, I'll do the rest. Drink water to run that turpentine out of you. Don't pour whiskey on top of it. Did you vomit?

Yep.

Well, keep doing it. It's a skill not to be undervalued.

Bridger listened and nodded gloomily. He didn't want to be on his own.

Bridger rode the black in and went to the livery. He talked to the tender, explained the treatment he wanted the horse to get — special, to compensate for the past days. The tender had a used saddle and Bridger bought it.

The hotel Bridger went to was plush beyond his imagining. The front windows were enormous and clean and let in bright swaths of sunlight that lay across the polished, dark floor. The check-in desk had a fat leather book on it bracketed by oil lamps, lit though it was day, and he noted the opulence implied by the waste, wanted to say, What th' fuck y' got lamps lit fer? but didn't.

Good afternoon sir, may I help you? The clerk said, turning to Bridger from the wall of cubbies behind the desk. He blinked and recoiled a little when he saw the tangle of misfortune that was Bridger at this moment. He was a clean, happy, and friendly man, impeccably dressed in a white shirt and black vest with gray stripes and sleeve garters gripping his arms. Bridger, expecting to be scoffed at for no reason, thrown out because of his ragged appearance, or poisoned, hesitated a moment. The clerk looked at him, like Bridger's hesitation was a most normal form of communication. The man's scrubbed face beamed at Bridger, framed by the globes of the lamps.

Yep, Bridger said. I wanna...I'd like a room.

Certainly, sir, the clerk replied. Are you looking for a modestly priced accommodation, or something more elaborate?

Ah...'laborate.

Very good, sir. We have a room that has a balcony on the street. It has a tub in the room and receives southern light in the afternoons. How does that sound?

Good.

Excellent. You look like you've had a rough time on the trail. No doubt you'll be wanting a bath and something to eat, and perhaps some brandy? There is only a nominal charge for the liquor, the hot water is included. I can have it brought up to you immediately if you like?

Bridger was mute. This was the happiest and friendliest person he'd ever seen, and he was a stranger. Bridger wanted to believe that he cared for his well-being. He wanted to throw himself at the clerk's feet and thank him. He didn't know what brandy was but he wanted some.

Yes, Bridger said. That'll be goo...that will be fine. Got smokes?

Of course. We have Bon Tons, I hope that will be satisfactory?

Yep.

Very good, sir. And how long will you be staying?

Jes th' night.

Fine. It seemed that made the clerk happy too, but then it also seemed that everything did.

If you could just sign in here, I'll have your bags brought up. And if you could just pay now, I will hold a bill for anything else you might need during your stay. A night is three dollars. Bridger fished Mary's bills out of his pants. They were wet and wadded. He pulled at them, separating them out until he found a fiver, and handed it over. The man handed him a pen and turned the book towards Bridger. Right here, he said, indicating an empty line in the ruled book with his forefinger. Bridger noticed his fingernail was carved into a spotless, soft, glowing curve, the skin around it plump and smooth. He grasped the pen with his claw and was going to print his name. Then he thought he shouldn't use his real name. He groped for a fake name, the strain combining with that of the fact that he had never held a pen before, only a pencil, and the ink was blobbing off onto the book.

The clerk took the pen from him. I'm very sorry sir, I dipped far too much ink into the pen, he said. He blotted the page and tipped ink from the pen onto a stained cloth he whisked from sight, and handed the pen back to Bridger.

Bridger printed out, Willem Pilgrin. He hadn't printed any word in a long time. It was pleasant, after the panic had passed. He looked at the name stumbling across the paper as if shitfaced. His pride diminished as he noticed other names marching across the lines and ending in flourishes, with his sad scratching beneath them.

Thank you, sir, the clerk said. I will have your baggage brought up right away.

I...don' got any, Bridger said. His saddlebags were on the floor, his rifle in his hand. Uh, there wuz a fire at th' mine. Got everythin'. 'Cept th' gold.

A very good plan to make gold so it doesn't burn, I believe. Would you like me to have your clothes cleaned while you bathe? Or if you like there is my store right beside us where you could get new ones of quite fine quality. You seem like a gentleman who would not like to be seen in those tatters.

I do? Uh, yes...I'll git me a...new outfit. An' wash these. It seemed best to just say yes to everything that was suggested to him.

Fine. I'll have your bath prepared directly.

The clerk in the clothing store was stamped out of the same die of helpful friendliness as the hotel one. He sized Bridger with his cloth ruler, a process that startled him as the man whipped the strip around his body. He brought out a black broadcloth suit, similar to the one Mary had given him. He held the jacket up. How is this, sir? he said.

Good.

Excellent. He helped Bridger out of his trail coat and into the suit coat, pulled at it, fussing.

Do this, he said, and raised his arms in front of him. Bridger complied. The sleeves rode up and the cloth tightened across his shoulders.

Hm. A size up, I believe, he said. You have abnormally broad shoulders. He took the coat off Bridger, left, and returned with another. This one worked.

An overcoat, sir? he said. For the night chill?

Yep.

He rummaged through a rack of them, and came back with a deep brown, knee-length wool coat with a high collar.

Brown? So you don't seem to always be in mourning?

Aright.

He helped Bridger into the coat and Bridger raised his arms.

How does that feel?

Good.

Enough room?

Yep.

Perfect. He took the coat back, laid it aside, and handed Bridger the trousers and pointed to a brocade curtain.

Whut? Bridger said.

Why, I'll need to hem the trousers for you, of course. You can't have the cuffs dragging in the dirt.

I gitcha.

He stood there on the stool the man put before him when he came out reeking. Without his boots on the smell was intense. The man grew less cheerful crouched down there by Bridger's feet, but he quickly jammed in a pin, straightened, and said in a burst of exhalation, I will have all of this to your room within the hour. A white shirt for you, as well? I believe I can guess the size of that, so no need to take your shirt off.

Yep. Thanks.

Would you like it to be put on your bill?

Yep.

Bridger returned to the hotel and asked the clerk where he could get a razor, and the clerk said he would be happy to get him a set of toiletries for a nominal fee, to which Bridger agreed.

The bath was warm and soapy and Bridger lounged in it, masturbating to a tangle of Mary and Ilya and guilt at being unable to separate them, drinking what he now understood was brandy from a clean, stemmed glass. The first glass was hard to swallow, but by the second he was sure he'd found his drink for life.

Bridger worked with his knife for a long time to get his fingernails to resemble those of the clerk, but couldn't — the tips of his fingers looked gnawed, the skin flaying. He examined his hand and decided not to go to a doctor. There was little physical ache now. The finger would probably just stay half-dead forever. He sliced himself twice shaving, standing pressing the wet, sweet-smelling towel against the cuts, feeling astonished at the persistence of his blood. The cuts from his father's bullet were almost healed. His suit arrived in the hands of a boy and he took it in through the door, towel around his waist, and handed his trail clothes out. The whole of this experience felt awkward, frightening, and something he never wanted to do without.

Before dressing he looked at himself naked in the full-length mirror, another first. It was novel and numbing, but also disturbing and disappointing, his assumption of his appearance dismissed and crushed, and he was forced to accept that he was excessively hairy but fascinating.

He turned away from the glass, dressed, and walked out to the balcony to stand in his shirtsleeves with his brandy in the sunset glow filling the valley with murky and soft redness, out of which the snowy palisade of mountains rose — the western side of the Jeffersons. Standing above the street he had the sense that he was powerful and competent. It was a quieter time, the town's bustle subsiding as people fled darkness. He watched for Ilya, afraid he would lose her, or that she would abandon him. Her absence was the only detraction from his sense of power.

From a restaurant across the way he could hear voices, the clatter of tableware, and he could smell the food. He was very hungry but also not, his stomach feeling flattened. When he imagined food, his hunger left. The image of himself eating alone in a restaurant was repugnant. He didn't want to leave his room. The thought that he might be recognized and arrested seemed to justify this, but didn't seem like the real reason. He lit a Bon Ton and stood at the railing, raking the street for her, stomach in a twist. For fifteen minutes he stood as twilight came on.

There she was, walking slowly down the boardwalk on the other side of the street, wearing a deep, green dress made of a fabric that glistened faintly, with white lace around the neck and wrists, and a deeply scooped bosom. Her hair was up and a small hat that looked silly to Bridger perched on it. She carried a new bag. He'd never seen her so gussied up, and excluding the hat, she was breathtaking. Bridger watched the men that passed her stagger and drop dead in her wake, saving him from having to shoot them. He wanted to call out to her.

She stopped and looked at the front of his hotel, lifted her eyes and saw him. She frowned. This was her second pass down the street, and this was the only hotel in the town of any refinement. She was filthy beneath the dress, having bought and changed into it at the modiste. Her stomach gnawed and she craved a drink, more so looking at the glass in Bridger's hand. She made her decision, put her hand up to Bridger in a 'stay' motion, crossed the street, and went into his hotel.

She checked in, noting the name 'Pilgrin' babbling in the book. She chose Mrs. Violet Plymouth as a name, and intimated to the clerk that her husband would be along to join her within the week. She requested, and got, a room with the balcony and bathwater brought to her.

After bathing she stood on the terrace outside Bridger's room and watched him through the window. The night had not become very cold, and the French doors to his room were held open by brass, spring-loaded pegs pushed to the decking. He sat at a circular table cleaning his weapons, the black steel stark against the blonde wood. A glass of brandy sat at his elbow, a decanter on a tray with other glasses beside it, as though he was expecting friends. A new, unopened bottle of whiskey stood next to a cigarette burning in an ashtray, and she noted his priorities. His face, shaven and clean, looked serious and soft, the brow furrowed, and a lock of brown hair in a long curl over it. Critically she assessed his clothes, deciding that he'd made a good choice, because of Mary most likely. She half-expected that he would have decided on some glaring, peacock horror of an outfit. But he needed a haircut. He looked raffish and handsome and competent.

Hello, Bridger, she said from the doorway. He started and his hand darted for the pistol, knocking it off the table where it clattered across the floor. Ilya laughed a little. She stepped through the door, her hands up.

It's me. He stopped, looking at her, crouched with his hand on the gun. Relief and embarrassment fought for control. Then he looked irritated and stood.

Jesus. Y' scared th' fuck outta me.

You need practice being surprised. Clearly. He snorted and shook his head, frowning.

Brandy? he said, sitting back down.

Yes, please. He poured her a glass from the tray and set it before her as she sat down across from him. Then she rose, crossed to the windows and closed the drapes all the way, and shut the doors, which had dense, lace curtains over the glass, stretched between rods at top and bottom.

He resumed cleaning his rifle with the kit he kept in his saddlebags, looking into the breech as he worked the lever, watching the parts move, looking for flaws, for rust, for something that looked broken, or worn and ready to break. And he enjoyed watching machining work, and couldn't imagine how it was done, but knew it was connected to mining and didn't like that. He was relieved to see her, and angry at her for humiliating him. She sat back down and lit one of his cigarettes.

You selected a nice hotel. Willem. Bridger nodded and smiled wryly at her.

I like your choice of name, she added.

Thanks. All I c'd think of. Who'r you?

I am Mrs. Plymouth. Of the New York Plymouths. Here to see to our mining interests when my husband arrives from New Orleans.

Nice t' meetcha.

Thank you so much.

Yer very welcome, madam.

That's enough.

Ain't it?

Bridger was upset that Ilya was married. It was worse than her being his sister. He arranged the weapons on the table and drank down the rest of his brandy, looking at her over the glass. He began feeding cartridges into them after looking at each.

Why so fussy about your bullets?

They ain't always good. Fuck up th' gun if they're bent, or nicked. Casing jams. Sometimes they git th' wrong caliber mixed in. Now'd be a bad time t' have th' guns bust.

So true.

Bridger kept himself from looking at her. She was fine and beautiful in the dress, but it removed her from him and he wished to be back in the cave with her.

Why'd y' come t' th' same hotel?

'Why did you come to the same hotel?'

Aright, I git it. Bridger wasn't in the mood to go through the humiliation of repeating himself for her. I thought we wuz gonna stay apart.

I wasn't going to let you have all the luxury. You seem to have instinctive upper class tendencies.

He shrugged. Jes stopped at th' first one I seen.

'I stopped at the first one I saw.'

That too.

Ilya saw that he was drunk but not out of control. She realized that this was a poor time for language lessons but it was hard to hold back, given the surroundings.

I decided it was worth the risk. I wasn't going to spend a night being chewed on by vermin after that cave.

Don' blame y'. You.

I should think not.

Glad yer here.

Thank you. And I thought that since we could die at any time, it would be best to enjoy life.

Anybody c'd die any time.

Yes. However, in our case it is more likely than in most. Most people do not have others actively wanting to kill them, though many more do than one might think...civilized. They all trust one another not to act on it. Sensibly, I suppose. Though now that I think of it, there is war, so...I suppose everyone always has someone who wants them dead. That's cheering to know. Somewhat makes our position less...disturbing. And yet less special, which is in and of itself disturbing...

Bridger followed her sentences like he was watching her disrobe. It was arousing, if he could get to the other side of the humiliation of not understanding. He shifted in his chair, easing his erection without betraying that he had one.

Ilya glanced at his erection. I think we can go unnoticed in a town this size, she said. At least, it's possible. I didn't see posters of me, or us, at the sheriff's office. Perhaps there hasn't been enough time to make one. Or they met that hotel woman and decided it wasn't worth it because of having to listen to her. Maybe I should have killed her. Or they saw who we killed and are feeling grateful not vengeful. I don't know. I don't care. We don't have to be seen together. And if we're killed or captured, that won't be worse than getting through those mountains. What could be?

Somethin's bound t' be worse, Bridger said. He had an image of them sitting and eating together, not worrying about being shot at or arrested, while raising forks and glasses to their mouths and being happy. He'd never eaten in a restaurant, and the thought of sitting together while other people brought them things made him crazy to do it.

Wanna eat? he said.

Ilya wanted to see other people, have them around her, have someone to feel contempt for, feel some sense of activity and life. She was exhausted in a way she'd never been before, and having other people want anything from her but an order for food was repellant. Both of them had come to the point where their hunger didn't feel like hunger quite, just an abstract need for food that didn't feel like appetite, and food itself seemed faintly disgusting. Their fatigue was buried beneath trembling anxiety and tension, as if they'd been stretched on a rack and kept awake but not torn apart. Thinking was a kind of aimless rummaging.

I think we have earned an evening out, Ilya said. We should try to have some fun. Chances of success are remote. If we have to kill some more people, well, nothing is easy.

Should we...go some'ere else? What if they see us t'gether here, the...hotel...man...I mean...

Clerk.

Clerk.

Ilya considered. Yes. It's true I am a married woman. It would soil my reputation to be seen in the company of a fledgling *roué* — it's a young, amorous...oh never mind. I don't know. I don't know what people's morals are out here, and I'm sure you don't either. I'm sure they're horribly restrictive. For me. I suppose we could pretend that we know each other and have met here coincidentally. That seems unbelievable however, especially so considering that word of us must be here, and seeing us together with that flimsy an explanation could easily destroy everything if one attentive person hears of it. If there is one attentive person in this town, which is not likely.

Bridger frowned. All he wanted was something to eat and to not worry. He took up his pistol and spun the cylinder.

Say something, Ilya said.

I think...it comes down t' two things...either we stay up here where it's safe, or we don'. An'...it ain't...isn't...sure, that it's safe up here.

It's safer.

Fuck, let's go out. He felt he should display some sense of daring to her, but was also getting bored and tired chewing the problem, and he was too drunk and depleted to follow it well.

Ilya looked at him. Alright. I want to go to the restaurant downstairs. It is the most refined. I don't want to go among the...rabble. We'll have to trust that we now differ enough from the two killers at the mining town to not be detected.

Aright. One thing, Bridger said. Where's yer horse?

In the livery. I saw yours there.

Aright. I bought a saddle for the black, so we ain't so gimpy.

Very good. We'll resupply tomorrow and leave early.

Bridger began to arm himself.

No guns, she said. This is not a situation we can shoot our way out of. And it's *gauche*.

He looked at her and snorted. Don' wanna be 'goshe.' He collected his guns and tucked them under the mattress.

No, we don't. Anyway it might be disarming to others not to be armed, she said, getting up and going towards the door. Less suspicious. Come to the dining room in ten minutes. I will tell the clerk that you and I are distant cousins who have met here by chance. Unless you would prefer to be my son. I'm indifferent.

I don' give a shit no more.

I was kidding about the son part. I'm not old enough for that.

She went to the clerk, who was looking more vibrant and happy in the excitement of evening.

Good evening, madam, he said.

Good evening. I have had the most serendipitous event just now.

'Serendipitous!' Really? The idea pleased him, as if it were part of the mandate of the hotel to supply serendipity and he was responsible.

Yes. As it happens you have a young man of my acquaintance, a cousin, staying at your hotel.

The clerk beamed. How very exciting, he said. Isn't it astonishing that as large and empty a place as the West is, things like this happen as often as they do?

It is exciting, yes. At any rate, his name is Willem Pilgrin.

Yes, of course, Mr. Pilgrin.

Just so. I have just met up with him in your corridor. What I would like is to supper with him in your dining room. Would you be able to give us a table?

Of course. This way.

And would you please direct Mr. Pilgrin to the table as well? He will be down shortly.

Of course.

Ilya was drinking claret when Bridger arrived with the clerk. They grasped the back of his chair to pull it out at the same time, but Bridger let go quickly and took a small step back.

Been in th' mines too long...sir, fergot my fuckin' manners...sorry...

Of course, sir. I understand.

Bridger sat. He had cigars sticking from his breast pocket. Looking as self-possessed as was possible for him, Bridger took a cigar and put it in his mouth.

No, Ilya said. Wait until after we've eaten. If I'm going to allow you to smoke that disgusting thing at all.

The room was choked with cigar smoke and the gray haze drifted in front of the lamps. Bridger was relieved that he didn't have to smoke it, his eyes were watering.

Ilya's craving for a good meal was dashed upon seeing the menu, though it was a printed menu, surprising her. Meat, potatoes, turnips, cabbage in various forms. No fresh fruit or vegetables. No oysters. No fish of any kind. She had been hoping for a tomato. It was Stewart food and she got angry, being reminded. She drank her claret in a long swallow, put her glass down and looked at Bridger. He looked puzzled for a moment.

Oh! he said, and poured her a new glass.

Thank you.

Welcome.

Ilya looked around the room. Some couples sat as she and Bridger did, the men looking petulant or annoyed to be sitting alone with their women, looking over at the saloon entrance when any burst of noise arose. This was a tableau she hated, the look of a woman as an accessory to the posturing of men. There was a table of loud men she had already decided to loathe beside their own. They smoked and talked of money, mines, equipment, drifts and veins and dredges and stocks and the tiny amount they had paid to a chump for a claim now worth an inestimable amount. They were bursting with their prowess. They reminded her of creatures born with their organs on the outside, but these somehow able to survive it and prosper in the world in which they found themselves.

She realized now the foolishness of her anticipation of an atmosphere of warmth and conviviality and civility in which to immerse herself for a short time, and realized she had been thinking of Jacques and Zoe without seeing herself doing it, since they were the only ones she had those feelings with. Now she was furious and hurt that what she got instead was a collection of overweight Henrys, but more bombastic and foolish and loathsome-looking, lower than Henry's cold, attractive competence.

Bridger was in awe. The men seemed terrifying and confident. The words on the menu were as foreign as the context in which they were bound. He drank hard to try to erode his sense of being a rock in a treasure chest. This experience was thrilling, but inaccessible and unbelievable. Most appalling and attractive for him were the enormous, gilt-framed mirrors that hung from the walls across from one another, reflecting the room on and on into itself. He stared at himself in the glass over Ilya's shoulder, measuring and assessing, and then shrinking away and out of sight, numbed by the amount of activity around him. The congestion made him think of when their ranch had had cattle, the howling chaos when they were rounded up and confined.

Smiling a little, Ilya said, Not that you're not looking very fine, but it's not polite to look at oneself in the mirror while at dinner. Not continuously. You should most often look at me. Don't emulate these men. Emulate me.

She ordered for both of them when she realized Bridger couldn't decipher the menu, then they just sat there, dazed, stretched, and feeling pummeled by the place.

...they killed three of my miners, laid up another three...one of the men at the next table said.

Ilya and Bridger heard and stared at one another.

...marshal still hasn't returned from investigating it. He got held up by an early snow over the Jeffersons. All we know is it was a low woman dressed like a man, and a man. The woman killed three buffalo hunters and a shopkeep...

'Man?' Bridger thought.

...a woman killer, it's a nice change. I approve of them acquiring equal rights. I've never seen a woman stretched...

Ilya stopped herself from turning to him and saying, 'Here's a stretched woman.' She looked at Bridger. We're notorious, she said, leaning towards him, voice low. But they have no descriptions, and no marshal. We're safe, but we should remain cautious.

Don' want me t' shoot nobody this time, then? Ain't pissed at nobody?

No.

Aright. Y' let me know anythin' changes.

I will do that. I'm glad you're mastering sarcasm, it makes you more interesting.

Their food arrived and Bridger clutched his utensils.

Stop, Ilya said. Mary didn't finish this part, I see. You don't have hooves. It will make everything better if you watch me before eating. Your table manners alone will get us shot. Everything you do is suspicious, when you're not shooting people or lighting fires or being my hero. All of which I quite like about you, so don't take offense. She laid her napkin in her lap and took up her fork and knife, sliced a small piece of meat from the slab and chewed it, mouth closed, looking at him, though she wished she could spit it out, since it was tough and tasteless and enraging. He studied her. She took up her glass, held it in her fingers like holding a flower, and took a sip. Bridger felt he should start shooting or leave. He took his napkin and began to tuck it into his collar as the men around him had.

Put it in your lap. When you do it as these men do, you're announcing that you intend to slobber over yourself, since you look like an infant. I would prefer if you just avoided doing that.

He moved the napkin. He pulled his glass away from the palm of his hand and drank, feeling like he would drop it. He moved the fork around in his fingers, studying the placement of hers.

Ilya's disappointment with the food was profound, and her stomach struggled to take anything in. It was better than goat meat, but not good enough to please her. There being a table cloth and true silverware was supposed to substitute for good cooking and flavor. This establishment had apparently decided that location was enough. She ground through the meal.

Tears flooded her eyes, she thought of Jacques and Zoe, and she longed for Mariani but they had none in the town. She'd asked, no one had heard of it.

The men beside them grew louder and louder as they drank, their voices blending, rising and falling, and she tried to block them out, block everything out. It should have been comic to watch Bridger struggle, but under the circumstances it was demeaning and sad. She felt she'd ruined the only restaurant meal he'd ever had by making him eat it properly. His obvious relish at eating something in a restaurant had become a laborious task because of her. He was diligent however, and by the end of the meal he was more or less keeping his face clear of grease, and the fork had stopped twisting in his hand like it wanted to escape. He cared enough for his new clothes to protect them.

Ilya tried to hold onto caution, but was angry that she had to be cautious, was expected to be by some sickening 'they,' some mob, some obscene world to which she couldn't explain that she was in the right and be believed. A wisp of hair escaped her coiffure and dangled over her brow. Her spine took on a forward curve and her glass crept down her fingers to her palm, and she longed for New York, where there were places she could go and be left to be as she chose to be. A malevolent and slurred cast came to her eyes. She made no attempt to converse with Bridger, who, though relieved by not talking, thought they should be.

The dessert — a foul, sneering attempt at a fruit tart with canned peaches, the whole dish swimming in a sickly sweet syrup mixed with butter burned to the point of blackening, and a crust that had to be chopped at — smothered the last of her tolerance. She ordered coffee and brandy, and plucked a cigar from Bridger's pocket.

Give me a light, please, she said. He looked at her a moment, took a box of matches from his breast pocket, poked one above the flame of the table lamp until it flared, and held it to the end of the cigar. The hot fumes in her mouth stoked her brain. She grinned at him, her countenance hard, the skin around her eyes drawn tight and seamed, her beauty now clawed.

Is that...lady...like? he said.

No. That should make you happy, but it doesn't does it?

I dunno. It might. The room had begun to hush around them. Bridger looked around. They were surrounded by expressions of disapproval. She continued to stare at Bridger. A faint voice inside her entreated her to regain her self-control.

Everyone's lookin' at us, he said. That ain't good.

Ignore them. I was tired of their incessant gibbering.

'Gibbering' sounds pretty bad.

Ignore them like you would a herd of cows that wasn't your own.

Fuck's that mean?

I have no notion, Ilya said. An urge to get up and go came over her but she felt like she might not be able to stand up, and wanted to vomit.

Me neither, Bridger said. He lit his own cigar, the coarse thickness of it odd and vile in his mouth, and strange the extended time it took to get it to burn. They smoked together, Ilya continuing to stare at him, and Bridger assembling his face into a mask of unconcern. The room around them began to waver with small tides of murmuring and noise began to rise. The clerk came to the doorway of the dining room, the lack of noise having drawn his attention. His face turned to dismay when he saw Ilya and Bridger.

The attention terrified Bridger. And the way Ilya stared at him was hard to stand. She seemed to want to tear his eyes from their sockets with her own.

Ilya felt that her self had split apart and she relished the feeling. She was waiting for a great fracture to consume her and everything around her.

Bridger's attention reduced itself to the pistol he didn't have. He wondered who he should shoot first, anyway. Himself, he thought. Get it over with. Whatever was good in life lasted so short a time, why bother?

What do you think we should do, Willem? Ilya said.

We should go.

Then you don't want to defend my rights as a free and equal human being in the land of liberty and equality?

Not right this minnit.

Ilya laughed with genuine mirth and appreciation, and the feeling of having lost all control and the anger lifted some, and fatigue flooded her. Excellent, she said. Sometimes you can be perfectly entertaining. It was beyond Bridger to laugh with her but he was glad she could.

Yes, you're right. We should retire. She looked around wearily. I'm stupid, she said. She dropped the cigar into her coffee cup with a sharp hiss. Foul things, no wonder these wretches suck on them. Well, it has been lovely, but I'm feeling quite faint. I believe I may swoon, like a lady. She held out her hand, palm up, and raised her pressed-together fingers up and down twice, looking at him with an eyebrow raised.

It took him a moment, but he then, with stoic grace that surprised her, pushed his chair back, dropped his cigar beside hers — his did not sizzle because hers had sucked up the dregs, so it stood in the cup smoking — and took the back of her chair. Ilya placed her folded napkin beside her cup and raised herself as Bridger pulled the chair away from her. She stood still for a moment, almost in fact fainting. People watched but did not fall silent.

Take my arm, she muttered.

They walked to the door and passed into the hotel lobby. The clerk had returned to his desk and was dealing with someone. As Bridger and Ilya weaved to the bottom of the stairs, he stared at them, his previous obsequiousness missing.

Good evening, Ilya managed to say, staring back.

9

Bridger had to close one eye to see his cards. Three aces. A ten. A deuce. He grasped some bills from the top of his pile and dropped them in the center of the table.

The man to his left contemplated a long time. He was prone to this and the others at the table hated it. But this contemplating man was also known to covet any slight for a long time, so he was countenanced. Finally this man turned his head, leaned over, spat an extended stream of tobacco juice into the cuspidor at his feet, and wiped his lips with the back of his hand. The slobber glistened on the skin around his mouth. He saw Bridger's bet.

The man across from Bridger saw as well. This man was sharply dressed in black down to his black shirt, and the glossy black stone that bound his string tie. His face had been pressed into a permanent sneer, which Bridger had woozily assumed was due to the man's malevolence, but which he had come to realize was due to some accident or ailment which had frozen half the man's face. The contrast of viciousness and helplessness in the man's expression invited his stare.

The man to Bridger's right also contemplated for a long time, though not as long as the first. This man had a habit of turning and looking into the eyes of whoever had bet, as if hoping to catch them revealing their hand. This was a disturbing move because one of his eyes was mottled brown while the other was gray. He saw the bet.

Bridger laid his ten and his deuce face down in front of him. Now the contemplating man, who was called Juice, fell again into deep thought, regarding his cards out of narrowed eyes. A flicker of irritation traveled across the face of the man dressed all in black, or tried to cross it — it began on the one living side then stopped as it reached the center. He was called Bit. He made a tiny gritting sound with the functioning side of his mouth. Juice looked at him, trying to detect the insult. This effort took a long time, during which Bit looked at his cards. Juice turned back to his cards and thought some more, laid one down. Bit immediately laid down two cards. Juice looked at Bit and decided that his suspicions were correct, and he was being slighted.

The third man, the dealer of this hand, called Geoff, laid down three cards. Geoff never grew irritated with Juice because he had great patience, which was often mistaken for incomprehension. Bridger also didn't grow impatient, because he was having a fine time flying above everything on his brandy, which had taken him past the fatigue from the last few days, turned it into part of his high. It was a state he loved, and which was still new to him, the sense of warmth and assurance overriding the clumsy drunkenness and slurred words, but mostly the sense of uncaring about whether he should or could speak at all. He had floated past his fear of the saloon and felt an intense warmth and happiness.

Geoff distributed the cards. Bridger looked at his from his cloud. His silence gave him an air of, if not mystery or danger, than at least oddity. He had picked up two nines. He tossed an unexamined amount again into the pot, forcing the others to count his bet. This practice was irritating them, but also bollixing them, because they couldn't tell whether Bridger's carelessness was a deliberate ploy or genuine uncaring. If the former it was a device to be deplored though reckoned with, if the latter it was demeaning to everyone to have a serious game treated frivolously. Bridger refilled his glass, and in a burst of camaraderie those of the others as well. The men viewed this and said nothing. Bridger was not insulted by this lack of gratitude and politeness. There was very little he cared about right now. It was the best night of his life thus far, that didn't have Ilya or Mary in it.

It seemed to take several minutes for Juice to raise his glass to his lips. It was like watching the progress of the sun across the sky, but without the warmth, brightness or wonder at the celestial mystery of it all. Bit was only barely containing his desire to shoot Juice, and gulped his liquor down on top of his rage to smother it. Juice raised. Bit quickly saw, further irritating him. Geoff darted his piercing look at Juice, but Juice had grown used to, and tired of, this maneuver, and would time his slurping discharge with it, forcing Geoff to look at something he otherwise tried to avoid seeing. Geoff, not prone to annoyance, was becoming indignant. Geoff folded.

Bridger had lost track of the game again. The four had been playing for two hours, but had not played many hands because of the aching slowness of the game. Bridger's attention would wander and he would look around the room with a sense of giddy well-being. He looked with indulgence at the other games going on around them, which were much more animated than his own, so the saloon was not steeped in tense quiet, but was active and loud and crowded. The noise came to Bridger from some muffled and far away place. A bent old man was jamming his rigid fingers down on the keys of a small piano, tickling the ivories with hammers. Men and women in various states of blowsy contentment hovered next to one another as though they were the sole source of the others' survival and happiness. A mixture of refined and bloated-looking men, and stringy ragged wastrels leaned against the bar and either shouted their opinion, or gazed around, or in the case of one wretch, sobbed. All of this took place in an atmosphere of, to Bridger, enormous warm conviviality and easy excitement, though at some moments of what might have been clarity, it also seemed squalid and fetid and dangerous. Whores who smelled too sweet would come to him, touch his face, look into his eyes, and say things he didn't hear, to which he would say nothing, but smile and look at them with incomprehension that they didn't know he only wanted Ilya to touch him, that if Ilya saw them touching him, he was sure she would shoot them down.

Bet, Bit said. Bridger turned his attention back to the game.

How much?

Twenty to you. Bridger fumbled twenty out of his pile and slurred, What th' hell, eh? and threw in another ten. At this raise Bit very nearly had another episode like the one that had paralyzed half his face. The prediction of how long it would take for the betting to come around to him again seemed too much to bear. As his good eye bulged his skull filled with blood, and his good face twitched madly. Juice spat and regarded his cards. Geoff, with no reason to look piercingly at anyone, sat looking dead-eyed at the table. Juice finally saw Bridger. Bit, distracted by what seemed like his exploding head, didn't notice that Juice had made his move and did nothing. Juice regarded this as suspicious and gave Bit a look. Eventually Bit came to, and saw Bridger as well.

Bridger laid his cards down in a diffident way, which looked to the others as if he were not interested in the game. This, and that Bridger's full-house trounced Juice's straight and Bit's three of a kind, and that Bridger had won throughout the game, and that Juice was now cleaned out and Bit was near broke, increased the tension. Bridger was unaware of the increase. When he realized he'd won again, which took some time, though not as long as it took Juice to make a bet, he pulled in the money, smiling but not gloating. The three men sat there watching him. Bridger collected the cards and prepared to deal the next hand, not noticing that Juice was broke and the atmosphere at the table had degenerated.

Trying to shuffle, Bridger fumbled the cards and they flopped onto the table.

Geoff said, I'm out, and got up. Bridger smiled at him and nodded. Thanks, Geoff.

Dropping the cards galvanized an alliance between Bit and Juice, as they became convinced now that Bridger was cheating. If Bridger had realized this he would have been astounded that anyone could think him capable of that kind of cunning, never mind the moral turpitude to cheat.

Ilya snapped awake in the wee hours, her head aching and her tongue parched, fearful and angry. It hadn't been sleep, it had been an anxious collapse. As she laid there, the muted sounds of the saloon coming from below, the pillow soft against her cheek, the events of the previous evening played out. She realized that they should leave. Right now.

Fuck, she said. I'm so stupid. She rolled from the bed, stomach clenched, and drank water straight from the white pitcher on the stand, splashing some on her face, shaking her head hard. She dressed in her trail outfit, now clean, tucking her hair away in her hat, covering her neck with a handkerchief, and her body with her coat. Her new dress she tucked at the bottom of her new bag. When she found Bridger's bed empty she stood a moment, stunned, then cursed and thought to leave him. She decided if he was with a whore she would. She trussed up his rifle with his range clothes and the unopened bottle of whiskey, noticing that wherever he was he had his pistol but not his coat, threw all of it over her shoulders and went out to the balcony. Light leaned into the dirt from the saloon beneath, and torches on tall poles burned at intervals down the street. There was no moon but the stars shone. She threw their bundles off the side of the balcony into the alley and clambered over the railing, hanging from the spindles, kicking free and dropping into the dust.

When she peeked through the windows Bridger was in the middle of his game. Bastard, she said. She went to the livery, woke up the tender, and got him to help her get the horses rigged, paying him heavily. When she returned with the geared-up horses and tied them up in the alley, Bridger was pulling in the money from the final hand. She saw the reaction of Bit and Juice. She saw Bridger's face, glowing and oblivious.

She considered leaving him, again. It was not so much that he would probably be killed or beaten that stayed her, it was more by whom he would be killed. She got the insane thought that it could only be she that killed him, the biting, possessive sense that he was hers to slay.

She waited a moment to see how things would play out. Maybe the men would do nothing. Maybe Bridger would come to and find a way out on his own. No, she thought, looking again at him. He was very gone. She clicked her nails on her pistol butt. Two burly men in sleeve garters came through the door to the boards outside with the sobbing wretch sagging between them. They pitched him into the street where he continued to sob, face buried in the crook of his elbow.

She could hear people thanking the two in a loud chorus as they came back inside. She waited a few moments, concealed herself as much as she could with her coat and hat, then stepped into the room and stood leaning against the wall to Bridger's side. Bridger's face had changed to an expression of stiff, wary comprehension. She was relieved. It would be very difficult if she had to wait for Bridger to be shot before he understood what was happening. She wanted to let him know she was present. It would make him braver if he knew he had to save face in front of her, or if he got the sense that he should protect her. His money remained on the table.

Ilya saw Bridger's lips move as he said something to the two men. Both shook their heads. The one in black, who Ilya saw seemed strangely half-frozen, said something out of the side of his mouth. The piano went into a clattering, discordant trill that indicated some sort of finale, then ended to no applause, and the room grew louder with voices in the abrupt absence of music. The other man at Bridger's table spat tobacco juice. She laid her hand over her pistol butt inside her coat.

Bridger had realized that he had a problem when Juice informed him that he thought Bridger was a cheat and was going to kill him, or at best Bridger was not going to leave the table with his winnings. For a moment Bridger had sat there stunned, his smile melting, until he looked wistful. His cloud of elation, this place of excitement, well-being, and peace to which he'd never been didn't disappear, but had removal and resignation layered into it. He believed Juice when he said he would kill him. In his current state that did not frighten him, but more seemed a kind of inevitable intrusion by an unwanted, nameless person he wished would leave him alone for once, but just wouldn't, wouldn't ever. The same cocksucker kept coming back, just dressed differently. He thought of Spunk Pilgrim and remembered with a small shot of mirth that he was Spunk at the moment. He looked into the eyes of both of these men. He had to squint to do it since their eyes narrowed so much. It was like everyone was forced to develop this squint because it was so damned hard to see into anyone's eyes. It must have been started by some innocent but nearsighted man long ago, and had now become this requisite quality.

Bridger gulped down the rest of the brandy in his glass and set it down. It seemed like the substance on which he depended to exist at all. It saddened him that this was his last glass for a while, or forever. His heart thudded but felt far away, as though he were feeling the pulse of another person, or the heart of a horse to whose chest he had pressed his ear. The feeling of being fed up with the stream of trouble that pestered him made changes in his fear. It was not that he was not afraid, it was that he was becoming more helpless, unable to effect at all the things that happened to him. He didn't think that things were this way for everyone. He was starting to feel special.

He wanted to explain to someone that he'd played poker only once before, barely knew how, and was learning as he played, that he didn't really care about the money. He thought to try that on the two men facing him, waiting for him to respond. No. He hated them now. He looked around the bar, wondering if there were a way out, if anyone was paying attention and might intervene, if they had ways of dealing with situations like his. He saw Ilya looking hard at him and felt a surge of warmth, like she'd just made him drunker and angrier. He smiled and raised his hand, waggling his fingers at her. He was not thinking of the men across from him at that moment. As he turned back to face them, they each looked to see who he was waving at. Bridger pulled his pistol, swung it up over the edge of the table and shot Juice in the chest. Ilya pulled her own pistol and shot Bit through the chest twice, walking at the table as if to push the slugs.

Ilya screamed, Run! The room erupted into scrambling chaos and flight as Bit and Juice slumped to the floor with strange propriety. Juice knocked over his cuspidor and his spittle joined with the blood in a gentle pool of black, white, and red. A bartender pulled a scattergun from beneath the bar and pointed it at the tangle of bodies. He fired one barrel as Ilya and Bridger went for the door. The blast was absorbed by a fleeing man who crossed in front of the muzzle. The bartender shifted at Ilya and Bridger as they crashed toward the door among panicked others, and fired the remaining barrel. People went down screeching. A piece of the delicate curve of Ilya's lower earlobe was flipped from her skull in a tiny shower of red that dressed her cheek and she shrieked. Bridger grunted as his back was struck. The bartender stood there, people moaning in the sting of powder and the smell of blood.

Ilya yanked Bridger after her into the alley and shoved him at his horse. He was growling hard. He saddled himself and roweled his horse behind her as she ran them out behind the hotel and down the dark lane behind it, then cut back into the main street and bolted for the edge of town.

It was almost dead black beyond town and their horses started to falter and skitter.

What the fuck?! she shrieked.

Goddamn it, stop! Bridger shouted. We're gonna break a fuckin' leg out here!

Ilya reined in and Bridger came up to her. The town was in an uproar behind them.

Well, what do we do then? she said, voice half shriek, half whisper, heart pounding, breath coming in ragged heaves.

Jes fuckin' give 'em rein, an' let 'em figger out where t' step, Bridger heaved out. They c'n see better'n we c'n, but they ain't gonna let y' jes fuckin' pound 'em out faster'n they c'n see th' damn ground.

Alright, Ilya said, alright. Let's go.

They stayed side by side and the horses found a cantering pace, and they kept it for a half hour. They could hear no pursuit.

Oh, this is so slow, Ilya said.

They ain't gonna be able t' go no faster 'n us, Bridger said. An'...fuckin'...ain't nobody in that damn bar gonna wanna come poundin' out after us less they wanna die real bad. They gotta git some law, an' they gotta mount up, an' gear up. Fuck, if th' marshal ain't there, who's gonna come after us? Jes keep on steady. He tried to clear his head, shaking it and sucking in deep breaths. Hell, y' got any recollect a which way outta town we took? Way we come in or th' opposite?

Ilya thought. Opposite.

Bridger grappled with the brandy, trying to remember what the terrain that he had been able to see from the balcony was like. Fuck time is it? he said.

Four, about.

Hold on, Bridger said, and reined in. Bein' on the road's shit. These horses is beat, an' they c'n jes run us down. An' we's bound to come across somebody they c'n ask if they seen us, come light. He strained his eyes looking into the dark. The starlight was enough to make out a little. Fuckit. Let's go this way...it's 'bout west. Jes give 'em head...don' direct 'em, jes...urge 'em...let 'em pick a way.

They pushed the horses up off the road and into the sage and grass, and let them choose a pace. The horses settled into a fast walk, and they sat being carried through the dark. The ground stayed low and rolling. Bridger's back burned, and Ilya's ear leaked an astounding amount of blood, the kerchief she had pressed against her ear was saturated. They rode in silence for a time and came to the bank of the Jefferson River. There was a seam of light growing between the profile of the Jefferson Range and the sky behind them.

Fuckin' hell, Bridger said. Gotta stop. Can't cross in th' dark.

They swung down and stood in the cold, and the sound of the burbling water.

Shit! Ilya screamed. Shit, shit, shiiiit!!

Bridger went to his knees and bent over, his back on fire.

Why the fuck were you playing poker!?

Bridger drew in a breath. Why th' fuck wuz y' smokin' a cigar!?

Because I wanted to smoke a cigar!

Well, I wanted t' play poker!

Smoking a cigar didn't result in killing people!

Then why'd y' fuckin' git th' horses ready?

I don't know. I panicked. Ilya held her forehead in her hands a moment. Why is this happening? she said. She got a sharp urge to shoot herself.

Ohhh, *fuck*, she said, hopelessness coming over her with the light.

Bridger stayed on his knees, forehead pressed into the ground, hands clenching the grass.

What's wrong with you? Ilya said.

Got shot in th' back.

Ilya stood a moment. Then why aren't you dead?

Dunno.

Well...what should I do?

How y' feel 'bout killin' me?

Torn.

Figgered.

So...it hurts...obviously...

Yep.

She sighed. Her ear was starting to clot up. She shut her eyes and marshaled herself. It will be light in a few minutes, she said. Then I can look at it.

Obliged.

Think nothing of it.

Aright.

She walked back a ways and listened for pursuit but there was nothing. Dawn suffused the air with the distant cousin of the blue of the river, and the birds began to harass them with their cries. Yellow came into the seam to the east, orange behind it.

She returned to where Bridger still hunched. He was wearing his new suit coat, white shirt, and his long underwear beneath it. There were six small holes punched through the suit coat.

Take your coat off, Ilya said. I can see well enough.

Bridger stood up, stripped out of his coat and dropped it on the ground.

There were small blood stains around the holes in his shirt. He took off the shirt and lowered the top of his underwear to his waistband.

Ilya stood looking at the small, angry-looking, bloody welts scattered across his hairy flesh. I don't understand, she said.

Whut?

How can this be lead? I don't think...

Don' reckon it would be or I'd be more fucked than this. Burns.

This is going to hurt, she said, and took her knife point and fingertips, and probed at one of the holes. Bridger growled. What is this? she said, holding a small, jagged, white pellet.

Lemme see. She held it out to him. He took it, looked at it, frowned and put it in his mouth. Ilya rolled her eyes at that.

Jesus, Bridger, she said. You don't have to impress me all the time.

Fuckin' salt, he said.

Salt?

Yep.

Why?

He shrugged. Hell if I know. Reckon it scares th' fuck outta people and hurts like hell, but it don' kill nobody. Guess it calms folks right th' fuck down.

I see. I do feel calm, it's true. Do you feel very lucky?

Life's good. Pick th' rest a them bits out.

The sun crested, straight sunlight flooded them and they were standing in a world of glittering frost. Ilya picked the salt out and stood uncertainly. Will it get infected? she said.

Dunno. It's fuckin' salt.

Doesn't seem like it would. Seems like you would use salt to keep lead from getting infected.

Hell if I know. You the one knows docs. Slop some whiskey on it. If it hurts, must be good fer y'. We gotta git on. He bent at the waist, and Ilya slogged whiskey over his back and rubbed it around with her hand. There, she said. All better.

Bridger straightened and grimaced, dragged his underwear back up, and looked mournfully at his new shirt and jacket. Jes can't keep me in clothes, he said. He went to his horse, pulled off the bundle Ilya had made, untied it, shrugged into his range shirt and coat, freed up his rifle and put it in the scabbard. He hesitated. Fuckit, he said. Guess time fer lookin' good's over again. He sat and pulled his boots off, shucked his pants and replaced them with his jeans, put the new shirt into the bundle with the pants and jacket and overcoat, retied it, and strapped it behind the saddle of his horse. He plopped to his ass and pulled his boots back on.

Are you alright? Ilya said.

Yep. He looked at her. There was blood down her neck, soaked into the collar of her coat. Are you?

Oh yes. Perfect.

Lemme see that. He came up close to her and pulled her hand with the sopping kerchief in it away from the side of her head. There was a big nick in her earlobe, which still leaked blood. He took the kerchief from her hand, went to the river's edge, washed it out in the water, folded it, returned to her, put it back in her hand. Jes keep pressin' on it. Nothin' else t' do. It'll stop bleedin' directly.

They stood on the river bank looking west.

What range is that? Ilya said.

Bridger shrugged. Fucked if I know. Don' matter, it's where we're goin'.

Mountains again.

Yep.

He fetched the canteen and filled it in the river, came back and handed it to Ilya. Drink a fuck of a lot of it an' refill. We git up in it, ain't no sayin' how much we'll find this time a year. Least the river's shallow.

She stood there drinking, looking at him, then gave him the canteen and he drank. Her head throbbed and she longed for Mariani, the sense of health at being without it gone. Bridger lowered the canteen, and blew. Fuck, he said. His drunk was wearing off and fatigue and headache were sidling in, and his back felt like bees had settled on him and were going to sting him forever.

He picked up the whiskey and took a long pull.

Are you just going to stay drunk? she said.

Nope. But I sure as shit ain't gonna feel like this all damn day. He took another swallow and handed her the bottle. She tipped it up and measured in a dose.

Bridger rubbed his face, straightened himself, and said, Aright. Be a while 'fore they see where we went, but this fuckin' frost'll lay right in r trail. Let's git on.

They mounted and splashed across the river and out onto the plain beyond. Bridger pushed them up into a trot and held them there, measuring the distance to the next range. The day was another autumn bluebird. After three hours they were up against the range, and stopped.

They'll be dumb and careless the first day, I think, Ilya said. They'll be angry. They'll have fresh horses, like you said, and more of them, and they'll assume they can just run us down.

They got a point, Bridger said.

We should kill them now is what I'm saying. Or scare them.

Ain't gonna scare shit. Fuckin' happy t' kill any damn thing right now, though.

This is as good a place as any to do it.

No, it ain't. It's too low. We can't git close enough to 'em. And we'll be runnin' uphill from any of 'em that live. We gotta git up higher.

Mm. I was thinking of your prowess with the rifle.

I can't git that many of 'em before they git hid. It ain't gonna be three men. Gonna be a lotta men. 'Specially cuz we kilt that bunch before.

Strange how it seems to snowball.

Yep. Anyhow, it ain't practical t' stay here.

'Practical?' Your vocabulary is exploding in front of me.

He looked at her.

'Vocabulary', she said. How many words you know.

'Vocabulary.' Ain't that some shit. Let's git up high.

They mounted, and stared back down the valley. No one yet.

Ilya followed Bridger as he trotted straight towards where the aspens and the pines began to tangle with one another among the bushes and shrubs in their fall colors, their yellows and reds running down through the pines. He hesitated as they approached the crease where the piedmont met the valley floor, and drainages cutting up into the range were before them. The whiskey and water were working in his skull, Bridger could feel his judgment wavering, and the anxiety of making a bad choice rustled in his gut with the memory of being snowbound, and the thought of heading right back into the high country. He shook his head. That one, he said. He pointed at a tight, narrow cut going up toward the ridge.

How do you know if we can get out of this one?

I don'. How d' y' know we can't?

I don't. But I know we have only so many fingers and toes to lose, so we need a new tactic besides just running uphill. 'Tactic', a...

I git it. Ain't no other fuckin' tactic fer this. When a new problem comes, we c'n git a new tactic.

Alright, I agree with you.

Don' fret it. There's always a way over if y' ain't chickenshit 'bout it. Them other cuts 'r big and wide. I want 'em t' suffer and I want 'em t' bunch up.

We aren't chickenshit. We're very brave.

Ain't it th' truth. Bridger put a shushing finger over his lips, got down wobbling from his horse, and put his ear to the ground for a few seconds. Then he squatted, gazing down the valley. He picked up a clot of dirt, looked up into the trees, sniffed it, broke it up, and held the remaining dirt to his ear.

Ilya watched, brow furrowed.

Well?

There. He pointed below them at the men coming into view.

She smiled. You're good company when you're at the right stage of drunk. That's terrible news for me.

Did I have y' fer a tick?

Yes, Bridger, you had me for a tick.

He mounted, then sat and waited.

Well?

Wait a tick.

Where did you hear that word, 'tick?'

Las' night...gent at th' table kep' usin' it.

Another thing about talking, since you've decided to be ambitious about it.

Whut's 'at?

Some words shouldn't be used too often. If you keep saying 'tick', I'll kill you myself.

If I c'd write I'd put this shit down.

We'll get to that another day. If we have any left.

Aright, Bridger said, watching the riders. Six of 'em. All bunched up an' comin' hard. No extra horses. Dumb.

Only six. What does a girl have to do to get some respect? Oh well, it's something I've come to be able to count on, the arrogant stupidity of most men.

Wouln't git carried away with countin' on it.

No. That would be stupid. Arrogant even.

Yep. Let's git on. They seen us by now.

Why do you want them to see us?

Gonna know where we went anyway. Fuckin' blind man c'd track us this time a day, through this grass. Make 'em stupider mebbe, seein' us jes run.

You're a natural.

Bridger followed the dry creek choked with a savage tangle of dead trees and boulders for a short while, but then broke through the wall of brush beside it, and they scraped uphill through the rich, sweet smell of the dying leaves that reminded Ilya of Fleishmann's bakery — the yeasty, delicious sting of Viennese baking. She thought again that she wished she knew what all these plants were called, was surprised at the number of them, the different kinds, the strange spiky lushness, her image of the West having been of a barren place where only the most desperate and stubborn vegetation would grow, compared to the East, where any old seed at all could flourish in what seemed now a crass and reckless way. Western flora seemed strangely elitist, harsh and fragile, as opposed to the democratic and indomitable vegetation of the East. She wished for a time when they weren't pursued again, a time to be in this world instead of crashing through it. She remembered Jacques' admonition that she had to learn to like something, and silently reminded her that she'd been busy, and managed to master the overwhelming craving for her, for her body, for the feel of her eyes and approval on her. Bridger's back dipped and wove around branches as though he were dancing. I feel safe with him out here, she thought, then thought, Stop. Keep proper distance. He is, after all, a killer.

When they were up the hill some the brush thinned, and they picked through trees and across open stretches of dead and dying grass and the bony stalks of wildflowers, the horses struggling at sidehilling, they struggling to stay mounted.

Let's walk, Bridger said. We gonna bust their legs. We got time.

They climbed for eight hours, until an expanse of stony wasteland with lone pines and slashes of shaded snow was before them.

Where's the snow? Ilya said.

Bridger shrugged. Dint dump s' hard here. Musta melted. Ain't as high, mebbe. Gits more sun right onnit. Best learn weather out here's fuckin' crazy.

On the other side of the expanse was a band of cliffs, on top of the cliffs was a ridge with a peak like a balled fist jammed up out of it, and a second ridge to the north, curving down to intersect this one somewhere out of sight. Ilya felt tearing worry at the disorientation she felt at these elevations, the way the mountains looked simple and comprehensible from the valley floor, and when she got up in them it was as if someone had rearranged them on her.

Bridger shrugged off his own sense of disorientation by not thinking about anything but the immediate worry, and scanned the cliff band that arched around in front of them and merged with the ridges going down each side of them like arms.

That'll work. He pointed to where a thin stream of water tumbled over a point where a slope of scree reached high enough for them to scramble over the cliff onto the high shelf.

Won't they think that's where we'll ambush them?

Yep. That's jes' th' way over I'm sayin'. Now we know we ain't caught in this bowl and gotta go back. We'll take 'em right here. 'Fore they got time t' think that thought.

Can the horses get over that?

I'll git 'em over. Or I won't. Back ain't possible, noway.

Maybe we should just run. Get out of this...bowl, get over and go on.

Maybe. Ain't practical though.

So you pointed out. Though it's not practical to kill them, either. There will always be more.

But less is better. Gits us outta a fix right now. Choice between havin' somebody chasin' us or not.

Yes. If it works.

There's six. They'll likely still be bunched up cuz there ain't no other place to go right here.

What if they're not bunched up?

Then we's right fucked an' this'll likely take a while longer. Most they can do is spread out their line. Likely they'll be stupid, like we wuz sayin'.

So let's just run.

Then what?

Make that decision later.

Rather decide onna new problem later, solve this'n now.

Are you sure it's not that you've come to enjoy killing?

Nope, I ain't sure. You?

Mixed emotions.

Well, right at th' time you's doin' it they ain't no mixed emotions.

Yes. I know. I think that's what people like about it. And maybe it's what many people dislike about it. I mean right now I have mixed emotions. And later I will.

Guess there's only so much unmixed y' c'n ask fer.

We could discuss it until they come and ask them what they would prefer.

Could. Probly wouln't like whut they come up with.

Probably not.

They ain't in a forgivin' mood, I'm bettin'.

No. Taking revenge is popular.

I ain't too much in a forgivin' mood my own self.

Forgiving of what?

I dunno. Does it matter?

Well. Your friends might be interested to know. Out of...self-preservation. I perhaps wouldn't want to get to where I need you to forgive me for something. If forgiveness is something you struggle with, you see.

Bridger looked at her. Y' ain't got much t' worry 'bout. Anyways, what friends?

Ah, yes. Friends. You struggle with that. It's not as easy as some make it seem. Well, that could change. It's possible. Counting on it would be foolish. And of course, there's me...I'm fairly friend-like.

Yeah. Well. Now ain't th' time t' shoot this particular brand a shit.

True, we'll have plenty of shit for our shooting pleasure when the time is right. What shall it be, then? A bloodbath, or graceless futile flight?

Ain't flyin' nowheres now. They catch us tryin' t' make it 'cross that empty stretch we lose th' top spot. They can jes rain slugs on us. Talked ourselfs outta a choice.

It feels like it isn't our fault, now. We had to reason it out and ran out of time.

Don' reckon there's many gonna see it that way.

Ilya thought about what could happen to her up here if these pursuers caught them, about who they could be.

Well, she said. Fuck the many.

If yer there in them rocks an' we start shootin' when they git right here, how many c'n y' hit? Y' don' gotta kill em. Ain't gonna happen with that little wheel gun y' got, anyhow. Jes make it so they can't git away an' I'll kill 'em.

Oh. Three. Four. If I don't run out and try to save them like a woman.

Not sure what woman yer thinkin' of, but try 'n keep that feelin' reined in. Aright. That'll do. I c'n git the rest. I'm gonna be over there. They'll more'n likely be in a line one behind th' other, so they c'n git through 'tween this ledge and this slope. I'll take the front, shoot to the middle, you take th' back, same shit. Soon's the first rider clears this tree, I'm gonna shoot.

Have I said what an honor it is to be present as your talents show?

Bridger was right. The men crossed the ledge in single file, and as the lead rider passed the tree they were cut down. Two of the middle riders, unable to go forward, back, or up the hill to the side, went over the edge. Bridger executed any that weren't killed straight away. It took six seconds and they didn't shoot back.

Bridger and Ilya came and stood in the massacre quiet. The wind made its applause in the trees, and the sun sat in the bitter, blue sky. Bridger stood and pushed cartridges into his rifle. Ilya shot a hard, short stream of vomit, and wiped her mouth.

And I promised myself I wouldn't vomit, she said. So stupid. She looked down on the men. How could they be so stupid? I always know they are, but I'm always surprised.

Folks like t' start off figgerin' th' thing'll be easy. They gotta be showed it ain't. That's what Mary said.

Ilya crouched and put her arms across her knees, her head in them. She looked up. I don't want to be this, she muttered.

Bridger waited, not thinking for what, rifle dangling muzzle down, looking over the ledge into the gorge axed into the earth, checking back down their trail for more men he maybe hadn't seen. The horses nosed and ate what there was. The smell of blood infused fall.

I ain't mindin' it, he said. Before wadn't good either.

Ilya stood, clapped her hat on, pushing strands of hair into it, rubbed her face, drank a slug of whiskey and a lot of water. This feels like an excessive response to that problem, she said.

Still might be others comin', Bridger said. Might be why these come so hard. He rounded up the four horses that hadn't gone over the edge and strung a rope to make a train of them, lashed the rope to his pommel. He went to each dead man and took their cartridges, took two rifles, loading them all onto one horse. He took a rifle scabbard from one of the saddles and put it on his own so that two rifles were to hand for him. Ilya rifled through the saddlebags, found a bottle of whiskey, some salt meat, clothes.

We's equipped now, Bridger said.

Not the kind of shopping I had in mind, she said.

Better'n stealin' a dress off a clothesline.

More manly for you.

Yep. Not so scary.

They stood a moment in the buzz of flies and the dry heat mixed with chill air.

Wanna say somethin'? Bridger said. God shit?

There's no God.

That's what Pap said.

He was smarter than you've portrayed him.

I jes don' give a shit either way. Well, Bridger said, looking at the men on the ground and trying to think of something appropriate to say for the moment. Guess they won' try 'at shit agin.

10

Robert was behind the group when he heard the shooting. He figured from the even and brief series of shots that the firing had been one-sided, and didn't think it was the fugitives who were on the sad side.

He got off his horse and sat down on a small outcropping. He looked at the sun, measured the distance to a tree, and sat there staring back down out of the notch of the drainage at the expanse of sage and grass stretching out toward the far range, watching the slate-colored cloud shadows on the golden land moving like aimless armies. When the sun hit the tree he went on.

He hadn't seen the saloon shooting. Had his room not been across the street he'd not have been awakened by the commotion. He'd dressed, come out, and gotten the story from the bartender he respected — the one who thought the one with the shotgun was deranged for shooting into a crowd. When it was clear that these were probably the two who'd shot up the dredge camp, he geared himself and joined the sheriff, because he'd been thinking about them.

Thing was, the sheriff who'd fronted the pack was young and desperate to prove himself, carried on as if there had never been a Custer. Robert had told him that they should split up and go steady and slow. That they could catch them easily over time, because he knew the terrain. That despite being a woman and a young man it wasn't smart to assume they were dumb or scared, seeing as how they'd shot their way out of that saloon and shot down the men at the dredger. That the old days were over and getting lost in the West wasn't as easy as it used to be — they'd turn up somewhere. That they should wait for the territorial marshal to return that day, since he had authority, and would have information from the dredger that might prove useful. That all the telegram from 'Ginny City had said was that it was a woman and a young man, that the woman had shot a storekeeper and three hunters, that the man had gunned down some miners and that they'd run like hell. That was it. That, in fact, it was just an assumption that these two were the same two from the dredger, though a good assumption, certainly. That they hadn't even waited to get any kind of thorough story of what had happened in the saloon.

But the boy had only said that it was he who was in charge and had intimated that Robert was a coward. When Robert had found the spot where the two had left the road and headed west, it had only made the boy pissier. So Robert had gone slowly and let them pull away. They weren't anything to him. Just anxious and ignorant boys, bored and overcome with their own imaginings, hankering for an earlier time when the West was better, wilder, more dangerous, when there was room for a man to be a man, all of that incredible insanity their brains stew in when they're young. Not that Robert hadn't once been similar but it wasn't the kind of company he liked to keep, now. Not then much, either. Nor did he like to be reminded of ways he once had been. When these men or boys or whatever foul mixture of both they were had made their idiotic comments about how they were going to shoot down the fugitives, reserving special animosity and clumsy salaciousness for the woman, Robert had had pangs of embarrassment as his own mean, women-hating silliness when young came back to him. Women-hating he was used to, didn't really notice, but it seemed to very much enrage these boys that this woman had shot men down and gotten away with it — it was her they seemed to really want to get and punish, it was only she they mentioned as they threatened the air to each other. Robert noticed that special animosity, thought it was interesting, and wondered why it was so. That one of the killers was a woman didn't make him angry, it made him curious, and he wanted to protect the woman from these men if he could. At least until it was clear who she was.

He reached the site of the shooting and looked at the downed men from his horse. He shook his head and frowned. It was like they'd shot up a crib of infants. Much as he disliked these boys, they were just boys. It didn't make him mad to see them dead, just melancholy, like he'd been reminded of some sad but long ago thing that had happened to him, but which he didn't let himself ponder anymore.

Hell, he said. It's hard to be upset about you boys gettin' dead. Wonder if that means I'm a piece of shit.

He sighed, squinted in the direction the killers must have gone since they hadn't shot him, fished the tin that had once held candies from his vest pocket, and took a cigarette from it. He rolled these himself each evening in preparation for the next day. He remembered watching this sheriff here groping around with his tobacco sack, tobacco blowing around, trying to do it one-handed whether he had two free or not, pulling the bag shut with his teeth, the whole thing a sad show by a desperate, small-feeling man. Robert had rarely seen someone so taken up with his appearance to others, so to the point of unreasonableness and impatience, so unwilling to go through the effort to learn and earn stature. He had just wanted it right now, all of it, everything that went through his skull in the form of a desire, why, he had to have it, he had a right to it. Robert had thought a man like that would be just a sight to behold, just some kind of visibly pained monster whose every act and word was some form of obvious craziness. But he hadn't been like that, he'd seemed like just a normal kid, a bit crazier than most, maybe. But then, after a while, Robert came to realize that there was never a thought of any kind that passed through the meat in his head that didn't have to do with getting what he wanted. That never a concern for another had passed through. He was pure, and a rare one because of it.

Robert pulled the smoke into his lungs and coughed. His chest was tight and ached. He only rolled six cigarettes for a day, trying to cut down some. But it was hard. He didn't much like the smoke anymore, but it was like deciding he should cut down pissing and shitting — just not really up to him. But it had been an awful long time since he'd taken a true, deep breath. He took it very slow and easy with his horses, not wanting to have to walk even a step.

He dismounted to look closer.

The killing had been neat and efficient, as it had sounded. The sheriff lay there, a hole in his forehead just off center. Robert thought that was interesting. Even at close range, to choose the smallest available target, though a good one to be sure of no shooting back, it took confidence. It took good shooting. It took ruthless steadiness, which often if not always depended on a feeling of righteousness in the cause. He wondered which of the two was responsible for it, and smiled a little when he felt the foolish hope in him that it would turn out to be the male.

He shut the sheriff's eyes. Fuckin' asshole, he said.

The next boy in the line had two holes in his chest, both fatal, and Robert could see that he'd been cut down before he'd had a chance to do much of anything. It was plain that the one doing the shooting was smart enough not to try to shoot this one in the head, since the chaos would have begun by then. He shut this one's eyes as well, remembering the sad fact that the biggest quality this one had had was his excessive regard for the sheriff.

Robert peered down at the two who'd gone over the edge — no way they could have survived the fall. A pang went through him looking at the horses contorted on the bloody rocks. That vision made him want to catch these two more.

The last two men of the posse were a little messier, but still executions. Or abortions. None of them had suffered long depending on how you measured such a thing, though the ones that went over the edge didn't have a good time.

He walked around until he found where the one who'd killed the sheriff had been hidden, and sat among the empty casings. The efficiency was troubling, since based on the little information he had these weren't experienced road men, or thieves whose motives were always clear. There were very few of those in any case, the ones that went at it like a job. There were many more lucky and crazy ones. The ones that just seemed to be being dragged around by some invisible force pulling them through the right moves to get away with things for a while. Or like the bunch that used to dominate his town, men that just went around jumping and robbing and killing anyone that came along in a brazen and ruthless way, and kept doing it as if no one would ever mind, and went on living in the community to boot. Come to find out it was because the sheriff was their leader that they were so brazen. They were just animals, those kind. Hanging them from the top log of their own shitty cabins had been a pleasure, though, being a lazy, verminous lot, the top log was often not far enough off the ground for them to strangle, and they'd have to dig a hole underneath their feet. That had been one serious drawback to cutting down the trees that the townspeople remarked on, being indignant about law-abiding citizens having to work that hard to kill a miscreant. Though, it being a mining town, there was no shortage of the proper tools and experienced hands for the digging, so that was lucky. Behind that experience, the council had passed an ordinance saying that some trees had to be left standing, now that they'd all been chopped down, and lacking inclination to build a proper gallows. It had been at that meeting that Robert's disgust with the people he was protecting had started to thrive in earnest.

He dreaded this pursuit. These two seemed to be able to act recklessly and win, and thoughtfully and win, and were ruthless about both. He didn't have to chase them, wasn't a real lawman anymore. He'd gotten the job behind his experience leading the vigilantes, but once he'd shot, hung, or driven off that crew, the job got more annoying and tedious than anything else. When this dumber-than-loose-stool kid came along and wanted the job, Robert said, Have it.

Robert looked down the slope at the body. Guess I coulda prolonged your life if I'd kept the job, he said. Then he thought of the time this kid had gotten a complaint about a dog biting somebody, and had gone out to the cabin to deal with it. Instead of trying to figure out what was going on, this kid went out, tied the dog to a tree in front of the cabin, and shot it while the children watched, the parents not at home at the time. Not only had the dog not bitten anybody — the complaint had come from a neighbor with a grudge — the dog didn't die. The kid had just crippled it. And with a rifle. The owner had to kill it himself when he came home. And why tie it to a tree to shoot it? Robert waited for the townsfolk to do something about this sort of idiocy, figured they'd come to him and ask him to take his job back, but they didn't do any more than bitch to one another about how stupid lawmen were generally. It was then that the sense he'd always had that to be a lawman was to be reviled no matter what you did, went crystalline. He'd figured the town and this kid were a nice fit for one another, and the desire to move on, get further away from people, at least people when they settled together like silt, had begun to burn hotter.

Probably not though, he said to the corpse. You was beyond my help. You was never long for this world with that snot on your shoulders. After he said that he felt mean, and admitted that, much as he disliked the sheriff, he had wanted to try to protect him. It wasn't personal, the dislike, and he'd thought the boy would eventually figure out that being a complete asshole didn't pay long term dividends. The protect-the-sheriff part of things hadn't gone well today, but he wasn't going to sacrifice himself to do it, so it was an easy failure to forgive himself for.

He watched the buzzards circle and lend grace to the scene, debating whether to go on. What with this shooting he had to think harder about why he was doing this, because these two just felt to him to be more dangerous than your average outlaw. He always worried some about getting killed but he always figured if he did, it would be luck on the part of the one who got him, not skill, not brains. This felt different. He admitted that he missed this kind of work, and that the silly odd-jobbing he'd been doing to eke out a living had become intolerable, because generally, he was bad at it. The thing got done, but it was painful, to do, and to watch. He could more or less accept the pain of doing it poorly, but having people know he was bad at it, that shamed him. He wasn't all that touchy about feeling shame, felt it was part of the deal of life, but being shamed in front of these townspeople, to have them, some of them, enjoy his shame, it was too much. And these townspeople were not the sort to give out pensions — it was un-American. They weren't all bad, in fact most were decent folks, but the good ones had a knack for letting the assholes have their way, and that was hard to stand.

He got to his feet and stretched, closing his eyes and letting the sun heat his face. He got up on his horse and sat in his dread. It was an unfamiliar feeling, and he hated it, and it pissed him off.

Hell, he said, looking at the notch which was the only possible way out of the bowl. I gotta meet you two.

He tugged the brim of his hat at the downed men and said, Hope God likes you better'n I did, and spurred his horse toward the ridge, leading his spare.

On the shelf he crouched in the last red sun of the day, panting. He stripped his coat off and opened his shirt to let the sweat dry, before the night cold came down with its painful suddenness that made one think of dying.

Struggling up through that notch had given him another piece of information about these two — they were good with horses, or one was anyway. Robert had just barely managed to get his two up and over, and he had a love affair going with them and they trusted him. Still, they'd snorted and backed and resisted, hating clambering over the scree, for which he didn't blame them what with hooves being bad equipment for the task, and he almost lost them on the last ten, steep yards through the narrow notch, with the merry trill of the coldest water in the world beside them. These two had managed to get six horses up and over, four of them strange ones who'd just had their riders shot from the saddle.

Before him, the shelf dropped off but not sharply. He could see the land beyond rise back up and continue off into the distance — more of this same plateau. He'd been up here before but not coming from this direction. Somewhere over there it dropped back down into the next tangle of valleys, but this shelf went on for a long way and was hard to get down from, especially with horses. There was no more 'up' to be had, except to go all the way up to the looming peaks — harsh, gray knobs mixed with crushed rock, with no vegetation, no cover.

He deeply wanted a fire but fear of these two made him hunker under his blankets and do without, gnawing meat and biscuit and thinking he was an asshole for doing this.

The deep chill in the hour before dawn got to him and he awoke with a gasping shudder. He was surprised he'd fallen deep asleep, he'd just gone under like he was lying in his own bed. Sadness clouted him, followed by the slithering knowledge of his waning potency. He'd always been able to sleep pretty much anywhere, but he'd also been able to stay awake when he wanted to and could sleep light if needed, which had been his intention. He'd just gone into heavy, dream-fraught unconsciousness, sitting wrapped in his blankets. He gave a hard fart like a curse, stood and lit a cigarette, stamped around getting warm in the chilly stillness and the growing light, and prepared to move on.

Ilya stood and dropped her blankets to the ground when dawn came. Whatever that was she'd been in, it wasn't sleep. The previous evening, they'd dropped down into this gully that got enough water coursing through it for a few tormented pines to make a copse, but it was dry now. It had been a long, wretched night, with no fire. She shivered and writhed inside her clothes and blew into her cupped hands. Her frostbit finger ached.

Don' blow on 'em, I toldja, Bridger said, when he noticed her. He was standing at the lip of the gully staring back the way they'd come. Do this. Throw 'em. 'Member?

Ilya began doing that. Yes, yes. I feel like I'm arguing with the cold. Is that what it's always like here in the West, you always feel like you're arguing with something that can't speak and is more powerful than you? You're always the stupid one?

Never heard that, but...sounds right.

Lovely.

She walked to her horse and hugged it, stealing its warmth. She watched Bridger peripherally. He looked tall, straight, warm, at ease in his element. It pained her to admit, and she knew it was stupid that it pained her, but he just didn't feel the cold like she did and she now realized that made her angry. She regretted having gotten so shitty last night, so bitter and removed, and told herself she must treat him more gently as Mary had wished, though at this point Mary's wishes seemed very inconsequential. But, this incessant trouble! This ridiculous running! This constant discomfort! This killing! Why hadn't she just run away from Herbert? He wouldn't have chased her and killed her! Why was she so stupid? As the memory of that night came to her, as it did daily, she kicked it aside and clamped her jaw against the sudden sadness and panic it brought, a practice at which she was becoming expert.

Bridger hadn't asked to be in her blankets last night, which she expected but didn't want, but she had almost asked him because she was cold. It was the blankets from the men they'd killed that had kept them apart, there were enough for her to keep warm. She got the urge to ask him why he hadn't asked, but didn't. She pushed her face into the horse and fought for control of her tears.

Bridger hadn't asked because he hadn't wanted to be told 'no,' and could feel that even if it was 'yes,' the meaning would be 'no,' because of Ilya's carriage and her demeanor. Privation made her grim beyond belief and made her beauty painful and forbidding, so there was a way in which not asking had not been difficult — he just hadn't wanted to be shot.

Do you have cigarettes left? she said. Be nice to him, she thought.

Bridger patted his pockets, came out with what was left of his Bon Tons, and walked down to her.

This cold camping is horrible, she said.

Yep. He lit two cigarettes with one swift movement before the match went out in the wind.

You do that well, she said, taking hers from him.

He looked at her eyes for a moment. It's my vocabulary.

She smiled in a sad, small way. Alright. You're articulate.

He looked.

You speak well.

He nodded. Thought y' wuz callin' me somethin' bad.

You'd know if I was. I was being metaphorical. Meaning...

He smiled his flat, thin line. I git it. I 'member that one. From th' cave. Metaphor's shit that means somethin' else.

She gazed at him a moment, surprised. She put her hand on his cheek, Yes, that's right, she said. Mostly. I didn't think you would remember. I didn't think you really cared about all that.

Who says I do? Seems t' me shit jes means what it fuckin' means. You cuttin' my finger off don' mean yer my friend, fer fuck's sake. You bein' my friend means yer my friend. In this fuckin' story, anyhow.

She pulled her hand away and snorted a laugh. There is that, yes, she said. Then, what he'd said hit her more and she started to laugh harder, her warm, throaty, 'ha-ha-ha,' and he joined her with his high-pitched, shrieking trill.

She stopped laughing and stared at him in astonishment.

That's your laugh!? she said, and then mirth and hysteria fully overtook her and she bent over, laughing to the point where her own register rose to a shriek. When she started doing that, Bridger flushed and stopped laughing. When she looked at him again, expecting him to still be in it with her, and saw that he had turned away, looking grim, she reined herself in.

Bridger! Bridger, wait! She put herself in front of him and stopped him from walking away. He stared at her. Please...She was still having trouble controlling her laughter. I...please, there is no possible way you can think I was laughing at your expense. No possible way. It was just...funny. No metaphors, no tricks, just...funny. And I'm grateful to you, because I haven't laughed so hard in...maybe never. And look where we are! Look at how hard a place this is to laugh in! Look at our...situation! I mean...and here I thought you could only kill people and look unhappy, and here's this new, hidden talent! Please! Don't be hurt!

He stared at her for a moment and the grim hurt hung there in his face, then melted into a wry sadness, and the corner of his mouth lifted.

Aright, he said.

The good feeling he'd produced in her, and her desire for him to not be mad or sad, almost made her blurt, I love you. She caught it and swallowed it.

You cannot be ashamed of your laugh, she said.

'Cept fer I sound like a fuckin' girl.

Well yes, that's true. But...oh, so what. It won't stay that way. Probably. If you use it more it might deepen. And remember, if someone gives you a problem over your laugh, you can just kill them and that will be that. You can do that now.

A small, short shriek of laughter escaped from him. Fergot 'bout that, he said.

Thank God. I thought I would never amuse you. You're too hard.

She went to the saddlebags, pulled the bottle, took a hit, handed it to him, he took a hit, gave it back to her, and she replaced it.

So, are we alright? she said.

Yep.

What do we do now? Not to sound ungrateful, but if we could avoid another episode with the cave and the snow and the goat, I'd appreciate that.

Ain't no guarantee, but I doubt we'll git a dump like that agin 'fore we're down.

Alright then, Jedediah, which way?

Bridger shrugged and stepped away from the copse, standing out on the stone. He looked west over the green ranges below lapping over themselves, another high spine of white peaks behind them. The air was cold and wet, bruise-colored clouds had settled over them, and to the east, in pale white spots that looked like wounds, yellow sunlight glowed, and sometimes a sharp beam would shoot clean through and light up the ground.

Well, we gotta git down, Bridger said. Snow's comin' soon one way or th' other.

Ilya looked at the glowing white spots in the clouds. Aren't those an indication it might be clearing?

Nope. Sucker holes. Be shut back up inna minnit. Gonna be shit all day, I'm thinkin'.

Excellent. I'm a sucker now. Where are we?

Bridger shrugged. I dunno this country any better'n you. There'll be trails or roads down there somewhere, but where, and where they go, I dunno. Runnin' crazy inta th' woods is a bad way t' travel.

We should continue to assume we're being followed. We don't know for certain there weren't more of them than we killed. She rubbed her eyes. She looked back the way they had come.

Alright. There's only one thing to do, she said.

There's more 'n 'at.

There's only one smart thing to do.

Yeah?

Wait to see if we're being pursued.

Nope. Gittin' down is what we gotta do. Y' need t' learn when t' shoot an' when t' run. Now's time t' run. Shoot, then run. Not shoot, then stop an' talk 'bout it. We git down now, while we got th' chance. When we're down, and not sittin' up here fer th' snow t' bury us, and where there's water, we'll worry 'bout if there's anybody followin'.

Oh, fine. Is there a book you're supposed to read for this non-sense?

Got me. Bridger was silent for a moment. Seems like there's always a bunch a things y' could do. Never seems like y' have that choice when y' want it, though. So, it seems like ain't nothin' a choice.

No. It doesn't seem that way. But it is. It's what gives life its delightful piquancy.

'Piquancy' sounds goddamn fuckin' great.

Oh, it is.

Aright, fuckit. Let's jes keep runnin' down this damn edge 'til we find a place t' drop off it.

Alright.

All day they skirted the precipice. Short shots of rain mixed with snow came but didn't stay. The rock they traversed was an endless stretch of tiny spines sticking straight up, mixed with crazy piles of boulders, and clots of pines growing down the spines of small ridges that seemed like the offspring of the bigger ones on whose backs they rode. The edge curled in a huge sweep until they were heading almost directly back the way they had come, without offering a way down. Twice Bridger led them out off the stone and into the woods, but each time the land was so steep the horses couldn't manage it, and they had to return. Ilya was disoriented altogether, Bridger as well. The hooves on the stone were like angry bells.

Fuck, we're gonna cliff out, Bridger said, and stopped. He curled forward in his saddle, laid his forehead on the neck of his horse and stayed there. Ilya stared at him for a moment then looked away. She waited. The sun was breaking out of the black skein behind which it had been all day, and the ragged tear of cloud line on the western horizon was glowing like a cut. West was altogether in a different direction than she expected. A slate-colored hue came over the permanent snow in the north-facing valleys, and sat below the russet on the exposed flanks of stone which looked lit from within.

Are you alright? Ilya said. Bridger straightened up, took his hat off, rubbed his hair back and in the same motion brushed his eyes clear, looked away from her, put his hat back on, turned up the collar of his coat and shirt, adjusted his kerchief.

Yep. Sorry. I reckon that rock bridge back there was th' one t' take. If any. This here's shit.

God himself would get lost up here. We'll go back. It's alright.

'Cept now I took us right out inta where we gotta run a gauntlet t' git out. If they's comin' they can jes wait fer us.

Assuming they know the terrain. Don't worry. She dragged out the bottle, drank, gave it to him.

Let's return to that spine where those pines were, she said. We can get a fire up. I'm not cold camping again. We'll find a way. You've done enough. If they come we'll let them kill us. I see no reason to cling to this earth too hard. Bridger nodded and looked at her.

Aright.

Robert wasn't able to catch sight of them throughout the day. The shelf rolled and dipped and turned, with ridges and spines and the juts of peaks blocking his vision. He continued winding around, not having to track, there being only one way to go. He came to a spot, a sheer face rearing up on his left, and the shelf he was on winding off around that face, and to his right, two gorges coming together to make a bridge. On the other side of the bridge was another shelf dipping out of sight around the bottom of a ridge cutting straight into the sky.

Six horses left enough scars on the stone for him to see that they'd done what many in this spot did—they took the route the land itself seemed to pull them in, that seemed to be heading downward faster. There were no real trails up this high, and there was no obvious way to tell which was the right way. They were caught in there.

If he stayed here and waited, it was another night in the dark with hungry horses. If he went in there he could walk into an ambush, something at which these two had demonstrated a certain expertise. He got off his horse and laid down flat on a stone, pressing his back against it, pushing his aching spine straight, and looked up at the deep dark of the clouds above him. He listened to his horses breath, snort, agitate. Between the two parties, they had a herd of them up here where there wasn't much to eat or drink. He closed his eyes and smoked, arms clenched across his chest.

Aright babies, he said, onward. He twisted to the side and got to his feet. He took his horses' heads in his arms and pulled their warmth into his chest for a moment, then took out his canteen and watered them each in turn out of his palm.

Tell you what, he said. You'll have graze by tomorrow, I promise. I ain't in no mood to let this foolishness go on longer than that. If I'm dead you'll make better decisions than I ever did.

Robert watched the fire lick at the night and the shape of the one person standing beside it. The shotgun blast of stars shone out of bitter black. The air was sharp.

Goddamnit, he breathed. Couldn't just be sittin' there drunk like normal criminals. Then he cursed himself for having had the hope. He was getting younger. He started out having foolish hope for the unlikely to happen, grew wiser, and now it was as if the muscle he was losing from his body was becoming foolishness in his mind.

Maybe I could just stay out here 'til Judgment Day and God can fill me in, he muttered. He rubbed his eyes. He was hungry and exhausted. He considered shooting down the one he could see and seeing what came of that, though shooting in the dark was an amateur move. And of course, then the other one would know where he was, while he didn't know where the other one was. And maybe this here was the woman. He didn't much like the idea of shooting the woman, not many things felt as wrong as that did. In fact, he didn't want to kill them at all, he wanted to capture them. He wanted to see them.

The person turned and walked out of the firelight into the trees.

What the hell is this, now? Robert muttered. He waited. After a long time the person had not returned to the fire. They weren't pissing or getting wood. He felt like just throwing his guns down and walking out just so he could explain to them that they weren't playing fair. Maybe he'd get a hot meal before they shot him.

Ilya found a spot, pulled her collar up over her neck and hunched into her coat. She rested the rifle in front of her and glowered at the flames. She'd wanted to stay by the fire and chance it, but Bridger had insisted on getting warm then waiting in the dark, and not staying together. She sat and waited.

Robert was torn between caution, and the need to do something. A long time passed, and he became incredulous that no one moved. He was very angry with these two. He was also just bored. Not only because it was boring to sit for hours in the dark. But because he'd done it before, too much, and it began to seem like an asinine way to spend a life. He was reminded of being a kid and playing this sort of game with his brothers. He hadn't known at the time that the kids' game was going to go on all his life. If he'd known he would have thought about it harder at the time. But hell, it had seemed fun, then. This was just dull, and the threat of getting shot didn't seem to make it more exciting. Maybe duller. He always won those kids' games, and adult ones for that matter, because he'd just wait for the adversary to lose patience and walk out in front of his guns in some form or another, and they always would. Could be that's why his brothers were dead now. They just never learned to wait.

The fire was dying. Robert wanted to pull out, but mostly he did what he set out to do, and he didn't want to change that. He tried to think straight and quick but his mind kept trying to get away from the circumstance, like a bird banging against a window.

Ilya had been listening to a faint sound for a long time before she noticed its strangeness. It was low, and mixed with the rustle of brush and pine boughs. The wind, when it rose above the constant sighing that was beginning to annoy her with its mournfulness, would take it away altogether, then when it died down far enough, and came from the right direction, she could hear it again. It was steady and low and bestial. A bear or something. She considered that. She'd never seen a live bear. Ironic, to manage to avoid death at the hands of the purportedly intelligent apes, to be devoured by a bear as she sat in the dark waiting for someone she didn't believe was there.

She strained to hear. When the wind softened and shifted to come from the left and stayed that way for a while, the sound was clearer. A realization grew in her mind and a memory of her father slid in with it, and for a while she just couldn't believe it, but she knew.

Robert awoke when his rifle was wrenched from his fingers and a pistol muzzle was pressed against his temple.

Good evening, Ilya said. Robert laid there staring into blackness.

Shit, he said.

Bridger saw the two shapes come out into the open.

One of them built the fire back up and he saw it was Ilya, and the other was kneeling with his hands on his head.

Come in, Bridger.

11

No, Robert said. I'm alone.

Ilya looked at him across the flames, Bridger beside her.

A little insulting, just one, she said. And one that falls asleep at the penultimate moment. Skillful of you to get so close, so congratulations on that. Proved to be your undoing however, which I quite enjoy. Irony is so pleasant when one is not the victim of it. I feel like we've worked hard and showed true potential, and we get a one man posse? That's what you call them, correct Bridger? 'Posses?'

Yep. You gittin' real wordy. A vocabulary, I mean...

Well, Robert said, staring at Ilya and letting the way she talked sink into him. I was part of that bunch y'all killed. Kinda.

No way t' be sure he's alone, Bridger said. Why wadn't y' with 'em when we shot 'em up? No sense jes one man hangin' back.

I didn't wanna get shot up. They seemed to cotton to the idea.

That's an excellent argument, Ilya said.

Still...Bridger said.

Well, actually, Ilya said, I believe him. If he's telling the truth that means that out of seven men, one was smart enough to be a little cautious, and confident enough not to go along with the rest. That still sounds like high odds, but plausible. Also, I am so fucking tired of this shit I don't care if there are ten more of them about to ride in and kill us all. I want to drink and I want something to eat, and I want to be warm and I want to sleep. If we're still here tomorrow, we'll make some decisions then. Dante never lived in the damn Rocky Mountains, clearly. Jesus, just the banality of the name — 'Rocky Mountains,' that's the best they could do? That alone is worse than death. Anyway, if there were any more out there we'd be dead by now. We already made our mistakes and we're still here. There's no certainty. We should be adults and stop looking for it. Especially up here.

Hell yeah, Bridger said. Let's git hammered. He pulled his pistol and pointed it at Robert, who flinched hard then went still, looking down in front of him.

Wait, Ilya said. You're going to just kill him?

What else?

Hm. Like many geniuses you have a certain...narrowness to you. Let's think it through.

Aw hell...been a lotta thinkin' aready t'day...still seems t' come down t' who shoots first. It ain't pract...

'Practical,' I know. Remember what I said about overusing words?

Still true...

Well, be fair. Thinking it through got us to the point where we had a plan that we both understood and agreed on, and we absolved ourselves from guilt because we found we had no choice but to shoot them. The same applies here. Oh and we're alive, if that escaped your notice.

That ain't no fuckin' bonus right now...how we gonna rest if he's sittin' right there? And fer shit's sake, why we gotta talk about it agin if it's th' same damn talkin'?

Because it's not the same circumstance. He's right there. We've met. In fact, he's kneeling, which is particularly disturbing. Stop kneeling, it's irritating me. I've discovered that irritating me can produce a profoundly violent reaction.

I can believe that, Robert said, and stood. Seems like you two like to overreact.

Bridger made a pissed-off hissing sound and lowered his pistol.

Don't pout, Bridger, Ilya said, getting angrier. She glared at Robert, and a burst of relief ran through her that someone to explain herself to had fallen asleep beside her camp for her.

I think we react in just the right way, she said. Those men at the dredge made a huge mistake, and it cost them. I made the only possible decision killing them. I used to just be very sarcastic when I got that irritated, but I've evolved. That ridiculous shopkeeper was talking down to me, among other things. Now, how would you feel if a feral, fuckless shopkeeper talked down to you for the amusement of men who chose to kill every single animal on which they depend for their livelihood?

Pretty puckered.

Yes, I believe so. And a man who intended to extend the insult and touch me, and much more than that, but I'm not going to think about it, I'm sure you can imagine where they were going. The thought itself would kill me. Oh! And I almost forgot, these are the descendents of the people who murdered Jews, my forebears. Burned them alive, ran them off, took everything they owned and said they caused the Black Plague, and that is only the very beginning. I don't like to hold a grudge, and I agree that Jews can be difficult and disturbing people whom I sometimes would like to burn alive myself, but using a plague as an excuse to murder them and steal from them, or to believe that they caused it? Sir, I submit that one has to be cautious with people like this.

Sounds...Robert groped.

Practical? Bridger said, and deadpanned her. She smiled small approval.

Among other things, she said. At any rate, I think of shooting the shopkeeper as a kind of...investigative surgery. I was trying to converse reasonably with the man, which requires brains, but he was a very poor interlocutor and I wanted to find out why. As I suspected, he had no brains. I'm sure I don't know what that was on the wall behind him when I shot it out.

Probably shit, Robert said. Well, none of that's surprisin'. Didn't figure them for the innocent type. Know what the joke about the folks in that gulch is?

Ilya shook her head.

How do you circumcise a boy from that town?

Ilya shrugged. Bridger thought, 'circumcise?'

You kick his sister in the head, Robert said.

Ilya smirked. Bridger looked stony and knowing.

Anyways, Robert said, you didn't hurt nobody's feelin's killin' them, but people 'round here are real touchy about people that act too independent. There was some very bad times with that kind of thing, and we just got to where it was gettin' pretty peaceful. There was an argument over whether we should try to find you when we heard about the gulch shootin', because no one actually gave a rat's ass about anybody you killed, but they decided justice was blind or some shit, and the marshal went out there. I was of a mind that bein' blind just means you have to smell the shitheads instead of seein' them, but they was dead set on doin' it right because we wouldn't get to be a state or somethin'. I would of just bought you a drink and let you go. Before you shot up our town, anyhow. That was different.

Well, let us buy you a drink now, then. You almost did catch us after all, that's something.

We can't trust 'im, Bridger said.

We don't have to. But he knows things we don't know. For example, do you know this country well?

Better'n most.

I like knowledge in a man. Intelligence is so rare one often has to settle for it. Stand guard out there if you want Bridger, but I'm putting down this penny dreadful we've been trapped in, just for the night. She threw wood on the fire, sat on her blankets, lit a cigarette and drank whiskey, staring into the flames.

Son, there ain't no one out there, Robert said. He looked Bridger in the eyes. You got my word. You'd be dead now if there was.

Don't call him 'son,' Ilya said. He overreacts. Things went poorly with his father.

I'm sorry. Meant nothin' by it.

Where's his guns? Bridger said.

I have them.

All of 'em? Y'sure?

Yes, I'm sure!

Aright, aright. Gimme yer boots an' set.

Obliged, Robert said, sat, and began pulling his boots off. Gettin' shot would have been a truly sad ending to a terrible evening. Fallin' dead asleep and snorin' while tryin' to capture two fugitives who killed a passel of people ain't proud time.

Not a great time for us either, Ilya said. We usually keep people very aroused. Maybe we're past our prime already.

We still got some days ahead, Bridger said. He took up the bottle and drank, then gave it to Robert. Anyways, probly yer best play. Hard t' shoot a man sleepin'.

Good thought. Reckon I'll try to remember it next people I try to sneak up on.

I almost wish you had not fallen asleep. It's more complicated to capture you than kill you, or be killed by you. I'm tired of complications.

You and me both, ma'am.

Don't call me 'ma'am.'

Alright. Sure are prickly about names. Might wanna have that looked at, I know a guy. 'What's in a name?' Shakespeare said.

That hack. Anyway, 'ma'am' isn't a name.

That's so, I stretched for it. But, now, I differ with you on Shakespeare...that was a man who could rustle words.

An over-rated writer who barely stood out in a field of one.

Was he an Injun 'r some shit? Bridger said. 'Shakes Spear?'

Robert laughed loud, Ilya snickered.

Hell, kills folks like nothin' and funny too...this boy's goin' places...

Ain't no boy.

Alright, alright, hell we keep this up I'm gonna get shot for being friendly. Maybe you could clear it up?

Bridger.

Alright, then. Robert.

Ilya.

Pleased to meetcha.

Don't mean we won't kill y' in th' mornin'.

Oh, no. No.

Makes it harder, however, Ilya said. He knows that.

I do, yessir...

Don't call me 'sir.'

Now, that there was a figure of speech.

I know. You westerners need to work on your sense of humor.

Not to sound ungrateful but, my horses are just standin' out there freezin' and starvin'. And there's food in my possibles. You was in a real rush leavin' town, and those youngsters didn't have but jerky and water, stupid like they was underestimating you. There's some salt pork and beans ain't spoiled yet in my sack. Few biscuits that'll toast alright. Couple tomatoes.

You have tomatoes?

I do. Know a woman can grow fruit from stone. Gotta glass house.

Bridger stood. Don' seem right. Hell's th' point a bein' an outlaw if y' gotta tend th' lawman's horses?

Don't call me 'lawman.'

12

Ilya rolled over and sat up. Bridger was sitting, pistol in his lap, watching Robert, listening to him snore.

Git any? he said. He looked stunned.

Not much. It's impressive, isn't it? I've never heard anything like that. It must have driven his wife mad, if he had one.

Do th' same t' us in a minnit. Worried he was gonna pull in bears with that shit.

My, Ilya said, head pounding, tongue huge and parched. I didn't quite predict that these mornings would be worse and more numerous out here than in New York. She looked around at another shocking and splendid Western morning, the horrible, redundant, red, dawn sun. I suppose it makes a certain kind of sense. All this beauty that has nothing to do with you, and cares nothing for you. No wonder people prefer cities where the streets run with shit. Maybe this is what it's like for a man to be around beautiful women, and that's why they're so...impossible. She drank water and sipped whiskey, shuddered, lit a cigarette. Did he have coffee in his bags?

Made some. Right there.

I love you. Bridger flinched. She grabbed the pot and a cup, poured coffee and a shot of whiskey in it, picked up a stone, stood up, and hit Robert with it. His roaring hitched, coughed, and stopped. He rolled over and blinked at the sky beginning to flood with yellow light, and the fading stars.

Hell.

Close to, Bridger said. Time t' git up. 'Nother day, 'nother chance t' kill somebody.

Don't be maudlin, Ilya said, then hesitated. Fuck, I don't know how to define it, just don't...overtalk. Christ, now I'm just making up words. Maybe I'm shooting people because I can't think of anything to say anymore.

You? Hell, that ain't it. Damn, never had s' many rules since...well, ain't never had s' many rules...

Lucky for me.

Mind? Robert said, sitting up and pointing at the pot.

Bridger shrugged. Funny time t' git selfish.

You never know with folks.

Often you do, Ilya said.

Robert poured coffee and whiskey, lit a cigarette, pawed his stringy, graying hair down against his scalp, ran his hand over his small, pointed white beard. I gotta...

Bridger motioned with the pistol and Robert went off a ways in his sock feet to pee, picking across the cold stone.

They sat around the embers and ate, finishing Robert's food.

Didn't pack for a party, he said.

When the whiskey had begun to bring her back up, Ilya went behind the trees and did a wretched toilet, dumping water over her head, and finger-brushing her hair out long, and tying it back in a loose tail. Her scalp hurt from having the hair stuffed into her hat and pinned down, and itched from the filth caught in it. She had a small mirror but didn't look. She fished the handkerchief out of her pants and washed it, tucked it back in. A lovely bit of timing, this new arrival, but there was no good time in her life right now.

She brushed off her clothes, walked back to the fire and strapped on her pistol belt, taking the gun out and checking the loads for no reason, then stood, gun in hand.

Bridger fussed with the horses. Robert squatted, poking the embers with a stick, feeling disheveled and old, weak.

You see the difficulty of the position we're in, Ilya said, looking down at Robert. He looked up at her, smiled with half his mouth, and looked back down.

I do at that, he said. It's a twisty one.

Kill 'im or leave 'im. Ain't twisty, Bridger said.

He's right. And it really pokes out when that happens, Ilya said.

That fuckin' mouth a yers is gonna git y' somewhere y' can't git outta one day.

It'll be worth it, if this is to be my life. Be calm, Bridger. That was meant to make you laugh. You're right a lot. It won't do to be too sensitive.

Gotta headache.

I know. Me too.

Think we all is feelin' south of good, Robert offered.

We should kill you. There's nothing to lose, and everything to gain. It's quite simple, really.

Well, my own fault. I made it easy on you.

And we appreciate that. We do.

Don't mention it. To nobody.

Of course not. If it comes to it we'll say...you were hit by lightning, will that do? How do you want to have died? You choose. Anything you want, this is your day. In any event, who would we tell? There are few people who seem to want to converse with us these days.

Reckon that'd be true. Ain't a whole lot to palaver about now.

To 'what' about?

'Palaver.' Talk.

Oh. I think I'll skip that one. There isn't a dearth of things to say. There's a dearth of people who will listen.

I come to understand the same thing myself. Seems to really bother folks, listening. Me now, I ain't got any pressin' business today, and I like to listen.

You're good, Ilya said. Charming. Hard to kill.

Well. I didn't get to be old by bein' a pissy fuck. Though, I seen that work for some.

She toyed with the gun. My, every day with the hard choices. I suppose I see why most people just do what they're told.

There's a sense to it. No offense to Bridger, but I'm thinkin' there's a possibility ain't bein' considered. A third way.

Which is?

I'll tag along with you. Been meanin' to move on, anyhow. And I ain't so spry now, but I also wasn't born in the woods to be scared by an owl, and that can be helpful.

'Born in the'...what? Never mind, I can feel you rotting my brain. You want me to believe you will switch sides of the law?

Well, now. Everybody knows 'law man' and 'good man' ain't the same, and I ain't neither. First thing I had to do when I got to that town was stretch the old sheriff, because he was the leader of the bunch robbin' and killin' folks, and wouldn't nobody brace him. What I'm about is sayin' that I believe you did what you had to do. You two just don't seem like the bad-seed kind. I'm sayin' at this point in my life, it comes down to who am I gonna spend whatever time I got left with, and ma'am, I mean Ilya, the notion of pissin' around with those self-important stumps back there in that town, and helpin' them spoil what used to be a good part of the world with their housewares, and cowshit, and rootin' around in the ground for bits of metal like they was hogs...it don't really appeal to me. I hate to be one of them kind that just bores the shit out of people with talkin' about how it used to be better, and mostly I don't say nothin' about it, but that don't mean I didn't prefer it, and that don't mean I gotta like this. And I ain't ready for retiracy. Anyways...it ain't a good idea to make an important decision after a night of drinkin'...whiskey head mars your judgment. And your aim.

That's a point. But I'm drunk again, now. I feel sharp enough. How are you, Bridger?

Bridger came over, took a drink, looked at Robert. I c'd hit 'im from here.

Hell, now...

I have a question for you, however, Ilya said.

Shoot, Robert said. Now, hold on...

Amusing. Who have you killed?

What do you mean 'who?'

Excuse me. Unnecessarily murky. My position, one of them, right or wrong, is that we didn't kill anyone we didn't have to.

That's a popular stance among killers. My years as a lawman taught me that. It ain't original. It's either 'they had it comin'', or 'I had no choice,' or 'I didn't do it.' Every once in a while there'd be a 'I did it an' I'd do it again.'

I'm saying that they had it coming, I did it and I'd do it again, and I had to, to save my own life. And any other justification your years have made you familiar with.

That's keepin' things under good cover.

I'm not looking back thinking that I'd rather any of those people were still alive.

Now, you ain't in a position to say when it comes to that posse you just shot down. You two held a proper killin' bee there.

For a man whose life isn't up to him anymore, you aren't being very submissive.

You'd like that better? I think you'd shoot me quicker.

Probably. Regarding the posse I am and am not in a position to say. I didn't have personal contact with any of those men, true. But I know that they had no intention of finding out why what happened happened. They just wanted revenge, and a few other things, all of them bad. I'm a woman, and what that means is that all men want something that's going to hurt me. They may not do anything about it, but it's right there. Always. And if they don't act on it, they get self-congratulatory about their self-restraint...so much so that one wishes they'd just rape me and leave, because it wouldn't take so long. Oh, and it can't be that bad a thing that men so stupid as to ride into an ambush like that aren't around anymore.

No fight from me there. Though, without stupid men, who's gonna dig the holes in the ground?

Stupid men without guns.

You got you a thing about stupid, I'm seein'.

I do, yes.

Well, I ain't stupid.

No, just sleepy. You'd be dead if stupid was your problem. Did you ever kill someone you wished you hadn't?

Robert got out of his squat, knees cracking. He stooped and picked up his hat, put it on, looked away, and pushed his fingers into his eyes. It took a moment for him to speak.

Now...that's gettin' into somethin'...

It's your life. It's unlikely to ever get more intimate than this. I am in this position because I killed a man who was trying to kill me. He wasn't a bad man, but he wasn't much of a man to say the least. And there was no recourse to justice, there was only law. I like the law. It's a fine invention with many admirable people administering it. I had to accept that I was not going to be one of those to whom justice would be forthcoming, though there would have been plenty of law. Maybe. I don't want there to be no laws. I want to sleep in a bed and I want men to leave me alone.

That ain't gonna happen. They gonna buzz around you.

Yes. So I kill them when they fly too close. I try to be judicious about it, but sometimes...

Bridger said, C'n we kick this here inta a trot? I ain't likin' this ledge, and I ain't likin' them clouds.

Well?

I kilt a couple maybe I didn't have to.

The story of the one that made you tear up just there. Tell me. Just the broad strokes, like Shakespeare, which is why he was a hack.

Shot the wrong kid. Didn't have a gun. Wasn't part of the boys I was after. It was dark.

There. A lovely haiku. Neither of us has done anything like that have we, Bridger? It's getting hard to know without a playbill. Maybe we should start a ledger or something.

Don' 'member.

Well, good on you, Robert said. I never started shootin' without someone else strikin' up the tune first, myself. That boy just walked into a fight wasn't his.

Is that the only important part? Who began it?

Ain't the only one. Signifyin' one, though.

What if it can't be said who started it?

Mostly it can.

No. There's not a clear beginning. We step into a river already running.

More like a rockslide already fallin'.

That's funny.

There's always somethin' in front of things, true. You was forced, you're sayin'?

Bridger sighed as he saw this was going to go on, lit a cigarette, drank, and sat.

No, I didn't say that. I was given a couple of options. None of which were good. I chose the one that put me in front of everybody else, because that's what they were doing to me. And I find it offensive that a superior person like myself should be brought down by cattle. I have no intention of dying in a stampede.

Sounds sensible. How come everyone don't just go killin' folks?

They're not me is the biggest reason. But, maybe they should.

Have to get mighty tall boots to wade the blood.

They are getting fashionable in New York, maybe that's why.

Wouldn't know. Well, I ain't gonna say nothin' against what you done.

Those two men in your town died because they were not gracious enough to lose a card game to a boy. I'm sorry, Bridger.

Huh?

Who cares about them? Ilya said.

Well now, just so we're clear on that...it's real unlikely Bit and Juice was gonna hurt Bridger. They call him Bit because he's always gettin' chewed on by smarter folks. They call the other Juice because tobacco juice runs outta him like pisswater. They do that kind of shit all the time.

Neither the two of 'em can play poker for damn because they drink too much and forget what they're doin', but are too proud and dumb to admit it. I've seen 'em just start playin' a different game altogether in the middle of a hand. Juice pulled his pistol on a man that give him his two cards in draw poker, said they was playin' stud. Bit's been known to just walk away from the table in the middle of a hand and never come back, then bust out the next day, 'Where's my money?' If Bridger had just got up, taken his win and walked away, they wouldn't have done nothin' but drink more and complain. Neither of 'em had the sense God give a hoof. And hell, Bit did have a way of thinkin' he was always under the outhouse instead of in it. Got worse after the ailment froze him up. Juice now, he was just teetered. No loss there, for sure. I ain't gonna be the one to say you're wrong, no way for you to know any of that. Just maybe sayin' usin' more um...wiles, to get through shit might be somethin' to consider...you know...in the future. Everybody actin' dangerous ain't.

Bridger thought of Spunk.

Why did you let them keep doing this?

Ain't my job to asswipe folks. I told 'em eventually somebody wasn't gonna be polite about it. And I did it when they was sober just to be sure. This ain't on me, and I don't give a shit. They didn't have no friends because you can't be friends with folks like that. Just seems there's a lot of people that gets knocked into the mud, and they don't every one of 'em get up and start shootin'. And I reckon that's better than if they did. Somebody gotta hold back.

You're right. It just doesn't matter that you are.

You ain't the first to notice me bein' right ain't a powerful thing.

Bit and Juice for one example.

Exactly.

Maybe in a hundred years or a thousand people will all hold back. But not now. Right now, I am not going to be the one to hold back. I can give compelling reasons and have, but in the end it's because I just don't want to. I hate this life, but I hated the other one, too. Though, being outside all the time, this is no good. I'll risk my life to be inside.

Alright.

And the posse? Ilya said. Weren't those your partners, friends, whatever you call them? Don't you want revenge for them?

Robert looked into her eyes steadily for a moment.

The truth, she said. I'll know if you lie to me, and you know which side I will err on if I'm not sure. I believe you about the dredge. I believe you about the poker game. But, you haven't dealt with the posse to my satisfaction. You dodged it. 'Mind'...is that the expression? 'Mind?'

Robert nodded.

Mind, I don't miss much.

Robert smiled. Snagged on that. He shrugged. I got mixed feelin's about it. 'Mind,' I didn't have no care for them boys, they was assholes, but most all boys is.

Bridger isn't, Ilya said. Bridger looked at her.

Well, excuse me, Ilya said, he can be. I wouldn't want him to be wholly without the capacity for it. And I'm not saying I knew those men in that posse, obviously, I had to guess. Did I guess correctly? You knew them.

Well...what exactly was your guess?

Aside from that they were presumably doing their job, and that they were bad at it? That they wanted revenge, not justice. And they wanted me, especially. That as soon as I took my fancy dress off, I became prey. That if they caught us up here in the mountains, away from others, it would go very poorly for me. Was I right?

Seem to recall they had some special meanness goin' for you.

Why?

Didn't say.

Why do you think?

Robert snorted a short laugh, shook his head, and looked at the ground. He'd never had a woman poke icepicks into his head. He'd been wondering the same thing.

Hell...I...

Ilya cocked her pistol and pointed it at his face. It's important, she said. Bridger watched them and smirked at Robert's expression.

Good luck, he said.

Ilya felt icy rage slink into her. So, you need help? she said. Alright. If those men had caught us, and tried to do what I think they wanted to do, what would you have done?

Robert looked her in the eyes and raised one hand. Give me a minnit. I thoughta what you're talkin' about, but I didn't take it to the point you're at, I was tryin' to catch you. I'll tell you straight, but get that black eye outta my face.

Ilya lowered the pistol.

Robert thought, trying to imagine. If...if...things had played out so I had a minnit to see who you was...I'd of come down on your side.

See...thing is...I'm guessin' they was just talk. When they seen who you was, I think they woulda gone limpy.

And if they hadn't?

I'd of killed 'em. Mostly outta mercy, I'm thinkin'. Because I don't think they woulda survived it, knowin' you now. But...

Yes?

I think you got somethin' in your eye. I don't know what it is. But...you ain't seein' as clear as you think you is. But that ain't no matter. I woulda come down on your side, if it come to that. I just...don't think it woulda. Seems like you're goin', 'I'm smart,' then forgettin' how bein' smart makes shootin' stupid. Makes *you* stupid.

Bridger stared at him, then looked at Ilya to see her response to being called stupid. Ilya looked at Robert. He was standing, looking at her, looking like his bones were sad. She got a stab of wishing that Herbert had been like this man.

I say we keep him, she said, and turned to Bridger. You?

Hell, if it'll stop you two from backin' and fillin' and shut th' fuck up, I'll take his guns and shoot us both dead for 'im.

Forgive him. He gets cranky when he hasn't killed anyone for too long.

That can rankle, Robert said. Anyway, you two get a guide outta the whole deal.

What if he guides us inta some shit? Bridger said

Oh hell, son, I'm not...sorry, sorry...

More important is the issue of the snoring.

Hell, I fergot 'bout that, Bridger said. We gotta kill 'im. They won' hafta track us with that shit goin' on at night.

You're really lowerin' the stakes on the provocation deal, now. You gonna start shootin' folks because they farted in their blankets? It's easy. If I'm on my back I'm quiet like a dead man. Just whack on me, or roll me or whatever. I'll stop.

Let's go! Bridger shouted.

13

We need water, Bridger said. Where's some?

Hell, I don't know.

Yer th' damn guide.

That don't mean I know every trickle in the country, I ain't John Colter. Especially in October. Ain't gonna be much new water 'til spring.

We got thirsty horses.

They'll drink, bye and bye.

Boys. Men. Whichever. Please get along.

Might be helpful for me to know just where the fuck you're goin', Robert said. Hard to guide seed puffs. Fuck, my head. Gimme that bottle...

I see it doesn't take you long to make yourself comfortable and be irritable.

You wanna guide or a scratchin' post?

I reserve the right to go back and forth.

Understood.

They kicked the fire apart, saddled. Bridger started to hide the camp.

Wouldn't bother, Robert said. Like I said, ain't nobody comin' behind. They're in front now. Matter of fact, you're surrounded, by the world. Wire. He made rapid motions with his forefinger, clicking noises with his mouth.

Bridger nodded, shrugged, took Robert's guns and strapped them to what was now the gun horse.

Lotta weight, Robert said.

Lotta people out there, Bridger said.

Do you throw away each gun after you use it on a fella or somethin', so you need a lot of them?

Nope. Mine was a carbine, now I got a rifle, too. This one got a scope on it, never seen one b'fore. Seems handy. This one's a Sharps.

In case we gotta kill a country with a rifle.

That may be what's happening, Ilya said. It's nice to have someone around to supply these unintentional homespun metaphors.

How d'ya know they're unintentional?

They sat on the edge of the shelf, morning sun warming their backs, frigid wind in their faces. Ilya clenched her hands over the pommel. Robert reached into his bag, fetched out leather gloves and whacked her in the arm with them. She looked at them, him, took them, pulled them on over her woolen ones, which didn't block wind well.

Thank you.

That time of year.

So it seems.

In front of them, dark green mountains rifled with snow were piled to the horizon.

More mountains, Ilya said.

Be a while before they stop, Robert said.

It's cold. She thought of what this scarifying wind was doing to her skin.

We're on the edge of passable here, with the weather comin' on. Could shit snow all over us any day. This what we're on is Death Canyon Shelf. That there's Hell's Canyon. Can't recommend it, invitin' as it sounds. Satan's Tooth right there. Devil's Stair'll get us down off of here, but what the fuck we do after that is anyone's guess.

Alright, alright, Ilya said. Just point out the river Styx and we'll cross and be done with it.

I was joshin', Robert said. They ain't called all that shit. Ain't got names, far as I know.

Ilya looked at Robert and smiled a little.

Guide's supposed to keep clients entertained, Robert said.

Ilya said to Bridger, See? Isn't this better than shooting him?

Bridger shrugged. He didn't want another dick around.

We need water, he said.

Aright, Robert said. We'll drop down into this drainage and there'll be a flow down there, somewhere. You woulda been fine if you'd taken the bridge. Never woulda met me then, though, that'd be sad. Just...where do y'all wanna go?

San Francisco.

Shit. On a horse? That'll take weeks. Can't be done in the winter anyhow, not off the road. I take it you don't wanna be on a road.

Well. A railroad is out of the question.

Why San Francisco?

Because it's a city. It's easier to be lost there. They care less on the coasts what happens in the middle. And it's a port, so if I, or we, want to leave the country altogether we can do that. Perhaps Europe. They seem to have stopped massacring each other for a while and decided to try to be civilized. Won't last. And we're on the wrong side of the world for that. And I want a decent meal, my god, how do people survive out here? Why would anyone stay?

Maybe you just haven't had a good cook. Me, I'm handy with fire.

It's the provisions. I want vegetables. I want garlic. I don't want to be a cowboy. If the Indians weren't dying of disease and sadness, they'd be laughing themselves to death that we want this place.

Some was doin' just that at first. Then they seen we was serious, and now they got them long faces you see in the pitures. Ain't no way you're gettin' to San Francisco overland in October. You might make it, but more 'n likely you'll die. 'Specially with the gear you got. Lotta guns don't do much for four feet of snow in a day — can't shoot clouds. You might head straight south and get out of the worst of the weather, down towards Salt Lake, but you'd have to find a way to keep from shootin' Mormons. That's hard on anybody, for you two it'd be outta the question. Then you'd have to get to the coast down where most of the people are, then go north to get to San Fran. That point you might as well head for Mexico and call it good. Up to you. Could go to Butte City...

What's Butte City?

From what I hear, people been tryin' to figure out what Butte City is for a while now, without a lot of success. It's a minin' town, for one thing.

No minin' towns, Bridger said.

You're just full of 'no.' I don' like 'em either, but Butte City's maybe some different than others. People who would know say there ain't no end to the metal in that hill.

Seems like something people would always say.

That's so. But this hill is a lot of copper, and that stuff is gettin' dear now. It's like one big rock made of copper, gold, and silver...and a bunch of other shit people ain't figured out how to use yet. Lots of it. People are streamin' there from everywhere...Cornish...Chinee...Irish...

Ugh, Irish, Ilya said.

I hear they ain't many Jews in Butte City, if that helps you.

That means when the metal runs out, it won't take so long to blame them, rob them, and burn them.

What's a fuckin' 'Irish?' Bridger said.

It's best you don't know unless you have to. I'll try and protect you, but it's inevitable you'll meet one. Don't worry, you'll know.

That's a life-changer, for sure. Point is, Butte City's gettin' big. Population's blowin' up, and it ain't like California where they're pannin' and scrabblin', and just hosin' down whole mountains. People are sinkin' sure-enough shafts, goin' deep, and what I hear, deeper they dig, more they find. You might be able to blend in there for a while. Railroad's comin' but it ain't there yet. There'll be better food, and a lot more people to get lost in. Shit, I don't know, I ain't never been a fugitive I just follow 'em. Do what you want. Just sayin' it's a pretty big stew to float in. Could resupply, anyhow.

Bridger, you've killed enough people now, you should have a say. Why no mining towns?

Well, y' seen that dredgin' operation. They cut down all th' trees. Dig up th' ground...turn everythin' inta shit...air's shit, ground's shit, water's shit...them boys...they git greedy an' then don' care 'bout nuthin' but that...Comstock's a fuckin' dirty shitpile now...same with 'Ginny City.

He's right. Minin' turns people into maggots...feed until they's none left, fly away fat. Around my town was pretty once, until folks found shiny stuff.

Hm. Men to maggots. Not much of a transformation. You weren't at the Comstock, Bridger.

No. Jes heard. Mary said.

Well. You two are making it sound like a place not to be missed. 'Butte'. How do you spell it? Not b-e-a-u-t. That would be far too ironic.

They spell it B-u-t-t-e.

Mm. French. How far is it?

Might get there in three days if we go full chisel. Probably more, comin' from where we are. And we should go at a good clip, with the weather. And no food to speak of. And nothin' much to shoot, because hunters cleaned out the corridor supplyin' the miners. And we gotta take that corridor, because we ain't bushwhackin' all the way there.

Bridger?

He shrugged. We don' like it there we c'n shoot some folks and pull foot fer th' next town. Seems like that's what happens anyhow.

Alright, Ilya said. Butte City it is. Good food, good whiskey, and a nice bath in a blighted landscape crawling with maggots. Lead on, Macduff.

Believe it's 'lay on.'

Well, I said he was a bad writer.

They rode steadily and switched out horses often. The weather held, became beautiful, the hard, pale sun taking off the edge of the night cold but not getting burning hot. Robert led them down into a short, steep canyon which took the rest of the day and all of the next to get through. There was no trail — it was thrashing through brush and ducking live branches like someone was swiping a broom at them, and dead ones like someone was jamming a skeletal finger at their eyes. But there was live water still running through the bottom, and the horses ate and drank. Robert told them that he was aiming for the valley to the west wide enough to follow the road and not be seen from it. It was treeless and open, but vast.

Robert was unarmed, which was strange for him. It made him see the sense of the word 'unarmed,' because it was very like having no limbs, being defenseless. The last time he had not had a gun to hand had been childhood. But in a sense, it was a relief for him, made him feel lighter, unburdened, and in this situation he felt strangely protected by the others, and calm about not being in charge. He liked only being responsible for getting them somewhere.

At first Robert was amazed, and instinctively disapproving, of the way Ilya and Bridger worked together. He couldn't say it was comfortable to have a woman run things, but couldn't say it was comfortable to feel that way. She was talented at it in a way men weren't, a way he couldn't name to himself. Most men who wanted to lead told themselves it was the perfect time to let the asshole inside run free. Ilya was annoying and sharp, but Robert acknowledged that he never thought 'What an asshole' about her, though 'What a cunt' came to mind often enough. And he couldn't help but be scornful towards Bridger that he accepted her as the leader, and her scorn when it came. Robert had never seen anything like this arrangement. Tough women were not rare, there was a thick vein of foul-mouthed, dumb sluts with scales for skin that ran through this country, which the melancholy preponderance of males worked until it was tapped, but a woman that directly ran men was rare. And he'd never encountered a woman whose refinement itself was her toughness — not that alone, but for sure, the fundamental substance of it. Robert figured that if he'd been younger, this woman would have been one to be cut down some, to be quarry, and he'd be the man to capture it. Now it seemed both that he'd be the one cut down, and that the effort itself, and the impulse, were unnecessary, futile, stupidly motivated. Getting old made things more acceptable just on account of the fatigue that set in. You only learned what was going on when you were too fagged out to give a shit. The strangeness of the arrangement wore off under the brutal riding, along with the capacity to care about anything but getting out of this canyon.

The privation and sense of being under attack ground the three of them down. Without the sense that they were being pursued, there was little tension except that which made one duller, the tension that came from just straining to put up with something awful, the numbness that came from the constant attention paid to staying in the saddle, avoiding branches, keeping the horses from breaking themselves, thinking for animals. Bridger's back burned and itched, and he longed for the simplicity of someone to shoot. Ilya longed for a bed, and her ear throbbed. Robert shut all of himself down but attention to what was ahead of him, he just moved forward, lapsing into the familiar state of patient, controlled attentiveness. As the tedium of spending all day in a battle with the terrain grew, the three went silent.

They ran out of whiskey and cigarettes halfway through the first day, collecting in a small clearing, each taking a final swallow. Robert twisted the last of his tobacco into three thin cigarettes. Robert got very grim behind this. He'd had enough for weeks until these two smoked him dry. They weren't much into conservation, understandably, probably.

The harshness of the traveling brought tears to Ilya's eyes and a constriction in her throat. Her arm still hurt, and her ear. Cramps rode her, the ache in her belly that whiskey could ease, and when the whiskey was gone, the pain was intense, made worse by the saddle. She wanted to shoot the other two down, reload, and keep shooting until she felt better. Robert recognized the problem and kept away from her. Bridger noticed an excess of bitchiness somewhere back in his head, but didn't think about it and just kept away, there being no other option. His feeling of wanting to go toward her, to help her, turned into something slightly bitter and rancid in the back of his head. He liked the reticence of the party and accepted Ilya's constant expression of barely-controlled rage and contempt as a fair price.

Midday of the third day they pushed out of the canyon and emerged onto a bluff over a vast plain, a thick, slow, gun-blue river winding back and forth through it. The beauty was so shocking and unexpected Ilya at first got angrier at being surprised, after bashing through the wretched ugliness of the brambly hell they'd traversed. The floor of this valley was flat and the color of pie dough. Trails and bunches of russet, gold, green and everything in between coursed through it like spatters of errant paint, and the clean blue over it made the scene seem to pop out of the earth like a cry of despair that one couldn't live forever only looking at this. Across the expanse, a wave of flowing, opulent bluffs rolled, fleshy and voluptuous, and made Ilya think of Rubens. She reined her horse hard, and trotted away from the men to whom she couldn't mention Rubens, or painters at all, dismounted, and laid in the grass on her side in the sun, facing away from them.

Robert and Bridger watched her. Robert pressed his finger to his lips and shook his head. They dismounted, picketed the horses and sat, taking their coats and shirts, boots and socks off, and laid in the sun, starving.

That afternoon the going was easier. They weren't fighting branches whipping at them or scrabbling around deadfalls and fields of ravaged stone. But it was slow, winding through the withered, bony branches of the sage seeming to reach out and tear and grasp at the horses' legs. The horses were streaked with welts and tears in their skin, some leaking blood that streaked their chests. Bridger believed he could feel in them a collective mood of 'I-ain't-doing-this-anymore' coming on.

The faces of the three were slashed as well, making them look as though in war paint. They pulled out of the valley and into a cut to camp that night. Fire, but no food, no whiskey, no cigarettes, no talking, except for Ilya saying, You said three days, and Robert saying, Maybe more, I also said. Bridger and Robert fussed with the horses, Ilya sat wrapped in blankets staring at the flames.

All the next day was the same, Robert in front leading them, Ilya next, Bridger behind, winding through sage and sun, the beauty of the place an impertinence, an insult.

Midday, Ilya said, Wait. She pointed at a broad-leafed plant close to the ground. What do you call that plant?

Robert glanced at her and smirked a little so she wouldn't see.

Injuns called it 'Don't-wipe-your-ass-with-this,' until the whites come. Now they call it 'Please-do-wipe-your-ass-with-this.' Can't recommend it. He fished deep in his saddlebags and threw her a clean kerchief.

Ilya took it and scraped off through the sage out of sight.

Robert sighed. We don't get that girl under somethin' solid soon, we ain't gonna make it, Bridger.

She's gnarled enough fer this.

No question of that. Question of her decidin' she just don't like us.

They turned into another cut at dusk to hide their fire from the road, which went up the other side of the valley. At night they could see a necklace of fires marking it.

They saw a fire in a grove of mature cottonwoods, a small flicker tucked far up where the cut narrowed to an impassable drainage.

Ilya was glaring at the fire as though it were responsible for something. Why are we running across people? she said. All this vastness, and still, people underfoot. We want to avoid them.

'Why?' Robert said. Well. One thing, this is the main road takes you to Butte, and I said folks is goin' that way. In a bigger way, people tend to be like water and all flow down where things are easier, and this valley's easiest. Worth considerin' that these people right here are doin' what we're doin' — stayin' away from the main current. Bit of a question what they're doin' this far off the road instead of in a caravansary, or just...where there's provisions to be had. And protection.

They'll have food.

Possible, Robert said. And tobacco, maybe. He breathed easier but was in an irritated clench of craving.

Let's go see, Bridger said, cutting off the talk before it could take hold. He'd enjoyed the last couple of days when things had been too horrible to be spoken about. He started his horse trotting towards the fire.

Don't reckon ridin' right on in is a good plan, Robert said.

We'll creep up on 'em, Bridger said over his shoulder. I jes don' wanna walk all th' way from here. They're fuckin'...a mile off right now.

They left their horses and walked towards the fire, crawling the last few yards to a point where they could see down into the small clearing beside a rivulet under the arching reach of cottonwood branches dropping golden leaves.

There were four horses hobbled around the camp. Right at the verge of the firelight a gutted deer hung, a stick wedged into the abdomen.

Beside the flames a dark, humped shape heaved in steady rhythm with low groans and growls mingled together from two throats.

Aw, hell now, Robert breathed. He was flushing slightly. Seems like a private party.

Bridger watched the shape moving and felt a prickling rush in his crotch. He wished to both leave and to see better.

Goddamnit, Ilya said, and put her head into her arms. I suppose this isn't the time to invite ourselves to dinner.

Might rile 'em some, Robert agreed. Though we sure enough got the drop on 'em right now. Be impolite though, to just be settin' there with a pistol sayin' 'howdy' when they surface.

I see you were properly raised, Ilya said. She noticed right then that her voice had taken on a constant vibrato of bitterness, that the sarcasm and incisiveness had toppled over into a seamless tone of contempt over which she had lost control, or the presence of mind to try to control. She told herself to ease up.

Yep, Robert said, letting the anger at the way she spoke to him pass through. I like to consider the other side.

Bridger's mouth was dry. The grunting became more urgent. He felt like he was along with the writhing shape as it became more violent, his insides tightening and seeming to move around out of his control.

Don't sound like it's gonna be long, Robert said, and rolled onto his back.

In any case, they won't be enthused about an intrusion. Not many welcome a post-coital visit.

Nope. They seem pretty satisfied with their own company.

Well, they'll be receiving guests whether they're happy about it or not. We'll give them time to compose themselves. But, I'm eating tonight.

The shape bounded about more violently, and the moans turned to desperate-sounding gasps and snorts, which profoundly affected Bridger, and pushed his pulse higher. The sudden keening that died down to a sigh and silence seemed to him like a slide down a mud bank into chill water. He felt drained, jacked up, and disappointed. Robert glanced at him. Bridger's rapt gaze and quick breathing amused him.

Don't shoot your own foot off, he said. Bridger flushed and glowered at the fire. Ilya gave Bridger a quick appraising look, frowned. Robert reminded himself that this wasn't a good person to fuck with much, being the fresh one in the mix.

What was presumably a man pulled himself out of the shape and stood up. He was indistinct from this distance, and when back-lit by the flames, his head seemed to have a wild array of spikes coming off it, like a crude drawing of a black, shining sun. He put his crotch in order and then bent to the fire, poked at it, threw in wood, and the flames went higher.

They waited a few minutes. The bedding from which the man had emerged stayed still. He sat by the flames.

Ilya almost said, 'Can you two do this?' Then she remembered Robert wasn't one of them. She nudged Bridger. Circle around. Stay out. Wait for me. He got up and walked off.

Don't leave 'em much time to loll in it, do you? Robert said.

Not when I'm hungry, Ilya replied. Anyway, this is the time when you feel bad when you should feel good, and don't know why, except maybe this person you just fucked was not a good choice. We're doing them a favor interrupting. Giving them something else to think about.

Robert smirked and shook his head a little at the lawless way she talked. He said, I remember that feelin' some.

Come with me but stay behind, away. If I hear you coming close, I'll just shoot you.

Givin' you space won't be hard.

She crept forward, then stood up and walked into the firelight, pistol at her side. Lucky these ain't the worried type with guards an' all, Robert thought.

Pardon me, she said. The man grunted, stood, and whirled around, his stick in his fist.

Easy, Ilya said.

Well, hello! A tall, spectral man came out of the darkness from the side and was upon her.

Jesus! she said, and tried to put her pistol on him but he was too close, and as she swung it, it hit his up-swinging arm and broke out of her hand. She started to pull away, but he put his arm around her shoulders and his pale face close to hers and said, Welcome to our camp! His foul breath washed over her face, and he waved his other arm in a long sweep at the clearing.

Fuck! she said, and yanked herself out of his grasp, stumbling over a root and going to her knees.

Oh. Hm, the man said, sadness in his voice, and turned away.

Bridger had raised his pistol to shoot the man, but didn't trust himself not to hit Ilya, and saw the man had no gun. Robert, entirely flatfooted, watched, and Bridger walked into the firelight.

Git away from her, he said. Ilya got to her feet and snatched her pistol from the ground, backing away and pointing it at the man.

What the hell? she said.

Robert started laughing.

The man came towards her again in a completely non-threatening way, a giant, pale face over hunched shoulders, a bashed in billycock on his skull, a long nose, and an errant eye coming out of the dark. Guess what I did last night? he said.

Bridger leveled his pistol.

Wait, Robert said.

Ilya stared.

I slept with my sister! the man said, nodded hard, and smiled. Hm! Yup! He stood still, looking at the fire, the tip of a forefinger in his mouth, gnawing at his nail.

Wet, white buttocks shone for a moment as the man on the ground threw off the hide beneath which he lay, got up, and stood there fixing his drawers. Ilya moved her pistol to this man as Bridger waved his between the others. The six of them stayed there for a long moment.

Hell, Robert said, and laughed. Never seen a couple bulls at it before.

Bridger was trying to grasp things. Goddamn, he said. His asshole was clenched very tight.

We aren't going to shoot you, Ilya said to no one in particular. I suppose...

Hard to think what to do with 'em, Robert said. Hard to think at all, right now. Momma didn't talk about this moment much...

The man at the fire was wrapped in a brown, matted, hairy tunic tied about his waist with a curled and torn length of hide. Grease and sweat-blackened leather breeches stuck from under it, disappearing into knee-high moccasins strapped on with criss-crossed leather. His head was a wild array of braided and tied ropes of gnarled hair, bits of once bright-colored cloth and threaded beads bobbing when he moved. His beard came down over his chest in three heavy prongs, thick and stiff enough looking to stab with. A long blade hung from his waist in a crude, handmade leather scabbard. His nose was a scarred lump with two dark nostrils — the tip of it was gone. He gave out a stream of grunts and singsonging whistles.

Pardon me? Ilya said. The man gave out a shorter version of his previous outburst. The other man emitted his own stream. This man was heavy, his torso a thick stump with four short muscular limbs coming from a shirt with a ruffled collar and no sleeves. His face was clean-shaven and hawkish, the hair dead black, and hanging straight down to his belt beside it like a curtain through which he peeked. He wore army breeches, the stripe down the side still visible. His boots were tall pipes of scarred leather. There was a long, curved sword thrust through his belt, the naked blade catching glints from the firelight.

Now that's some, Robert said. They keep their blades on. That's feelin' rushed. Must be a man-on-man thing.

You'll have to give up those swords, Ilya said. All we want is to eat. We don't intend to harm you. I think we're safe in thinking that these are not lawmen who are after us, Robert.

'Less things've changed a lot since I wore tin.

The two men talked to each other.

What are they saying? she asked Robert.

Ain't no language I ever heard. Some kinda Injun, I guess. But I normally recognize it, though I can't speak it or understand it. Somethin's real fucked up with these two. Three.

You're perceptive. Christ, Ilya said. She gestured at the sword of the first man with her pistol, trying to tell him to give it to her.

He stared at her.

Oh, not again, Ilya sighed. She cocked her pistol, pointed it at his face and held out her hand for the blade, motioning.

Give it to me.

The men stared at them.

Mm, mm, can we, is...is anyone else comin' over tonight? the spectral man said, coming close to Ilya, pushing his face toward her. Can we have a party? She moved away, putting her hand against his chest to ward him off. He was all bone.

Not to my knowledge, she said to him. No party tonight.

Oh, he said, sounding disappointed, and moved off.

What is this thing? she said.

A spudbrain, apparently. Be glad you ain't his sister, anyhow. Appears they been out here a spell, Robert said. A hell of a long spell. Guess we can figure why they ain't over on the road with folks. Be an ugly reception for 'em.

Not to dwell on it, but if he slept with his sister, where is she?

Wouldn't count on it bein' a recent event.

Are they white? Bridger asked.

Well, this tall one here's whiter than anything 'cept snow. Damned if I know 'bout the others. Use to be it was pretty clear who folks was out here. Now, hard to say for sure. Don't seem like it's important for 'em now, anyhow. Looks like they're mostly dirt. That's a Confederate sword the one's got, but that don't signify much.

Based on their private life, they're Greek, Ilya said.

Well, I don' wanna stand out here all night, Bridger said.

Robert held his fingers to his lips and chewed at the men, who were now standing beside one another. The spectral one moved into the dark, murmuring. Then, his voice came to them in a louder, conversational tone.

Who's he talking to? Ilya said. Bridger went out, came back a few moments later, shaking his head.

Got a mirror on a tree. He's talkin' to it.

Travelin' with you two beats all, Robert said. You gotta shine for findin' fun shit to do. What's he sayin'?

Dint wanna horn in on it.

Decent of you. Food? He motioned like eating to the men again.

The spiky man mimicked the move, nodded towards the deer.

Reckon everyone understands that, Robert said. They don't seem like the greedy kind.

Well, this consorting is nice but if they don't give up the swords, we can't be friends, Ilya said.

Don't look to me like they care to do that. But it don't look to be because they're wantin' to be difficult.

Then we have to shoot them.

Well now, why's that? They don't seem anxious to battle.

How could you possibly know that? Look at them.

There's such a thing as bein' too suspicious.

I know that, asshole. That's what I'm doing. Being too suspicious so we don't get hacked to pieces.

Alright, then. Jesus, you're a meat ax when you ain't eaten. Anyhow, you got guns. That's one up on blades where I'm from.

Fine. Fuck! I don't care. Her abdomen ached. Go get the horses, she said to Bridger. You start cooking, Robert. I'll watch them. If they want to join us they're welcome.

Accommodatin' of you.

When have I not wanted to get along with people?

Ilya tossed through their belongings for weapons. There was an old flintlock rifle with the hammer entirely missing and the barrel hacked off short, but no other guns. There were two small bows, and a bunch of tiny arrows with beaten metal tips.

Are these toys? Ilya said.

No. Those are what the Blackfeet, well, any of the Injuns up this way, use to kill shit with. Hard to get to, ain't it?

They wouldn't kill a sparrow.

Kill buffler with 'em. Took a shitload of 'em, but it worked.

The first rifle they saw must have made them feel quite...impotent.

Probably had a bunch of feelings.

Like dread.

That's what'd take me over.

Ilya made the men understand that all they wanted was something to eat by not trying to get anything else from them, sitting down, making gestures intended to mean they were harmless. They stood a long time in the same spots and watched the three of them move around. Eventually, they squatted. The spectral one stayed off in the dark, talking to himself.

Robert crossed to the deer and looked at it. Well, one or both of 'em is Injun. Least partway. They're the only ones could take a deer with bows. Or find one at all around here behind the white hunters. I'd be put to it if it was me.

Why is he missing his nose?

Don't know. Blackfeet like to lop off women's noses when they cheat. But then, who don't? Why this buck got his lopped off beats me. Could be that fuckin' we walked up on done it. But, I heard Injuns don't frown on that so much as white folks. They think it makes you special. 'Course, I also heard they torture and beat you to death for it, so who knows?

I suppose that will make one shy around others.

Pretty clear things in general haven't gone the easy way for 'em. Least they got each other.

Ilya, Robert said. She looked at him. She was sitting leaning against the pale, gray bole of a downed pine, holding her pistol with one hand, the other on her stomach. He gestured at the deer. I need a knife.

She pulled hers and tossed it to him. Don't think I'm not watching.

Oh, hell no. Well, now. The loin's still in. We'll eat good. Conversation ain't gonna be much, I guess. He worked the knife in and started stripping the cut out. He came back into the light holding the meat, crouched, and sliced the strip into one-inch-thick discs on the downed trunk. He held the knife up for a moment, and placed it on a stone in front of Ilya. She nodded.

There was a pot with a lid on it sitting to one side of the flames, small wisps of steam leaking from it. Robert sniffed at it, wrinkled his nose.

Don't know what that is, he said, moving it aside. Ain't coffee.

Spiky man made a soft grunt, leaned forward and lifted the top off the pot, a bit of rag in his fingers, and stirred the mixture with a stick stripped of its bark. A rich, bitter, wet aroma, not foul not food, filled the air. He set the pot far enough away from heat for it to cool.

Tea, I guess, Robert said. He raked coals away from the flames into a pile, fed wood into the other side so it leaped up high and threw light hard, and crossed to the man with the sword. He held up his palm in a calming way. Easy, hoss, he said, reached out, and slid the blade free. The man made no objection.

These are some highly peaceable...whatever-the-fuck-they-ares, he said, and threaded the steaks onto the blade and laid it on rocks over the coals. And that's some, thinkin' about what they look like they been through, and them not gettin' violent over it.

Maybe they decided they were always outnumbered in this world and resistance was futile.

Could be that. Or they're wily fucks just waitin'. He sat, leaned back, and groaned. Hell, slab of tomato, an onion, and some garlic, and we'd be pretty.

And wine. And cigarettes. And brandy. And coffee. And a bed. And a bath. And oysters.

The sort to keep your eye on what you got, I see. We could just give these boys some odds and bits of our gear in trade for the meat, Robert said. Your gear, I mean. Do it right now maybe, give 'em the notion we ain't just stealin'. Looks like they been doin' without the finer things for a spell. Seems politer than killin' 'em, seein' as how they don't seem to want a problem. If that's what you was plannin' for.

I'm not going to kill them. I have standards. I like to at least know what it is I'm killing.

That's a policy. Lemme get 'em a couple blankets, and we got the extra shirts from those innocent young boys you relieved of their lives.

And I'm still waiting for a thank you. Go ahead.

Robert went out, came back with an armful of blankets and clothes, and put them on the ground beside the men. He waved his hand. The two nodded. Their faces eased a little.

The cold brought the spectral one from his talk with himself to the fire, where he stood there, looking back into the darkness, gnawing his fingernail.

This one here brings a nice feel to the proceedings, Robert said.

Yes. Puts one at ease somehow.

Hard to figure how these three fell in together.

I shudder to think. It doesn't seem altogether a bad arrangement.

Nope. They seem shot through the same barrel.

Jesus, these sayings of yours...

Easy. I just wanted to perk you up.

Thank you.

Bridger finished with the horses and came up to the fire carrying Robert's food bag and put it beside him.

You read my mind Bridger, he said, rummaged in it through the cook-ware and came up with a tin of salt and crushed pepper mixed. Ain't alto-gether out of the civilized world. They gettin' infected?

No sign yet. Startin' t' scab aright. Have t' look better in th' mornin'. Hard t' see.

You washed 'em with the creek water?

Whattaya think?

Aright. My fault. Just askin'. Buncha horses with festerin' sores bleed-in' pus ain't a good thing.

Thought that m'self. We c'n git t' Butte, we can git somethin' fer 'em.

They sat staring at the meat roasting, Robert turning it.

I'm callin' that done, he said, took the sword by the haft and extended it to Ilya, the point at her chest, looking at her eyes. She looked at him, reached out, and slid a steak from the blade, putting it on her knee to cool. You'll want this, Robert said, handed her the tin, and went around the fire with the blade until they were all gobbling.

This is excellent, Ilya said, struggling hard to allow enjoyment. You have a genius for it.

It'll do. Robert went to the carcass and returned with another slab, and started over. This one ain't gonna be as good, but better'n any restaurant.

Not 'any,' Ilya said.

Alright. I can do this all night, he said, satisfaction that looked to Ilya like sanctimony on his face. She felt a stab of envy at his easiness, at his unencumbered relish for things, the lack of resistance he could get to when he'd reached a place where none was needed.

The spectral one ate standing, and continued to stand over the rest of them sitting and lying about, gorged.

Ilya frowned. She waved her arm until she got his attention. Why don't you sit down? she said, putting gentleness into her voice.

Oh! Is anyone else comin'?

I don't think so, no. He certainly seems a social sort, which is perhaps the saddest thing I've seen today.

Hm. I'll sit right here?

That's fine. She watched him put himself into a contorted, half-sitting, half-crouching position, and pose there. She frowned harder. Sit all the way down. Stretch your legs out.

Hm. He put his ass all the way to the ground and stretched his impossibly long legs in front of him toward the flames. He looked wooden.

Robert snorted a laugh and said, Don't he beat all. He waved his hand at the two men to get their attention, then made a motion like smoking a cigarette. Tobacco? he said. They stared at him. Shit, he sighed. He made a gesture at them like drinking from a bottle. Whiskey?

Why don't you look through their things? Ilya said. I didn't see any, but I wasn't looking. I didn't check their horses. Simpler than trying to talk to them.

Damned if I won't, Robert replied. Don't feel good, but if they got a smoke...He got up and rifled through their belongings. Bits of smooth, twisted wood, knife hafts with the blades snapped off, bits of quartz and garnets, mangled feathers — some with just the spine of them left, hanks of hair tied with string, a hairbrush, the leg of a child's china doll, broken off mid-thigh. There ain't shit in here.

Robert held up what was left of a flintlock pistol — no ramrod, no cock, no flashpan, just a short barrel with a touchhole. Spiky man grunted and waved his hand, alertness in his eyes.

Well, guess they can't hurt us none with this, Robert said and tossed it to the man. I don't even wanna know what they want it for.

Spiky man caught the barrel and poked the muzzle into his mouth and sucked at it. Air hissed through it. He fished around beneath his tunic and came up with a little skin sack, and a small, carved bit of wood. The wood fit into the touchhole, and he pinched some tangled crap out of the sack and tamped it into the wood.

Hell, I wouldn't of thought of that, Robert said. These boys shine at some things. Bathin' and talkin', not much for that, but...

Spike took a stick from the fire, lit the pipe, and puffed. He handed it to his partner and he sucked deeply, then held it out to Ilya. She hesitated, then took the pipe and drew in fumes. The stuff was a vile combination of bitter and sweet and weedy. She held the smoke in, handed it to Bridger.

No opium in it, sadly, she said, and coughed.

Bridger frowned at the taste, held out the pipe to the spectral one, who took it but just held it.

Skip him, Ilya said. He's perfect the way he is. Bridger took the pipe back and passed it to Robert.

Robert smoked and coughed hard. Damn, I smoked horseshit that outshined this...whatever the hell it is.

Spike restoked the pipe and it made the rounds again.

Smokin' a peace pipe, Robert said. Been out here a long time, never had me the chance before now. Way this shit tastes ain't no wonder it was war got chose.

Spike got up, went to the pile of their stuff, came back with two metal cups and a hand-fashioned wooden ladle, dipped out of the pot into the cups, gave one to his partner, and settled back.

Hell, I'm havin' me somethin' hot, Robert said. He pulled cups out of his kitchen sack, ladled one full, gestured at Ilya, who was nearly asleep. She shrugged, took the cup, sipped, and gagged a little.

Vile, she said. Warm though.

Not a tea man, myself, Robert said, and drank. He forced the liquid down, face clenched. I'm seein' why now.

Bridger drank the cup straight down, craving whiskey. His stomach roiled but he clamped on it.

The two men watched them and finished their cups, put them aside. Spike took the blankets Robert had given them, laid them out, made a bed, and the two of them stripped to skin and crawled in together, laying flat on their backs and staring upwards.

Didn't need to see that overmuch, Robert said, drinking more. Grows on you, this shit. He emptied the cup.

Ilya had almost gone to sleep, cup in her hand. She snapped awake, drained the cup, sat up. Can you stay awake, Bridger? she said.

Yep.

First you, than me. Don't sleep. If you think you're going to drop off, wake me.

Aright. He rose and went through the dark to the creek, slashed his face and neck with the water, and wound through the brush back to the fire. Ilya and Robert had bedded down. The spectral one sat. Ilya looked at him.

Hey, she said.

Hm!

Go to bed.

Oh! He rose and left, came back into the light with a bundle. The sight he made trying to put together a place to sleep set Robert to laughing.

This'n here...he said.

Ilya cursed, threw her blankets back. Here, she said, stop, and took the blanket from the man's hands. Jesus, the reek of this stuff, it's not odd he doesn't want to go to bed. She threw the bundle into the bushes. Bridger, we have more bedding?

Got a couple more blankets.

Get them. She took them from his hands when he returned from the horses and laid them out, pulled a saddle up for a pillow, and gestured at it. There, for you, she said.

Mm, he said, and started to get himself in, looking like he was crawling head first down a cliff face.

Take your boots off.

Oh!

When he was as settled as much as it seemed a man such as himself could be, Ilya crawled back into her bedding.

And I was thinkin' there was no mother to you, Robert said.

Be careful. That was all of it.

Ilya came awake because there was something wrong with her. She laid there staring through leaves at stars. The camp was quiet, the fire a low glow. A soft wind touched leaves from their holds and they drifted down. The creek chuckled.

I know what this is, she thought, and sat up, taking up her pistol, and trying to marshal her mind against the easy illness slinking through her, but failing. The feeling of the gun had changed, become more solid, it had become more beautiful. She fell into an examination of it. It wasn't ornate, but the lines of the weapon, and the smooth metal machining in careful perfection curving to meet with the wood grip seemed wondrous and impossible, and she was reminded of the woodwork in the house at Washington Square, and teared up because since she had left there she had not seen such craftsmanship. She couldn't imagine how anyone had done it, made something so beautiful. It didn't seem like a weapon now, but like an ornament made for no other purpose but to please. The ache in her abdomen had receded, but her hard mind held onto the pain, tried to use it to resist this other person who'd slithered into her.

Robert never fell all the way asleep, but began to feel uprooted. His boots seemed to be moving away from him. He pulled his legs back, thinking his feet were in the coals of the fire. He felt at them, wondering where the burning was. They weren't hot. There was a vile taste in his mouth and he was salivating madly, and spat a lot. It felt like a small stream of bile was flowing up out of his innards. It was strange to him, but not entirely alarming. He rose from his blankets and threw wood on the coals, feeling like the air itself had taken on a solidity through which he had to move.

The fire had more facets than he could believe, and he frowned, thinking he was seeing every piece of flame rising. He wanted to grasp them, didn't. He felt like he could grasp the burning end of a stick without being harmed, felt like he wanted to, felt like it was impossibly stupid that he never had before, like he'd missed something that had been sitting in front of him his entire life. He felt like crying, but didn't feel ashamed of it. Like it was also something he'd been missing somehow, not the feeling of sadness and loss, but that of an unshackling too long in coming. His mind tried to poke at him, tried to tell him that something was quite wrong when the commonplace felt like this. He waved a mental hand at it, as if dismissing the irritating person he felt his old self to now be.

Bridger crawled away and vomited explosively and plunged into a paralyzing fear, curled on the ground, trying to hold onto himself. The image of Spike sticking the pistol in his mouth swelled in him, the gun firing, the back of Spike's head showering blood. The pipe sat there on the rock, gleaming, growing. He couldn't understand why it was just sitting there doing nothing and being devoured and writhing in the maw of this man at the same time. He couldn't face the image at all and couldn't drag his gaze away, but it didn't seem like his gaze, it seemed like he had too many gazes, splintering off and flitting in front of him, and all of them had this vibrating quality, this...squirming, everything was squirming. He couldn't understand where he had gone and he had a block in his throat that seemed the size of a wagon, and the block was made of alternating hilarity and terror and gorge rising up out of an inside that seemed bottomless and completely dark and filled with nameless things that oozed out of it as stark, seamless realities. He couldn't move anything but his eyes, and looked around, panicky, but no one paid any attention to him, if you didn't count the phantoms. He made gurgling sounds that no one could hear and he couldn't tell if he'd made them, though to him they seemed like a crack of thunder along with the sudden deluge of a rainstorm. Ilya became naked and enormous leaning over him, mouth wide open and smothering breasts with nipples like gun muzzles and then it wasn't her but his father, fleshless and yet leering and hissing through the broken teeth hanging from the jagged line of bone and saying only, 'Howdy,' over and over and over until Bridger was screaming but he wasn't making any sound at all, and though he knew it he couldn't change it. He put his head back and gulped air and tried to marshal himself, looked up at the sky, trying to expunge these images, and the stars shot down straight at him in a downpour of lights in long thin ropes, the quarter moon a white-hot blade descending to slice him.

Robert was watching Spike and friend fondling each other beneath their blankets, their movements seeming melodic and deep. He could hear the sounds of a fiddle player he'd once heard who had known how to play more than just rapid and ragged notes, but could pull long, low strains from the instrument that were at once melancholy and uplifting. The sense of disgust at the sight of the men was like the cry of a man about to strike earth at the end of a long fall. He was filled with a sense of profound engagement and appalled wonder, like he'd felt watching a stallion mount a mare, the huge tool of the animal impressive and frightening, like a hammer wielded by a skilled hand, but he realized that image was coming only out of his mind, because the two men weren't fucking, they were just squirming together, and he felt he understood that, because he felt an attraction to Ilya, an intimacy and affection, an urge to crawl to her, but no lust, and his equipment was fallow. Mostly he felt contented and entertained by the flood of images and recollections suddenly re-revealed to him, the same as they ever were but vivid and deep, and the associations from them somehow wild but indisputably right. Whispering behind it all was his own voice, one of them, a trusted one, saying, 'I have heard of this stuff.' The way everything in the world seemed to be taking place behind a rippling curtain of water made him alternate between fascination and panic. Occasionally, he happily threw up.

Ilya also watched the two men. The first feeling was that of mild shock, and the sense that she couldn't quite understand anything. Her eyes kept pulling themselves away and wandering out into the dark through which she thought she could see through the softly waving curtain someone had draped over everything. She was sure she could see night creatures scuttling though the bushes, and they rearing up on their hind legs to look at her, becoming like stuffed animals rather than real, with eyes that glowed. This alarmed her some and she pulled her gaze back to the two men, and suddenly it seemed absurd and funny and she was laughing. She couldn't stop laughing. It began as a burbling rising up in her throat and came out in a chattering moan as she tried to stop it. But she couldn't, and it escalated out of her reach, becoming a high, ratcheting keen that stole her breath from her, became less like mirth than alarm. She curled on the ground, pistol still clutched in her hand, and the laughter became a decrescendo of her own gasping breath, but then she looked over at the two men, and she laughed again. Tears poured from her eyes, and she stopped trying to stop the laughter so she could keep breathing.

Robert caught her hilarity, chortling and snorting into his palm. And then he was laughing hard, and he recognized that he had never laughed this hard and wanted to stop. The two laughed, sides aching, as the other two continued fondling, and the spectral one sat staring at nothing and just being more spectral, and Bridger laid trapped in the screech he couldn't voice, finally jerking himself to his feet and bolting into the dark.

14

Ilya surfaced and sat up. The spectral one stood looking at his mirror talking. Robert roared in his blankets. A cold mist obscured everything but what was close to her. The cottonwood branches looked like black bones in gray flesh. The fire smoked one tendril. She was cold to the marrow. Something flitted through her vision and she flinched.

Ah, fuck, she said, and got to her feet, shuddering hard. She walked to Robert, teeth clacking, and kicked him, and he burst upright. She went to the fire and scraped at it with a stick until embers glowed and she knelt there and built it into a crackling roar and huddled by it. Robert came up beside her and sat on his haunches, trembling.

Mornin', he said.

Of what age?

Stone, maybe. Not the one to ask. He looked around. Our numbers are some reduced. Spike, his partner and their horses, the deer, were gone.

Ilya nodded at the spectral one. They left us the best of them.

Mmm. Thankin' us for our company, maybe. Might be his usefulness ain't showed itself yet.

It will be a long wait.

Likely.

Bridger! she shouted. Lovely, she muttered, when nothing came back. Did you see him at all?

Hard to say for certain what I seen. Be a bitch if them boys made a straight trade, this'n for Bridger.

Funny but doubtful. I don't think they were Bridger's social set. Do you know what that...tobacco...was?

Not from experience. What that was we was smokin', I ain't got any notion. But my feelin' is that tea was cactus from the South, 'peyote' the Mex call it. Injuns down there use it to spirit walk or some shit. It's religious.

I've heard of it. I've never had it. Better than drinking Christ's blood, I must say.

Didn't peg you for havin' done that.

I didn't. I would if it would finally kill him. I've seen others drink it however, and they didn't behave the way we did.

Nope. Blood must be better, judgin' from the popularity. Don't suppose it was real bright us doin' that.

We lived.

If you call this that. I feel like Satan shat me out. Not lookin' like Bridger lived, at the moment.

Did you know what it was when we drank it?

I'm wonderin' that myself. It was like I was two-minded. I knew I was drinkin' somethin' that wasn't usual...but...ridin' like we done all that time with no whiskey and no tobacco...it'll make you hope for the best even when you got shit in your mouth.

I had something similar happen. I wanted something good to happen so badly I would drink anything to have it.

Well. Here you go, he said, waved his arm around. The good.

Ilya felt warmed and stood up, flinched. Are you seeing things flit by?

Yep, some. Guess that's the last of the spirits.

We need to find Bridger.

Not in this fog. It'll burn off in an hour. He might find his way back by then. Best figure not to travel today. Bear could be devourin' us, we'd think it was us havin' breakfast.

Ilya went to the spectral one, thinking he must be cold. In daylight she could see that he was wearing three pairs of pants, so many socks his boots were split open, more shirts than a store kept in stock, and every pocket he had bulged, stuffed with things she didn't want to think about at the moment. He was so tightly wrapped in clothes his blood must have been stuck in his heart. He was quaking violently.

Come, she said, taking his arm, pulling him towards the flames.

Mm. When's Mike comin' back?

Who's Mike? He gestured to where the two men had slept.

'Mike?' Robert said. He was named Mike? I was hopin' for 'Sitting Bull' or somethin'.

I think Mike and his friend have moved on, she said to the spectral one, and stood him close to the heat. My god, why is he wearing so many clothes?

Got me. Maybe folks like to take 'em when he ain't got 'em on. If he come from a sanatorium somewhere, he ain't gonna be real trustin'. Not a tough one to take advantage of, neither.

When the fog burned off some they looked for Bridger. Fingers of mist wound through the brush and red boulders. The landscape kept jerking around on them. Robert would be moving along, feeling foggy but more or less alright, and a bush would seem to move and freeze in place again. He would flinch hard and grab for a pistol he didn't have. Then it would seem very doubtful that the bush had moved, but he would watch it anyway. And after a period, it would happen again with something else. When a grouse blew into flight from under his feet, his heart bounded and he shrieked a little. Residual laughter would come roiling up out of him like gorge rising without warning, and he would double over as if retching. None of this had anything like the pleasure of the previous evening.

Ilya had it worse than Robert. More things jumped around more often. She was gritting her teeth and willing the world to hold still, and trying to attain a sense of self-control that kept flitting away on her. The waving curtain of water from the evening before would come over her vision, then recede. She giggled without humor. Moments of her old self, possessed and confident, came up, but they seemed uncomfortable, felt false, and she doubted she was those things anymore, maybe never had been, and much as she wanted to feel steady, some of her didn't want to go back to it, didn't want responsibility of any kind, wanted to be a flit that kept shooting by her. At one point, she shot a stump that threatened her. The shot scared the shit out of Robert, who jumped hugely, then willed himself to calm.

Did you get it?

Oh, Ilya said, and laughed softly. That stump won't be a bother any more.

Good work. Might wanna...I don't know what...the gun...Bridger sticks his head up, you might overdo the welcome...

A thought. She dropped the cartridges out of her pistol.

I have him, she called out a few minutes later.

Things had not gotten better for Bridger after fleeing the fire the night before. After reeling around and screeching low, every sound and movement around him magnified to terrifying proportions, his own body either seeming to be detached and off away somewhere where he had to pursue it, or to have itself grown to massive size to the point where Bridger felt he was damaging the earth to step upon it. When things steadied a bit, he threw himself to the ground and dug his fingers into the grass, trying to stop everything from rippling. He tried to keep his eyes shut, but what would come whirling out of the depths of him was more frightening than just watching the world swell and constrict and contort itself for his terror, so he stared at the ground, singling out a blade of grass that came to seem wondrously detailed if only it would stop writhing like a snake, and laid there wanting to die.

It took both Ilya and Robert to get Bridger to his feet, fistfuls of grass tearing out of the ground in his hands. He couldn't talk, and his eyes kept skittering about. Nothing was funny to him. Ilya and Robert kept chortling periodically, one starting and the other joining in. Ilya got angry at Robert for getting her started. She wanted to get rid of this feeling of being out of control but didn't want to have to do anything. It had come to seem very dangerous now, although her efforts to get on with things also seemed questionable. She couldn't at all figure out what she was doing with herself or why, couldn't travel from one thought to the next. The whole notion that she was out here in the wilderness with a couple of men, running from other men who wanted to kill her, was absurd, and she wanted to go to those men and say, Kill me, or leave me alone, but this in between is not going to work.

Bridger was soaking wet. We gotta get him warm, Robert said.

They got him back to the fire, stripped him down, replaced his clothes with blankets, put a canteen in his hand and stood staring at him as he sat staring into the flames. He blinked his eyes a lot, his head occasionally twitched, and he didn't speak.

Well, that shut 'im up, finally, Robert said. I was gettin' tired of the constant chatter. I'm just gonna come out and say we might wanna keep him away from the firearms. I'm just sayin'. He won't be worth a pisshole in the snow for a while.

We'll be fortunate if he ever comes back. I suppose.

Now I reckon I see how come those boys were so...so. They ain't even in this world. Couldn't of killed 'em if we wanted to.

A wise choice on their part, leaving, judging by what we have to return to.

Yep. I wouldn't of minded stayin' a while longer. Hungry again now, though. Real hungry.

We can't move on today. How far are we now, do you think?

I'm gonna guess one long day or two short ones. Depends on how these two travel. Bridger'll be fine if he comes back, but this other one, be like towin' a cannon around. The James Gang, we ain't.

No. Though, between your snoring, this one's breath, and Bridger's general air of malignity, we could be rich without firing a shot. They would just hand over the money.

Hell yeah. And you could pretty much just insult folks for a spell and they'd pay us to stop blackin' up their world and go away. That's if your bein' beautiful didn't make 'em crazy up and kill themselves.

Ilya looked at him and smiled a little. Would that that were the effect of beauty on people, she said. Much more time out here and I won't have any beauty remaining. She looked sad and wiped at her face, looking at the filth on her hand afterward. She twitched, made a small move for her pistol, stopped. Goddamnit.

You gotta lotta looks left.

Ilya looked at him. I don't want you on that road, she said.

I know that. Who would? I stink and I'm loud and I'm old. Not sure I'd envy the boy who was on that road, neither. Don't hurt to make it known I notice, though.

Alright. It's not personal. She sighed heavily. What should we do?

Well. Occurs to me that I ain't in fact done much wrong but join you, and nobody knows that. If there's money around, I can ride over and maybe get food off of somebody on the road. Wouldn't take but three hours out and back.

If you came back.

There's that.

I have some money left.

Some outlaws take money while they're at it. Just a thought for you. We can sit here all day with nothin' to eat. Wouldn't kill us. But I'm thinkin' we're gonna wanna be pretty pert tomorrow, and if we're hungry...it ain't good. Bridger here...he might not hold it down right off, but when his boots hit the ground again, he's gonna want chow bad.

I suppose I could go with you and not show myself.

Leavin' these two alone? What we come back to might be dark.

Yes.

Might be I can get whiskey, to boot. Not good whiskey, probably, but somethin'...least we know where we're gonna end up with a bottle of Ol' Snot.

Ilya stood and went to her gear, fished in her saddlebag, came back to Robert and put bills in his palm.

If you don't come back, I'm just going to assume you want me to shoot you.

He nodded. I'll be back. I was just gonna drink myself to death you two hadn't come along with a better idea. You got a knack for makin' things interestin'. That's a fuck of a lot more dear than what most got to offer.

Ilya shrugged. I'm not in a position to think everything through, nor to worry about you. Take your guns out of his armory. I'll thank you now for killing me, if you decide to.

See now, that's the kind of spirit makes me wanna stay with this party. I ain't interested in killin' you.

I know. Go quickly, please. This is going to be the longest day.

15

The following morning brought cold, bitter clarity that was welcome to them after the previous day. They smoked, drank, ate from what Robert had bought from a wagon bringing resupply to Butte City.

Didn't push the topic, but I didn't hear nothin' about you two floatin' around the caravansary. Might be a good sign. I figured you'd be everybody's favorite topic right about now.

It's becoming insulting how little attention I'm getting. Why bother to be exceptional if people don't notice?

They were finished packing and stood together around the dead fire. Ilya stood to the side and looked up into the blue beginning to color yellow beyond the gray branches and rust leaves. She felt strong again, self-possessed, new energy moving through her, the current from which tugged at her fatalism and pessimism, made her think of leaves caught in a backwater of the creek, one by one being caught up and taken downstream.

They had just left Bridger alone, once they were sure he wasn't going to bolt again.

How do you feel? Ilya said to him. She felt good enough that the question was more than a way to coldly assess his capabilities. She noticed that she felt warm enough to care about someone else a little, and cupped her mind around the warmth.

Able, Bridger said.

Ilya nodded at him and touched his shoulder. Well said.

Bridger had steadied down and the world had reassembled itself the way it used to look, for the most part. He couldn't get his mind around their circumstances much, and mostly felt like he wasn't up to the task in any case, and just wanted to be moving, using his body for something. In short bursts he'd feel a sense of excitement at the adventure of it all, and he would review what had happened to them, what he had done, and he would make up a story, change things that had actually happened, make them better. He became a fictional character of his own making who would come right to the moment of a shooting, and make it as if it were seen through the eyes of a rheumy-eyed windbag next to a stove spinning yarns.

Then the sense of adventure would disappear into a kind of deep incomprehension about the real events. Then he couldn't believe that he wasn't dead and the others were. That just seemed impossible. The yarn about the outlaw that was him would draw itself up, like sucking venom from a snakebite, into the crystalline moment when Juice had turned his head back to face him and had seen Bridger's pistol muzzle pointing at him, and his face had scrunched into abjection and terror, and that face disappearing in the blue burst of smoke and the hard bang of the gun.

Ilya turned to the spectral one, whose routine of hovering and talking to his mirror had remained until they had geared up to go. Then he had gotten more and more still until he was standing to the side, his long body in a submissive, heartbreaking curve, as if he expected to be left there.

We need a name for this, she said.

You ain't leavin' him, I guess, Robert said.

You know I'm not. He'll die horribly if we leave him out here. Maybe there's a place for him in Butte City.

Now that's a funny notion by itself, 'a place for him.' Only places I ever heard of for folks like him is where they stick 'em in a room and try and make 'em believe God wanted 'em this way and he was thinkin' of 'em the whole time. Meanwhile they eat their own hands off, like this one seems to be on his way to doin'.

He's eaten his fingernails to bleeding, Ilya said. This is a personal foible I hadn't expected to contend with. Listening to them, the spectral one put his fingers in his mouth.

Stop that, Ilya said, crossed to him and pulled his arm away. She pulled her gloves from her coat pocket and gave them to him. Put these on and leave them on.

Oh, he said.

Can you ride a horse?

Yup! Yup, I can! I can ride a horse like...like...hm!

Can't think of an apt comparison, eh? Ilya said, smiling a little.

He's that good, Robert said. Caps the climax, this one.

Havin' him ain't gonna help us any, Bridger said.

We're not leaving him, so put that from your mind if it's in there, Ilya said. At any rate, it's really too early to say. Get on your horse...ah...we need something to call him...

Didja ask if he's got a name?

I didn't, now that you mention it. What's your name?

My name?

Yes.

Mm. Cup?

Cup?

Mm.

Are you certain?

Pipe?

Huh. This boy seems not to get the distance between him and the rest of things.

Ilya sighed. It's probably an adequate measurement of the extent of his experience, Cup and Pipe. It would be fine if he were a pub.

Guess we get to name 'im. It's like he's our firstborn.

We're not calling him Robert Jr.

Damn.

What do you want to be called? Ilya said.

Me?

Yes.

Me?

You want to be called 'Me?'

Yup!

Can anyone think of an objection?

Confusin', Bridger said.

That's so, Robert said. 'Course, things ain't been clear as crickwater up until now. How about 'Spud?' He's dumb as one.

It's alright with me, Ilya said. 'Spud' is less of a mouthful than 'You Fucking Stink.' Get on your horse, Spud.

Watching him get astride the animal was taxing, but he did it. His feet hung close to the ground and Ilya put them in the stirrups. You two are going to have to help with him. If you think I'm going to be the only parent here, please rethink that.

She mounted and nodded to Robert.

Butte City had best brace itself, he said.

III

1

No, Ilya said. Please tell me this is not it.

I'm thinkin' that's it, Robert said. It's gotta be. That's the butte it gets its name from, right there, that big, fuckin' volcano-lookin' hill.

Hell, Bridger said, and looked angry.

Mm, oh, oh boy! Spud said. Look at that! Isn't that nice! When's...when are...hmm...hungry...can we, can we go out to supper tonight?

Don't chew your hands, Spud, Ilya said. Put your gloves back on. Yes. I think we can go out and eat tonight. His enthusiasm is quite something.

And we was worried there wasn't no place for him with us, Robert said. Not catchin' though, his enthusiasm, judgin' by your two faces.

They sat on their horses on the crest of a treeless ridge that stuck out of the Pioneer Range, from which they had emerged. Across an expanse of grass and a maze of gulches laced with trees being felled, two buttes stuck up out of the bottom of a massive dipper, the spout of which flattened and eased through the ring of mountains to the northwest. Across from where they sat, close to the ridge line, huge, blackened wood-frame buildings poured smoke into the sky from tall stacks, where it curled up and was trapped by a flat palm of gray cloud. Scattered across the hillside in front of them were more buildings, most of them pouring their own smoke, wreaths of which slunk close to the ground and wrapped buildings like they were to be pulled below. Chains of dirt roads carried wagons, and spindly trestles carried coughing engines pulling small cars across gulches, and from one building to another. The place gave out an incessant, faint clatter which carried across the valley floor to them, and the smell of pine smoke tinged with something acrid was the air. Through the smoke they could see a cluster of substantial masonry buildings arranged in a grid, surrounded by heaps of shattered stone, ponds of still water, long pyramidal piles of burning ore, and cabins and frame houses freckling it all.

I ain't stayin' here, Bridger said.

What are they burning? Ilya said, scrubbing her face with both palms, and working her eyes with her fingers.

I don't know, Robert said. They're makin' metal.

That incessant pounding, what are they doing?

Hell girl, I ain't no miner. They're bashin' and burnin' rocks to get pistols and pots and coins out of 'em.

You thought that we would want to be here, guide?

Well hell, look at it. The air's so thick the law couldn't recognize you if you was standin' right in front of 'em.

This place is shit, Bridger said.

Goddamn, you two is some fussy fuckers for people who can't keep from killin' someone for more than a day. Go to hell and leave me out of it.

You brought us to hell. And I believe the fussiness is behind the killing, to a certain degree, Ilya said. She forced her voice to soften. I expect you to understand that. She sat looking at the buildings in the grid of streets. Anger and the urge to cry passed through her like the phantoms from the day before.

Well, she said, looking at the gridded cluster, at the very least they've grasped how to make a primitive city. Why exactly they decided to locate it where they bash and burn their rocks is somewhat hard to fathom. Why couldn't they put the city over there where there are no...factories...or whatever they are?

Don't like walkin' to work, maybe, Robert said.

Fuckin' lazy maggot bastards, Bridger said. I dunno what th' fuck they're doin', but it's poisonin' everythin'.

Ilya looked at the sky. What time is it?

Comin' up on candlelightin', Robert said. And the mercury's fallin'. We gotta choose. Well, what's it gonna be, boss? Gonna let a little smoke keep you from a bath?

No, I'm not. Bridger, I understand your feelings and I share them. But we have to get indoors. We can make a new plan and leave soon. If you want to stay out here, or go off on your own, please do. But I'm staying in this...furnace...until I'm warm and clean and properly fed again. If being clean is possible here. What would you like to do?

Dunno, he said.

Them horses is proof of guilt, Robert said. Just sayin'. Brands. Gotta find a way to deal with that.

Such as?

Could picket 'em out here, the condemnin' ones, until we see what were goin' into.

Ain't doin' 'at, Bridger said. They need nursin'. If it snows, they're buried out here. An' they could git pinched.

Alright Bridger, you're right, Ilya said. We'll risk it, for now. Everyone who has money, give it to me. Ilya counted it. Shit. We have sixty-two dollars. How long will that last us here?

Two days, maybe, for four. Plus puttin' up horses. If we're scrimpy.

We're not going to be scrimping. We're going to live for a day. Alright, Bridger? Darling? Why care where we are right now? We light up this...city, for an evening, we face our troubles tomorrow. Alright? Some whiskey? Steak? It won't be the same without you and your irrepressible spirit.

Bridger's face cleared, and he snorted. Aright, aright. Fuck.

Good. Robert, you're our innocent one. Go in, get us rooms, somewhere nice. Look to see if our pictures are all over. See if they're just waiting for us to blunder in.

What about ol' Spud here?

Yes. Our Spud. Well, he's been wanting to attend a party, so we shall have a party. Yes, get him a room of his own. It will be a first, I'm sure. We'll give him a coming out ball.

That'll put a quick end to a buddin' city, Robert said. Alright. Could be Fred's here. He said he was headin' this way because he had a line on a constable's post. I'll see if I can maybe give us some cover with the law with my so-fine reputation. Carry on like you all is somethin' other than you are. We could be family, or somethin'...

Yes, thank you, do that, you all do feel like my family, Ilya said. My, that's not something I ever thought I'd say. Wait. No, don't do that. It's too complicated, and...disturbing. We're friends, for now. Traveling companions. Something. Keep it very simple, or say nothing at all about it. Nothing is best. I'll trust your judgment. Not because I think it's good, but my choices in life have narrowed drastically of late.

Alright, boss.

Go. Be quick about it, please. 'I got me a turrible dry.'

Hell, Bridger, listen to that. We soiled her.

She wuz dirty aready.

2

Oh, I love Butte! Ilya said to her gang as they sat at the table in front of the steamed-over window of the French Restaurant, and emptied her wine glass between her red lips with rouge smeared around them. The tabletop was a battlefield of glasses, plates, bottles, and the remnants of devoured food on a destroyed white tablecloth, golden lamplight shining over it and their sweating faces. Around them the well-heeled of the city gabbled, and the place had a lovely, ambient odor of food, burning kerosene, the occasional blast of clean, outside air when the door was opened, and the more-or-less bathed and perfumed.

I love everything about it, she went on. They have Mariani here! Do you know what that means, you fucking bumpkins?

Means you're a fuck of a lot cheerier, Robert said.

Means yer on a path t' git us kilt with yer mouth, Bridger said

I very well might, my hero, I very well might. But I'll take many of the enemy with me, with words alone. Guns. Pah. I don't need a fucking gun. No, Mariani means we drink like the Pope tonight! We have the true blood of Christ right here on our table.

Mm... Spud said, and curled his forefinger toward his leering, happy face, in a 'come close and listen to me' gesture he often used which Ilya had now come to recognize, but was hard to acquiesce to because of his carrion breath. He was now shiny and clean, and his seventeen layers of filthy clothes had been removed, disposed of, and replaced with just one dapper, crisp, gray suit, with a black cravat. His bashed-in hat was now a black, flat-brimmed number which made him look deadly until you got close. All of which was not the improvement she had hoped for because without the dirt it was clear his skin was a devastation, but it very much was an improvement.

Yes, yes dear Spud, what is it?

Can...can I...can I have some more wine?

Of course, of course, it's your coming out ball, my disgusting debutante! No, not the Mariani, here, drink the Bordeaux. If you drink the Mariani you won't stop chewing yourself until you've devoured your own skull. I suppose we could have made tonight your bar mitzvah, but I wouldn't wish that on your poor, utterly irredeemable soul. Now you see, Bridger, you see how superior this is to skulking about out there in the bushes freezing? They have a french restaurant called 'French Restaurant,' and the food is good. Very good. They have bohemian chic! Wasn't it entirely good leadership for me to bring us here?

Reckon so.

Oh, come now! 'Reckon so.' It was genius. Sheer genius. And the owner already loves me! Jesse James, pah! A piker through and through. 'Reckon so.' I mean, really. Giving credit where it's due is not a sign of weakness, my dearest hero. Aren't I your favorite boss? Aren't I? Ah, I'm not a boss, I don't like 'boss'...what do you call someone like me out here, Robert?

Besides thoroughly fuckin' shitfaced? I ain't sure.

Well, there must be a name for me. The leader of the posse is the sheriff, and the leader of the gang is the...what? You see my point?

I reckon 'gang leader' is gonna hafta cover it, there, Ilya. And probably better to not go shoutin' out that we're a gang in a restaurant. If that's what we are.

You're right. You're right. Shhhh. Bad me. Bad leader. I'll use more discretion. She saw the owner across the room. Jean! Jean! You glorious frog fuck! Cognac, please!

People around them turned and stared at them, without approval, but without obvious malice, some with bemusement.

They have cognac here, Robert. And Velvet Mouthpiece cigarettes, my favorite. And hot water. I don't feel like 'leader' is a big enough title for someone of my stature and wisdom, do you? I mean truly, it makes me sound like the dog that runs in front of the other dogs. I am not a dog. And neither are you! My men are not dogs! Come, as long as we're on a taxonomical spree, let's dub everyone anew. It's safer. It can't be just Spud who gets a new name and new clothes and starts a new life. We're Buttians now! We need Butte names. I will be...Commodore!

Robert and Bridger sat there looking grim, eying other patrons, holding their pistol grips inside their coats.

Ah, Commodore, ain't this about how you got into a shootin' last time you was bein' civilized? Robert said.

Well perhaps, but we did all the good shooting last time. Because we excel at what we do, is that not so, Bridger? We shoot them before they shoot us. We should patent that idea, Bridger. I'll give you half of the proceeds, don't fret. Strange no one else thought of it. We're very likely the best gang west of the Mississippi. Ain't that what y'all like t' say, 'west of the Mississippi?' Or is it the Pecos? Where is the fucking Pecos, are we west of it?

We's good, it's so, Bridger said, but y' gotta fuckin' tone it down some, Ilya.

Goldarn, you two is strung tighter'n Montana bob wire after it...fuckin'... rains or some damn thing! C'mon now, we want ol' Spud here to have a good time, don't we? Spud! You havin' a damn good time, boy?

Yup!

There. You two could learn something from the dolt here. Or I'll throw you out of the gang, and it'll just be me and Spud against the world.

Your cognac, Jean said as he appeared at their table. He was a short, portly man wearing a white shirt, black trousers, and an expression of bemused grimness.

Jean, Jean, thank God you're here. You are the first culinary genius I've been around in...weeks. Except for Mary. I miss Mary. But my love, it was as if I was being slowly murdered by having my taste buds cut out one at a time.

Jean slid a chair over from an adjacent table, sat, and poured cognac around.

Oui, Madame, I know the feeling very well. It is part of being in America. The English eat their disgusting food in England, and shit it out here for your ignorant palates. And I love you very much, and I love your *bon* energy, but you must stop shouting, *s'il te plaît*, my love. Eh? These others, they are not so happy and free as you, and I must have their money as well.

Jean, I am sorry. I will of course calm myself. And thank you for using the informal 'please' with me. I know we just met.

Of course. What is the West for?

I was just very excited because of your bernaise sauce...on antelope! Your antelope is so good! The dullards in New York never had antelope like this. I hate New York. And you have tarragon! Do you bumpkins know how long it takes to learn how to make a proper bernaise sauce?

Bridger and Robert wagged their heads. Spud ate his fingers.

Tell them, Jean. Tell the bumpkins how long it fucking takes to learn to make a good bernaise sauce.

Ah, mine was quite good after a couple of weeks.

A couple of weeks!? My. I thought it took much longer than that. Damn men always told me years. Well, never mind! It's excellent. Do you know how long it's been since I've tasted tarragon?

A very long time?

So long, I dread considering it. Weeks. Maybe even over a month!

Then do not dwell on it. It is in the past. Enjoy. Quietly.

Of course. Is there a place where noise is not so...frowned upon? In my favorite city in the world?

Alas, the idiots who are in power have banned the dancing saloons, and the hurdy-gurdy houses, and the dancing houses. Now they have made fun illegal...again. They no longer even let *les enfants* coast in the streets.

Oh, fuck! Why do they do this to us, Jean? Why? The fucking wretched bourgeois. I'm so glad my Flaubert is dead. Butte would make him despair so.

Mm, I do not know if such a thing is possible, more despair. It is *triste*, so *triste*, they do this. And so American to make everyone work so hard while they ruin their lives. The French, they are bad, but they say, 'You are already too boring to work too hard as well.'

They did this in New York, Jean. They bundle up the poor people with the fun and throw them both away in Brooklyn. They made the Points into a church and the Bowery into a cemetery. They keep sending the blacks away after freeing them, 'You're free! Now please go away.' And it is harder to go to Brooklyn than it is to go to Butte. One has to swim through sewage to get to a pasture. Brooklyn is a horrible place, Jean, horrible...they still have farms...and now they're building a bridge to get there. Why? Who wants to go so badly, and why wouldn't we just make them swim over and stay there? We don't want them to be able to get back easily...

Stupide.

Very stupid.

However, there is, of course, a place for fun here that they do not close. It is very noisy. A secret.

Shh. Shh. A secret. A noisy secret. Excellent. Where?

It is very easy. You go down one block, you will be at Mercury St...

They have a Mercury Street, my men, do you hear that? Quicksilver Street! I want to live on Quicksilver Street, because I am very quick, and I need a quick street to live on! But why did they call it 'Mercury' Street? That's very dull...

These are dull men, *mon amie*. Granite Street, Main Street, Silver Street, bah, bah...

Then when they have a chance to name something Quicksilver Street they call it Mercury Street? What is wrong with these people?

No one knows, my dear, no one knows. They like to be numbing. But you do not have to be! So, you go left, you go one block, and in the alley, you see Owsley's Grog Shop, and in the basement there, you will hear stifled fun, and you knock. *D'accord?*

Oh Jean, thank you. Will they let me play, or will stupid men think I am there to fuck them for their money, when I would just kill them and take it if I wanted it. Will they let me be?

Oui. You say to the manager, his name is Henri, that you are from me, and you only want the fun men have. He will protect you.

Jean, I love you.

I love you, too, my dear. Also, in one hour or so, we are going to the Alice to see the lights. Everyone will be there. That will be fun, I think. A different fun, but fun.

Lights? What lights?

They are called Brush lights, I think so. I do not know what they are, but they are electric. Arc lights. No flame.

My bumpkins! Electric arc lights! In Butte! They didn't have them in New York when I left, except if you were invited. Always in New York, you must be invited. A 'dashed nuisance' that. Pah. You see how lucky you are, men? I always know where the best place to be is! I am the best Commodore in the world. We'll go and see them. It is like they knew we were coming. I said we would light this town up, and here, we're doing it! And you as well, Spud. Isn't this the best party you've ever been to?

Yup! This is the best party I've ever been to!

You are the only one who truly appreciates me, Spud. Jean, where is it?

At the Alice, up the hill.

What is the Alice?

It is the biggest, best mine and hoist in the city. And mill and smelter now, as well. Thirty tons of ore crushed a day, eh? Thirty tons? I am two hundred pounds, so that is three hundred of me shattered to pieces every day. And sixty stamps going all day and all night. The richest lode in the country some say, but everybody says that. Few come and crow, 'Ah, my vein, it is the worst in the world.' I am closing, and me, and my friends, we go in the wagon, and we bring some wine, and some oysters, and some bread, and we watch the lights go on. You may come with us, if you want.

We want! We want!

Oui, one hour, then...

An hour, yes...and another bottle, *s'il te plaît*, my men have nothing in their glasses.

Of course.

Yes! This is wonderful. The first night here and we are with the very best people. Now my men, names. Bridger you can go first. Think of a name for yourself. Something very...*chic!*

Bridger reached out and grabbed Ilya's hand and squeezed it hard, staring into her eyes.

I ain't dyin' cuzza you, bitch. Ease up. Shut up.

Ilya's mouth opened to retort, then she stopped, closed it, looked around at the gilded words 'French Restaurant' arcing backwards across the window glass, at the soft, yellow wainscot and the creamy plaster above it with photographs of the Pont Neuf, and the Louvre, and Notre Dame, and thought to mention to Jean that he really must get less commonplace photos. She looked at the beveled-glass mirrors lining the walls with their gilt frames and the menu written on the glass, and the pressed tin ceiling with the coat of arms of some house or other the design, and the pyramidal skylight with wire glass panes that was dark now but during the day would flood the place with natural light, the lot of it slurring in her vision as if she could hear it buzzing, and returned her gaze to his, remembering the last restaurant they had been in.

Yes. Yes. You're right, she said low. Very good. You are a good bumpkin Bridger, thank you.

That bumpkin' shit's gettin' to be towards enough, Robert said.

Yes. Yes. Alright. But we should have fun gentlemen, we should, but simply...less obtrusively, you would agree with me on that? And I realize how difficult fun is for you without stopping a woman from being the way she wants to be.

When it gets me kilt, yeah, Robert said. Rest of the time have at it. Now look, pay attention. There's posters for you two up at the post office, and Fred's office, but there ain't no photographs, and the drawings they done don't look enough like y'all for anybody to be sure, if you work at not lookin' like the piture a little. Bridger keeps that hair on his face, he'll be alright, maybe. Ilya, I don't know...

I'll dye my hair.

There you go. And they didn't find the posse you shot up, so the reward ain't enough to drive anybody into a fuckin' crazy. And Fred says in Butte ain't nobody gives a shit about fuckall but metal. And this place just crawls with people, and more comin' every day. I reckon with a little luck, we'll be alright here for a short spell then pull out, but not if you keep makin' a stink. I'm thinkin' I'm a hot guide for bringin' you here, an' you're about to spoil it.

Well said, Robert, well said. I lost my composure, I apologize.

Aright then.

How much is the reward?

Five hundred.

Five hundred!? That's all? What does a woman have to do in this hellish country? Booth got fifty thousand just for shooting that vainglorious fuck Lincoln for shackling us together with those bigoted Crocketts! There is no justice. None at all.

Best stop shootin' nobodies if you're all bent on bein' a bigshot.

No, I'm not bent on being a bigshot. Well, I am, I am. Excuse me while I lie right to your face. But I am being frivolous. Alright. Names. We must have names. Not me, because I have already changed mine to...mine. But Bridger, you cannot be Bridger any longer. And you can't be Spunk like at that hotel, I can't have one of my men named after ejaculate. So...name yourself.

Right fuckin' now?

Yes. Why not?

Cuz...be good t' have some time t' think 'bout it.

Nonsense. And not something like 'Slim,' or 'Tex.' Something as dignified as yourself.

I ain't changin' my name, Robert said. I'm still pure. Hard to beat 'Bridger,' now. That's a fine name. Anyhow boss, the names on the posters is Willem Pilgrin, and Mrs. Violet Plymouth. You're already hidin', usin' your real names.

Oh. Oh, yes. I forgot my own story. Where would I be without my trusted lieutenants?

Deader'n shit.

Nicely put, Robert.

They were the last table sitting, the other patrons having put on their coats and begun getting into their landaus and clopping away over the freshly-laid cobbles, and their thin coating of dry, glittering snow.

We are ready, *mes amis*? Jean said, standing and beaming with his wife and two friends, a big, white cloth-covered basket in his arms. He wore a huge fur coat which matched that of his small, brightly-rouged wife, whose smile was constant and shattering white.

Yes, let's go, Ilya said. She tried to hand Jean a handful of bills, and he pushed them back. Tomorrow, tomorrow, we will settle up tomorrow, my friends. I will keep a running *billet* for you.

It has been astounding good fortune to meet you, Jean.

And for me, Ilya, you are fun...you would be astounded at the stupid shits to whom I must serve food here.

Oh, I would not.

Ah. *Excusez moi*, you are correct of course, and that is why we are friends.

Precisely.

But, I do not know all of your names.

Jean, I introduce Bridger, and Robert, and Spud. Bridger nodded somewhat rudely. Robert said, Pleased to meetcha. Spud said, I am very happy to meet you! And put his face much too close to Jean's, grinning madly.

Oh! Jean said, and pulled away, smiling.

Spud, don't frighten people to death like that, Ilya said.

Oh, Spud said, pulled back, and looked away sadly.

He has a special way about him, Ilya said low to Jean. His enthusiasm is his gun, and sometimes it misfires. He means nothing.

Indeed. Fascinating, Jean said. And you are a gang of robbers? Highwaymen? Musketeers? Eh? Bridger flinched and Ilya put her arm out to his forearm, and slid her hand down to grasp his as it came up toward his pistol. Bridger's alarm fermented to wobbly, desperate need for her, her touch killing him.

No, no, Jean, we are here to root out riches from the ground like everyone else. I am the capital, Robert is my superintendent, and Bridger is my foreman. Spud is...ah, our steward, recently promoted from sickening toady.

Pleased. May I present my wife and partner Marie, and my *sous chefs,* Claude and Gustave.

Your food is divine, Ilya said, all of you. I am so grateful I could shoot you all down.

Merci, Madame, you are very welcome, Gustave said, and the three of them made small head bows toward her.

You will do very well digging, but you must hurry for ground, Jean said. The masters are gobbling up all of it like swine to truffles. Come, we will see electricity!

The wind had swept the bowl in which the city sat, and the air was bitter cold and clean-tasting, only the faint and delicious scent of pine smoke touched it, filtered through the feathery snowfall that tickled their skin. They climbed into the wagon, and Gustave took the reins and snapped up the horses. They sat on hay loosely bundled as they banged up the corridor of brick buildings of the sort and substance that Ilya hadn't seen since New York, and Bridger had never seen. There was a white ceramic bowl filled with grilled oysters with a fennel sauce, and they gobbled them out of their shells, the meat enormous and fleshy, except for Bridger, who frowned and shook his head, until Ilya grabbed his jaw in her hand and forced his mouth open and put an oyster in, and forced his mouth shut, then stared at him as he ate, her face warm and beaming and happy in a way Bridger hadn't seen the remotest sign of since the dinner at Mary's, and never pointed straight at him, and because of it, because of how it made him feel to see her like that, that beauty without meanness of which she was capable, he chewed and swallowed and nodded and smiled and told himself he loved it, and told her too, and she laughed and said, See? And he said, I see. She kissed him hard on the mouth, threw his chin playfully, and drank cognac, tipping her head far back to have it drain from the snifter, then slid out an unsteady hand, snatched the bottle from the hay, pulled the cork with her teeth, and filled her glass as it tried to get away from her.

Robert drifted on his private current of buzzing, warm, controlled contentment, and his own sense of wonder at having a sense of safety and pleasure and energy he may have never felt before, and the thought of that saddened him, but he took a cigarette from the box Jean passed around, him pointing and saying happily, Turkish, *c'est bon*! Robert held his match in his cupped hands and lit everyone's cigarette in turn, himself last, and settled back on his bale, arm over the wagon slat, sipping cognac which he'd never had before and now only ever wanted to drink. They all eased back from the action of themselves and watched the glowing, growing city unwind, the lamps glowing from windows from as high as four stories overhead, the fenestration receding into the distance behind them as they rolled uphill. The valley below them was a pox of shining yellow light, and hard, bright flame bursting from the stacks in strange, industrial syncopation.

People roamed the sidewalks and the streets in a melee, whistling and waving bottles and shouting, Edison said, let there be light! And, Franklin lives! And, America, America! And, Butte City! Butte City! The first city! The best city!

As they left the city core the buildings dropped away, and the people came together into a stream walking up the hill, and they were in a convoy of conveyances of every description, filled with revelry laced with the grimness of those who disapproved of too much revelry. The wagon jolted down off the cobbles onto dirt, and they were grinding past hoist works with their engines huffing and throwing red and yellow light through their open doors onto the bright, new, freshly-soiled snow. A pair of miners in blackened clothes and ecstatically filthy faces shouted at them and pawed for the back of the wagon, both swinging bottles, and Jean cried, *Oui, oui!* and waved his arm at them. Robert and Bridger reached out and grabbed their hands and got them up in the wagon, where they sat and drank and gabbled what presumably were thank yous in a language none of them remotely recognized. Ilya grabbed oysters and handed them to them, and as they saw her leaning toward them in the swaying lamplight they were transfixed for a moment by her face, and then nodded and smiled and devoured oysters and shouted at one another as they skirted the precipice of dangerous exultation.

The road swung to the left and the people and wagons all began to clot up, until Ilya's gang was hemmed into a crowd, all arranged around an enormous structure, Gothic and fearsome and throwing light and flame and noise, and from another building, connected to the first by a tall trestle that appeared made by a spider and which looked too flimsy to hold anything of substance, came the drowning racket of the sixty stamps banging up and dropping down and shattering quartz into dust and pebbles and wealth. The exhalation of people and horses puffed into the falling snow, and in front of them on the far side of the sea of people they could see a rudimentary dais on a timbered scaffold with a group of men on it they could not hear speaking. Shushes rippled through the crowd and the reveling quieted, but still all there was was the crashing of the fabrication of a country, and the fires of smelting one, and Ilya sat there in her fog of appalled wonderment and thought, It's so Dickens...over and over, until a light atop the building burst into life, impossibly bright, and crackling and sparking with white energy. The crowd appeared starkly out of the suddenly absurd and weak flame light, faces turned up at first, then blinded and turning away from the ghastly intrusion of that which illuminated what none very much wanted to see. The snow here hadn't covered the choked-up effluent of their reduction process because of the ambient heat and activity, and the ground was a strange swamp of shattered rocks and neat stacks of cordwood that seemed endless, long, pyramidal pyres of glowing ore on roasting floors with blackened men standing with long pikes, and on the down slope of these piles, leech ponds of industrial sewage slicked with a shiny coat of worthlessness. Necklaces of battered ore cars rattled around on their rails, and the stinging soot of the incessant burning blackened and evaporated the falling snow before it reached the ground, and stung in the nostrils. Volcanic puddles of slag hit the air with a shattering hiss and flowed through the valleys of the endless range of tailings piles that stretched into the night.

Ilya's gang sat speechless and benumbed as the crowd went into an escalating roar, arms raised, bottles aloft in the glittering, white, first light.

3

Ilya stood at her window in her rumpled shift, hair exploded, eye sockets dark, head shrieking, feeling the cold bleed through the glass over her breasts and belly, watching the children enter the school across the street, and the men dismantle the timber scaffold used to build it, all of them scuffling and slipping around in the hissing, whiteout snowfall that seemed determined and malign.

Ow, she said, rubbed her forehead, smirked, and took a gentle slug from the Mariani, clamping hard, waiting for it to slink through her.

Fool, she said. She turned and went to the bed, snaked the blanket off it, wrapped herself, and stood in front of the arched mirror over the oak dresser. Stark white lilies coursed down the red wallpaper in militant rows. A rocking chair sat off the carpet on the maple floor. The carpet was fake Persian, an insane and ornate design that hurt her to look at this morning. The crown molding was not fantastically ornate, nor were the picture molding and chair rail, but they were there and that reassured her some. Paintings she had not yet summoned the courage to look at hung on the walls. There were two windows, each four-over-four doublehungs. Damask jalousies of not terribly tasteful design hung beside them. A small stove with a relief of what were evidently pieces of mining equipment of types that were for her nameless was almost out. In front of her on the dresser was a white bowl half filled with chilly water. She cupped her hands and repeatedly bathed her face, dragging her fingers over her skin. She dried her face with the white towel with more lilies on it in a red border.

For a moment she struggled to recall what had happened after the lights went on and hers went off, and then stopped trying, and slopped over into flinching dread, fear, and regret.

Why do you want to get us killed? she said to the glass.

Fuck you, she said. If I left it up to you, we'd never do anything.

There were three even taps on her door.

Who?

Robert.

Enter.

Robert came in carrying an armful of firewood. You should lock that, he said. He gave her one glance and snorted a small laugh. He crossed to her small stove, dropped the wood into the basket, opened the door, stirred the embers, selected an array of sticks that would catch, pushed them in, shut the door, and opened the drafts wide.

Like it cold for a reason? he said.

She shrugged, crossed to the rocker, sat, swigged, and stared out the window at the snow. The blanket sagged from her shoulders and her chest was bare to the insides of her breasts, her hair falling over her face. Robert glanced at the skin, smacked himself inwardly, laughed a snort, and turned away.

You look like a piece of slag, he said.

Thank you. I assume that's bad. She looked at him. He was in pressed clothes, his hair was plastered down, and his beard was neatly trimmed. Why don't you?

Best somebody holds back some. Made it me.

Smart of you. I'm sorry I was the stupid one.

S'aright. You was on your way to gettin' us lynched first night in. Least I could do. Be back directly, he said, and left the room.

He knocked again thirty minutes later.

Come, Ilya said. She hadn't liked her tone when she'd said 'enter' the previous time.

He came back in with an enormous wooden tray with a heavy, white cloth draped over it, and put it on the bed. He had snow on his coat. He locked the door and left the key in it.

This is one asses and elbows city, he said, shaking his head. Never seen one like this. I don't think you got much to worry about, gettin' found here. Talked to Jean there, explained the situation. Set us up sweet on credit again. Got in 'tween the breakfast and lunch folks. Robert pulled the writing table from the wall into the center of the room and put its chair on one side. When he lifted the cloth from the tray, a burst of steam and aroma filled the room.

Got us a little *petit déjeuner*, Jean called it. That's French for 'breakfast.' I says, 'Aright, but make it a big *petit déjeuner*, we got deep holes to fill.'

'Little *petit déjeuner*' is redundant.

Looks tasty, too.

He took one of the lamps and lit it, setting it on the table.

While I'm at it...he muttered, and lit the other two in the room. Dark as fuck in here, you wantin' to be a bat? He spread out eggs in cups, butter, jam, orange juice, a plate of antelope from the previous night's dinner, now in trembling aspic, a battered pewter pitcher of coffee, a tall, glass beaker of clotted, brown-red liquid with lemons and jagged bits of ice floating in it with other things harder to identify.

What's that? Ilya said, pointing at the beaker.

Hair of the dog, Jean says, his own recipe. Wine, *consommé*, lemons, crushed up tomatoes, some other shit I can't remember. Sounded like the whole pantry. I'm just gonna trust *'consommé'* is some good shit. Sends his regards. Says eat it all, even if you don't wanna.

Consommé is broth.

Alright. He put an ill-looking baguette down. He said to apologize about the bag...bag...what...?

Baguette.

...*baguette*. Says his oven ain't no good for it and can't get a right one yet.

A very sweet man. I'm sure we'll manage, somehow.

Ilya sighed, stood, dragged her rocker to the table, threw a pillow on the seat and sat, wrapping the blanket tight around her and staring dully at the food.

Looks great, she said. She put the Mariani on the floor beside her, gathered her hair and tied it into a loose knot at the nape of her neck. The wine was quietly buzzing through her, making her feel better and worse, up and down, male and female, dead and alive.

Where is Bridger? she said.

Looked in on him. Wasn't movin' but wasn't dead. Figured I'd leave 'im.

Good. He's earned a rest. How about Spud?

Same.

We'd probably better be careful he doesn't get up and start wandering around the hotel pissing on things. Or trying to make new friends. He'll get us arrested.

I locked him in.

Oh. Do you want to be boss? You're doing a lot of thinking and...correcting. Maybe it's a farce that I'm doing it. I would hate that to be the case and not know it.

No thanks, Commodore. Done my time bossin'. I'm aright bein' the schoolmarm checkin' your work. Anyway, you're better at it than I ever was. Never cared for tellin' folks what to do.

Understandable.

Robert poured her coffee, motioned with the creamer. Ilya smelled at the cup, then shook her head.

I'll drink it black. Jean gets good coffee.

Gets good everything, seems. Got a real shine for it.

The French do. For your information.

Heard that. Ain't seein' the point of an egg with shells on, though.

It's still hot inside is why. On the other hand, what the fuck does a fool like me know?

Not all sweet on yourself today, I'm feelin'.

No.

Didn't do no permanent harm. Probably. Folks seem pretty loose here.

I hope not. I am well sick of trouble. Thank you for getting this.

Welcome.

They stopped talking, and sat in the sounds of eating and the city. Spoons tapped on eggshells. Children shrieked. Men shouted outside and their hammers made dull thuds as they beat the scaffold apart. Horses clopped and wagon wheels banged, but all of it was strange and muffled by snow, as though a hand were held over the mouth of the city.

What language is that? Robert said.

Swede, perhaps. Scandinavian something, I would guess.

Ain't no American speakers here, seems like.

None with a flair for it like you.

Damn straight. Not to give you a problem first off, but we're busted. Told 'em downstairs we'd pay today for more time, but the clerk didn't look happy. We're supposed to be out by now, and they ain't no shortage of folks lookin' for rooms. What we'll pay with is a problem.

Yes. Well. I suppose I could fuck or shoot someone.

They're pretty close to the same this mornin', I bet. If anybody'd fuck me I'd do it for you.

I doubt very much that you would.

Suppose you're right. But the wantin' to help's real.

I believe you.

No notion what I could do for scratch. I'm useless, now.

You're valuable to me. Money isn't that important. What am I saying? Of course it is.

Ilya chewed the antelope in aspic slowly, thinking, watching Robert slice himself a piece of it like it was composed of blasting powder.

It's an acquired taste, she said.

It's an acquired look.

True. I can wire for money, Ilya said. I was trying to avoid having to do that.

How come?

Ilya looked at him steadily for a while, measuring.

She sighed. I guess there's no point in holding anything back. The man I killed in New York. It was my husband.

That so?

Yes. He was the son of a very wealthy and powerful man.

Who don't care for you much about now.

I assume not.

Robert leaned back and wiped his mouth, poured himself a stein of the concoction, and sipped it.

How is it? Ilya said.

Kinda disgustin', but kinda refreshin'.

That's the French.

Seems. So now, if he's such a swell how come the whole US Cavalry ain't after you?

I don't know. And it's abrading my nerves to not know.

Care for his son, did he?

In his way, I suppose, but even if he hated him, he wouldn't do nothing about my killing him. He is not that sort.

They usually ain't. Maybe he's not wantin' a crowd involved.

It must be that. But if he doesn't, what is he doing?

Robert thought. Ain't a lot of options. He comes himself, or he sends somebody without a loose flapper. Private army, maybe. But why would he want to be so hushy about it all?

He is plutocratic scum. Sometimes it's very important to them that they believe others are ignorant of that, so they hide things. There has always been a shroud of secrecy around him, and I do mean shroud, and presumably there are reasons for that. Possibly he simply does not want publicity or scrutiny of any kind. He is one of the very upper crust that does not want to be known, does not want notoriety. He can't be certain that I don't know something about his business dealings that would reflect poorly on him. He wants to be behind it all, pulling the levers of the country. He was very forceful about me not gossiping about leaving his son, or his family, or that I'm a Jew that married into his family, and aborted his grandchild.

'Leavin' his family?'

We agreed that I would leave his family, and he paid me to be quiet about anything that I might know that would besmirch his sparkling reputation. I did happen to kill his son and take his money before I left. I have kept up my end of the bargain about gossiping, until now I suppose, but now it doesn't seem so important for some reason. The killing his son part, it's true, I went beyond the contractual agreement in that regard.

Hm. Pretty serious add, that. Took his chips and killed his kid, eh? And killed his grandkid? That's innovatin' as you go.

Like I said, the killing wasn't on purpose.

Didja kill 'im before or after you took the money?

Before.

And that's why you're the Commodore. I believe you you didn't do it on purpose. Well. Maybe he wants it quiet, and maybe he wants to be the one to say what your punishment is, instead of the law. Maybe he's got somethin' special in mind for you. Maybe hangin' ain't gonna satisfy him. If you're sayin' he's the private sort.

A chilling thought.

I'd say so.

The doorknob rattled.

I have to teach him to knock? Ilya sighed into the air. Yes? she said.

Bridger.

She waved at Robert and he stood and threw the key and opened the door.

Bridger came in like something falling out of the back of a wagon. Robert laughed, Ilya smiled and shook her head.

Guess minin' towns don't like you no better than you like them, Robert said.

Fuck, Bridger said, and looked like some sad combination of dying and pounding excitement.

Go get two chairs and Spud and join us, Ilya said. Can you make it?

I'll make it.

Drink a dose of this, she said, holding out the Mariani. It has marvelous curative powers if you keep it in check. Like I do, because I have responsibilities. Bridger took the bottle and slugged from it.

Here's the Spud key, Robert said, and held it out. Bridger slopped over, took it, left the room.

Well, let's figure we's right about all this. He got any idea where you are?

I don't see how he could. It wouldn't take this long to find me if he knew how I'd left New York, he could have wired ahead and taken me off the train. If he'd found the body before I left he could have stopped me there.

And now you got them wanted pitures out there. Think they'd make it back to New York?

Ilya shrugged. You're the lawman.

Ain't likely the pitures would make it back there. The story, that's a sure thing, just because people like murder, especially Western murder.

He wouldn't know it was me just from a newspaper story.

Reckon not. Ain't a lot of women killers, though. You're special that way.

Yes.

And if they find the sheriff and his boys up there, then it gets twisty. But if it snowed like it's doin' now down there, ain't nobody gonna find 'em this year. Likely never, gets to that point. I'm thinkin' you might of got away clean with that one. The territorial marshal's the only one might take it on himself to go lookin', but even then...wouldn't be any way to know where to look. Them townsfolk ain't gonna run up in them hills of their own mind. And you all was way hell and gone up there when you dropped 'em, and way off any trail. All anybody could know is they didn't come back, and that doesn't prove nothin'. For all they know, that sheriff is still after you.

A Bridger decision, by the way, to get up high before killing them. I would have botched it.

No questionin' his smarts.

Enough time has gone by, I think, that if they were going to find those men they would have.

Likely so.

Bridger and Spud came into the room, Bridger dragging chairs.

Well! Good morning! Spud said.

Good morning, Spud, Ilya said.

Howdy, chum, Robert said.

Oh...look! Look at...this! He waved grandly at the spread.

It is something, isn't it? Ilya said.

Yes! Yes it is! It's beautiful! Is...is anyone else comin' over?

No, I'm sorry, this is it.

Oh.

Boy just ain't happy unless it's a do every time.

It is strange, isn't it? It makes me feel guilty we aren't more popular.

What's this? Bridger said, and sat down, put one elbow on the table with his chin cupped in it, and waved at the food with the other.

It's your breakfast. Take your elbow off the table.

But, what is it? he said, and removed his elbow without being apparently affronted.

I'm not going through this again, I just finished with Robert. Just eat it, it's all there is and we've nothing to buy anything else with. Spud, stop standing over us. Sit down here and eat.

Why, certainly!

Spud sat down and didn't move.

Could you? Ilya said, and motioned to Robert.

Why, certainly! he said, and made a plate for Spud. He put the fork and knife in his hands. Reckon he gets the way of these already, after last night?

We'll see.

Spud began to eat with painful-looking but effective motions.

Lookee there. Does aright if you get 'im there.

Amazing. Ilya shook her head and looked around the room. Did anyone end up with cigarettes?

Robert fished and came out with a box of Turkish Orientals. I like these Turkish ones, he said. Like smokin' a spice cabinet that wants you dead.

Ilya stood, dragged her rocker back to the window, sat and smoked, looking out, an egg cup in her lap for ashes. Robert got up, slipped off his boots and laid on the mussed bed with his own egg cup.

Gonna be a long powwow I'm thinkin', he said.

Indeed, Geronimo, Ilya said, and didn't tell him to get off her bed. Alright. I'll talk to the hotelier and get us more time. I'll wire to New York and get us money. I've been trying to avoid that.

Why's wirin' for money a no good? Robert said.

Because the person to whom I would be wiring is the one Henry would think would know where I went.

Do he?

She. No. But she knows how I went, and the general direction.

So this friend then, wouldn't he already have fucked with her?

Perhaps. She's not a good woman to anger. Henry is fortunate that he is still alive, given how much Jacques despises him. If those two houses decide to declare war, it will be the New York equivalent of the States War. I miss her. I hate not speaking to her.

You're worried the wire'll get caught by this Henry, then.

Yes. But I have no choice. There is no possible way in life to avoid doing things you know are stupid.

Well, hang on now. You're doin' a lot of supposin'.

That's why I am the Commodore. It's alright. There is no other option. Jacques can see to herself. It's really only me that is at risk, if the wire is intercepted. And she would want to know that I am alive. I feel like I am being cruel to her by not telling her.

Ain't gonna know that if it gets intercepted.

I'll send two. I'll send a hundred.

Ain't barely got money to send one.

It will be fine. If I want something from someone, I can generally get it. But the money she sends will help us only in the short term. It can't go on forever. I can't support us all. Or ask Jacques to, though she might do it for me. But, she may not have it. She might be poor-rich, now.

Well, Robert said. We's criminals now. Don't that mean that's how we get money?

I don't feel like a criminal, Ilya said. I don't want to be a criminal. It's far too much work.

Hell, gettin' out already? Right after I come in with you? Ain't it my luck. That leaves workin', as I recall.

I'm not going to work, Ilya said. It's far too much work.

Hell you gonna do then?

I don't know. Sit at Jean's until he kills me with his food.

There's an honorable death.

I'd be doing what I love.

I c'd work, Bridger said.

My Frankenstein, Ilya said, you're alive. I must remember the curative powers of aspic in the morning. Bridger working. I love the idea.

I don' like bein' a criminal, neither.

What don't you like about it? Robert said.

I don' like all the time thinkin' somebody's gonna kill me.

That'll wear on you. But goin' to work ain't necessarily gonna stop that from happenin'. Right person from the past walks in you're cooked, what you already done.

But his chances improve, Ilya said. And mine. And look at this. She held back the curtain more to show the snow coming down. It hardly seems wise to return to a life of crime when you're snowed in to the community in question.

Guess I could see about gettin' some job where I stand around with a gun guardin' shit, Robert said. All the metal 'round here, must be drownin' in thieves. Probably make a livin' shootin' Chinamen. Or I could be police, help Fred.

Boring, Ilya said. And savage. It doesn't feel right for you, with your tender heart.

Well, Robert said, you sure as hell ain't gettin' me underground.

Nor me, Ilya said. What job are you thinking of getting, Bridger? A greeter?

I c'n carpenter some.

In this shit? Robert said, waving at the snow.

It doesn't seem like the weather slows them down, Ilya said. They're quite insane. The Swedes are still out there on those boards, banging away. I suppose if they fall, they land in snow.

Drunker 'n monkeys, I bet.

Can't all th' carpenter jobs be outside, Bridger said.

You sayin' you're gonna go in a hole? You hate minin'.

Bridger shrugged and stared out the window exhaling smoke, gulped down a wallop of the concoction, looking like all of the world's misery gathered into one bag.

What c'n I do? he said. Th' Alice looked like they c'd always use a body. Can't live on somebody else's dollar.

If I had it you could, Ilya said. I don't encourage anyone to work if they can avoid it. But I have your same problem, myself. Well, excuse me. Yours is worse, because mining is an option for you. I am fortunate that it isn't for me. Though, I will likely have to be a whore.

Ain't havin' y' whorin', Bridger said, with strict venom. I'll kill the sonsabitches that git on you.

We could team up and be panel thieves, darling, but instead you could murder the sap before I have to fuck him.

Hell's zat?

You hide behind a secret panel in the room, and while he is fucking me you pinch his wallet. I was joking. I won't do that work again. Once as a sort of necessary lark, but no more. Not enough men know how to fuck well enough to make it bearable.

Jean might hire you, Robert said.

I'd get fat. No matter. I will be fine. It's Bridger I worry about. Darling, you'll be doing something you hate. That is no life. They'll turn your sense of discipline and duty into a daily horror for you. They'll turn perhaps your most beautiful quality into something that hurts you and helps them.

He shrugged. We'll leave when th' weather clears. An' if I'm in there, I c'd blow the fuckers up. Burn that damn building t' th' ground.

You want to be a terrorist, darling? How very Russian of you. You're gloomy as one, so it may work. You could kill Henry as they killed the Czar. But dear, if it disturbs you to have others wanting to kill you, being a revolutionary is probably not a good choice.

Well hell, Robert said, least he'd be fuckin' shit up for a good reason.

Our reasons were good.

Small though, I'm sayin'.

I'm not small.

Hell, woman...

I understand you. I'm just concerned about our young Bridger becoming political. Better to be a simple murderer than someone with a cause.

We need money, don' we? Bridger said.

Yes we do, but I very much doubt the wage one is paid for digging in the ground provides for a very good life. Not like this one we're enjoying right now, certainly.

Yet folks do it, Robert said. Don't seem like somethin' I'd like, but they must be payin' somethin' to get folks down there.

I have no idea what industrial wages are nowadays, Ilya said, but I know how picayune the pay was for New York piece work and so on. Enough to make suicide attractive, but not inevitable.

I don' mind workin', Bridger said. I liked doin' stuff fer Mary.

He likes somethin', Robert said. I'll be.

This could be the start of something truly enormous, Ilya said. You could become an optimist, Bridger, and rule the world.

Ain't gonna happen, he said. Tell y' what I don' like, I don' like fuckin' 'round out in th' snow tryin' t' keep starvin' cows alive an' freezin' my fuckin' ass off.

There's that fussiness we love you for, Ilya said.

An' them machines they got. I ain't never seen nothin' like them. Dint know y' could even build somethin' like that. That big. Fuckin'...makes hangin' a door look damn puny.

Oh my, Robert, we're losing him. Our young killer is going straight.

I'm right proud.

I c'd learn how t' do that shit, then blow it up.

That's good thinking. The best terrorists come out of that which they want to destroy. That's where the animosity comes from. You're a natural.

Soundin' like everybody got a purpose in their life but me and ol' Spud here, Robert said.

You're my Praetorian Guard.

Slick.

And evidently, you're our waiter, Ilya said. And a fine one. Oh, she said, held her forehead and tried to rally. What day is it?

Wednesday.

Alright. Forgive me, I'm about to give some terse orders. Do we have any money left at all?

I got ten, Bridger said. Held it back.

Good man, Ilya said. For the first time, Bridger didn't repeat the word 'man' in his mind when he heard himself referred to that way.

I got a fiver, Robert said.

Alright. That's enough to get us through until tomorrow. Robert, take all this back to Jean and give him my regards. Tell him we'll dine there at seven and to please hold that same table, and that I will talk about money with him then. Pick up all the newspapers there are in this city, get some New York papers if there are any. Old ones are fine. In fact, ask specifically for old ones. And see where the telegraph office is. I have to get cleaned up and then I'll get us money, and fend off the hotelier. Bridger, please get yourself presentable, get some clothes on Spud, find the apothecary and take him there and ask him if they have something for that skin. He's like a shedding snake, and makes us look conspicuous.

Could be Spud's good cover, I'm thinkin', Robert said. What killer'd want to be nurse to a boy like him?

Perhaps. I could pretend I'm here to open a sanitarium for lunatics. It never occurred to me before becoming one that being a criminal means you get to change who you are whenever you like. Anyway Bridger, ask the apothecary if there's a place in this town to buy a wig, a costumery, or a dress shop or something. Tell him your mother is sick and her hair is falling out, and she's ashamed to come outside. If there is, get me one, a red one. Long. With curls. And look after the horses. See if there's any unscrupulous types that would buy some of them, regardless of where they came from. We don't need this many horses. We need money.

She stood up and yanked the drapes over the pouring white, as the others stood.

Robert, please ask them to send up hot water to me right away. I can't bear to be filthy on the outside as well.

4

As Bridger walked through the black snow toward the Alice, panting from the walk up the hill, the man he'd seen the previous day pointed at him with one hand, and at a man standing apart from the group of miners outside the doors with the other.

What's the crack, boyo? Cathal said, as Bridger approached him.

What? Bridger said.

What's the crack?

What fuckin' 'crack?'

No need fair that talk, nooh. The story. Yer dooin's. The crack. How are ye?

I'm aright. Bridger looked away from him, because he was hard to look at because of the frightening state of his clothes. They were a horrifying collection of filthy rags that made Bridger's old getup seem precious. His face was clean but his hands were gnarled, lumpy, scarred up pieces of flesh that looked like they belonged on a reptile.

Have y'ever dug a hole before, then?

Dug places t'shit in.

Same shite, a hole's a hole. We do that here as well, but mostly we just follow the metal. But Shifty wants us jackin' inna shaft, an' he's hot that I'm after bein' down there two shifts to make one blast. I says to 'im, 'Ye can't singlejack in that feckin' hole, because we're runnin' straight through a knob harder than the quartz, like.' An' he's after thinkin' I'm actin' the maggot down there, but I'm beatin' away with all there is in me. What c'n I do when the partner he gives me is a feckin' cod?

I dunno.

We should be alright now, we can doublejack if you can hold a bit. We'll let Patrick and Colin keep up wit the chunkin', an' if ye got enough bang in yer arms, we can blast end of shift.

Sound's like somethin' I oughtta be able to do. 'Course, I ain't gotta fuckin' tiny notion whut yer sayin'.

Then ye'll fit like a peg on this crew. But many's said the same that they could do, an' left with broken arms. But they're breathin' on us like George's dragons to get the shaft down to the eight hundred by Christmas, an' we're only at the seven fifty now. Lucky you, y' simple feck, yer getting yer first whacks in the shaft, an' not out in the drift. Jackin' straight down's easy. Drift jackin' likes to kill men.

Aright.

'Aright,' says he. Four months, three shifts a day, bangin' on that knob, an' we can do fifty feet in a month. A daft one, this...let's see how you feel doon innit, boyo.

You c'n do it I can, Bridger said.

That's the spirit we're after, noow. C'm, they're ready t' start droopin' us...

They walked to the doors and joined the throng of filthy flesh.

Inside, the men stood gathered in a rumpled herd with a harsh but not disgusting smell coming from them. The gallows frame reared up eighty feet above them into the dimness, shot through with the stabbing white light of the arc lamps throwing crazy, angular shadows through the structure. Empty ore cars surrounded them, battered as though being beaten was their function. The engineer rode his machine sixty feet away, standing on a platform six feet above the main floor, flat cables in massive spools before him, like thread to stitch the veins below back together from their volcanic rending, the cables vibrating into the air and lapping over the wheels perched at the top of the frame. The engine to the right of his dais seethed, stack towering over him, and men worked transferring cord wood toward the firebox. The massive, bolted boiler rumbled and pushed out a steady hiss that mixed with the roar of contained flame. The engineer grasped his two levers which stood in front of him at chest height coming up out of the floor, pushing them forward and pulling them back in turn, watching the arms of the depth gauges in front of him move around the discs like they were lunatic clocks, sewing the cables up and down according to the gauge, timing it all according to the butler's bell that dangled in front of him and tinkled commands from below. Men filed onto the lifts and dropped into the earth under his cables.

Bridger stood there, heart thudding in slow, heavy beats, in a state of angry, speechless, terrified wonderment. The gallows frame was a thing he couldn't take in, the timbers larger by far than any milled piece of lumber he'd ever seen. They made the timber in Mary's building look frail to the point of giggling. The structure stood within the confines of the booming building like something that would punish him if he even tried to describe it to himself. His brain cramped as he tried to picture how they managed timbers that big for milling, how they even got the hubris to fell a tree that big, how they figured out how to make their cuts and manhandled them around and into the air — the frame they assembled seemed like the frame they would need to assemble the frame. The tightness of their shoulder cuts depressed him — it had taken him so long to do his on a tiny scale, and these were gigantic, and reckoned at precise angles, and the angles weren't the same all the way around the structure because the rear legs were braced back into the ground like those of a man pushing against that which would crush him. He looked at the men around him and marveled that they weren't gigantic themselves, they were wiry, paunchy, a boggling hodge-podge of heights, stooping and straight, who had somehow managed to learn to converse over the grinding, incessant racket that was pushing against Bridger's ears.

The wheels at the top of the legs of the gallows frame were huge to the point of Bridger not believing they could turn, the ponderousness of them seeming to make mockery of the idea, but as the engineer threw his levers they banged and shot sparks and whirred into a violent spinning that seemed too much to be held in place even by timbers of this size. The shattering racket that came from this complex of steel and flame and men was overwhelming, and the sense of being absorbed into something that was inexorable, and planned, and had no weaknesses, had nothing that could be exploited, in fact was designed to only find the weaknesses of the men feeding themselves into it, was breaking Bridger's stoicism. He felt a mixture of gorge and fear clotting in his throat, and he looked at the faces of Cathal and the other men, watching for the expressions of terror that must surely be there, because there couldn't be any other reaction to this place, to this extinguishing, this feeding frenzy, but the men looked placid.

The shuffling flow of men continued until Cathal and he filled a cage with four other men, and Bridger's insides were rammed upwards by the sudden drop. A small shriek came from him and Cathal looked at him and winked with an expression of concern and reassurance and smirking mockery. The cage plunged out of the light of the hoist house and into the darkness of the shaft. The sound of the guides on the fir rails that kept the car straight was like Bridger's shriek amplified and made permanent, and they could smell the wood burning from the friction. They plunged past stations lit with the sad, yellow light of lamps, the process like watching someone slowly blinking at them as they flashed by. The other car zipped by going up empty to fetch another mouthful of men. The fat, horizontal members of this tall, timbered shaft flashed by them — the cage in which the men stood had no walls or roof, just a floor, and steel ribs at the corners leading to a cable sling connecting to the hook connected to the hoisting cable. The men stood pressed together, hands cupped over their crotches, buckets in their hands dangling between their legs as if to catch their testicles, facing away from the outside of the cage and leaning in, wordless and solemn and avoiding each others' eyes, holding themselves together as if one body so nothing would make it outside the plane of the edge of the platform and be sheared off.

The cage began to slow, then went into a hard deceleration that bent the knees of the men and forced them towards the floor, then the cage stopped altogether.

Good marnin', ye hopeless fecks, the station tender said. Hop smart, we're two cages behind. The men stepped off into the hot, sopping dark, the tender pulled his string, and as Bridger laid his first step on the floor of the inside of the earth, the cage whizzed up the shaft behind him, and he felt the push of air on the back of his neck.

An' what's this, noow? A fresh faggot for 'r fires, is it?

Donal got his silly self sacked, he did, Cathal said. This is me new jackin' boy, Bridger.

'Bridger?' An' what land is that name from?

I'm 'Merican, Bridger said, and stumbled over a few steps and vomited down the wall.

Didn't have to say it twice, lad, the station tender said, and he and Cathal laughed.

Doona worry, Cathal said when Bridger had straightened up. There's some that don't spew on the first drop, but we doona like 'em. Ye didn't do it in the cage, an' that's a good thing.

Thanks.

Yer very welcome, sir. Let's go, noow, let's get to it, Shifty'll be doon in an' hour and he's a right feckin' Cornish prick, but he c'n dig like a bloody badger.

Cathal held out a candle holder on a belt-type strap. Strap it on yer noggin', he said, and did the same to himself, over a cloth skullcap. Yer goona need to get some prooper gearin' sir, ye won't last in surface clothes. Shifty didn't say nothing to ye, aboot havin' some proper shite fer workin', then?

Said show up, find you.

Well, yer doin' a right job then. He likes to punish ye fer bein' hired. If ye can last out a week of it, he'll turn Paddy on ye, much as a Janner can.

What th' fuck's a 'Janner?' Bridger said.

A Cornie...a Cornish bloke. Y' niver heard of a Cornish person? Cornwall? England?

Nope. Grow a lotta corn there, do they?

Oi, laddie, he said sadly, shaking his head. Yer startin' right doon at the bottom in every possible way. Y' do know what a feckin' Irishman is, then?

You are.

Aright then, ye pick up things quick, anyway. Ain't yer cosmopolitan parts we're after usin' doon here. Git in there noow, we can't natter anymore, charmin' as ye are. Cathal pointed at the top of a ladder coming up out of a hole below a platform of heavy planking that closed off the bottom of the shaft below the lifts. Bridger noticed that the seven hundred feet of timbering above them rested on these planks, which should have been shattered and crushed by the weight. He stared at the timbering in the flickering of the station lamp, and saw that the timbers had no bolts into the granite holding them in place, only blocking and wedges slammed into strategic spots against the sides of the shaft, pinning the entire frame into place with compression alone.

Yer fuckin' shittin' me, Bridger said.

Why would I do that now, sir? Because I'm Irish? No. It's doon y' go, or out y' go, an' y'd better be after makin' yer choice right noow.

Fuck, Bridger said.

Noow yer seein' it clear. Cathal struck a match, lit his candle, then Bridger's, shook out the match, and crawled through the hole onto the ladder.

I'll see ye or I won't, he said, and disappeared.

Bridger stood there with a candle attached to his forehead, and looked around. The men that had come down with them had vanished into the holes punched into the sides of the station, winding off away into the dark. The station tender had hopped the cage to another level. He listened to the sounds of the operation, the faint taps of steel on steel, the crashing of the skips and the lift gear, the dripping of water oozing out of the rock around him, and the gushing of the water being pumped out of the shaft by the heavy plunge and pull of the pump timbers pushing into the sump. The earth made soft, groaning noises. He wanted to flee, but even had he wanted to, there was no cage to get on, no one to talk to about how to get out of this hole.

Choose t' come doon, I see, Cathal said as Bridger landed on the uneven granite and stood there. Up ain't so much, noow, I find. All they got is fresh air, an' light, an' stones doona come crashin' down on ye with no warnin'. This'll feel like yer mother's tits doon here, bye an' bye.

That's good, Bridger said. So, what th' fuck r we doin'?

We're goona drill us some holes inta this floor right here, sir. Soon as I c'n git the water outta me way. Light a bunch a these and put 'em 'round so we can see, but doona put 'em close t' the wood. Ye can see why that'd be a don't-do, yeh?

I c'n see the thinkin', Bridger said, took the handful of candles and box of matches, and started feeling around the sides of the shaft in the light of his own head candle, finding places a candle would stand and lighting them, figuring out to melt the bottom of the stub first when his first dropped with a hiss into the water. His boots were wet immediately, and he couldn't keep his footing because they were without tread, being meant for riding.

Cathal made pouting noises and said, I'll ask Shifty if he'll let me poop out at break an' git you some prooper boots. I've got spares. Ye can't stay doon here all day in them. Feckin' shiteater shoulda told ye to bring 'em if he didn't have a metal heart. He handed a handful of candle holders on long spikes to Bridger, with a hammer. Find cracks, yeh, and bash 'em in.

Cathal got enough water off the floor to find his holes, sweeping it into a depression where a reservoir had formed and the end of the pumping pipe was, and took long, thin blades of wood to mark their locations.

We can work with that, I think, sir. That'll do on the lightin', noow, they'll feckin' blow out on us all day, anyway. Let's bangit shall we?

He went to an array of bits leaning against the side of the shaft, selected one a foot long.

We'll go with a sharty 'til yer swingin' an' holdin' right. He selected one of the twelve holes he'd begun, dropped the bit into it so eight inches of it stuck into the air.

C'mere sir, this is where ye earn yer wage. Bridger crouched beside him. Take the little fecker in yer paws. Bridger reached out and grasped the bit in his hands, one over the other — an inch of the mushroomed head of the bit stuck above his flesh.

Yer not goona be wantin' to have yer paw s' close t' the end, the mushroom'll gash ye good if I doon't. Change yer grip on it....that's not too bad, I might not hitcha...course, I might...

Cathal stood up, grabbed a sledge hammer with a head that came to what looked to Bridger like a very small striking face for the size of the bit he was holding.

Doona move, noow, he said, raised the hammer and struck a slight, careful blow. The steel vibrated in Bridger's hands, and wanted to bounce out of the hole.

Turn it a wee dram, sir. Too much. Aye. Cathal struck another light blow. Turn. He struck another. Turn. He struck another. It'll go easier far ye, if ye pick the one hand t' do the turnin' and use the other t' hold her steady. An' best if ye lift the bit a mite on each turn — get more bite. Bridger tried this, saw what he meant. His knees cramped up.

Hold on, Bridger said before Cathal struck another blow. He got off his feet and knelt down on the wet, spiky granite. Shit, he said as he realized he could not stay in that position, and began to try to clamber back to his feet.

Hoold on there, Cathal said, if you wanna that poose, take the helper. He handed Bridger a short length of plank wrapped in denim cloth. Put yer knobbies on that an' try.

Bridger put the board down, knelt on it, and grabbed the bit again.

Ready?

Yep.

Cathal struck lightly again, Bridger turned. They went around one revolution of the bit.

Are y' feelin' coomf'tarble? Cathal said.

Right fuckin' cozy.

Mind noow, I'm goona swing like I gotta job to do here, a little more.

Aright.

Cathal swung and struck the bit harder, and it wanted to jump back out of the hole more, and Bridger realized he had to push down hard until the blow, then lift and turn. Bridger's heart leaped as he felt the force of the blow, and a hard chill ran through him, followed by a hot flush. He turned the bit, and Cathal hit it with very little time to spare from the moment Bridger had the bit steady. The candle on his head went out from the breeze of the hammer coming by him, and in the lack of light, locating the head of the bit was difficult. He wondered briefly if the light going out was a cause for stopping, but Cathal just kept machining on. Bridger clamped down on himself and put all the attention he had in him on moving the bit in its proscribed series of turns, and trying to keep the head of the bit in the same spot as much as he could from blow to blow. The blows began to come faster, and the swings were harder, and the vibration of the steel began to become numbness in his hands. What there was of the world other than this bit he was holding left his skull. The panicky sense of futility that Bridger felt as he recognized how little the bit went into the rock from each blow began to recede from him as the bit began to disappear through his hands at a much faster clip than he would have ever believed possible. Cathal fell into a rhythm and his blows evened into a steady beat. He didn't seem to be expending much effort, he'd just found some motion that his body had always wanted to have, and he was punching into the earth in a natural way, and all that was missing was the pleasured cries of the woman smart enough not to come down here.

They kept at it until there was so little bit left above the stone that Bridger was having a hard time holding onto it without getting his hand smashed. He was about to say stop, when Cathal held his blow and straightened.

There lad, a longer bit we'll be after needin'. And noow, whatever happens to ye, ye can always say ye doublejacked the Alice. An' trust me, she doona kiss.

5

Thank you, Jean.

You're welcome, Ilya, he said, and replaced her pot of coffee. *Le repas* is good?

Perfect again Jean, thank you.

Bon.

Finish your food, Spud. It's very difficult to keep meat on you.

Mm. What are we gonna do t'day?

We're doing it, my dear. We're going to sit here and read and be warm and watch others pass by on their way to work. Later perhaps we'll take a walk. I'm on holiday until the start of December. Then I'm going to take seriously this problem of idleness and purposelessness and being a near pauper. Does that meet with your approval?

Yup!

Good. I feel very safe with you.

What's Robert doin'?

Robert is probably keeping company with his friend Fred, talking about old times and drinking and the like. Be thankful they aren't doing it here. Nostalgia can be excruciating.

Oh.

Your skin is clearing up. That's good. Does it feel better?

Yup. It don't itch.

Good. You're beginning to talk more. That's good also. In an odd way.

She turned the page of *The New Northwest*, and sipped coffee. Listen to this tripe, Spud,

> His only love was a lady of Louisville, lo! These many years ago, who, woman-like, gave the staid, sober-side young chum the go-by, and wedded a wild, devil-may-care fellow, who ended life's journey by sailing into eternity's sea through a river of whiskey.

Well, cheers dear lady, I say, Ilya said, lifted her glass, and sipped brandy. She got the fun from him while it was there to be had, and now he's dead before he became a burden. Would that I had her judgment. Oh, I do. Who is the poet? Oh, Whittier. Sad that he didn't sail into eternity himself before he became a poet, eh Spud?

Yeah! Why didn't he sail into eternity?

You're such an agreeable fellow, my dear. And quite the critic. Perhaps you should get a job at the paper and review the cultural life of our fair, sooty city.

Yeah! I could get a job!

Ah. And they now have undercover detectives at Coney patrolling for immoral bathing suits. Hm. I wonder where they conceal their pistol and badge? Their bathing suits must be highly moral. Perhaps a gun isn't necessary when arresting people over bathing suits. Doesn't say what the punishment is if your bathing suit is immoral. Hydropathic torture, perhaps. Always effective, and plenty of water right nearby...breakfast caps will be in favor in the fall, a relief that...oh, and velvet will be the rage next winter. Again? Hm. I thought it had been the rage two seasons ago. I must wire Jacques and confirm...this local paper, who knows where they get their fashion news? Salt Lake perhaps, where suits of armor are always in style. Ah! Spud! Look! 'Morocco a Paradise for Jews'. Finally, eh? The Zionists are only off by several hundred miles. Oh, well. Better to be close to the Spanish, they're so very tolerant. Let's see about this paradise, Spud...

> According to law the Jews cannot possess lands or horses nor cultivate the ground outside of their ghetto. Nor are they permitted to accept lots and houses as mortgages. They are not allowed to ride horses, and may employ only mules and asses for the purpose. They are not permitted to lay hands on a Mussulman, even in self-defense, except in their own dwellings.

> They cannot bear witness in court, and may not speak to a Mohammedan judge except in a bent position.
> In the markets or at the booths a Jew may not outbid a Mussulman in a purchase of victuals. They are forbidden to read and write Arabic. They may not, while on a journey, approach a spring at which Mussulmen are standing; nor are they permitted to sit down directly opposite a Mohammedan, but must take an oblique position. On an encounter in the street they must always turn to the left, and on a journey must, when mounted on a donkey, descend there from at a considerable distance, in order to allow Mussulmen to pass on foot. They aren't permitted to wear a red fez, but must don a black one, likewise, black slippers instead of red or yellow ones. The Bournous they must wear in such a manner that the opening is on the right side, and hence they cannot make any use whatever of the left arm.

Well, that all sounds dreadful, particularly not allowing them to outbid. That's simply cruelty beyond the pale. Though it's hardly a punishment to have to wear a black fez with black slippers. That's what I would prefer. What do you think, Spud? You'd like the yellow slippers wouldn't you? They would match your eyes.

Yup!

Hm. And it says here some cigarettes have opium and arsenic in them. But they don't say which brands so we know which to buy. Bad reporting, I say...

The door opened, a chair at Ilya's table scraped back, and she looked up to see Henry's face descending before her.

Good morning, May, he said.

Well, hello! Spud said. Welcome to our restaurant!

Henry looked at him. Thank you, he said.

As Spud spoke, the bolt of alarm Henry's appearance caused ran through Ilya, and continued out. She put the paper on the table, put her hands in her lap, and clenched them together. After quietly shutting the door, Rex sat at an empty table, crossed his legs, and stared at her. His green suit was a despairing wail in her restaurant.

Good morning, Henry, Ilya said. She reached out, slid a Velvet Mouthpiece from her case, and lit it. Her hands were steady enough, she noticed.

Henry removed his hat and set it on the table.

There are hooks for that, Ilya said, and gestured to the wall where her wrap hung.

Henry hesitated, then stood and hung his hat and overcoat and scarf, and returned to his seat. He adjusted his chair so he was facing slightly away from Ilya and could look out the window, straightened his gray suit coat, crossed his legs, and sat with back straight. He slipped a case from his inside pocket, selected a thin cigar. Ilya struck a Victory match and held it out for him.

Thank you, he said, and let smoke trail up his face over his self-satisfied expression. He gazed into her eyes. The maddening pull toward her wrestled with his desire to crush her, save her, and kill her.

Care for something? she said, shaking out the match. I'm having coffee and brandy. Shame I've already eaten, but please order something if you're hungry. Put it on my bill by all means. I love to see a man eat, as you know.

Coffee and brandy would be fine.

And your...what is he? She gestured at Rex.

Henry smiled. A friend. Would you care for something, Rex? Henry said.

Wouldn't hate a wee dram.

Jean! Ilya called. He poked his head out of the kitchen door.

Some glasses and more brandy and coffee, *si'l te plaît*, for my friends.

Oui.

You're looking well, Henry, she said. Pursuing quarry agrees with you. Not strangely.

If it is worthy quarry.

I will accept that as a compliment.

Do. You should take as much enjoyment as you can with the time you have left.

I see. You've quite made up your mind as to my future, then?

Oh yes, Henry lied. Yes. Herbert will have had a lovely time compared to what you will be subjected to.

I daresay Herbert had a very good time with his last moments. At any rate he was...excited. Such a state can be very difficult for a man such as himself to reach.

C'n I clap the smirk, guv? Rex said.

Henry raised his hand to stay him.

No Rex. I'm enjoying this. It sounds like insolence, but it's terror. We will have our moment later.

Jean approached the table across the small, white hexagonal tiles with the *fleur de lis* mosaic in red in the center of the floor. Gustave slopped a string mop across the tiles, the odor of vinegar bleeding through the air. The restaurant was empty of other patrons.

Please *Monsieur,* forgive the smell. I must clean for the lunch people.

It is no bother, Henry said.

Jean set a decanter of brandy, and a tray with many cups and glasses, on the table.

Another *fête* you're having, perhaps, Ilya, eh? he said.

A good word for it, Ilya said.

Jean placed a snifter and cup before Henry. He set another cup and snifter before Rex, took up the decanter and coffee pitcher, and filled the cups and glasses.

C'est bon, Ilya? he said, putting them back on her table.

Oui, she said, looked up at him intensely, and gave a small nod toward Henry as he was occupied by his coffee. Jean saw it, nodded a little, a crease above his nose, perplexity in his eyes. As he passed Gustave on his way to the kitchen he muttered, listen.

Persisting in wanting to be French still, my dear? Henry said.

Oh yes. Who wants to be a Jew, after all?

So true. Unfortunate that, for you. Though it makes the festivities of this afternoon all the more interesting. Much more to look forward to. It's sad. Had you known your place, much of this could have been avoided. Not that I'm not enjoying it immensely.

Well. America is not a Jewish paradise Henry, like Morocco, so knowing one's place is not so easy. Is it possible that you are too sure of the outcome of your efforts?

No. It's never happened before.

Ah. I have never happened before, though.

But you have, Henry lied again, and smirked at her arrogance. You are not so original. I made a small miscalculation regarding you, I admit. But a small miscalculation befits a small person.

Small? *Moi?* Henry. That's simply beneath you. Do by all means insult me, but really, can you find no actual quality of mine to attack? It's something of a compliment I suppose, that you must resort to an obvious falsehood to slander me. Perhaps I am perfect. Small? No.

You will soon be very, very small.

I see. Are you going to put me through a jaw crusher? They have many of them in Butte. The height of advancement, or so I hear. They make rocks into powder.

I know what a jaw crusher is, I own many. Henry's face held the small smirk, and his eyes glittered. He'd found her. His heart pounded as it hadn't for a long time, as it had in his early days watching crude emerge from the ground like it would never stop, as it had when his competitors went down around him like stricken boats. He observed with approval her fearlessness under the threat of horrible death, or her ability to conceal her fear. Either way suited him.

He said, I prefer to let your fate be a surprise. You were unlucky in your choice of a place to hide from me. I now have an owner's share of Butte's best shaft, and had to come see to that. You made things very efficient for me.

And you do so prize efficiency. You are in on the Alice, then. I didn't see that in the paper. I only read the fashion and travesty stories. You know me. Frivolous.

Oh, yes. The very word I associate with you.

The Alice is a fine hole, from all reports. Well congratulations, Henry. Though, that you have further enriched yourself is hardly surprising. And you continue to underestimate me, which, I must say, if I were a thin-skinned sort, would offend me. But since it benefits me to have you do it, I can only say, *merci...*

De rien.

Oh, the informal as well, Henry. You charmer.

He shrugged. Who doesn't know French for 'nothing?' It's all they're good for.

Ilya sipped brandy, reminding herself not to drink too much, and looked out the window.

Though, she said, it could be that your underestimation of me is a trick. That could be amusing. At any rate Henry, do you think that if I truly wanted to hide from you, I could not have done it? Don't be silly. In this wide world of ours? If I wanted to be lost, I would be lost. I decided that being lost was too uncomfortable. And frankly, I am not a woman who needs to hide.

Not anymore, no. You will soon be very hidden. Henry watched to see what this last threat of physical violence would do, predicting the result.

Ilya made an annoyed expression and said, how discomfiting for me.

Henry nodded.

The bawd's a perfect richardsnary, ain't she? Rex said. A right earth-bath you'll be havin', me shkeney.

Ilya turned to Rex for a moment, then back to Henry. She raised an eyebrow and tipped her head at Rex. 'Richardsnary?' 'Shkeney?' You've decided to amuse me to death with a clown?

He has a special Englishman's ruthlessness that I find attractive. Every mark is an Irishman to him. And it's a nice hobby, learning a new language. I know what a 'shkeney' is now.

It's a Jewish thief. But what have I stolen?

My son's life.

Petty theft at best.

Henry opened his mouth, the door swung back, and Robert stepped inside behind Henry. Rex stiffened, and Henry shut his mouth, watching Rex to gauge the threat.

Howdy, Ilya, Robert said, glancing at Henry then back to her, eyebrow cocked.

Hello, Robert, she said, meet my friend Henry. Robert's eyes narrowed and he stood there, noting Rex and looking at the suit with surprise, waiting for what he should do to show itself.

Pleased, Henry said, not turning to him.

Me too, Robert said.

This is a Rex, Ilya said, gesturing at him. The two men nodded at each other.

Howdy, Spud, Robert said, shutting the door and walking in. Gustave nodded at him, slopping the mop about with aching slowness.

Hello, Robert! Spud said. Did...didja...see Fred?

I saw Fred, yes I did, Spud.

Is he good?

Yes, he is. Fred is feeling good. The council decided to outlaw opium dens, but they also decided to fire one policeman, but not Fred. That means he can keep his job and still go to the vision shop, because there ain't enough police to shut 'em down. Guvment now, there's some folks don't know how to pick a road so they pick all of 'em.

Why don't you join us? Ilya said.

Why don't I? Robert sat in his customary chair facing the street, poured himself brandy and coffee. He realized this put Rex out of his direct line of vision, got up, swung his chair against the wainscoting, took up his drinks, and sat in it with a cheery sigh. He put his coffee on a chair beside him and swigged brandy.

Jean got any of them croissants?

He always does, Ilya said. We were just discussing our itinerary for the afternoon, Robert.

That so. What we got goin'?

They're being somewhat secretive, but I'm beginning to suspect that it will be unpleasant for me.

It has nothing to do with you, Henry said, looking at Robert.

Now, I'm thinkin' maybe it does. I'd hate to be the sour one and not partake of the fun.

As you wish.

More sanguine the better, Rex said. It's all ruby when I leaks it.

Ilya rolled her eyes, genuinely amused, and looked at Rex, trying to see if this was a show he was putting on. This one, she said. Really. I haven't heard talk like that since New York. He's not an actor?

I'm not certain he knows, Henry said, smirking. He slid toward her down the slope of shared amusement, and stopped himself.

I knows, Rex said.

Well, Ilya said, it's making me positively nostalgic, so thank you. She halted her own slide. So then, Henry, is it your intention to make a scene here in my locale? Drag me out by the hair? I'd have to remove the wig, but then my hair is too short to get a grip.

I'm flexible. I can wait until you come willingly. As long as you understand that the outcome is inevitable.

I disagree. I have my trusted henchman here, now. She gestured at Robert. You're in my lair. And you've now informed me that the Alice is an important part of your empire. That was not smart. If something happens to me, I have a young gentleman friend who works in your mine who could cost you some money...

Robert looked at her and frowned. Ilya realized she'd just exposed Bridger. Panic and remorse danced in her, then she plowed on,

...ah...he quite loves me, and I have a lot of affection for him, and he's already predisposed to blowing it up on principle. He is something of a freedom fighter, my friend. He has compassion for trees and water and the like. In my short time here, I've come to understand that mine fires can be deadly, and costly. Quick to start. And very common. Easy to conceal.

Henry watched her for a moment, brow now furrowed, then looked at his cigar. I see. Who is this man?

I think I'll withhold that information for the time being. I'm sure a canny businessman like yourself can understand that.

I'll fire the entire crew.

Will you? Three shifts, several hundreds of men, all quite angry at having lost their employ for no reason, wanting revenge? And one extremely angry, somewhat unbalanced man wanting to avenge the loss of his beloved at your hands? You won't be able to hide your involvement in that, unless you try to kill everyone in this building right now. And make no mistake, there is nothing this man would not do for me, or to avenge me. Except, perhaps, to listen to me talk. He's sensitive in that regard, and may have a moment of hesitation when he realizes he won't have to listen to me anymore if I'm dead, but it will pass. And seeing him in one of his rages, it's quite...disturbing. He's a horde of one. He does not become a raving lunatic, he becomes as silent and ruthless as syphilis. And of course, I have Spud here, but I would not unleash Spud on you, Henry. Even you deserve a better fate than that. No, I reserve Spud for special occasions. Like Rex here, perhaps. That is a showdown not to be missed. Isn't that so, Spud?

Yup. Showdown!

Rex stared at Spud with perplexed bloodthirstiness.

Ilya lit another cigarette and decided that further was the only place to go. Robert, she said, could you go and fetch croissants? I don't want to make Jean come out here while he's cooking. Oh, and tell him what we're talking about, you know how he loves gossip.

That smart, I go? Robert said.

I'll be fine. I'm among friends.

Robert stood and Rex put his hand into his coat, Robert the same. Spud mimicked them, but had no gun.

Henry put his hand out to Rex. No, he said.

Robert and Rex stared at one another for a long moment, both landing on loathing for the other easily, then Robert walked to the back. Gustave turned and followed him.

And, Ilya said, if you discharged everyone, quite a number of shareholders and partners that know nothing about why you would do such a destructive thing would be upset, wouldn't they? Hire all new men? It hardly sounds like any way to run a business. All to see me dead? Bad business. Simply to avenge the death of a weakling child of whom you were ashamed? What if I simply said I was sorry? And returned the money I took, at interest of your choosing? She hesitated, then leaned forward and said, Truly Henry, I am not without conscience, without remorse. I only killed Herbert because he tried to kill me. If I thought that information would matter to you, I would have simply explained. But you would not have cared. Witness your senseless fantasy of my suffering at your hands.

You know nothing of my fantasies, Henry said. Which is fortunate for you.

I believe that, Ilya said. You're a gentleman, and would keep such vile things to yourself. Though it surprises me that you have fantasies at all, practical and realistic as you are.

Robert put a plate of croissants on the table, took one, and bit into it. Ain't fresh no more, he said, returned to his seat, and looked at Henry. Ain't this a hell of a boodle, now? Jean said he was plumb interested in anything that touched on his favorite customers. Got all Napoleon there for a minute. Had to calm him down some. Them frogs...wouldn't wanna be on the other side of one of them in a tangle.

There was a soft, clacking sound, and they turned to see Jean taking a seat at a table beside the kitchen door, a shotgun beside his coffee cup. Gustave was standing behind a rifle laying on the bar, its muzzle pointed at the group, mop handle leaning beside him, face impassive.

Henry looked at that, turned, and stared at Ilya for a long moment. He nodded at her, his mouth making a quick downturn of appreciation at the corners, and looked out the window. It was shift change and miners flowed by, their shiny lunch pails the cleanest thing about them. He waved his hand at Rex, who stood, walked to their table, and placed the wanted poster down, smoothing it out flat. He returned to his seat. As he did, the poster rolled back up. Henry took it up, rolled it again with the face out so it would stay flat, and put it back down.

Ilya looked down at it, mastered the chill it produced. Yes?

That's you.

That's an exceedingly poor rendering of a person I don't know. It looks like many people. That person is nowhere near as beautiful as I, for one thing.

But I have a photograph of you that will make things rather clear when put before someone who saw you. Your wedding photograph, in fact. And I'm going to guess that this, Henry poked his forefinger straight down on Bridger's face, is your terrorist friend.

No, Ilya said. Not at all. I don't know who that is.

Oh, but you do. When I saw the story of these killings in the paper I thought, 'Now, that sounds like my May.' And then I saw this poster, and, so it is. What if a man like me were to contact people I know and tell them the whole sad story of this fallen woman?

Ilya's lip curled at the characterization of her as fallen.

You could do that. But then you would become a very interesting person to everyone in the world. I would talk and talk. And Jacques would hear about it, and she's a perfect dribble-mouth. Imagine the stories in the New York papers, they do so relish attacking your sort. Henry Stewart and his rebellious son, and the Jewish daughter-in-law he paid off to silence her about being Jewish. Unseemly, after fighting a whole war over bigotry.

Henry smiled at her. Feeble, he said. Beneath you. Perhaps I would feel threatened by that if you were a black who married my son.

I am not so lucky. But I'm not finished. I've been reading some old newspapers, catching up on my business news. There is that small matter of the South Improvement Company. You were involved in that, no, with Rockefeller? Squashing independent oil producers by colluding with the railroads and doubling their shipping rates? 'Drawbacks,' were they called? Hiding that Standard Oil was shipping for half of what they were, by having the railroad give you...what were they called? 'Rebates?' And having the railroads provide you with information about the independent producers' shipping destinations, amounts, things of that nature? Planting spies, but calling them representatives? Underselling the little guys until they have to sell out to you? Very smart. Such lovely words for extortion, bribery, and conspiracy. Oh, and monopoly, which in this country is a word more foul than Jew. So American, to tout competition as the foundation of capitalism while crushing it. Good of you to let dear Mr. Rockefeller receive the publicity for that venture. Too bad, really...you're so much more handsome than that lizard-eyed monster. You'd make a better figurehead. In any event, modest of you to lay back, since the public has been nothing if not supportive of your brand of hypocritical brigandage. Using a public utility to enrich yourself, they'll love you. The people of Montana, and Butte especially, are so very approving of your way of doing business, they will surely welcome you into their community.

Welcome into our community! Spud said.

Henry turned and looked at Spud and laughed a little. He looked back at Ilya and nodded at Spud. This one, he said. Really.

He has a dolt's ruthlessness I enjoy.

As do I. Well Ilya, that was a very interesting story, but it means nothing to me. People can complain as they like, but the fact is that anyone is welcome to use those tactics. If they don't, it is their poor judgment.

Mm. That's so. But Jacques has sent me some other invaluable information. You played both sides, didn't you? You allied yourself with Standard so you could get cheap rates shipping on the railroads. And you allied yourself with the independents, the 'National Refiners Union' if memory serves, so you could use their pipeline, which is far the more economical way to transport. I wonder what either of these sides would do if they knew your duplicity? Especially Rockefeller. He's mean. And rather a stickler for loyalty in business, paradoxically enough.

Henry's face had gone stony and his cheek muscles twitched.

Uh-oh, Robert said, looking at him with a pleased expression.

Rex made an infuriated sound and shifted in his chair. Jean put his hand on the breech of his shotgun, and Gustave did the same with his rifle. Robert stared at Rex, poised and smiling. Rex grinned back with his wretched teeth.

How? Henry said, glaring at Ilya.

Perhaps you were premature in beginning to groom Herbert as your replacement. You have no idea how chatty he could be with me when he was drunk enough. I mean before he decided I was the source of all his troubles and elected to hate me.

What exactly did he chat about?

You used your name for Pure Oil to keep your alliance with Rockefeller, and Lillian's maiden name for Pristine Lubricants, so you could be in with the independents. What's behind that, I don't know. Irony Crude, perhaps. Herbert told me the names, but I didn't care at the time. Jacques found out the rest. And I'm sure there's more to your doings than I know.

Henry looked at her, impassive. He smiled and nodded. Very good. I knew your silly bohemianism was a waste of your talents. And an act.

Wasting talent is a talent. And an act, I suppose. And all bohemians aren't silly, though there are some that make us all seem that way. It surprises you that I know what I know, doesn't it?

No, in fact it doesn't, he said. It does a little, he thought. I believed you were an enterprising woman, and you've shown me to be right again, by finding these things out. Though, how enterprising you are is beginning to be a powerful irritant just now. But it is no matter. My involvement in those ventures is ended. This information can't hurt me.

Perhaps not in a way you can't handle. But it can be inconvenient. And it can lead to lawsuits. And public opprobrium that can be a nuisance. You were smarter than Rockefeller, because you kept hold of your secrecy. Now, he will be stared at for the rest of his life. He will always have to defend himself. But, not you. I can ruin your secrecy. And it's never good to have powerful men unhappy with you, as I can now attest. Be reasonable,

Henry. I didn't kill Jesus, I killed Herbert. A distinction even you should be able to see.

You think I am going to let that you murdered my son go by the boards?

It was not murder. It was not. Even given that you don't know the story you know that I am not so foolish as to outright murder my source of money. Your son knew that he wasn't the man you are, but also felt he had to be. Rather a bind that, I think. And the only person in the world whose love for him wasn't contingent abandoned him. She contracted pneumonia and died, and she did it before he had a chance to get rid of me and redeem himself in her eyes, so perhaps he believed he helped kill her. Though, it was me he decided was entirely to blame.

Tell me how it happened.

Ilya sighed. Why does it matter?

It matters.

She rubbed her face with one hand and looked at the ceiling for a moment. Alright, Henry. That night, we had a conversation in which he said that he was throwing me away, with nothing. I agreed to that, though I felt that he was laying all the blame for the failure of the marriage on me, which was unfair. Some blame, yes. I didn't adjust well to the role I was supposed to play. But he was scapegoating me, and as it turns out I'm sensitive to that. Nor do I care for being just...tossed away. Not me. That was a very foolish decision on his part. He felt powerless and inferior, and like many who feel that way, he grasped at the most brutish and unjust solution.

Ilya stopped and moved her gaze from Henry out the window, and her breath hitched as that night came back to her with force. She pushed herself into cold, then thought that a small, actual display of remorse would be wise, let herself look stricken for a moment, which came off somewhat well since she was stricken, then resolved her features.

Please continue, Henry said, watching Ilya's face go through its moves and gauging how much authenticity was behind it, figuring not much. I'm fascinated.

I'm certain of it. My verbal acuity is quite something, isn't it?

Indeed it is. 'Something' may be the best word for it.

There are better ones I'm sure, but even I am at a loss for what they are right now.

A pleasure to see your weakness show.

I'm sure. A relief that there are so few of them.

Yes. A relief for both of us.

Robert snickered, shook his head, lit a cigarette, then leaned back in his chair and relaxed. He toyed with his new realization that there was a lot more going on between these two than he knew. Maybe you was right, Ilya, he said. Shakespeare was a hack. This is some fun shit, right here.

I'm right often, she said. I cannot recommend it.

It is a burden, Henry said. So then, my son attacked you simply for being better than he? That doesn't sound true.

It isn't. I pointed out that I knew the...intimate nature...of his relationship with Jackson. Ilya waited, looking at Henry.

Henry smiled at her. You think that is news to me?

It isn't?

You think me blind?

Far from it. But...I only understood it relatively recently myself...

So you assumed I would lag behind you in this discovery? Who is wrong now?

Apparently I am.

Ain't this a day for firsts, Robert said. Ilya's wrong, and Ilya admits it. He was mad at her on Bridger's behalf.

Stop it, Robert. You know that's not a first.

I do, I do. Seems awful true, though.

'Seems' and 'is' are different.

Damn good thing too. Shit'd be too boring.

Then, Henry said, when Herbert found out that you knew, what happened?

These details, they're necessary?

Yes. People enjoy making men like me out to be monsters, but what I am is a creature whose attention to detail makes it better adapted to his world than others. All comes from that. So yes, I want detail, I have decisions to make. Are you having trouble giving it? Is your memory failing you?

My memory is sadly flawless. But it is not a memory I like to evoke.

Do it anyway. For me.

Alright. Perhaps I owe you that.

And more.

It is graphic. Are you certain you want this picture drawn in your mind?

Do you believe I have none now?

I suppose you must.

I want the actuality, not the supposition I have now.

And you trust me to give the truth to you?

Yes. Your discomfort with lying is perhaps your greatest weakness, your greatest arrogance.

Hm. That could be.

It is, believe me. Tell it.

Alright.

Robert pondered that this was one of the few times he'd ever seen Ilya do what someone else wanted her to do, and it was this man. He tried to remember if she'd ever done it for him, and drew a blank.

Ilya said, I walked to the fireplace where Herbert was standing holding the fire poker. I was only going to get my cigarettes and was preparing to leave. I almost didn't say anything. I regret that I did. But, I...could not...let him believe he had won...I...could not...accept...his...dominating me...no...he was humiliating me...and...being humiliated by someone whose superiority revolves only around his social stature...his money...I couldn't...

Ilya got angry at the way she was struggling with her words, and she realized she was starting to slump forward in her chair, was starting to go limp, and she pulled herself up. Henry watched all this happening to her, watched the look of fury pass over her features, watched her go straight in her chair, and the look of hauteur and supercilious bemusement retake her skin, and had to again smother the sense of arousal she provoked in him. But he now had no doubt that there was authenticity to her remorse.

Ilya let herself return to that night and, trying to get her tone to a good mix of power and softness, said,

So I pointed out to him that I knew where he went for his sexual pleasures, and that was something he couldn't bear to have known.

Which you knew would be the case.

How could I know something like that? I am smart, not a god. You accepted that quality in him?

Henry shrugged. It is an abomination. But much of the world is. It is senseless to object to abominations, but wise to utilize them.

For example?

The willingness of human beings to be duped into being chattel by men like me is my personal favorite. Go on.

He turned and swung the poker at my head.

Violence is uncharacteristic of Herbert. Was.

Yes. But I believe I pushed him very far that night. And I think about that moment often, more often than I wish to. I believe that he was not altogether committed to killing me. I think, had he been, I would be dead. I think he didn't have all of himself in his blow. I pulled back, and that helped, but I was surprised, though perhaps I shouldn't have been, and if he had been committed...it would have gone differently. But when I didn't run from him, when I fought, then I think it became...primitive for him. For us. The line for Herbert was not fully crossed when I mentioned Jackson, it was when I didn't run. It was when there was a risk that a woman was going to best him even in a physical contest, after doing it intellectually. Irony was not your son's strong suit, Henry. Oh, and he was very much drunker than I.

Henry nodded and looked at the ceiling, twisting his cigar in his mouth.

One does not grow up a lower-class Jew in New York and not grow accustomed to physical conflict, Henry. One learns that in order to avoid violence, you have to turn your back, not your cheek, which is a far more dangerous position. A problem with Jesus' thought, that.

There are serious drawbacks to the privilege my son enjoyed, Henry said, appreciating Ilya's statement, and wishing he'd thought of it.

Perhaps you are to blame. If you had made him box and wrestle in school, he would be alive.

Henry barked a short, bitter laugh. Forcing someone to do what they don't want to do works in business. In family it is not so easy. His mother cosseted him. And knowing what I came to know later, I imagine there would have been some awkwardness that would have resulted from my son rolling around on the floor in the arms of a man. Then what happened?

He lost the fight. When the time came I did not hold back, and I struck him in the side of the head with all my strength, which, as it happens, is considerable. I crushed his skull. I watched the life leave his eyes, such as it was. Ilya cursed herself for adding this last. Henry smiled at the remark, at the rebelliousness and self-destruction it signaled, the gorgeous recklessness.

Hm. Tell me, when you struck him, what posture was he in?

'Posture?'

Yes.

He was on his knees before me. Ilya realized she hadn't thought in depth about that point.

Murderous, some might call that.

They would be wrong.

'Wrong?' You killed a man who was helpless before you at the time.

To stop him from killing me.

But he couldn't have, at the time you killed him. Detail, you see.

Detail which is irrelevant! Did I forget to mention that he tried to strangle me? Oh, and he didn't swing the poker at me once, he did it twice.

He wasn't stopping. Believe what you like. I was there. I am the authority on this matter. I did what I had to do. The end.

The end isn't here, yet. How was that for you, the moment you struck him?

'How was it?'

Yes. Be cautious.

It is blurry

Clarify it.

Ilya thought. It was horrifying.

And?

It was exhilarating.

Well saved.

Thank you. And then, it was not exhilarating. It was dire. And absurd. And insultingly stupid. It was...an abomination.

How did you respond to this abomination?

I would call it brief hysterics. I'm a woman, after all.

In a manner of speaking. So you elected to utilize this abomination. Steal from me and flee.

I was at a loss for something to do with my time. Living on the run seemed a better vocation than schoolteacher or nurse. Or whore.

Or pointless bohemian. So then, Herbert set you free.

Yes. By using me to commit suicide. He so hated to do things alone.

You believe Herbert wanted to be dead?

She thought. She'd never questioned the idea before, really, she'd just clung to it.

Well...how could I know? I...believe...Herbert was in a horrible crucible. Perhaps he didn't literally want to be dead, but I also doubt he wanted to live, under the circumstances. There was no place for him to be...whatever he was. Not with me, not with you, not with Jackson, not even with his mother. I think we failed him.

Then you feel guilty?

Yes. To a point.

What point?

To the point where it is not my job to have bottomless sympathy for a man who has decided I am the root of all his problems. I had sympathy, perhaps not much, but I had it. Then, I did not. It was he who decided that throwing me away in every possible way was the proper move. I didn't care about his sexual life, on the contrary. I didn't care that he wanted me gone. I cared that he decided to be cruel to me and blame me, and felt that I had earned nothing. At that moment, the responsibility became his. And you? Do you feel guilty?

Yes, Henry thought.

No, Henry said.

Liar, Ilya thought.

Why should I feel guilty? He was given everything. There are those for whom nothing will be enough, and there is nothing to be done about that. As you've demonstrated.

Damn, Robert said, just got colder in here than outside. Havin' you for a Pa musta been damn cozy.

Henry shrugged. If a man does not respond well to the terms life sets for him, that man is not one, as has been shown. He was treated in the way appropriate to the job he was to have in life, so that he would succeed at that life, so that he would not be devoured. If he wanted another life, he was free to have it. I would not have killed him with a poker over it. He would not have starved. He wanted another chance to be my heir, I gave it to him, and he betrayed me.

Which is an interesting point, Ilya said. I killed the man who betrayed you...for you. Perhaps I am your real hired gun, and Rex is just for show. Which he excels at, there is no question. Rex tipped his hat.

Henry looked at her, the thought making its way through his mind. It was both absurd and true, and, he decided, currently irrelevant.

He said, One takes risks, and sometimes one loses. But I never lose everything. Ever.

'Cept your damn soul, I'm thinkin', Robert said.

Henry turned to Robert and, for the first time that Ilya had ever seen, grinned broadly, grinned in a way that was not controlled, not designed to frighten, to dominate. The rarity of that, combined with how handsome and indomitable it made him look, the graven profile, gave Ilya's heart a hard yank, which released the realization that this man wanted her to a depth she hadn't grasped. She'd had him loosely clumped in with all the other men in the world that wanted to bed her, wanted conquest. The realization that he wanted more from her than that had been concealed behind his intensely private nature, her reflexive contempt for him, and now her fear of him. She smiled. And after all her abuse of him. What did she have to do to be rid of this man? Then she realized that it had been her attraction to him that had revealed his to her, and she frowned.

You're a father? Henry said, still grinning at Robert.

Hell, no. One of me's enough.

They're not you. That's the trouble.

So I'm gettin'. 'Course, seems there's a hitch between your kid takin' a cut at Ilya, two cuts accordin' to her, and you bein' here takin' cuts yourself. So they ain't not you, neither.

Agreed. Though, you'll notice I carry no poker. Either way my soul is intact. But I do not indulge it. And I do not indulge the souls of others.

Obliged. Gettin' my soul indulged by you? Damn Inquisition sounds like more fun.

What will you do, Henry, Ilya said, about having no heir? You're quite alone, now.

He looked at her.

A problem easily remedied, he said.

Is it? I suppose finding a walking womb would not be difficult for a man such as yourself. Though those tend to yield Herberts, an outcome I assume you'd like to avoid. I can't say I know what is important to you Henry, your opacity is admirable. But I think that perhaps your legacy is important to you, and progeny are generally considered representative of that. And that is why you go to such lengths to conceal yourself. I don't think you want to be reviled as a ruthless, cheating, bastard robber baron, like Mr. Gould, and depicted as a despicable Jewish spider in cartoons around the world as he is, despite the fact that he is not Jewish. Though now that I've said that, it would be amusing if you were accused of being Jewish, and I could do that. That would be entertaining.

For me as well. Henry smiled at her and said, It was his name that made it possible to depict Gould as a Jew. It wouldn't work very well with mine.

True. Though, I could just lie. Journalists love lies.

Henry felt the urge to tell her what motivated him, but it was no longer clear to him. The ambivalence of youth he'd put to rest in himself long ago had reawakened, she'd shaken it awake, brought back the vitality Lillian and her puritanical piety had bled from him. And now he had the Alice, a new war, renewed business intensity. It was exhilarating, being a childless widower. He now had the choice to create a new family but with the benefit of experience, or to not bother, to live only for himself.

He would not say anything. Not yet. Not until this fog inside him had dissipated, this fog he didn't entirely hate, because it gave life novelty and brought a strange transformation of the dull clarity he'd fabricated.

So then, are we finished? Ilya said. Are you still set on hurting me? Killing me?

Oh, not today, Henry said. Rex pouted.

Were you ever?

Well, that, you see, that would be a very hard thing to be sure of.

Henry. That was complexity. How dare you.

I leave nothing off the table, however.

You were testing me then, earlier, with your threats?

Another case in which what is true can't be known. Anyway, there is no satisfaction in victory attained too easily. That was a masterful performance on your part. Bravo.

Thank you.

Certainly. I give credit where it is due. But that is all it was, a performance. No my dear, this is not over. Don't run. I'll chase you.

Ilya made an exasperated spitting sound. Oh, Henry, she said, what more do you *want?!*

He stood and put his coat on, gestured to Rex, who stood, opened the door, and held it. Frigid air blew in. Henry put on his hat, tipped it at all in the room, smiled at Ilya, and said,

'More' will do.

Yeah! Spud said. More!

end

ABOUT THE AUTHOR

Photo: Ginny Newsom

Scot Crawford is a writer, carpenter, artist, and general gadabout. His short stories have been published in *The Brooklyn Rail*. His political satire has been published in *The Shackle Report*. He has performed his work at *The Happy Endings Reading Series*, *The Brooklyn Library*, *The Cornelia Street Cafe*, and the *Bowery Poetry Club*, all in New York City. He lives in NYC, Idaho, Montana, and New Orleans.

facebook.com/DoublejackIlya